MW01514811

SHADOW OF THE SCAR

The Book of Jasher Part 2

BILL W. SANFORD

To Debra...always there

ISBN: 1542349729
ISBN 13: 9781542349727
Library of Congress Control Number: 2017900092
CreateSpace Independent Publishing Platform
North Charleston, South Carolina

A New Attack

From the Austin *American-Statesman*, May 9, 2025 (page 1):

Terrorists Destroy Lago Vista Neighborhood
By Elaine Douglas

The recent events in Austin, Texas have now been linked to a world-wide terrorist organization. That, at least, has been the official word from local, state and national law enforcement officials when asked regarding this horrific attack which left not only several homes devastated, but half a dozen government agents were dead and several more were in critical condition.

Sources who have requested to remain anonymous have pointed out that a number of those officers were actually agents of the Central Intelligence Agency. Given the CIA would normally have no mandate for operating within the borders of the United States, it is curious that they would have been asked to participate in this action with Homeland Security. No comments have been forthcoming as yet from that agency.

Homeland Security has revealed that the incident is the work of Benjamin Jasher, an antiquities dealer and citizen of Israel.

Their investigations have disclosed Jasher as one of the master-minds of the international terrorist organization known as ISIS. As a result of an ongoing investigation which placed Homeland Security in pursuit of this group, Jasher and several of his followers had run to ground in the quiet Austin suburban village known as Lago Vista. According to those same sources, a home was selected at random and Jasher took control of the residence of William Bedford, a professor at the University of Texas. With him in his home at the time was Isaac Levinson, also a professor of the same university. Both men were held captive for several days while government officials had closed in and surrounded the premises.

Jasher, realizing that he was surrounded, attempted to make a public declaration and coerced the two captives to cooperate, but it was determined this was a ruse to allow the terrorists an escape. As agents closed in on the home to free the hostages and capture Jasher, high explosive charges were detonated in the upstairs and basement area, killing and injuring several of the officers assigned to the assault team. Once it was determined the property was spread throughout with explosives, only the professional training and quick removal of those devices by the task force prevented further loss of life and damage to the neighboring homes and streets.

Nevertheless, in the confusion of the detonations, Jasher and his men slipped away and the two university professors were believed taken as hostages. An international manhunt is underway to bring the terrorists to justice and to recover the two United States citizens being held captive.

Austin Police Chief, Nathan Riley, also told reporters …

Once on the tarmac of the Nicosia Airport on Cyprus, Benjamin Jasher calmly removed the telephone from the inside of his sports jacket. A moment later and he transmitted a code word which alerted his Chief of Security, Dov Hacohen, the ex-Mossad Israeli tactical officer he had used on a number of occasions. The message was short: Jericho.

Knowing that Jasher's flight plan would place him in Cyprus that morning, Dov had been ready for an hour with an extraction team. Immediately, Hacohen and the team he led drove up in three dark SUVs to the waiting plane. He and two others went up the stairway then exited a few minutes later with Jasher and the two professors, Bedford and Levinson. These all climbed into the middle SUV and all three cars sped off to the other side of the island.

Jasher turned to his companions and said, "Professors, we are driving to my home here on Cyprus. My security team will have the estate well-guarded and once there you can begin settling into your new accommodations."

Isaac Levinson, Professor of Ancient Languages of the University of Texas, leaned forward slightly and asked, "I take it then that our living arrangements will be free of danger?"

Jasher shook his head ruefully. "I doubt that there is any place on the planet where anyone is truly safe once Walker Cain decides to attack. Our advantage is that my estate is isolated and easily defended. Moreover, I have the best security team that money and past favors can buy."

Professor William Bedford, Professor of Paleology at the University of Texas, appeared skeptical. He should have been; since associating with Jasher, on two separate occasions he had had to fear for his live. "Suppose we are attacked again as we were in Austin?" he asked.

"I freely admit that our arrangements in Austin were a mistake. There was simply no way to know how committed Walker Cain would be in his efforts to halt or destroy our process of translation."

"Our security appeared sufficient. At what point did he realize what we were up to?" asked Bedford.

"I doubt he actually knew the particulars of our collaboration until Isaac notified the University President of our intentions to make public our manuscript. When he discovered our actual plans, I believe he panicked and the destruction to your home and neighborhood was the result."

"And if he tries another attack? Can your security force here provide us enough protection to finish the translation?" Levinson asked.

"He may decide upon another attack, but it will cost him dearly. I have friends in Cyprus who will alert the international news media should he attempt a provocative attack on my estate and he will be held accountable."

Two hours later, both professors were settled in for the night and Jasher breathed a sigh of relief that they had arrived safely, but he knew from experience that once his adversary had decided on a course of action, he would not stop until his goal had been achieved. Though he trusted his security team to ensure their safety, he hoped it would be sufficient.

Jasher was walking through the outer courtyard which overlooked the Mediterranean. In spite of the security lights around the estate, the night sky was alight with a full moon; likewise, numerous stars were also visible. He was pondering the activities of the upcoming day when Dov Hacohen quietly walked up behind him. Benjamin had long become accustomed to Dov's walk, thus he knew it was he without having to turn around. *Now what?*

"Sir, my intelligence sources tell me that Walker Cain is planning a counter-attack on your estate. He is sending in an experienced team from Europe under the control of Gustav Gottesmann. Our old friend James Perkins will no doubt be nearby though his team will not be the tip of the spear on this occasion."

Jasher shook his head in dismay, muttering, "So soon? I should have known Cain would waste little time; it is the smart move." Jasher, hoping to find some way to prevent any further disturbance to the work then asked, "When do they plan to attack?"

"My sources say probably late tomorrow night. How do you want to handle this?"

Jasher thought for a moment then replied, "I want to send a clear message to Walker Cain that we will not be intimidated. We need time to complete this project, so our response to his attack should be immediate and lethal as well as pre-emptive. Can we get to Gottesmann's tactical team before they reach Cyprus, preferably over international waters? I do not want this attack to occur on Cyprus and especially I do not want any international backlash."

Dov gave it some thought. "It could be done if we had the right hardware. I know a good pilot we could bring on board, but you will need to call in a favor to the Israelis and borrow one of the Eurocopter Tigers. Also we will need to move on this quickly; we are running out of time."

Jasher muttered, "We are always out of time."

James Perkins, aka "The Extractor", sat across the desk from Gustav Gottesmann, but didn't care for what he was seeing nor hearing. Word had come down from the Director himself that he was to give this man his full cooperation in the apprehension of the known fugitive Benjamin Jasher and his colleagues. Moreover, he was authorized to confiscate any records or manuscripts that might be in their possession. Jasher was to be captured alive, along with the records taken intact, and all other considerations were rescinded. This operation was designated as a national security priority 1A1, which meant that he was authorized to use deadly force to complete the mission. It was hardly the op that bothered him so much; clearly Jasher should have been picked up some time ago. What he didn't like was Gustav's condescending manners or his insufferable attitude of superiority, but most of all, he didn't like the idea that he was receiving his marching orders from some punk kid.

Gustav was outlining the scope of Perkins' role as well as doling out a hefty dollop of contempt and he seemed to be truly enjoying the experience. "As I was saying, Mr. Perkins, we are well aware of that debacle that occurred in Austin. It was unconscionable of you to have failed."

"Our intel was faulty. My men walked into a trap."

"Nevertheless, I have pointed out to Mr. Cain that it could have been handled more expeditiously by Homeland Security alone, but he insisted that your men should be brought in on the detail as you had prior dealings with the fugitive Jasher." Gustav's gaze was withering as he added, "Jasher made you all look like clowns at a Texas rodeo."

"Mr. Gottesmann, I neither care nor have any particular concern for your opinion. Jasher had help from professionals and we won't underestimate him again."

Gustav would not accept any of Perkins' lame excuses as a reason for failure. Perkins was a professional and the results never should have ended up with the cleanup that took place in Austin that night.

Gustav gazed at the agent and insisted, "Regardless, you will take orders from me. You and your team will not move on Jasher unless on my word. In essence, you will be there strictly as back-up for my own team. You are not to get in our way, and if they get past us, then and only then are you to engage. Are we on the same page, Perkins?"

"Yes, understood," he replied. "Where do we now stand? Sir." His tone conveyed how he truly felt about the arrangement.

Gustav, however, remained unruffled by the attitude of disrespect. Cain had placed him in complete control of this operation and he had no intention of giving this cretin any more information than he needed to do his job. He had decided, however, to throw the dog a bone.

"Two days ago, our intelligence sources intercepted a short call from the Nicosia Airport on Cyprus. It included a code word; moments later Dov Hacohen and his extraction team were seen entering a Learjet and then they disembarked with Jasher and two men."

"Do we know where they have gone to ground?"

"Three SUVs drove away to the western end of the island where Jasher has been known to stay occasionally. We suspect he and the two men accompanying him will hold up there until they can set up another press conference. We do not plan to give them another opportunity."

"For once we both agree on something. What's the op?"

Ignoring the remark, Gustav replied, "Your team and mine will meet tomorrow night in a remote air strip in Turkey. My men will fly out by helicopter and be dropped on Cyprus a few miles from Jasher's estate. They will then breach the estate and do the job you were supposed to have done last week, but due to your incompetence, were permitted to elude capture."

Perkins bit back a scathing remark. Gustav was long overdue for an accident and Perkins had some definite ideas how that might be arranged. The thought made him smile and so his next question was friendly enough.

"So, my team will not be in on this assault on Cyprus?"

"Quite right, Mr. Perkins," Gustav added dryly. "Though I seriously doubt that it will occur, the only scenario in which I can foresee using your team is if, by chance, Jasher and his security detail can offer enough resistance to eliminate my team. In any case, you will stand by in Turkey and wait for further orders."

Dov Hacohen had insisted upon accompanying the helicopter pilot as he left the Israeli Air Base in the Sinai desert. The pilot, an old friend by the name of Eli Lieberman, had been very enthusiastic over the mission. It had been far too long since he had used the "Tigercopter", as he called it.

"Dov, I must say, I was bloody well impressed that your friend Jasher had so much clout in the government. The PM called me directly and told me to give this mission my undivided attention. The last thing he said was he expected my complete success."

"Yes, our friend Jasher certainly knows men in high places. I have to admire the way he is going about this operation, though. He used the word pre-emptive and left no room for doubt that he wanted a clear message sent to our other friends in high places."

Dov was grinning in anticipation of the engagement ahead. He gazed around the helicopter in admiration. "Some serious piece of hardware, this 'copter, what?"

"You know it, mate! This is the upgrade to the Eurocopter Tiger containing the most advanced stealth equipment. It has the new composite materials on the airframe that results in reductions in the aircraft's radar cross section. Furthermore, it can discern, differentiate and track any plane type within fifty miles. As to the upgrades, measures were taken to produce minimal visual, radar, infra-red and acoustic signatures to improve battlefield survivability. We are virtually invisible."

"That's the way Jasher wants it. Negative boot prints on this mission, mate."

The Boeing C-17 cargo plane containing Gottesmann's tactical assault team had left an isolated air field in southern Turkey about an hour earlier. The men, all highly trained, were briefed on the mission and had been given the "green light" to engage any repelling force. The mission was: eliminate the opposition, capture Jasher alive and recover all records; all other considerations rescinded. The team captain was on the radio with Gottesmann for the final instructions.

"Understood, sir. Jasher, alive, the records recovered."

"Good luck, Captain. I will see you back at the base."

Eli glanced at his display that was telling him the cargo plane they sought was now on radar before them. "There it is, Dov."

Dov smiled and asked, "How close do we have to be?"

"I suggest we take it out now." He glanced over to Dov and said, "Say the word, Dov."

"Now. Light it up."

"Rocket away." From the undercarriage of the helicopter sped a 90 mm Mistral rocket with infra-red homing. The cargo plane had been marked; there would be no miss.

The two men watched silently as the rocket tracked the plane. Six miles away the Boeing C-17 went up in flames along with Gottesmann's tactical insertion team. Eli smiled and quietly declared, "Poof."

"They did what?" yelled Walker Cain into his desk phone. Instead of hearing that Gustav had accomplished the mission, he was being briefed that once again Jasher had found a way to thwart his best efforts to collect the records.

Gustav was in agony over this failure. "Sir, Jasher and his security team had to have received inside intelligence on this mission prior to our departure. They were waiting for our insertion team and blew them out of the sky. It is my professional opinion a mole exists in our security organization and the details of this operation were leaked to Jasher. There can be no other explanation."

Cain hung up the phone a few minutes later. Was it a mole or just plain stupidity? He didn't know which, but he would get to the bottom of it even if he had to dismantle his whole security operation and start over; he had done it before many times. His office in Manhattan overlooking the East River became deathly quiet as the echo of his last conversation slowly retreated into the silence. Walker Cain arose from his chair and walked with calm deliberation over to the window, his hands clasped tensely behind his back then began to watch a barge move sluggishly down the East River and out to the bay.

THE TRANSLATION

Professor William Bedford was deep in thought. To the world at large, he and Isaac Levinson had been abducted by a now notorious art dealer of antiquities, Benjamin Jasher, and a man-hunt was underway to recover them and bring Jasher to justice. It would have been impossible to reach out to his family or the authorities of his whereabouts and relate the true conditions under which he was now living. No doubt this would have alerted the wrong people to their location.

Now in a villa on the western side of the island of Cyprus, over the past few days he and Professor Levinson had slowly grown accustomed to the new surroundings. The living area where he was seated was luxuriously appointed with Spanish leather, Turkish tapestries and Persian *objets d'art*. Their quarters were luxurious and the translation room in the basement was fully equipped with all the tools necessary for a successful rendering. Nevertheless, Bedford felt since their arrival that he and Levinson were not so much guests as prisoners living in a gilded cage.

Professor Levinson entered the room quietly, wishing to minimize the intrusion of his friend's attempt at meditation. After a few moments he ventured a question, "William, where is our host today?"

Bedford slowly opened his eyes and gazed out through the vast picture window overlooking an exquisite courtyard. Marine birds of various varieties were circling then landed on a nearby table. An early morning breeze wafted lightly through the garden and the terns caught the wind and took flight out to the deep blue of the sea.

"He left a few minutes ago. He said it was time to meet with his guards and perform a perimeter check, as he put it." After a moment he added, perhaps as a deliberate understatement, "Jasher takes security quite seriously, doesn't he?"

Levinson commented dryly, "Our dramatic departure from Austin was definitely a testament to his foresight on the matter." After a moment he added, "Did you ever in your wildest imagination think that it would come to this?"

Bedford thought back a few months earlier when he was in the midst of attempting to connect a common cause between the decline of ancient civilizations and governments in modern days. He slowly smiled and replied, "Never. I suppose it goes back to the old adage that you should be careful what you wish for, you just might get more than you hoped."

Levinson grunted his agreement and added, "I have one even better by Henri Ameil: *"Destiny has two ways of crushing us – by refusing our wishes or by fulfilling them."* Both professors chuckled over Levinson's poignant quotation.

As they began to walk down the stairway leading into the basement work area, Levinson happened to glance in the direction of the rising sun of another day as it peeked then broke forth into the limitless horizon of the vast Mediterranean. He marveled at the scene and the wonder of so much history which had unfolded over and around this great body of water.

Jasher descended the downstairs then made his way tiredly into the basement study. He was feeling morose, but gratified that this latest attack had been successfully repulsed by Dov Hacohen and his friend in the Israeli Army. He had kept any mention of this incident from Levinson and Bedford, thus it had not distracted them from their labor nor had it caused any undue concern to his two colleagues; he had intended to keep it that way. They had been spared the details that he, alone, would have to carry around like so much excess baggage from this point forward. The two professors, Bedford and Levinson, were already busily poring over the latest translation pertaining to Noah. The two scientists were deep in conversation, but paused as Jasher entered the translation room.

"William, Isaac, don't let me interrupt your work."

Since arriving on Cyprus, work on the next volume of records had commenced. It was a relief to know that their acceptance of the reality of Cain was finally realized. There was, of course, much left in the records to be translated, and certainly more questions would be forthcoming as relating to Cain's Brotherhood, the Clan of the Scar, but he hoped their doubt regarding not only his own long life span, but Cain's as well, would be softened with time. This acceptance was the key to understanding and recognition of the translation as a credible, historical document.

The ancient bronze records, what Jasher was calling *The Abridgement*, lay before them on the work table. Nearby lay the translated manuscript and notes, including reference materials which the two professors had been using for translation. As Isaac glanced up from the work on the table before him, his eyes met Jasher's and his face became openly inquisitive.

He asked, "How is it you seem to know Cain so well? You speak of him as though you are relatives, though I am sure you would hardly claim him as such."

"Cain and I do not share a common lineage, but it amuses him to consider me a brother and, in some sense, I suppose our ancestral ties are close enough to be considered brothers. At least in our chance meetings I have permitted him to address me in this manner, though I doubt I could stop him if I tried. I know him quite well not just by his reputation and our chance meetings, but as an historical recorder of his works."

Bedford was looking over the records on the desk before them, and though Jasher still insisted on referring to them as *The Abridgement*, he and Levinson had taken to referring to them with a different name. Thinking about that difference, Professor Bedford asked, "I hope you don't mind us calling the finished translation *The Last Book of Jasher*. Assuming you don't have other translations in store for us, it would seem appropriate."

"This collaboration will be the last, so it seems proper, though inaccurate."

"How so?" asked Levinson.

"I would not like to take credit for the writings of so many. It is, after all, an abridgement of the observations of several men."

"You are too modest, my friend", commented William. "The world should know of your contribution to history."

Isaac pointed out, "There is the Hebrew text of the Book of Jasher. I have studied it, of course. Do you claim to be that man?"

"I am familiar with it also. That man had a different calling entirely and wrote of things outside the purview of my mission and I think that is all I should say on the matter."

Bedford smiled and commented, "But, that doesn't exactly answer the question, though, does it?"

Jasher shrugged then replied, "The new name you are calling *The Abridgment* will suffice if that is your pleasure."

Bedford had run across another reference to this Brotherhood of which Jasher had referred in his records. He asked pointedly, "Jasher, much of what you have described to us regarding this Society seems to corroborate my findings regarding the downfall of many great civilizations throughout history. Is this Order among us today?"

"Professors, the Society of Cain, or as he refers to it as the Clan of the Scar, has existed since well before the Great Flood, though over the centuries it may have gone underground for a short period of time, only to resurface with a renewed resurgence of strength. I can assure you, though, since the middle of the fifteenth century, it has ever grown stronger and its influence has been felt at every level of government in every nation of the world."

Levinson commented, "I gather, then, that Cain is still in control. The very idea that such a creature could still be alive today and in charge of a multi-national corporation is a matter I am still trying very hard to accept."

"It was he who was behind the attack in Austin, and I can assure you, he has not given up his plans to stop our publication of *The Abridgement.* A more modern version of Cain's original Society exists today and, as I have mentioned, and my abridgement will so testify, Cain is still actively at the helm. He is very much alive."

Bedford asked, "How deeply has his Society burrowed into our social fabric?"

"His Clan reviews every consideration of global governments at all levels for sincere, public-driven legislation. Under a cloak of well-meaning, concerned intervention, it subverts the original intent of those laws by placing the same laws in lock-step with his long-term agenda, which is to marginalize the agency of Mankind. In our day, Cain's society is not just secretive, it is invisible. It is the very opposite of public and its influence has been insinuated at all levels of government as well as the corporate-controlled media."

Levinson shook his head in perplexity and said, "It's incredible that in spite of his level of influence, none of his activities has ever appeared directly on any government radar."

"As our modern technologically-driven world has evolved and the works of men have become more transparent and visible on a larger, more public stage, now even Cain has been forced to remove his activities from the public light into what it is today, a shadow society."

Bedford was silent for a moment then asked, "What does he truly want?"

"He wants to emerge from the shadows and be universally acclaimed as our personal savior."

PART 1

THE DAYS OF PELEG

22 The children of Shem were Elam, and Sidon, and
Arphaxad, and Lud, and Aram.
23 And the children of Aram were Uz, and Hul, and
Gether, and Mash.
24 And Arphaxad begat Salah; and Salah begat Eber.
25 And unto Eber were born two sons: the name of
one was Peleg; for in his days was the earth divided;
and his brother's name was Joktan.

----- Genesis 10: 22-25

And unto a descendant of Shem, Eber, son of Salah
was born two sons: Joktan and Peleg. And lo, in the
days of Peleg the earth began to twist and shake to and
fro and was divided into two separate lands.
And many of the sons and daughters of Shem and his
brother Japheth were separated by the great waters and
now inhabited a land of promise, choice above all others and they were no more to be seen.

And Cain, agent of Lucifer, was wroth to be denied the hearts of those separated by the waters.

----- The Abridgement, Chapter 12

That men do not learn very much from the lessons of history is the most important of all the lessons of history.

----- Aldous Huxley

CHAPTER 1

THE FINAL DAYS OF NOAH

N oah opened his eyes on yet another day. Since the devastation of the Great Flood, he had counted himself fortunate to be alive and grateful beyond measure that his family and he had withstood the catastrophe. He recalled quite vividly the slow settling of the ship on dry land near a large mountain peak. Since there had been no way to navigate the ark, he had had to depend upon the providence of the Creator to position the ship in just the right place; and of course, He had. Noah recalled how he had called his sons and grandsons together and explained to them what was then expected.

"My sons, our Creator has seen fit to end our journey over the great waters at this location. Each of you has had responsibility over the feeding and care of each animal type and you must now ready each for their journeys over the earth. From here we will release the animals and allow life to begin again."

With a shout of triumph, each had jumped to his task and directed the animals to the exit of the ark. It was a scene never to be forgotten. As if with a solemn mission, each pair of animals, both male and female, began the long trek towards all points of the compass. A myriad species of birds and animals proceeded forward, some walking, some flying and others crawling, but all moved as if irresistibly drawn to some preordained location. Though the movements of some were slow while others out of biological design were much quicker, each seemed to grasp a certainty of their individual responsibilities to fulfill the measure of their creations.

Following the exit of the animals, Noah had called the next council a few days later, this time with all the family, including his daughters, granddaughters and their families. The message to them was no less significant than his earlier message to his sons regarding the animals.

"My sons and daughters, the Lord our Creator has spared us so that the human family can begin again. The task and labor before us is similar and equally as important as that of our first parents, now our ancestors, they who faced and sacrificed through toil and unknown challenges to provide a world of truth and love to their children. Our Earth has been cleansed and now we must restart this same process of building and procreation. There is nothing new about this. It has always been thus and will always continue to be done in this manner. So, if we hold onto our faith in the Creator then our direction is sure and clear and our success assured."

Nearly three hundred years had passed away since the Flood and Noah had given solemn thanks that all had proceeded so well from that point forward, and yet he was concerned. It disturbed and worried him that he was no closer to having access to the complete records of his people than when he had first walked again on dry land. His family was growing and now spreading throughout the earth, and although since the Flood he had maintained a written record in the language of his family, including an accurate genealogy, his descendants, up until now, had lived with only a limited written understanding of the distant past of their ancestors.

Moreover, though it might take time, he knew that Man's imperfections would inevitably lead to the same problems that had existed before the Flood and for that reason the Creator had been very specific on this matter. The recording and chronicle of the history and genealogy of his people from this day forward would be the responsibility of those through the lineage of Japheth, his eldest son, and would be faithfully maintained by those who would follow him.

Recently, however, in an effort to undermine the liberties of Man, Noah had become aware that Cain had recommenced spreading his nefarious society among his progeny. He realized that eventually they would fall again under his influence and that of the father of his lies, Lucifer, then mankind would yet again begin that long and terrible road toward darkness. To ensure the continuity of the work started by Seth and serve as an historical indictment against Cain and his Society, out of necessity, the next recorder had to be called to chronicle those historical events which would follow. They, too, would be recorded by someone of the lineage of his eldest son, Japheth.

The morning hour had grown late, but Jasher was still fast asleep. His father, a descendant of Japheth, was Elisha, a great-grandson of Noah, and he had allowed his son to sleep longer than usual. The previous day, Jasher had toiled long in the fields and so Elisha was feeling generous this morning. After his wife, Naomi, had prepared breakfast he decided that it was time to awake his eldest son from his deep slumber.

Elisha, always a man with a sense of humor, gave his son a quick shake and announced, "Jasher, rise and shine, my boy. The fields await your quick return. Your mother has prepared a fine breakfast to sustain us in our efforts." He paused then added thoughtfully, "Also, your grandfather, Noah, has arrived to pay us a visit."

Jasher, now a man, had developed a peculiar ability since childhood. Most persons require a few moments or even minutes to fully arouse themselves from a deep sleep, but Jasher, once awakened, became immediately alert and in tune with whatever was said or done around him. So, when he heard his father mention his distant grandfather's name, he quickly bounded from his bed and got dressed for the day. A few minutes later he walked alertly toward the breakfast area.

He halted just outside the dining room and watched with curiosity as his father and mother were deep in conversation with Noah. Looking around the room, he became aware that his younger siblings had been dismissed to eat out of doors while the adults remained inside. Judging from the tone and intensity of the subject of the discussion, it was clear that though his great-great-grandfather had grown older, his enthusiasm for talking had remained undiminished by time. Jasher reflected that Noah would now be nearing seven hundred years of age and the trip from his home near Mount Sephar had to have been especially tiring, yet he was here and that could only mean that his visit was more than just casual.

He recalled his last meeting with Noah. The man had been sickly and short-tempered, which for Noah was unprecedented. Usually affable and affectionate, he had appeared pensive and withdrawn, so his grandfather's outward demeanor appeared puzzling at the time. He was very fond of Noah, and given his current warmth and animation, he hoped that things had changed.

Jasher, himself, was usually open and garrulous, even chatty by nature. Lately, however, he seemed to feel something significant was about to happen to him and this had made him introspective and brooding; he was waiting for something, but as yet was still unable to define it. By now a young man of his age and maturity would have already been married with a family. By contrast, many of his younger siblings had already entered into such relationships and now had families and homes of their own. His parents were lately wondering why he was so reluctant to make such a commitment and move on with his life. He, too, was beginning to wonder the same thing.

Jasher entered the room and Noah, quickly for an old man he noted, arose and they both embraced and greeted one another with affection. "Grandfather, it has been far too long since we last saw you. You are actually looking better than I remember," he commented with a smile.

"Jasher," chided Naomi, "what a thing to say! You must apologize at once."

"Naomi," replied Noah with a smile, "the young man is just being honest and is quite correct." He added briskly, "Come, my son, and let us break bread and discuss things of importance." The four sat, and while eating, discussed matters of the family.

In the three hundred years since the Flood, the people were again prolific in their roles as procreators of the family of man. There were already the beginnings of mighty civilizations such as Canaan, Sumer and Assyria situated in the middle of the land mass predominately inhabited by the descendants of Ham and Shem. In the midst of this was the Ararat Mountains on which the ark had set aground. Many of those of the lineage of Shem had been divided with most of his descendants living towards the eastern side near their ancestral home of Sharon. Those descendants of Japheth had settled on the western side of the continent and it was to this location that Noah had traveled for his visit.

The breakfast now completed, Noah slowly rested his eyes on his great-great-grandson, Jasher, and with a clear, emphatic voice stated, "My son, as you may have guessed, my arrival was not simply to pay a friendly visit to family, though it would have given me great pleasure to do so. In any case, as you have pointed out, the last we met I was feeling old and troubled in my heart because there was still one more task that had to be performed before I go to my grave."

"What worried you grandfather? Surely it was not your old age. We all age eventually and die or so I have been led to believe." He smiled as he proclaimed what should have been obvious.

"No, my son, it was simple procrastination of something that I knew needed to be done. Lately, I was worried that unless the task was completed soon, I would not have the strength to perform it. This, of course, was foolish thinking on my part because when the Creator wants a man to perform a labor then he will provide him the means and the energy to complete it; in this matter He has."

Noah pondered the timing of his next statement. The difficult part of revelation, he reflected, was to know just how much to reveal and when. Should it be all at once or some here and another there? Noah knew that time was running out for him and he hoped that Jasher and his parents were sufficiently prepared to accept what he was about to reveal. Thus with some apprehension, he decided to reveal his entire message now and to extend a calling to Jasher. Moreover, his parents, he had reasoned, must be informed of the immediacy of the task ahead in order to fully support their son in the matter.

He began, "Before the Great Flood, our family had been devoted record keepers. There were many reasons why this was done, not the least of which was that the Creator had so decreed it, but from a purely practical standpoint, record keeping was a way for us to record our history, our genealogy and maintain our written and spoken language. Without the performance of these duties, our future civilizations would be bereft of our collective knowledge and advancements. Neither would they learn from our past mistakes."

He gazed at those around the table for a few moments as if deciding on his next point then proceeded. "The time has come for us to resume this duty. The Creator has decided that Ashkenaz, a descendant of my son Japheth, will take over this responsibility and he has been called to act in that capacity as well as his sons who will follow him. Those of the lineage of Ashkenaz will write of our genealogy and history since the Flood and those records will include not only names and locations, but a collection of our spiritual reflections as they proceed from our Lord and Creator to his children."

"I ran into one of my cousins the other day who was preparing to leave for some unknown destination. Did this have something to do with the calling you have extended to Ashkenaz?"

"Yes. For reasons known only to the Creator, I informed your cousin Ashkenaz and his descendants that they have been selected to relocate their families eastward toward the center of our land. Even as we speak, they have already begun the migration to the east."

Jasher sensed a premonition, almost as if he knew that his recent forebodings were about to be verified. "Grandfather, as you have said, you are not here for a social visit. Why do I fear it has something to do with me?"

"I have come to extend a different, but equally important calling to you Jasher, and though you will assume a similar role in the matter of keeping the records of our people, your task will be specifically historical in nature."

Noah was aware that Seth, his distant kinsman, had performed this duty for many years before the Flood. On one occasion, Noah had asked his father, Lamech, to share some light on Seth's calling. Lamech had responded that he had once asked Seth whether this duty had ever brought him complete satisfaction. Seth's reply was typically poignant as he explained: "Completion of the Creator's Will brought me satisfaction, but the duty was often disappointing. Seeing and recording men at their worst never fulfilled my soul's desire, thus I often had to look elsewhere to satisfy those needs."

So, knowing the trials that Jasher would face, it was difficult for Noah to express his excitement of this calling. Instead, he attempted to convey the gravity and importance of this singular duty.

"Jasher, it is the will of the Creator that your duty will be to record the rise and fall of the great civilizations of mankind and to observe in particular the influence of the Society of your distant uncle Cain upon their decline. This task will seldom bring a sense of personal fulfillment, but the Creator has decreed that this work must be done to serve as a witness to future generations against Cain in a day when he and the father of all lies, Lucifer, will attempt to obtain complete control over the hearts of men."

Naomi appeared visibly pained at the loss of her son. "How soon is he to leave, Noah?" She gripped her husband's hand for support.

"Jasher and I must pack and leave this same day on a journey far to the east where I will show him the resting place of our records. During our trek eastward, I will explain to him his duties and this special calling which he will carry for as long as the Creator has ordained it."

Jasher sat silently throughout Noah's discourse. Several times he had begun to speak and protest his disposition and preparedness for this calling, but each time he tried it was clear to him that what he had been expecting had finally arrived and the notion, he discovered, was quite exhilarating. Notwithstanding, as he later came to believe through experience, if pleasure seems greatest in anticipation, it is also true of trouble.

Finally, after a few moments of apprehension, Jasher replied, "If this is truly the will of the Creator, then he must be desperate. Surely there are others more qualified to perform this labor than I."

His mother was aghast at her son's reply, but Elisha only smiled, trying to hide his smile behind his hand.

Noah smiled and with a laugh Jasher thought improbable, given the serious circumstances, replied, "My son, you and I have so much in common. I expressed those same feelings of inadequacy to my own father, Lamech, when he extended my own calling. At the time, I was hardly much older than you are now."

Jasher brooded a moment then asked, "How did your father respond?"

"He told me that we are but the clay in the potter's hand. If we are patient, He will mold us until we become what we have been ordained to be."

Noah's wizened eyes looked over to Jasher's parents and he quietly declared, "Your son will be long-lived and will perform his duties admirably. I have seen it or I would have been more reluctant to travel this far and test my health. I hope you can spare him from the fields because his work begins the moment we depart for the east."

It was early morning as they made their way gradually up the glacis toward the cave entrance to the mountain depository. His mind seemed to be undimmed by the years. Though it had been over three centuries since Noah had last walked its pathways, he recalled the conditions leading up to the Flood as though they had occurred only the day before. Despite the effects of the Flood which had affected so much of the landscape, he noted that the valley itself seemed to be untouched by time or wear of weather. The glacier was gone now, of course, no doubt obliterated by the falling, torrential waters as was nearly everything else during the early stages of the event. But, he remembered a promise that was made and those who had kept it, thus he also suspected that the valley was still inhabited.

Noah was keeping pace with his grandson and seemed none worse from the wear. Since beginning this journey, Jasher had grown to admire the stamina of his grandfather. He had never seen a man of his age with as much spring in his step, especially the last few days. It was almost as if he had regressed back to a younger self, so instead of growing more weary with each mile, he seemed to gain strength. As they had begun the last leg of the journey this morning Noah had commented that he had never felt better in the last week than he had felt since departing from the ark so many years earlier.

To Noah it felt especially good to be alive today and he smiled inwardly as though divining the thoughts of his grandson. As they rested for a few minutes, he declared, "Jasher, do not be too deceived by the youthful strength in my old bones and sinew. The Creator has strengthened me enough to complete this climb."

Jasher commented, "That may be, but if you feel a need to stop for a rest, just let me know. I doubt that cave is going anywhere."

With a smile, Noah remarked, "Well, do not be concerned; I will not collapse before my mission is completed." With that said, he again led the way upward.

They followed a trail that had been carefully cut from the stone and rock leading through the tree line. Noticing the diligent manner in which the path had been tended, Jasher concluded that these were signs of human habitation in the immediate area. The pathway had certainly made the climb much easier and so he turned to Noah to offer a comment.

"Grandfather, it appears we are not alone in this valley. I suspect that if we had come in through the south instead of the north, we would have encountered settlements."

"Jasher," Noah explained, "You are quite correct. There have always been settlements of our people in this valley. I did not want to announce our presence just yet, but we may yet pay them a visit after our descent down from the mountain, especially of course if you have to carry me down on your back."

"Why do you think that?"

"After showing you the cave and the records, my mission will be essentially over. Then, our donkey will be too busy bearing our recording plates and I am afraid there will not be enough room on his back for my old tired bones."

"How much farther is the climb, Grandfather?"

Noah realized his memory was as sharp as it once was, an additional boon from the Creator, he reflected. "Jasher," Noah instructed, "from this point forward you will need to pay close attention. We are looking for a cat-like formation and as you pass the gently sloping glacis then through the tree-line, you will begin to see near the top of the mountain a rock formation in the shape of a cat's head. Stay on the path which will lead past the glacis though the trees, always staying the course toward the direction of the cat."

"I suppose if I go astray, I can always ask for directions at one of the settlements. Since they have been here, as you say since the beginning, they will surely know the way up to the cave."

"Of course, the people of the valley have done a marvelous job of constructing and then maintaining the pathways, but who knows how much longer they will remain here or for how long the path will be tended. You must take care to watch for the signs or you will miss the entrance to the cave."

Noah entered the cavern first and led Jasher down a short hall that opened up into a large inner room. Off to the left, Jasher noticed a large rounded rock which had been chiseled to form a solid wheel.

Now curious, Jasher asked, "Grandfather, the wheel over there seems peculiar. Would you know its purpose?"

"That, my son, was the only thing between the flood waters and the records; also, as it turned out, those who took refuge here."

He smiled as he reflected upon the amazing perseverance of the inhabitants who had to endure being covered up inside this cave for so long. "You will discover soon enough that they are your cousins and thanks to their willingness to assume the role of caretakers of the records buried in the mountain, they were permitted to survive the Flood when so many others perished." He added thoughtfully, "And that, Jasher, is a story for another time."

Jasher was amazed at the natural lighting of the cavern and realized immediately that this light emanated from all parts of the cave. Within one room were stacked records to the height of a man and each was exquisitely preserved in a manner in which Jasher was unfamiliar. Noah noted the expression of awe on the face of his grandson and he pointed out, "From this moment forward, this is now your cave and your responsibility."

Jasher nodded his understanding then noticed Noah had a slight limp. "Grandfather, you are tired and should rest."

"Yes, we will rest here for the night, so bring the food in from the saddle pack. As I recall, there is a natural spring in the next room, so we shall have fresh water."

The two men sat contentedly within the confines of the inner cavern. Noah was especially aware that, though his body was weary, his mind was clear and unclouded from worry for the first time since before beginning this curious life journey hundreds of years before the Flood. That is a very long time he reflected. His wife was long deceased and his sons and grandsons and their progeny were raised and had families of their own. New civilizations were beginning and the world he had once known was a distant memory. He suspected that he was no longer looked upon in the same patriarchal manner he once had been and with a sudden realization he knew that his life mission was coming to a close.

Jasher snapped Noah from his internal reverie with a request. "Grandfather, please tell me of our distant kinsman Seth. If I am to assume the same role, it might help if I understand who he was and how he went about performing this duty."

As if recalling an especially memorable meeting he replied, "I met him on a number of occasions in my youth when I was younger than you are now." He paused to gather his thoughts. "But, I fear that most of what I know of him I received second-hand from my father, Lamech. What I do know is that Seth received this duty as a sacred calling from his father, Adam. Seth was brilliant in a way that set him apart from every other man alive and he managed to see much change in his lifetime."

Jasher pointed out that, "My father once said, whenever there was a positive gain to our civilization before the Flood, it invariably can be attributed directly back to him."

"Very true. My father, Lamech, mentioned on a number of occasions that Seth had a keen intellect for science and mathematics and loved to discuss the movements of the heavenly bodies through the night time sky." Noah was pensive a moment then proceeded. "But, he was more than that. Most of us struggle with the little light we have and occasionally shine like the stars in the heavens, on especially good days, perhaps even like the moon, but Seth was always like the sun."

Jasher appreciated the metaphorical comparison and added, "Grandfather, I think you are greatly playing down the role you have played in the Creator's plan. Seth's wisdom must have been the result of his longevity." As an afterthought, he mused, "He must have been long-lived for you to have known him and he, like your father, must have perished in the Flood."

Noah, too, had made the same comment about Seth. "I know not of how my father, Lamech, met his end, but he did mention to me that Seth, being a just man, was taken away in the spirit, not having to taste of death in the same way as all other men."

"That I had never heard. What does it mean to be taken away in the spirt?"

"After delivering the final records to Lamech and showing him the whereabouts of this mountain and what it contained, Seth had concluded his days were done, his mission completed, so he hung back as my father departed down the road. Lamech turned to wave a farewell when he beheld a light open up in front of Seth then seemed to settle upon him. You may think Lamech may have imagined what followed next, but according to his account, when the light disappeared, he asserted that Seth was no longer on the road. He had simply vanished from sight or taken away in the spirit."

Jasher, upon hearing his grandfather's assertion, looked doubtful, then changed the subject slightly, "How did Seth go about the task of recording?"

"Seth, when moved upon by the spirit, would enter a land which had been corrupted by Cain's Society and make enquiries among the people. He would interview not only the common citizens, such as farmers and artisans, but especially those within the inner courts of governments and kings. When he had gathered enough information from the inhabitants he then made copious notes of his own general observations."

Jasher looked around the room at the numerous bronze plates and marveled at the painstaking time it must have taken to copy his observations onto them. "He must have recorded them on the metal plates like those before us."

"His knowledge of those times was vast and no doubt preserved on the records you see in the cave and here he safeguarded them for future generations." Noah continued, but with a personal observation. "He performed this recording task brilliantly, but it brought him very little happiness, you see. It took him away from those he loved and eventually he lived to see each member of his immediate family pass on in death before he died."

"He must have been very long-lived for him to have outlived even his sons."

Noah murmured sadly, "Jasher, it is a hard thing for a father to outlive his progeny. You must prepare yourself for that same eventuality."

Jasher felt the weight of a long lifetime of responsibility settle firmly upon his shoulders. "So, it is to be that way with me also?"

Noah shook his head and slowly agreed. "Yes, but who knows for how long that may be?" He further pointed out, "Seth had a special strength about him which only comes to those who have fully committed themselves to the Creator's will and if you will always remember that then you, too, will find the strength to do what is necessary."

Jasher looked around and shook his head in quiet despair. "All this seems too much for me. I am but a man and one lacking in the wisdom for such a calling."

Noah gently patted his shoulder and declared, "I only know that He would not have chosen you unless you were capable of fulfilling this mission in spite of the dangers inherent to confronting our ancient enemy and antagonist, Cain. Seth may have had a lonely and sometimes dangerous task, but he was never alone and neither will you be."

A concern had settled upon Jasher as he heard the words of Noah regarding this adversary. "So, I am to record the influence of Cain and his Society on future civilizations. I have never met him yet I fear him." He then asked, "What can I expect of this man?"

Noah paused for a moment to reflect how to describe civilization's greatest threat. "Cain is pathetically amoral and has allied himself with the Father of all lies, Lucifer, but eventually he will outlive the need to rely on him. If you ever meet Cain, and I fear you will much sooner than later, remember that his force is stronger and his actions are more cunning than Lucifer and will, in fact, eventually rule over him. He embraces no personal dogma save one, the elimination of our freedoms for his own self-aggrandizement. Everything he does and says is a means to an end and the end is always the same without change: the dominance of Mankind and the eventual overthrow of personal agency."

"It would seem to me that the control over all men would be beyond the reach of anyone. What possible reason would he have to do this, other than, of course, the gratification that comes with power over others?"

"Like his ally, Lucifer, he asserts that we are unworthy to have the right of choice and we all would deny it or avoid it if given the chance. This will always be the rationale of men who seek power for its own sake and usually Cain will be behind those efforts with his larger plan. He will build up whole civilizations committed to his beliefs and use anyone, including whole armies to achieve that aim just to prove his point. There is nothing or anyone he will avoid sacrificing to achieve that goal. Part of that aim is the destruction of every record relating to his diabolical society, the Clan of the Scar."

"What does he think to accomplish by destroying the records?"

After a moment of reflection, Noah attempted to explain. "In his self-deluded way, he wants to succeed at his purpose without being held account-able for the destruction and misery he causes along the way. That is why he seeks to destroy all the records in this mountain and every other record you will add to this collection. If you can deliver the records to this depository before he can destroy them, however, then they will be safe, for the land on which this mountain sits is hallowed ground and he will not be permitted to penetrate it nor anyone he sends. Seth and my father, Lamech, consecrated this land and it is holy."

"Then I should I fear for my life? If what you say is true, he will come after me and will not tire until I am dead in the ground."

"Even though Cain has limited power to destroy the records, his power is insufficient to destroy you as it has been disallowed. Nonetheless, you must be cunning and use whatever means necessary to safeguard them. Cain is well aware of these conditions so he will try every other method he can conceive to thwart your labors, including threats, lies and intimidation. But you must be strong and resist for the records must stand as a credible witness against him one day. That is your sacred mission and duty and that is the reason he is so dedicated to destroy the records from seeing the light of day."

"Then the records are maintained to stand as a witness of his activities among men?"

"They stand between him and what he desires most: justification for his actions and acquittal for his deeds, for without them as a witness, he and Lucifer will attempt to convince the Creator that Mankind is unworthy of our agency to make personal choices. Both have deluded themselves into believing that the Creator would reverse his position in this matter. In the end, even Cain will see that this freedom is an eternal concept and no one can violate it without consequences. The irony is that even Cain has his agency of choice, though he would deny it to others."

"Then why maintain the records?"

"Justice demands it and if they were not present, then our Creator would cease to be a just god."

Jasher could see Noah was getting tired, but he ventured one last question. "Will there be others like myself?"

Noah seemed taken back with the question. He pondered it for a few moments then replied, "Jasher, you will be the first since the Great Flood to carry this duty, but no other floods will descend to interrupt the flow of man's need to gather together in large groups. As these civilizations grow and spawn others, the time will arrive to call more chroniclers to assist in this work."

"If I am to get help along the way, from where will these men be called and how will I know them?"

"Primarily, they will come from your progeny, so teach them well. They will have a similar mission, but unlike you, they will have more or less a normal span of life, so in a sense you will be the only one to insure continuity of this calling throughout the ages. As they are called, they will seek you out and deliver their records to you, and in turn, you will deliver the records to this mountain for safekeeping."

"I gather then that the location of this mountain vault is to be kept secret even among my descendants."

"Cain will no doubt make it his life's work to prevent others and you from recording his deeds and he will destroy whole kingdoms in an attempt to discover this location by whatever means he can. You must not reveal its whereabouts to anyone else save those who you explicitly trust or those of your lineage."

"Is there any limitation on his resolve to find and destroy the records?"

"If he knows the location of the vault he will make a concerted effort to stop you even if it means destroying everything in your path to get them there safely. It is the one secret regarding your mission that must be kept and the only one worth dying for and, I might add, killing for."

"Killing seems harsh. I hope that it will never come to that."

"Nor I, but it is still better for a few to suffer than an entire civilization of people destroyed by corrupt men who may never receive justice for their crimes. Never deny others their right of choice and you will always be on safe ground."

Noah, the great patriarch from the time of the Flood, bedded down for the night next to his great-great-grandson. He discovered that, unlike previous nights during the trek eastward, he was exhausted from a long day of walking up the mountain; his feet and legs were beginning to ache and the distraction caused him to wince in pain. He observed that Jasher had little trouble dropping off to sleep and he smiled inwardly at the stamina and vigor of his grandson, so young and anxious to begin his life while he was at the end of his own time and quite ready to move on.

He had discovered that time had more meaning to those who carefully planned and thought out their lives. *It is something we think, therefore it is. Is time simply an extension of our minds,* he wondered?

As he was thus pondering, a light across the room got brighter and as he shifted his eyes in that direction, a man in a white robe passed through a brilliant gateway and stood there as though waiting. The man then beckoned Noah in his direction towards the light then smiling the man nodded his head knowingly. It was then that Noah noticed the man looked vaguely familiar as if he were an old acquaintance or perhaps a distant relative. Noah painfully raised himself up, now all at once feeling the full age of his life, his body protesting the shift from his arms, then his legs to his feet. He swayed upon tired and feeble legs now swollen from months of walking. The pain was terrible and his aches pure misery as the agony coursed throughout his body. In spite of the pain, with sudden joyful understanding, he knew his time had come around at last and without hesitation slowly made his way towards the light and the portal that led to beyond time.

Jasher awoke in the morning refreshed and anxious to begin this new chapter in his life. He expected to find Noah nearby, but after calling his name several times, he concluded that he must have walked away to be alone. When he did not return for a few minutes, Jasher looked about the cavern, calling his name. He searched each inner cave, but Noah was nowhere to be seen then he checked outside, but Noah was nowhere to be found. He spent the rest of the morning awaiting his return, but at some point it became obvious he would not; Noah was simply gone and would not be back. It was strange to be alone after having his grandfather's company for so many months, but feeling the time was now right and at peace with his decision, he began to descend the mountain.

He felt different in a way that he could not exactly define. On personal reflection, he realized his life seemed more directed and focused; a burden was evident, but it was manageable. To punctuate this personal reflection and seal a good beginning for his life's calling, he decided to pay a visit to the inhabitants farther south in the valley. Noah had been correct; there was something special about them.

Over thirty years passed away in the interim since Jasher descended the mountain. With him he carried several blank plates he would use for writing his initial recordings and this activity would consume the first decades of his mission. When asked about his great-great-grandfather Noah, he would invariably point out that the Lord Creator had taken him unto himself. This seemed to satisfy those truly interested, which over the course of time became fewer and fewer. It was sad, he supposed, but most of Noah's descendants were content to live out their own lives following their own paths and found no occasion to be overly interested in the whereabouts or final resting place of the great patriarch of the family.

CHAPTER 2

SARGON OF AKKAD

The insatiable need for heartless power and ruthless control is the telltale sign of an uninitiated man – the most irresponsible, incompetent and destructive force on earth.

----- Michael Leunig, Australian poet and cultural commentator

The name of the Mari people of ancient Mesopotamia can be traced back to Mer, an ancient storm deity of the region now known as Syria and considered the patron deity of the city of a similar name. It has been noted that the name of the city Mari was spelled similarly to that of the storm god and can be concluded that it was derived from that name, Mer.

The Mariotes worshiped both Semitic and Sumerian deities and established their city as a center of trade. Although these earlier periods were characterized by heavy Sumerian cultural influence, Mari was not a city which had attracted Sumerian immigrants, rather a Semitic speaking nation that used a dialect similar to Eblaite.

At the heart of Mari, a royal palace was built, which also served as a temple. Four successive architectural levels from the kingdom's palace have been unearthed and the last two levels are dated to the Akkadian period.

According to researchers, King Hidar of Mari was succeeded by Isqi-Mari whose royal seal was discovered and it depicts battle scenes, which suggest that he was responsible for the destruction of Ebla while still a general. Just a decade after Ebla's destruction, around 2300 BCE, Mari itself was destroyed and burned to the ground by Sargon, King of Akkad, who many believe to be Nimrod, the mighty hunter as mentioned in the Book of Genesis of the Old Testament.

The Akkadian Empire was an ancient Semitic empire centered in the city of Akkad and its surrounding region, also called Akkad, in ancient Mesopotamia. The empire united all the indigenous Akkadian-speaking Semites and the Sumerian speakers under one rule. This Empire controlled Mesopotamia, the Eastern Mediterranean lands of Greece, south to Lebanon as well as parts of Iran.

Akkadia reached its political peak between the 24th and 22nd centuries BCE, following the conquests by its founder Sargon of Akkad (2334 – 2279 BC). Under Sargon and his successors, the Akkadian language was briefly imposed on neighboring conquered states such as Elam, later to be known as Iran. Akkad is sometimes regarded as the first empire in history, though there are earlier Sumerian claimants.

After the fall of the Akkadian Empire, the Akkadian people of Mesopotamia eventually coalesced into two major Akkadian cultured nations: Assyria in the north and a few centuries later Babylonia in the south. In time, Assyria fell under complete control of Babylonia and ceased to exist as a separate nation.

The early Sumerian civilization, considered to be the oldest of all recorded cultural centers, can be traced back to around the region known as Mari, later to become the land of Syria. The first king over the land was naturally Cain who, once he had established a power base, began to send out the tentacles of the Clan and re-establish control, which he had lost at the time of the Great Flood. Over the next few centuries his rule was largely uncontested and those kings who attempted to invade his land with their armies found themselves in a fight that they discovered quickly was unwinnable. His Society had managed to infiltrate every neighboring territory and undermine every attempt by those kingdoms to take over the region. If Cain's forces were outnumbered, he simply called upon his spies or assassins to even the playing field. The kings were assassinated either before the invasion could begin or when it became clear that Mari might be eventually overrun. Then Cain attacked when they were at their most vulnerable, supplanting the king of the invaded nation with a new ruler of his choosing. This had been done in a protracted war with the Eblaites in what is now Syria and now a member of the Clan sat on the throne of Ebla. In this fashion he began to spread his influence once more over the land.

Cain's latest attempt at expansion had driven his arm of influence farther south and to the east along the banks of the Tigris and Euphrates Rivers to a land that he initially called Shinar. From Mari, he already controlled the headwaters of the Euphrates River as well as all the major trade routes. As it was more centralized to his proposed expansion, he decided to move his power base to Shinar and establish a new apex of control around a new city/state he later called Akkad, which would later evolve into the Assyrian then later the Babylonian Empires.

While Cain had found a capable but ruthless man by the name of Sargon to rule over this new land of Shinar, also known as Akkad, the Kingdom of Mari he left in the nominal hands of a trusted member of the Clan, Isqi-Mari. He, to his credit, had proven himself capable in battle to Cain against the Eblaites and it was unfortunate that that trust was about to be tested by his two willful daughters, Nisaba and Inanna, both wives of Sargon.

The man awoke from a deep, drug induced dream state. His first feeling was that of being wet, the second of being tied down. Though his reactions were still slow, he realized that his arms and legs had been bound together in a sitting position making it difficult to move. In addition to the loss of movement, the ropes had also disallowed normal blood circulation to his arms and legs, so his feelings in those areas had been cut off. His eyes, still slow to focus, managed to detect he was located in a near-empty room devoid of everything save himself, a few urns and a large cauldron in which he had been placed. Around the near sterile quarters, someone had displayed a few statues and pictographs of Sumerian gods: Anu, of the firmament, as well as Enli, god of the air and Ishtar, goddess of love. His condition prevented any movement, but his peripheral vision could just make out an adjoining room closed off by a translucent curtain made of light cotton gauze or linen hanging over the doorway.

As he became more aware and less under the influence of the drugs he began to speculate about his surroundings, and though still groggy, he tried to recall how it was that he had ended up in this position. As a captured soldier, for all intents and purposes, he knew that his life was over unless his captors were short of experienced men and he could be folded into their army. He began to recall that he had probably been dosed during the evening meal and so, while unconscious, he had been trussed and dropped into this vat of water.

Is this an act of ritual cleansing in propitiation to Akkadian gods, he asked himself. *If so, then why the elaborate use of the ropes? Why not just finish me off with the sword and give me a true soldier's death?*

At length, the after effects of the drug had worn slowly off and with it a sense of panic had set in. He began to feel heat from below and around him and wondered from whence it came and its purpose. He then threw an anxious glance again toward the curtain and gradually he became aware that behind the curtain sat a man, still, yet attentive, almost as if he were waiting for something to begin.

Sargon had been anticipating this moment for a few days now. He sat naked quietly behind the translucent curtain, his eyes were closed, his muscular arms crossed loosely around his stomach, the hands now dangling between his legs occasionally touching his inner thighs. The experience was totally intoxicating, wildly erotic beyond anything he had ever experienced. He waited in keen anticipation for the moment of discovery when the victim became completely aware of his helpless plight then later as the water began to slowly warm. *What would the victim say and how would he react to his absolute inability to change the course of his fate?* He knew the questions varied insignificantly between victims, yet there was always the moment of absolute truth and clarity which they all shared in common. As the water got hotter then finally came to a boil, the question of why would no longer be relevant. The only thought that would consume the man would be the removal of the relentless pain that would never cease until he passed out hours later either from the burning or because he had simply wearied himself from the constant screaming.

Sargon, King of the Akkadian Empire, had been ruler over the land for nearly thirty years and in that time had swept away all obstructions to his rule, but he was still an unhappy man. In fact, the only real interest of late was the anticipated expansion farther north into the land of Nineveh, the Kingdom of the Assyrians. Sargon was at his most contented when he was planning or expanding his borders or in battle, but when he wasn't thus occupied his moods tended to bounce between boredom, anxiety and even depression, the latter having led eventually to insomnia. He was still awaiting the final approval of a northern expansion into Assyria from the Master Mahan of the Clan and he was getting impatient over the delay. It was this anxiety which had led to his recent interest in what he privately considered as "boiling therapy".

He was in the company of a member of the Clan a few years earlier when this brother mentioned how he had cured his anxiety and insomnia attacks by parboiling a human being. He had gone on to explain that he had discovered, quite by accident, that if he slowly boiled a person, usually a man, it would settle his anxiety or depression long enough for him to function. Sargon had been skeptical at first, but later decided to try it for himself. He had been assured by the brother that if he sat completely still with his eyes closed, while the trussed-up, drugged man slowly regained consciousness and began screaming, first in terror then later with absolute pain as the water slowly came to a boil and the torment was at its greatest, his own anxiety would begin to dissipate and eventually permit sleep.

Sargon's first few attempts fell short of expectations, however, so he remained dissatisfied with the results. It seemed the water had come to a boil too quickly and so the process scarcely lasted long enough to completely relieve his anxiety; in fact, if anything it made it worst. One attempt had gone so badly that in a rage he had the boiler-man thrown into the cauldron after the other man had expired.

But Sargon, being a persistent man, had scoured the region until he found a master who knew how to administer just the right amount of fuel over time so the process would last from sundown until the early morning hours. The screams would begin to trail off sometime after midnight until only small whimpers could be heard from the hapless victim. Finally, perhaps an hour later, the man had passed out and only then was Sargon able to sleep. This activity would take place usually twice per week as the king's anxiety levels would begin to peak, but lately the screams could be heard on a third night. As one might imagine, this activity had just the opposite effect on the rest of the household.

Inanna and Nisaba were sisters and shared the same husband, King Sargon of Akkad. Nisaba, the elder of the two, was now seated in Inanna's dressing room in the palace, and while she busied herself brushing her sister's hair, Inanna was bemoaning their station, a common occurrence. In her usual puling voice she reserved for the current topic of discussion, she turned to Nisaba and remarked, "Sister, our husband Sargon is a beast and you know it! I wished our father could have found us a more suitable husband!"

Nisaba, with obvious annoyance at her sister's indiscretion and using the comb to emphasize her words, whispered, "You should learn to curb your tongue, Inanna. Sargon's spies are everywhere. I declare, I thought I saw one in my soup the other day."

Inanna, as usual, ignored her sister's warnings and replied more loudly than good taste and caution should have demanded. "Sister, his spies are the least of our worries. I swear, if he boils another man, it will drive me insane;

the noise goes on all night long. I scarcely got a moments rest last night and neither did you, so save me the lecture on indiscretion."

Nisaba knew well to what her sister was referring. Their husband was a callous, uncaring man and these things could at least be tolerated, but the boiling was completely unnerving and lately had been occurring sometimes as many as three times per week.

Ever fearful that her sister's complaints might reach the wrong ears, Nisaba counselled, "Sister, regardless, we must be careful how we express our dislike for this practice. We, too, might end up in the pot one day."

Inanna blanched at the notion. Of course, it had never occurred to her that anyone who questioned Sargon, especially his wives, could end up in a similar fashion as his enemies.

"You are right, Nisaba, but this is no way to live!" With a moan, she murmured, "I wish we were home with Father and Mother."

"I agree, Sister, but, nonetheless this is our life and we should make the best of it."

Nisaba resumed combing her sister's hair then began the process of braiding them into tresses. She had been deep in thought when the king's third son, prince Shar-kali passed the open room from the hallway. Now there was an attractive man, thought Nisaba, scarcely for the first time. He was handsome, yet considerate, and as he had demonstrated on many occasions in local tournaments, he was an expert with a bow. It was a shame that he stood to inherit very little of his father's throne; his two older brothers, one who was imbecilic and the eldest an oaf, stood to gain it all.

"Was that Shar-kali?" asked Inanna a trifle too casually.

"It was."

"But, Little Sister, his comings and goings are of no concern of yours," she warned.

Nisaba had observed her sister's interest in the young man as well, but Inanna lacked her sister's discretion in such matters. When she looked upon the prince, it was more open, less circumspect than the occasion and good sense would dictate.

"Whatever do you mean, Nisaba?"

"You know exactly what I mean, Sister. We have a comfortable life here and though it is far from perfect, we will hardly starve nor go without so long as we behave ourselves."

"I was just curious. No harm in being aware of who walks the hallways, Sister."

"Uh huh".

Nisaba had grown skeptical of most things, including her sister's supposed discreet behavior around the prince. The real problem was that she knew Shar-kali felt the same about Inanna. Nisaba had observed him giving her more than a casual glance at the evening meals and he always managed to position himself near her whenever the occasion permitted. His conversations to her were always respectful, of course, but his eyes told a very different story. Naturally, his mother would notice, assuming Sargon would allow her to grace the table, which he seldom did these days.

According to Sargon, a few years ago Shar-kali's mother, Queen Shala, had become barren. It was, of course hardly his fault, he had asserted, and he seemed to see no reason why he should be reminded that he was cursed with a wife who could no longer bare him children. In consequence, Nisaba and Inanna were packed off from their homeland, Mari, to become his wives in order to fill the void vacated by the Queen who had had the bad taste to grow too old to produce Sargon more progeny.

Nisaba would tell you, however, that a change of wives had changed nothing of his current childless condition. It was obvious the few times Sargon had bothered to exercise his conjugal rights for nightly visits to Nisaba and her sister that either he was past his years of siring children or his sexual interest was non-existent. Furthermore, Nisaba had concluded that Sargon's sole interest was expanding the borders of his kingdom and sex had precious little to do with any of that.

"Just remember, dear Sister, whatever happens to you, the same happens to me. We came in together and we will go out the same way."

Nevertheless, as many will attest, love pays scant attention to reason or common sense. So, when it came to her feelings for Shar-kali, Sister Nisaba's counsel had fallen on deaf ears. Inanna was attracted to Shar-kali and she knew he felt the same for her, and as far as she was concerned, the discussion ended there.

Shar-kali had fallen in love with Inanna almost from the first week she and her sister had been betrothed to his father, the King. Over the past two years, he could have had any woman he wished in Akkad and had tried many, but Inanna was the only one he ever thought about now. His love had made him only dimly aware of how dangerous it would be for the two of them if they ever wanted a relationship, but his feelings for her had grown so intense that the very thought of her had left him reckless and past caring. He had seen the way she glanced at him when he passed her in the hallway and later at the evening meals and her smile, as if reserved for him only, was always radiant and inviting. This evening, he had been so overcome with lust for her that later, when he passed her in the hallway, he had carelessly allowed his fingers to reach out to her own. They both paused slightly to allow him a light caress then she had returned his touch ever so wantonly and squeezed, insinuating more.

The desert days can be quite warm, but if they can be tolerated there is always the night to look forward to. The nights along the Euphrates were cool year-round and Inanna found them quite exhilarating, this night in particular. As she walked out to the terrace and felt the evening wind blow across the city of Akkad, her anticipation of the coming night left her a little breathless. Waiting in the shadows was Shar-kali and as she heard his light step from behind, her heart began to beat faster in anticipation of their first joining.

As she turned, she felt the desert breeze lightly wafting the gauzy material clinging to her near-naked body, outlining her taut, ready figure. As he came nearer, she beckoned him onward into her outstretched arms. Both came forward with neither care nor self-restraint. An embrace and a kiss, the melding of the two bodies in a sensuous swaying harmony convinced them both of mutual, heartfelt desires. As he tenderly lifted her, she placed her arms about his neck and their eyes locked of promises to come, their lips lightly met now sealing desires of hidden gifts to be revealed. Shar-kali slowly carried her back into the bed chamber and lay her down upon the bed she had prepared only minutes earlier. Their mutual unspoken desire consumed them and they became as one.

You silly fool!" cried Nisaba. Just how long have these ridiculous trysts been going on?"

"Over a month, but don't make it sound so cheap!"

She was furious that her sister would think her feelings for Shar-kali were less than genuine. "We are in love and there is hardly more to be said about it. We will continue to meet as long as it suits us. Besides, we have been discreet."

"I beg to differ, Little Sister!" Nisaba pointed out sharply, pulling her own hair in frustration. "You wouldn't know how to be discreet if it snuck up and bit you on your silly little ass. He is the third son of King Sargon and he stands to inherit nothing from his father. What he will receive for his night time visits to your bedchamber will be a loss of his silly head. Clearly his smaller head has been doing all his thinking lately."

"You say that because you are jealous and would steal him away from me the first chance you got!"

Any conversation with her sister was like talking with a child. Inanna seemed only vaguely aware of the danger in which she had placed them both by her affair. Nisaba shook her head in exasperation then sat down heavily on a nearby chair, her head in her hands.

"You will be discovered eventually and when your treachery reaches the ears of the King, our husband, and it will, then our lives will scarcely be worth more than two farts in a sand storm."

Hearing Nisaba's accusation, Inanna's indignation suddenly changed to tearful concern. "What should we do? I love him with all my heart and I couldn't bear to live without him!" Her sniffling quickly turned to an all-out cascade of tears.

"You little trollop! Shut up while I try to figure out a solution to this mess!"

Nisaba was sick of listening to her sister's silly prattles. Their situation was hopeless and she realized it would be up to her to remedy the dilemma they were in. Her mind began racing ahead, testing one avenue of thought after the next only to reject each out of hand as unworkable. Asking Inanna and her lover to give up their affair was beyond either of them; they would grow increasingly negligent until the whole household was aware of the betrayal to the king. Then it would be just a matter of time before all three of them ended up in a vat over a hot flame. After several minutes of fruitless considerations, Nisaba had to conclude there was only one workable plan left to them.

"We must escape back to the home of our father in Mari. He and only he can protect us."

"What about Shar-kali? I can't leave him here to be boiled in his father's pot!"

"Well, obviously he must come with us, you empty-headed girl! It would do him scarcely any good to stay here and try to explain to Sargon the details of your midnight humping."

Inanna ignored her sister's crude remark. "Do you think our father will take us back?"

In exasperation Nisaba rolled her eyes upward and replied, "Yes, and he will have much to explain to Sargon, but he is the only one who can help us and we must leave immediately. Inform your lover we leave tomorrow night and he must ensure our travel will be discreet or we may all end up learning how a boiled lobster feels."

Cain was ushered ceremoniously into the audience chamber, and while he found a comfortable chair, Sargon ordered cool drinks from the nearby attending servant. When the servant returned with the drinks, Sargon dismissed him to insure privacy. As a young boy will await a sweet treat with obvious anticipation, Sargon asked, "So, Cain do I now have leave to move against our neighbors to the north?"

Cain leaned back comfortably in the lounging chair. The day was warm, but the drink was cool to the palate. "You do, Sargon. Those members of the Clan who have been placed in the Assyrian government as well as the army have met with my spies and they all assure me that the time is now ripe for an invasion. When you cross the borders into Assyria, the field commanders will stand down and allow your victorious army to march in uncontested and the city of Nineveh will be yours for the taking."

"And King Mandaru?"

"Though I have given my operatives free rein when it comes to being creative, doubtless their king will suffer a sudden serious malady, probably a dagger to the neck. The end result will be the same, however, regardless of the method employed. His inner court and all guards without ties to our Society will be similarly dispatched and you will enter the city with minimal resistance."

Sargon appeared disappointed. "Frankly, I was hoping for an armed conflict. Unless a message can be sent, there may be those who feel I am too weak and can be pushed about. Eventually, Akkad may be invaded by an alliance that feels that I am untested in battle."

Cain suppressed his anger at Sargon's lack of vision. *What an ingrate!* "Sargon, please understand there will be time for such outward demonstrations in the future. Along with the resources to support my new territory, I want the cities in the north and to the south along the Tigris and Euphrates to be left intact. Once I have carved out this new nation, then you will be free to expand farther north and west toward the Great Sea. You may then use your armies to amuse you if our expansion into those areas becomes too resistant."

Though clearly he was bothered by the news, Sargon seemed to understand. Cain had uncovered Sargon's latest interest and wondered if it was affecting his focus at the end-game. He had explained his long term plans with him, but perhaps he needed to probe deeper to see just how far this affectation went.

"Sargon, it has come to my attention that over the past few months you have acquired a new interest that involves boiling alive your enemies. Would you care to comment on that?"

The king appeared surprised that Cain would have such intimate details. "I have found that this activity lessens my anxiety and helps me to sleep."

Remembering his own youthful propensity for inflicting pain, Cain could hardly stand in judgment of Sargon. Nevertheless, he warned, "Just see that it does only that and stops short of becoming an obsession to distract you from our goals."

"Of course, Cain," he replied, relieved now that Cain showed no disapproval.

Cain had made his point so he moved on to the specifics of the conquest of the Northern provinces. Sargon had appeared outwardly calm as Cain conducted the briefing, but inwardly he was making mental note of how he was going to address this business of idle talk around the palace. He reflected, *It would seem that someone in the palace has loose lips; probably the women.*

A week later, King Isqi-Mari of Mari and his wife Queen Lydda were surprised, but delighted, to see that their two daughters had arrived from the court of Sargon. Though the presence of the king's son, Shar-kali, was unexpected, it was assumed he had accompanied the women as a courtesy to ensure their safety. What he was not prepared to hear was the reason for the visit. After all had been properly welcomed and a meal had been prepared for the visitors, Nisaba reluctantly confided there was more to their arrival than a simple visit.

"Father," began Nisaba "we have arrived at our home here in Mari to stay. We will not be returning to Akkad."

Isqi-Mari frowned as though he had misunderstood his daughter's statement. Lydda, his wife, was equally disturbed and was the first to voice her concern. "Nisaba, you two are the rightful wives of Sargon, perhaps lacking the same stature as Queen Shala, but nonetheless are betrothed and therefore belong to his court." The more Lydda thought of the provocative nature of their decision the more she became concerned and asked frankly, "Have you two lost your minds?"

Nisaba, being the older of the two women, spoke for them both and declared, "Mother, our husband Sargon is a madman that treats us with contempt and is more concerned with boiling his enemies in the palace than attending to his duties as a husband." Inanna could contain her feelings no more and the two distraught daughters then began explaining the conditions of fear under which they both had been forced to endure.

Isqi-Mari had been listening to this exchange between mother and daughters when he thought he misunderstood a comment. "Come again, he does what?"

Inanna looked over to her father and with tears in her eyes blurted out, "Father, he boils people alive." She then went on to explain in detail what she knew as well as suspected regarding this ghoulish activity.

As though about to faint, the Queen, gasped, "Oh, my!" under her breath. Lydda could scarcely believe what she had just heard.

Isqi-Mari turned toward the young man from the court of Sargon and demanded, "Shar-kali, what is this we have heard of your father?"

Shar-kali shook his head miserably in disbelief of the whirlwind of events of the past month. His normally careful instincts had been severely weakened by the wonderful nights with Inanna and discovering their love, but, there came a time in which even love had to be tempered with self-preservation. When approached by Inanna to flee Akkad, he was quick to understand and accept the predicament in which all three were now under. He reluctantly agreed that once his father discovered his affair with Inanna, Sargon would spare little time in exacting his revenge on them all. But, he also realized privately that whatever explanation for his behavior he might have been willing to use in his defense, it went by the boards the moment he fled to Mari with the two sisters. He had been following the dialogue among the women when Isqi-Mari had provided an opportunity for him to offer some explanation for their actions.

"Sire, your daughters have spoken the truth. My father, the king, has taken into his head to instill fear into the minds of all those in his court through this abominable practice. My mother, the Queen, has been censured for her opinions on the matter and when she raised her objections my father had her banished to her bed chamber. Now she is more prisoner than wife and Queen."

The king pulled at his beard distractedly then looked at the women and declared, "My Daughters, in spite of all which has been revealed, I still believe resolutely in the absolute rule of the liege lord of the land. And perhaps, more to the point, my rule in Mari is dependent on the good graces of Cain and Sargon, his chief henchman. I can ill afford to have either of them as an enemy if I have any future intentions of rule in Mari."

He turned his attention back to Shar-kali and declared, "I, too, am appalled by Sargon's behavior and it does indeed worry me that my daughters have been subjected to live under the conditions you have described. Nevertheless, there must be more to this business of your visit than simple fear of the possibility of ending up as the enemies of Sargon, which I assure you there are many."

Shar-kali now realized the time had come to reveal his love for Inanna and the real reason for the flight from Akkad. Before he could say more, Inanna spoke up urgently and declared to her two parents, "Father, Mother, Shar-kali and I are in love and have consummated our relationship many times. We wish to marry."

Isqi-Mari and his wife looked at one another and could scarcely believe what they had just heard. "We are doomed," Lydda intoned quietly. "There is no way to escape this."

Conversations commenced back and forth for nearly ten minutes then Isqi-Mari remarked with finality, "You three must go back and say that you were just here for a visit and that Shar-kali had accompanied you for protection. I will dispatch Sargon a letter stating that my wife had suddenly grown ill and needed her daughters by her side."

Now looking at the two lovers, he declared, "Once you have returned to Akkad, you will cease this affair and you two will conduct yourselves with restraint."

The Queen looked over to her husband and nodded her acceptance of the story. "Yes, it should work," she remarked.

Inanna closed her eyes at what must be revealed. "I am pregnant," Inanna whispered.

Everyone immediately ceased any further conversation and personal thought. Now feeling as though the air had been taken suddenly out of the room, while Inanna sobbed despairingly, all others present simply sat stunned. Finally, her mother, Queen Lydda, a Semite from the lineage of Japheth voiced the obvious. "Oh my, that changes everything."

Two weeks later, an envoy from the court of Sargon arrived in Mari. He pointedly omitted any pleasant inquiry of the whereabouts of the two women, but instead delivered an ultimatum from Sargon to return his wives and his treacherous son or face an armed invasion. Being an old general and unaccustomed to being given a declaration of such severity, Isqi-Mari declined to agree to the request. He stated for the record to the ambassador that Shar-kali and Inanna were in love, that she was now pregnant and the two were to be married. The envoy was sent back with the short message: "Come and get them."

Cain and Sargon were both present when the envoy returned with Isqi-Mari's terse response. Within moments, Sargon was incensed and paced up and down in the audience room seething with anger. Aside from the personal shame he felt of his faithless wives and his treacherous son, Isqi-Mari had rudely declined to honor his reasonable request to turn them over to him. While Cain had looked on disgustedly, Sargon had railed on incessantly about his loss.

Cain was considerably more objective about the affair and commented, "Sargon, you should have consulted me before sending your personal envoy with an ultimatum."

In exasperation Sargon replied defensively, "They were my wives and one of them had the effrontery to have an affair with my philandering son!"

Cain replied dryly, "Do you even know which wife it was, Sargon?"

Sargon was momentarily taken back by the question. "The younger one, I believe, but it hardly matters." He pounded his fist on a nearby table and screamed dementedly, "I want their blood!" But, what he really wanted was to find three large cooking pots and light the fires himself.

Cain allowed the man to expend his energy until he seemed to be done with his ravings of revenge. Cain informed him, "If you are finished with your ranting, I will tell you what you are going to do. There doesn't seem to be any way to remove your wives and son without open warfare with Mari. Your precipitous action has left us hardly any alternative in the matter. Though I regret unleashing my army on my first home, I see no other way to save Akkad from our future enemies. We must fight and we must make an example of Mari or our plans in this region will come to naught. Sargon, your foolishness has cost me more than I would normally allow, but you will have your open warfare you have so desperately sought and you will get a chance to send that message to our regional neighbors you were worried so much about."

Sargon wore a blissful smile of expectancy. His days and nights would now be happily consumed with preparations for an all-out assault on Mari. There would be only a few special prisoners taken and they would languish in his dungeon until the evening came when each would feel the eventual heat of his boiling pot. As Cain looked on disgustedly, Sargon rubbed his hands together in anticipation of the battle to come.

CHAPTER 3

THE DESTRUCTION OF MARI

King Isqi-Mari was pacing with anxiety in his throne room when his wife, two daughters and Shar-kali were ushered into his presence by two of his military adjutants Beydar and Mozan. The king had every right to feel anxious; he had just learned that an army led by Sargon, King of Akkad, was only a few days removed from his nation. He knew from experience that if such an army were to invade his country, it would be a certainty that his smaller army would be overrun the same day of the attack. Nevertheless, he had decided to re-assume his old position as General of the Army and give them battle. He had come to this decision hardly out of bravado or some misplaced sense of duty in the face of sure suicide. He intended to get his family out of Mari and give them as much time as possible to gain distance from Sargon's revenge.

Lydda slowly became aware of the concern on her husband's face and now knew without asking that their lives were in jeopardy; the king's countenance confirmed it. Her hand went instinctively to her throat as though she had already felt the sure cut of the blade. "Husband, is it truly Sargon?"

"Yes, his army will be here within two days. I can hope to hold him off for only a few hours, a half-day at the most." He glanced over to his two military advisers for their conclusions of the current situation and both slowly nodded their heads at the king's assessments of the chances for victory.

At hearing this, Inanna finally realized what her infidelity to Sargon had produced. She began to wail hopelessly and threw herself moaning into the arms of Shar-kali. "I am so sorry, but how could I have known? Now we will be no more and my baby will have no life!"

Shar-kali, too, shared in her misery, but could think of nothing to say to assuage her guilt and personal pain over what was surely to come. He could only hold her and hope that it would be enough.

Nisaba fell into her mother's arms and she, too, began to weep, not for the sure, quick death which she hoped would come, but from the slow torture of Sargon's boiling pot. "Mother, what are we to do? Our husband is a monster and will show us no mercy!"

Isqi-Mari invited them all to be seated as he explained what he had decided. Once reasonable calm had again prevailed, he said, "I have come to a decision and it is final and there is no possibility of recalling it because we have run out of time and options." He lowered his head in sorrow and slowly raised it, now intoning, "My two adjutants here, Beydar and Mozan, I trust with my life and now I must trust them with the lives of my family. Lydda, you and our daughters and Shar-kali will quickly prepare yourselves for a long journey back to the ancient land of your fathers where you will stay and never return to this land again. I will meet Sargon on the field of battle and try to buy as much time for you as possible until you are clear of danger. My two adjutants will escort you and have my permission to stay with you as long as they are needed."

With some anger, Beydar announced, "Sire, my duty is with you and to protect my country from those who would invade it. Do not force me to endure this shame!"

Shar-kali's anxiety over the survival of his family finally burst forth as he announced, "I am your king and you will do as I command! My family and the future of my line are in question here and I refuse to allow Sargon to take that away from me as long as I have air to breath and a sword with which to swing in battle! You will fight to preserve my family and I will fight to give each of them a chance for survival." He looked at the two disappointed advisers and intoned flatly, "Do you both understand?"

The two men reluctantly agreed, but it was clear from their reactions that they would rather die in battle than to serve as family escorts to a strange land on the other side of the realm. Being a military man for many years, he understood their feelings.

Reluctantly, he shared with them all of what he really believed. "It is likely that Sargon will spare no one alive in our kingdom. His pride has been hurt and he has been searching some time to find a reason for open confrontation. He seeks to send a message of his preeminence to the neighboring countries in the region. As Cain has allowed him to invade us, Sargon will not ask for our surrender. For us it will be a battle to the death."

Lydda was aghast at what she had just heard. "Husband, surely as a member of the Clan you will have some influence upon Cain's decision."

"Lydda, the die was cast the moment I refused to turn my children over to Sargon for punishment. I have thought this through and my decision is made. There is no way to avoid what is now inevitable; you will all prepare yourselves for the long journey at once. Please do as I have counselled. Now, I wish to be alone with my advisers. Much planning is needed and I have very little time to accomplish it."

On the fifth day of the third month in the thirtieth year of Sargon's reign as king of Akkad, his army entered the Kingdom of Mari and the work of death began. Isqi-Mari had taken personal command of his own army and demonstrated great tactical prowess in the face of a superior invading force. Nevertheless, after only a few hours of intense fighting, the outnumbered soldiers of Mari were sent scurrying for their lives in a complete rout.

Now left alone with a small retinue, Isqi-Mari was eventually surrounded and cut down as the arrows of several archers found their mark. His head was brought back to the tent of Sargon and was spat upon by Sargon and his men until the head had eventually found a final resting place on a pike. With all the pomp of a conquering general and the head of Isqi-Mari proudly displayed, Sargon rode victoriously through the streets of Mari.

Sargon, in a brief moment of magnanimity, had decided that he would extend leniency to his son if he would personally take his two ungrateful wives, truss them up and prepare them for his pots. His victory lap, however, was cut short. Upon entering the palace, he found neither anyone to greet him nor to grovel at his feet for mercy. In a tirade of anger, he told his soldiers to tear the city apart and look for them. When they were unable to locate the three refugees from Akkad and the Queen Lydda, he told his soldiers to torch the city and completely destroy it. He brought back a dozen Mari soldiers in chains for his future amusement and the remainder of the city population, the countryside and the rest of the captured soldiers were put to the sword. When Sargon departed the land of Mari, there was no one left alive to see him and his victorious army march back to Akkad.

Upon his return, Cain was highly displeased at the excessive manner in which the Mari campaign had been consummated. As Sargon sat before him and gave a grim accounting of what had occurred in his old homeland, Cain reluctantly realized that Sargon had confirmed what his own spies had related to him earlier. When the king had finished with the grisly details, Cain shook his head in exasperation and exclaimed, "What did you think to accomplish by putting the whole country to the torch and the population to the sword? I said to send a message, not a valedictory speech!"

Sargon shrugged his shoulders and calmly added, "It is over, Cain. We should now move on and plan for our next conquest to the north at Nineveh. The Assyrians await our victory march."

Cain remained unappeased. He ordered, "When you are done with your next victory march," he added sarcastically, "You will rebuild Mari and re-populate it with the Assyrians. I am too sentimental to see my old home grow desolate and cold."

"I will make it so, Cain." After a moment, he extended a jovial invitation. "I am having a victory boiling tonight. Would you care to join me?"

Far to the west in the nascent Kingdom of Madai, now refugees and all that remained of the land of Mari, six persons slowly made their way on horseback until they had arrived at the country of Lydda's birth. Her kinsmen openly welcomed them and bid them to join them in their homes until a suitable dwelling could be located for their needs. Inanna and Shar-kali were betrothed and in short order Inanna delivered a strapping baby boy, the immediate darling of the neighborhood. Lydda mourned her husband, General Isqi-Mari, but honored his memory all the days of her life. Nisaba married a local millwright and they relocated north to Javan.

Before moving on with their lives, however, they were visited by a young man with a special mission who said he had come to chronicle the destruction of Mari. As they all sat down, he introduced himself as Jasher, a descendant of Japheth the son of Noah.

CHAPTER 4

A MESSENGER

Jasher had been a guest at the home of his distant cousin, Peleg, for a few months now. He had just completed his observations, interviews and recording of the nascent civilization of Nineveh, formerly the chief region of the Assyrians, now part of the greater land of Babylonia or Shinar as Cain was calling it. Peleg had offered his home there as a refuge and centralized location whereby Jasher could make his recordings in relative peace outside the view of the local citizenry.

Jasher had discovered that whenever he made his recordings more public, he invariably attracted more attention to his task than he would have desired. At first he had dismissed this feeling as a trifling more than simple paranoia, but in the land of Elam he had observed that the same men began frequenting the inn where he was staying. He abruptly changed inns one afternoon and discovered a few days later that the same men had followed him to his new lodgings. From that point forward, he decided that he would need a private location from which to record. In consequence, when Peleg had offered his hospitality he was eager to accept.

In addition to the gracious host, his cousin was also well-traveled as well as highly informed. Over the next few weeks Jasher had begun to hear disquieting news from Peleg of reports coming out of Akkad, the chief city. After some discussion with him, Jasher decided it was time to make his journey to the west to Babylonia and visit this land wherein King Rimush, the son of Sargon, now ruled Assyria. He had bid his cousin farewell and had set out with his donkey laden with his bedroll and recording materials.

Jasher had been on the road for a few days when he became aware of a man walking with some deliberation in his direction and a feeling of heightened curiosity came over him as the man stopped directly in his path. The traveler, somewhat taller than most, had clear blue eyes, dark brown brows and fine brown hair that seemed to be slightly growing out grey. As most men had scarcely the time to shave or had the inclination, he was clean-shaven, which among most persons seemed to be a curiosity, even a novelty. Moreover, it had always been the custom as a sign of manhood to sport one's beard as soon as it was possible to do so. However, Jasher sensed that the middle-aged man seemed unconcerned with the social norms of the time.

The stranger smiled openly with perfect teeth, also a rarity, and introduced himself. "Jasher, I am Joseph, a messenger from our Creator who has been sent to deliver you a message for your journey to Shinar." He did not offer his hand by way of greeting, but merely bowed.

Even with all this taken into consideration, there was still something uniquely peculiar about the messenger, but Jasher was unable to make complete sense of it. Wanting to be equally courteous, Jasher acknowledged his bow and stated, "Joseph, I feel as though I should know you. Have we met?"

The man smiled and modestly proclaimed, "In life I was known as Seth." He allowed that declaration to register and proceeded to explain, "Noah, your grandfather, mentioned my name to you on a number of occasions and declared to you that you would occasionally receive help in this work. Since my death I have been awaiting the moment when I could provide my services to you. As we are kinsmen, I would offer you my hand or an embrace in greeting, but it is not yet permitted. Are you prepared to receive my message?" He offered the question with a knowing, expectant smile.

Jasher's curiosity gave way to astonishment as he recollected the words of his grandfather. When Noah had asserted he would not be alone in this work, he had assumed, of course, that others would be involved, but there was no way to prepare himself for the extraordinary messenger. But the man, if he could be called such, appeared real, yet not quite entirely there or perhaps a little too perfect in the sense that he had trouble focusing on the messenger's form.

"Yes, of course." he stammered. Though he had performed several recordings of events, Jasher had felt his efforts inadequate, thus until now he had felt like an imposter, wandering around in a strange land with no idea how to proceed.

Joseph appeared happy to oblige, his manner was affable and he seemed to perceive Jasher's thoughts. "I have observed your work since your calling and I am pleased to report that your work among men has been exemplary, and fortunately, free of opposition."

Jasher was, of course, relieved to hear that his work and time had been recognized and had value. "I could never be certain that I was performing the work in the prescribed manner. And, yes, my work has been free of outside problems, though of late I have noticed men who seemed a little more curious at my recording labors than I would have expected."

"It was correct of you to take notice and adjust your routines. You are now about to enter a permanent phase of this mission in which you will be met with incessant, open opposition to your work. You will meet a man in Nineveh who will introduce himself as Cain. He will make foolish claims of power and control over the hearts of men, but you must resist him."

"My grandfather Noah warned me of this man. Should I make an attempt to avoid all encounters with him?"

"It would do you little good to try. Your mission will invariably bring you into open confrontation with him and this conflict will be ongoing for the remainder of your life. While in life, I too, had to deal with him in consequence of my calling."

"How shall I deal with his hostilities? I assume he will be clever as well as powerfully intimidating."

"You must avoid any prolonged conversation with him and say little except that pertaining to your mission. He will try to confuse you, perhaps even to encourage your sympathy towards his cause, but in the end, he will level threats against you and your work. Please know that you will not be alone and that I have been assigned to watch over you."

He gave Jasher a moment to digest this message then asked, "Do you understand my message? If so, then I must depart."

"Joseph, will we meet again?"

"Of course, but others will decide the when and where." He paused and humbly proclaimed with a smile, "I am merely the messenger." With his message now delivered, he bowed a farewell, and turning, he then walked through a copse of bushes off the road. Once out of sight, a light appeared within the trees and descended upon him then he disappeared out of sight.

Jasher, when he had recovered from this extraordinary experience, resumed his journey towards the land of Babylonia. Along the way he continued to replay in his mind the words of warning from the messenger Joseph regarding the inevitable encounter he was about to experience with Cain. He was still unsure how he would react to the meeting, but he was determined to put up a front of strength. One thing was certain, however, he no longer doubted Cain's existence; his grandfather's warning had not been mere exaggeration. He just hoped he was equal to the encounter.

CHAPTER 5

SIDON'S GIFT

Sidon had always been a careful, meticulous man. As a boy growing up along the western bank of the Tigris River, and while he went about his daily work as a stone mason near the city of Calneh, he had always shown an aptitude for careful planning. He was an artisan of the highest caliber, not because of any innate ability, but because he could envision the end result of the project before it was begun.

Unlike many in the area, he was a Shemite, a distant relative of Aram, youngest son of Shem. His eyes were hazel and his skin was light, which set him even further apart from those of that area of Shinar. The differences to him were immaterial as he was ambivalent by nature, but it did cause him occasional confrontations from the darker young men of the province. He may have had an indifferent demeanor, but even at an early age, he was quick to retaliate when provoked. By the time he had reached adulthood, the locals had either established a bond of friendship with him or simply kept him at a distance. He was a good man to have as a friend, but a bitter opponent if aroused.

Sidon would have spent the remainder of his life happily constructing houses and buildings for the new cities that were then being settled between the Tigris and Euphrates Rivers. Unfortunately, an incident occurred which would forever change his life. A son of a local magistrate found offense with

Sidon's brother over a trifling wager in a horse race when his brother had tried to collect his winnings. The magistrate's son refused to pay him, and in fact had set his personal guards upon him; thus, by the end of the day, Sidon's brother lay dead, his wife was a widow and his two sons were now fatherless.

As was custom, Sidon's father attempted to redress his son's murder, and when he became too insistent, he was imprisoned by the magistrate in his palace; an all too common occurrence. Malluch, the magistrate, was a feared and politically protected man, and such men always had armed guards on permanent retainer. His reputation had circulated that even with minimal provocation he would not hesitate to wipe out Sidon's entire family if he felt threatened. Consequently, now realizing that other members of the family could easily end up in the same dungeon next to his father or worse, Sidon had counselled patience.

While his father languished in the magistrate's prison, Sidon devised a plan to not only free him, but avenge his brother's death. He waited almost a year, cultivating friendships and associations which would place him in close contact to the magistrate and his murdering son. As it was, in time, Malluch's power and influence had grown, and now fearing loss of his personal treasures, he had decided he needed a new security wall to surround his estate.

An associate of Sidon mentioned in passing that the magistrate was seeking the assistance of a skilled mason for a project he was contemplating and asked whether Sidon might be interested if the opportunity arose, and of course, he was. When Malluch asked local contractors to direct him to the best artisan mason, Sidon's name was consistently mentioned as the logical choice. Before long, Sidon was interviewed and was subsequently contracted to perform the service.

Sidon began the new project and from that day forward became thoroughly familiar with the magistrate's home, the layout of the buildings on the property and the routine of the guards. Moreover, he took the time to mark the movements of the killer son who had had his brother murdered in the street. Within a short time, he had developed a working friendship with the guards and a cordial relationship with Malluch. Then after a few weeks, the magistrate expressed his desire to have Sidon join him on the terrace for a cool drink. Sidon, of course, accepted; the invitation presented the ideal opportunity he had been awaiting. Sidon dismissed his men for the day and joined the magistrate at his table on the terrace.

The magistrate was expansive with his praise. "Sidon, your workmanship is magnificent. I have the finest, most beautiful wall in the city and your use of the natural stone and brick will serve me well. Moreover, my guards assure me that my palace could now withstand the assault of a small army!" he exclaimed with pride.

Sidon noticed the guards were not on alert, and in fact were busy elsewhere. Apparently, they seemed to consider him no more a threat than Malluch. Knowing that his contract was nearing its end, he decided he would have no better chance for success than at this moment.

"Thank, you my Lord." He sipped his wine. He calmly looked at the magistrate and declared, "You are quite right, it could withstand an assault from without, but you are still vulnerable from within."

"My friend, for that I have my guards," he boasted.

"I see no guards," Sidon replied with a smile.

This response confused Malluch; he seemed to frown and looked around to locate his men. While he was thus occupied, he was a trifle too slow to take notice of the dagger that was now thrust at his throat.

"Make no sudden move nor alert the guards in any way. You will now take me on a tour of your palace, My Lord." To his delight, Sidon felt no anxiety over the matter. On the contrary, the experience was stimulating in a new and fascinating way.

"Sidon, you are a dead man. Even if you are just looking for my treasure, you are dead!"

"If I am dead, as you say, then you will have no reason to deny me my last wish."

He quietly walked the magistrate inside his residence, the knife at his back. From his reaction, Sidon was sure Malluch could feel the point up against his spine and knew he was not bluffing.

Malluch had decided to play along and let his guards finish him off at their leisure. Now giving the impression of cooperating, with an agreeable tone he declared, "Very, well, Sidon, where are we going?"

"Downstairs to the dungeon, My Lord," he replied amiably.

His job as an artisan was quiet, even peaceful and so he had not realized how much he would enjoy this confrontation, the closeness of the prey, his smell and watching him sweat. It was exhilarating in a way he had never anticipated.

"The dungeon? I don't understand. Why would you want to go down there?"

"There is someone I wish to visit, but before we descend, please invite your son to join us."

"My son," he stammered, "Which one?"

The man is rather obtuse, Sidon thought. His voice became more abrasive as he whispered fiercely, "The murderer, the one who had my brother butchered in the street a year ago!" He roughly pushed the magistrate forward against a nearby wall then placed the cutting edge of his knife near the man's throat.

"Sidon, I will have you hung for this. Your whole family will suffer, I swear it."

Malluch had responded with bravado, but it was false and Sidon saw through it. The man was sweating like a pig at noon-day.

Fortune smiled on Sidon for no sooner had the threat been uttered than the son for which he was looking entered the hallway from his bed chamber. Upon seeing his father held at the point of a knife, he rushed forward and Sidon never hesitated. He pushed the magistrate to the floor and thrust the knife upward into the throat of his oncoming son. He dragged it straight down cutting the esophagus and severing the windpipe then lithely moved to one side to avoid the spurting blood. Immediately, the front of the son's robe was soaked along with the floor and nearby wall.

Malluch tried to spin away from the falling body, but fear had gripped him and his movements were slow. As his son collapsed to his knees, he toppled forward to the floor and spilled his life's blood all over his father.

Sidon, noting the magistrate's terror, gripped him by the arm and pulled him up. Again, the point of the dagger was near his throat.

"We will now visit the dungeon," Sidon whispered into his ear. "But first, drag your son's body into his bedchamber and push it against the wall." Malluch was roughly pushed toward the bleeding corpse of his dead son.

Malluch was unused to dealing with so much personal anxiety. He was more accustomed to having others do his bloodletting for him and so was unprepared for the sight of so much blood, particularly since he was now wearing so much of it. Gazing stupidly at the bloody corpse of his son had only added to the queasiness of his stomach; thus, after he had disposed of the body, he became violently sick. He was now not only wearing his son's blood that had splattered all over his robe, but also the remains of his half-digested mid-day meal.

After the deed was done and the body was secured away in the bed chamber, Sidon forced the magistrate down the stairway into the dungeon. Another push sent him sprawling, and now off balanced, he tripped on his robe and ended up on the floor at the foot of the stairs. Sidon was a few steps behind, and gazing about the dank room, he carefully strained to see any occupants in the dim light. There, lying prone on a straw bed in a filthy corner of the cell was the bedraggled form of his father.

He called out, "Father, are you alive?"

Now too weak from a near starvation diet he had been administered as a result of his stay with the magistrate, his father could only move about feebly on the floor. Owing to the dimness of the room, he squinted to see, but detecting the voice of his son he uttered a thin croak of recognition.

"Sidon, is that you?"

"Let him out," Sidon commanded, appalled at his father's torn and filthy clothing and angry at his weakened condition. He backhanded the magistrate across his face, drawing blood, and pushed him toward the far wall where the keys were hanging from a hook.

Malluch staggered over to the wall and fetched the key. After opening the cell door, he was now hoping to avoid another blow to his face and get a chance to escape to alert his guards. He backed away quickly and, as Sidon made a move to enter the cell, the magistrate took that moment to rush for safety, but before he could reach the first step, however, he turned slightly. Sidon took casual aim, and without hesitation, flung the knife with all his strength into the escaping man. The knife hit him high in the neck, severing the carotid artery. Malluch stumbled and his forward momentum drove him into the steps and as the blood sprayed out and hit the nearby wall, he slowly blinked his eyes in bewilderment then died within minutes.

Taking his father by the arm, Sidon helped him to his feet and carefully walked him from the cell then leaned him against the wall near the stairs. Turning around, he walked over to the still warm corpse of Malluch and pulled out the dagger from his neck. He then grabbed the arms and dragged the body into the cell and tossed it into the corner where his father had laid for the past year. Now trying to avoid any evidence that might tie them to the violence, Sidon carefully walked his father around the blood smears of the magistrate on the wall and the stairway.

Once outside again, Sidon decided it was time to remove the guards. The trick was to get close enough to them without giving them reason to suspect foul play. While the guards were performing their usual security routines that he now recognized, Sidon quickly got his father to the terrace and sat him down on a nearby bench. As each guard rounded the corner of the building a few minutes apart, Sidon dispatched each with his knife then he threw the collapsing body off the terrace and watched as each tumbled down to the wall below. Once all were removed, he walked deliberately back into the house and killed every member of the magistrate's household; there would be no witnesses and no one to point an accusing finger at his family. He walked his father slowly back home and so, after a year of wasting away in Malluch's dungeon, he was reunited with his loved ones.

No one ever discovered who had killed the magistrate and his guards then murdered his household, but some locals had their suspicions. Nevertheless, they were too smart to open their mouths to the authorities and from that time forward, Sidon walked with a new respect in his neighborhood and no one ever dared to offend him or his family in any way.

A few months later, Sidon was approached by an associate in the burgeoning government of Calneh, some fifty miles south of Akkad. An influential contact from Akkad had requested to see him about a contract for work and Sidon had accepted the invitation. Within a day he was seated before a man having been introduced as a potential client.

The man came right to the point. "I am Cain."

Neither a sign of recognition nor any sudden dawning of understanding registered on Sidon's face. His only reaction was a quick bow and his own impassive introduction. "I am Sidon. How may I be of service?"

Cain looked him over and was immediately impressed. Sidon was self-assured and poised. He carried none of the fumbling obeisance that was prevalent among the lower class artisans of the kingdom when in the presence of superiors. In spite of his confident exterior, Cain sensed the man could be submissive if the role required it. He intended to proceed probing the depths of this man's natural reserve.

"Sidon, you come highly recommended. Regrettably, I understand one of your last contracts ended incomplete. It seems your employer was afflicted with a bad case of stupidity and made the unforgivable mistake of angering the wrong person. Would you know anything about this?"

Again, there was no register of emotion, only curiosity. "Lord, how would I know of such things? I am but a humble stone mason."

Cain rejected his disingenuous reply out of hand and decided to probe even deeper. "How did you enjoy the company of Malluch, the Magistrate? Surely you and he must have developed at least a cordial, yet business-like relationship?"

"As it turned out, the magistrate and I shared common political and social interests. It was unfortunate that we disagreed on how these interests should be best applied, but it was well worth the time it required to know him better." He smiled as if recalling an especially fine moment with an exceptional woman.

"It does seem curious that you were the last one seen in the area before the murders took place. Also, either by good fortune or exceptional skill, you were able to walk away from the slaughter unharmed."

With a shrug of the shoulders and a slight smile playing along his lips, he quietly declared, "Perhaps it was a little of both."

Cain was particularly impressed by the peculiar physical and emotional ease of the man. The questions neither seemed to evoke any outward denials nor cause any undue anxiety. Cain had concluded many years earlier that most men spent a whole lifetime avoiding acceptance of their true natures. There was always a reluctance it seemed which prevented them from this self-discovery and eventually embracing those natural gifts. It may have been a fear of failure or even success, so they rejected the possibility of becoming something greater than fate had ordained them to be.

Either because of an unexpected circumstance or a quirk of fate, this man had been thrown out of his usual mundane routine then he had displayed a natural cunning as well as a ferocity he was unaware he had. Cain was curious to know how he would react if presented with the possibility of following this self-discovery down the road to its natural conclusion and he had heard and seen enough to make his decision.

"Sidon, you are in possession of a rare skill and mindset which marks you apart from most men and makes you a desirable candidate for my business ventures that would extend beyond your usual labors. Would you be interested in coming to work for me?"

Since the incident with the Magistrate Malluch, Sidon had pondered his actions and had weighed his feelings at length. Having experienced minimal regrets, he had concluded that he had felt hardly any remorse or self-disgust at his deed; actually, he had felt fine. It had been necessary so he had taken care of the problem; moreover, the act of a well-planned execution had left him a serenity he had never before experienced. He had ultimately concluded that there was nothing wrong with how he now felt about his newly acquired interests, but had wondered how to proceed. Cain seemed to be offering him a chance to see where these skills and interests would lead him beyond his usual occupation and he realized he felt more than just idle curiosity about those possibilities. A more compelling life was beckoning and he intended to explore it to its fullness.

With a nod of his head, he came to a conclusion and asked, "And what would you have me do, My Lord?"

"I have in mind a job that will require you to use your trowel for something other than building walls."

Thus, for Sidon, began a compelling, but violent life of self-fulfillment and blissful acceptance.

CHAPTER 6

RIMUSH, SON OF SARGON

The King of Babylonia, Rimush, a son of Sargon, was in the ninth year of his reign, and while he sat fretfully on the throne throughout the morning, he had given audience to several members of his court. After having delivered their reports, each was dismissed in turn, leaving His Chief Adviser, Nadim, to present the final review of the day.

Nadim, a member of the Clan, was an adviser to King Rimush and his father Sargon before him, but regardless of his delicate skills of persuasion, his counsel had been set for naught on many occasions by the current ruler. Nadim had come to the conclusion, hardly for the first time, that Rimush was too dense for reason.

"My King," he began, "Our relations with King Mamagal of Kish continue to erode, and as you know, his third son, Elam, wishes to marry with your fourth daughter, Antu. As I have previously pointed out, in my opinion Sire, this marriage will solidify our relations with Mamagal and will forestall any aspirations he may have to jeopardize your success in the region. For the sake of the peace of both nations, I urge you to reconsider your last refusal for this engagement and to allow this marriage to proceed."

Rimush was quick-tempered and his tongue had gotten him into more trouble lately than Nadim could easily repair. The king brooded for a moment then, as usual, his passion got the better of him.

"Never," he spat. "The day my precious Antu marries that dim-witted lout will be a cold day in Ur." He fumed then resumed his rant. "To think our houses would be joined by such an abominable marriage is an affront to the memory of her dear departed mother, Ishtar, my favorite above all of my wives." He continued to seethe as he thought of how he would have to tolerate this union.

Nadim's assessment of the situation was more dispassionate and objective than that of Rimush. However, it was clear that the king's refusal to accept his counsel was beginning to be a source of personal anxiety. He had just come that morning from the inn where Cain had met him and they had discussed Rimush's stubborn attitude at length. Unsurprisingly, Nadim had recalled that Cain's final verdict had not gone well for the king. In fact, unless Rimush reversed his viewpoint on the matter, he would soon meet with an unforeseen encounter with a dagger, probably while he sat on his throne.

When Nadim had appeared earlier in the day, Cain was seated near the back of the inn in the shadows with a small drink in his hand, and finding a nearby seat, the adviser had sat down opposite him.

"Report," was all Cain said.

"Sire," he began with apprehension in his voice, "my master, the King, continues to be obstinate in his acceptance of the marriage between the Kingdoms of Kish and Babylonia. I have tried every means of persuasion, but he remains intractable on this point. I simply do not know what more I can do."

Cain measured the man with badly concealed contempt. "It was your job as adviser to convince him. If you are unable to appeal to his better judgment of the importance of this union, then you will remind him of his loyalty to the Clan. This reminder is extended only once. After that, the die is cast and his fate is sealed."

The Master Mahan leaned forward until his face was only inches from that of the now quaking adviser and accentuated each point with his finger. "This engagement must be announced by the end of the day. He can either accept this decision or be removed and you will assure him there is no other way." He let this last statement hang in the air then he leaned back in this chair. Dismissing Nadim with a wave of his hand, he said, "Now, go do your job."

Thus, Nadim had met with Rimush later that afternoon to appeal to his sense of self-preservation. After speaking with Cain, he was well aware that there was more than just the head of the King now on the chopping block. Having made note of the stubborn set on the jaw of Rimush, he stood appalled that the oaf who sat before him could be so willful and downright stupid. Nadim hated being in the middle of this contest of wills, but he now realized that Rimush had left him no choice in the matter and neither had Cain.

So, smiling and with as much humility as was possible, he quietly admonished, "Sire, may I remind you of your oath and obligation to the Clan? Cain has made his decision quite clear on this matter and he will refuse to recall his words. Your daughter will marry the son of Mamagal or he will be remove you from your throne." Nadim braced himself for the inevitable outburst to come.

"You impertinent fool! You dare remind me of my oath to the Clan and then have the temerity to threaten me while I sit upon my own throne?"

Rimush then swore by the gods that he would rather face a sandstorm than permit his daughter to dishonor herself with that clod Elam. "Guards," he shouted, "remove my witless adviser from my presence and let him languish in my dungeon for a few weeks until he learns his place."

Two guards arrived running and made haste to remove the unfortunate, protesting adviser from the throne room. As he was thrust out into the hallway, Rimush hurled threats at the retreating counselor. After a few moments, the king resumed his brooding meditation and was about to call for food and drink from his servant when he appeared suddenly by his side as if anticipating his need.

"Ah, Sidon, I see you have read my mind." Eating and drinking usually put him in a more amiable frame of mind. Perhaps, he reflected, I should have had a drink before dealing with that fool Nadim.

Sidon had served Cain in a variety of similar roles over the past few years and enjoyed the game of subterfuge, especially when it ended with dispatching the hapless victim. Rimush was a fool, thought Sidon, and he hoped heartily that the king would give him reason for a dramatic consummation of his mission.

His voice was submissive as he commented, "Sire, I do apologize for overhearing your discussion with your adviser regarding the betrothal of your daughter. Please pardon my impertinence, but it seems your last comments indicated there will be no marriage. Was this not so or did I misunderstand?"

Rimush frowned at the indiscretion of his servant. "Sidon, I realize that my voice had been loud and my discussion with Nadim was more like an argument and consequently more public than I would normally permit. Nevertheless, servants should serve and not listen to conversations on matters of the kingdom of which they have no part." Rimush prepared a frustrated rebuke and shouted, "But, to answer your question, there will be no wedding, at least not while I draw breath!" Rimush, still thirsty and now desiring food, snarled, "Now, bring me food and more to drink!"

"Your pardon, Sire, of course" Sidon replied deferentially. His manner was polite as he declared, "My King, Cain wishes to inform you that your services in his kingdom are no longer required."

With a quick motion Sidon pulled a dagger from within the sleeve of his robe and buried it deeply into the neck of Rimush. The King of Babylonia was caught completely by surprise, and rising off his throne, he began to stagger about the audience room, spraying the throne and floor with his blood. He tumbled to the ground and began kicking about the stone floor, holding his severed neck. Sidon rolled him over onto his stomach then found the sweet spot between the fourth and fifth rib and drove his knife home, slicing the ruler's vital organs. When it was obvious that the task was completed, Sidon made his way out of the room.

Before leaving the palace he found Manishki, uncle of Rimush in the courtyard awaiting his arrival. With a glance and rubbing his nose, the predetermined signal of the mission accomplished, Sidon's gesture informed the uncle of the condition of Rimush, his nephew. Immediately, Manishki ran to the throne room and sealed the doors then he left guards in front to discourage anyone from disturbing the corpse. Meanwhile, Sidon was on his way to meet with Cain.

Shortly thereafter, Sidon sat in front of Cain in the shadows of the same tavern from which he had delivered Rimush his orders earlier in the day. After placing an order for wine for Sidon, Cain leaned over the table and remarked pointedly, "Report".

"Sire, regrettably, Rimush will no longer be in your service. He chose bitterly to contest your preeminence of his kingdom by his unreasonable refusal to carry out your will. It was necessary to dispatch him in the usual manner of the Clan."

"And Manishki, his uncle?"

The barkeeper arrived with the drink and sat it down in front of Sidon. Both waited until he had left then Sidon took a sip then proceeded to explain.

"I signaled to Manishki in the prearranged manner. He made his way back toward the throne room, I presume to seal off the palace until further orders arrived."

Cain was curious as to whether Nadim, the adviser, had been in the throne room when Sidon had dispatched Rimush. "And what of Nadim; was he present to witness the king's dismissal?"

"Actually, Sire, Rimush set his guards upon Nadim after the adviser had reminded the ruler of his duty to the Clan. He languishes now in the dungeon."

Cain, as usual, was pleased with the thorough work of his asset, Sidon. "Very well, you are dismissed. Please report back to my manse and wait for further instructions. You will, of course, be reassigned as the need arises. As it turns out I may have a new assignment for you that should prove challenging and equal to your talents."

"Thank you Sire, and as always, it is my pleasure to serve the Clan." Sidon drained his wine cup, arose and left the inn.

Cain signaled to another man a few tables to his side to join him at his table. When the man was seated he said, "You will report to Manishki as his new adviser and you will tell him he is to clean up that lump of scum in the throne room. You will further mention that Nadim, my former adviser to

Rimush, is in the dungeon and is to be set free in a week; he is to report back to me upon his release."

"Yes, Lord." The man hesitated then ventured a tentative question, "Will the family of King Rimush be so quick to accept his death?"

Cain responded with a stony gaze and comment. "You are not new to the Clan so I scarcely need to remind you of how I operate, but I will explain this to you only once and it would be wise if you remember it." He paused for emphasis then declared, "At the moment a man accepts a throne I have given him, everything in his life, his family, his friends, his fortunes, even the breath he takes become subject to my law and my direction. Every so often, I have to send a clear message to reiterate this fact of life. The message has been sent and his family and the realm will understand from whom it originated. There will be no opposition."

Cain leaned back in his seat and thoughtfully sipped at his drink then added, "Inform Manishki he is to inherit his nephew's throne and soon he will take on an additional wife, a daughter of Mamagal of my choosing. Within the month following the marriage, he will be inducted into the Clan. Do you understand what I have just said?"

The new adviser quietly agreed then Cain intoned, "You are dismissed."

The man's bow was formal and he soon made haste to the palace to report to his new master and King of Babylonia, Manishki.

CHAPTER 7

A Tale in Nineveh

Cain was about to drain his cup then leave the tavern when he became aware of a traveler who had entered the doorway and quietly found a seat across the room. Cain studied the man while he made his order for food and drink. As his skin was light and his hair a brownish blonde, eyes probably green or blue, Cain concluded he was likely a stranger to Shinar. Moreover, his nose was slightly prominent, somewhat narrow and his demeanor almost patrician. Yes, he was clearly a stranger, reflected Cain, undoubtedly from some western province, obviously a Japhethite. It suddenly occurred to him that his spies had reported a stranger mingling among the citizens and courts within the area and asking questions about recent events. When he made the connection, his eyes narrowed and he began to seethe over the effrontery of the man to brazenly enter his realm and make inquiries regarding his business. Cain concluded it was high time he made acquaintance with the successor to his rotten, lying brother Seth.

With an arrogance born of years of conceit and entitlement, he sauntered over to the table and sat down opposite the stranger. "I am Cain and you must be Jasher, the new chronicler or should I say spy."

"Hardly a spy, but an observer and recorder of your works." Having been forewarned, Jasher was unsurprised, but apprehensive to finally meet Cain.

"I must say, you have some nerve barging in where you have been un-invited. My brother also had the same annoying manner of conducting his erstwhile business and attempted to interfere where he was unwelcome."

"I understand the limits of my involvement into your affairs, Cain, and interference is not part of my mission parameters."

Cain, now breathing deeply, leaned over the table in an intimidating fashion and uttered fiercely, "Understand Spy, this is my kingdom and it shall remain that way so you can crawl back to whatever backwater village that spawned you and report nothing."

"Cain, you know my mission and you know well that I am obliged to record all that I see in the realm. You can neither intimidate me with your bluster nor your threats."

"I also fully understand my limitations, Jasher, but I never forget I can make life difficult for you. From this point forward, you will be watched and if you expose the records, they will be taken from you and they will be destroyed. I refuse to allow you to record filthy lies in my own kingdom as my brother Seth once did. When he could find no evidence of any ill effects of my Society, he simply invented some." With a smile he then declared self-righteously, "I never had anything to hide."

"If you have nothing to hide then you have nothing to fear, Cain. I will report only the truth. If your Society can't abide the light of day, then I suggest you do a better job of hiding its effects."

"Jasher, you dare lecture me on what I will or will not do? I assure you that I am used to having my way and I always win!" Cain glared at Jasher and dared him to reply.

Jasher could think of only one instance that contradicted his claim. "Then what of Zion in the Kingdom of Enoch?"

Jasher's comment had hit the mark. Before the Great Flood, the City of Zion was renowned for its progressive and enlightened people. Though Cain had managed to plant several operatives in that nation to undermine the government, they nonetheless failed to subvert the rule of Zion. Legend had it that after Cain's operatives were exposed for subversion, the entire territory was removed from off the face of the Earth. His failure to take control of

Enoch's government still curdled his memory while Jasher's comment was an unwelcome reminder of that missed opportunity.

For a moment Cain was too stunned by the remark to respond. Instead of showing anger he became defensive, even wary. He muttered an excuse. "That was an aberration and a violation of the rules." With sanctimonious indignation, he pointed out, "That kingdom would have been mine if it had been left alone. Instead it was ripped from my grasp without a proper test. If I had had a reasonable opportunity to try again, I know I would have been successful, but I was cheated just as I have always been cheated. I was robbed of my chance to show I could influence the misguided citizens of Zion to give up their so called rights of personal choice. It wasn't fair to remove them from me when I was so close to success and I curse my God that he snatched them away before I could make my point." He angrily demanded, "If Seth recorded that event then he had better have the story correct."

Jasher smiled slightly and replied, "He did record it and the story was correct."

Cain stood as if to turn and go, but abruptly knocked over the chair behind him. He pointed his finger directly at Jasher and angrily pronounced, "Jasher, I curse you and your detestable mission. There is nothing for you here and you are unwelcome. I suggest you leave."

"Cain, I will leave when it suits me." He paused and glanced about the room then returned his focus on Cain. "Rumor has it that King Rimush is about to be dethroned. Or is that now in the past tense?"

Cain's first impulse was to jab his dagger into Jasher's eye. He gloried in how that would look and feel, but knew better to even think it. *Those accursed rules are ridiculously one-sided,* he silently screamed.

With restraint he informed Jasher, "I would know nothing of such rumors or falsehoods. Whatever happens to King Rimush, it will not be my doing. So, take care of recording such calumnies and assigning them to me." He added a last threat, "Don't cross my path again, Jasher. It may go badly for you." With disgust, he turned angrily toward the door and slammed it on the way out.

Jasher had watched as Cain made his exit. He reflected that if the messenger had not alerted him for this visit, the confrontation would have gone badly for him and he would have appeared fearful and weak. He had to admit that Cain's presence had been formidable, even unsettling, and so, in the future, he would have to take his threats seriously. To minimize capture of the records, he decided that he would have to make mental notes of his investigations or risk being publicly accosted for any observations he might write. Moreover, any records or notes that he wrote would have to be thoroughly secured at all times.

Jasher waited a week until after the news of the death of King Rimush had fully circulated the region before he decided to begin his official inquiry into the matter. Having suspected that the Clan of the Scar was behind the king's murder, he naturally would have wanted to begin his interviews with members of the inner court as well as family members. As he suspected, members of the family were unwilling to speak out, understandably fearing reprisals. It appeared that the fear of the Clan had outweighed the outrage caused by the loss of their ruler and family member.

Nadim, the former Chief Adviser to the supreme ruler, had been recently released from the jail by King Manishki, the uncle of the unlamented, lately deceased King Rimush. Jasher had sought out the adviser and requested a short interview and, in short time, they met in a different and less public inn than the previous one in which he had encountered Cain. At the meeting, Nadim had appeared agitated but eventually cooperative. When he spoke, he had a slight lisp and his mannerisms were somewhat effeminate once he became anxious, but nonetheless, in spite of the distraction, Jasher was determined to extract the information he needed.

Nadim began, "I know I should avoid talking with you. If word ever circulated that I had spoken of the king's death, my life would be as worthless as a three-legged dog. I was Chief Adviser, you know!"

Jasher placated the ex-counsellor to Rimush by appealing to his pride. In a consoling voice he stated, "Nadim, thank you for talking with me. It pains me to watch a man of your influence and stature being treated in such a shameful manner. I am sure your service to King Rimush was exemplary and your knowledge of his affairs was vast."

Though he realized he was being flattered, and clearly enjoyed it, Nadim nonetheless wanted to vindicate his part in the murder by telling his side. With a slight pout, he proceeded with his story, "Well, yes, of course, I was indispensable to Rimush in guiding his decisions. It was hardly my fault he decided to ignore my warnings and refused to allow the marriage of his daughter into the House of Mamagal. If he had been less stubborn he would still be alive today."

"Nadim, a man of your obvious intelligence would want the record correct regarding your handling of this affair. Would you be willing to explain your relationship with Cain, his Brotherhood and eventually your dealings with Rimush?"

"I will talk with you, but you must understand that I am only doing it because I was unjustly treated in the whole matter."

"Of course and you do not have to worry. I will ensure that your story is properly accounted and my writings discreet."

As if recalling a fond remembrance, Nadim smiled and related his first encounter with the Clan of the Scar that had begun some twenty years earlier as a young man. His father, Dedan, was providing service as Chief Adviser to the court of Nineveh and had secretly been a member of the Society of Cain for nearly two years. Dedan had realized, as had others, that eventually Cain would prevail in his bid to control all nations of the region, thus he had been quick to change his loyalties. Nadim related what few knew, that Cain had allowed the King of Akkad, Sargon, to expand his control into Nineveh of Assyria, as well as neighboring lands, resulting in the formation of the Kingdom of Babylonia.

Due to Dedan's influence to the court of Mandaru of Assyria, he and other advisers had subverted the government of that country on behalf of the Clan. Their influence in the conquest made it possible for the capture and subjugation of that kingdom with minimal bloodshed.

Nadim went on to explain, "In general, once under control of the Clan, as long as the appointed ruler paid homage to Cain and recognized his sovereignty over the realm, he was allowed to retain his pretention of power. Wars were never fought within the realm to satisfy the power lust of one supreme ruler over another. They were fought only to bring one country under control when a ruler decided to controvert Cain's agenda or, like Mandaru, he was slow to relinquish control over his territory. So eventually, without exception, the king, along with his inner court, was invariably part of Cain's Society or they were eliminated. For obvious reasons this was done to ensure that Cain not only maintained actual control over that kingdom, but could respond faster in the event that his policies were not being followed. It was this, more than anything else, which made it possible for Cain to depose King Rimush and install another ruler so quickly over the region of Babylonia."

"How were you inducted into the Clan?"

"My father, Dedan, was an exemplary adviser and taught me in all the ways necessary to prepare me for a special posting in the realm of the Akkadians, the new rulers of Nineveh. When I became of age I was naturally approached by the Clan and extended an invitation to join, but like all members, I was required to provide a sign of my obeisance before I was permitted to join, otherwise, the Society would not accept me. This concession tied me and all members together in a mutual conspiracy of loyalty to one another. As it was explained to me, this had always been the way of the Clan of the Scar since the first oaths were administered."

"And you found no objection to this?"

"I objected, of course, but let me describe my position in the matter:

It was a blistering afternoon in summer when my father and I were in the family courtyard discussing this same topic. "Father," I began, "You have taught me in all the ways of your craft and I am ready to assume this posting in the realm, but as to the matter of the Society, I would rather avoid any entanglements. It seems to me that once I have become involved with them, my first duty would be to the Brotherhood instead of the kingdom I am to serve."

My father was appalled at my naïveté. He replied, "Nadim, don't be foolish. Of course this is the way of the Society, but I assure you that it would be no different elsewhere. No one ever arrives at any position of worth in this world without a sponsor and that sponsor always requires a show of loyalty before trust is extended and then and only then is your success made assured. If you seek to be a person of stature and one who controls the flow of events, you have to be someone who can be trusted to act for the greater good." Then he paused for emphasis and declared, "The Clan represents the future and the greater good for our realm."

I considered his words and after a few moments I asked, "How does one go about making the proper compromise?"

He replied, "Very well, my son, you have asked the correct question and are now on your way to attaining your ultimate goals. Sargon has asked me to serve on his council in Akkad, and after giving the matter much though, I have proposed to the king that I allow you to serve with me on his council."

"Will Sargon approve my posting?" I was understandably doubtful.

He said, "Being an intelligent man, King Sargon will no doubt see the advantage to have someone I have trained and available should I ever need to be elsewhere."

"Once I am posted, will I be approached by a member of the Clan?" I asked.

He pointed out, "Once on the council, someone of wealth will no doubt desire you to represent him favorably. A modest gratuity will be extended then you will show your appreciation by proposing legislation or laws that will benefit either your benefactor or those who he represents."

I was appalled, but asked, "How will the king react, given such a blatant bribe is accepted from a member of his council?"

My father responded, "The king will have no problem supporting any such laws, as he too, will benefit from the negotiation. When it is obvious you have gained their trust then someone from the Inner Clan will discreetly reach out to you and your admission will be a mere formality."

I freely admit at that moment I was saddened at my lost innocence. I asked, "And this is the way of the world, Father?"

I can recall my father averting his eyes, but he stated, "It is my son. It always has been and always will be. It will be best if you avoid dwelling on the moral dilemma. From this point forward, just assume there is none."

And just as my father had predicted, I was approached, a favor was asked and I accepted the bribe. Quickly thereafter, I was met by a member of the Clan and from that moment forward I prospered and my success grew. After several years Dedan grew ill, and knowing he must soon die, he called me to his bedside to convey one last counsel and said, "Nadim, your role as adviser has been exemplary, but you have long basked in my shadow and you must now cast your own. Consequently, I have asked King Sargon to favor you an appointment to his court as his Chief Adviser and he has agreed."

My father seemed to gather his remaining strength to explain his final impressions. "There is only one last bit of advice that you should understand: At the center of all you do within the realm is the Clan of the Scar. You may disappoint the king and even incur his wrath, but as long as you remain true to the Society of the Clan, you are protected."

I pointed out, "King Sargon is very powerful, father. I realize the Clan controls many aspects of social matters within the realm, but can Cain be so omnipotent as to control everything?"

He shook his head sadly and informed me, "You will be Chief Adviser soon and so I will point out to you a very hard fact of life in our realm under Cain. The king cannot harm you without harming himself, thus the only person you must avoid disappointing is Cain, and of course, his Inner Clan of Advisers. Cain will see every failure to him as a personal affront to his leadership and once your failure to him is clear, there is no way to reason with him and there is no rationale that he will accept. He, alone, holds your life in his hands. I am sorry, my son, for having postponed this admission to you until now, but there was never any alternative if you had any chance for a successful career."

I told him, "Father, as a member of the Clan, I suppose I always suspected Cain was the controlling force in the region, but after having served and dealt with Sargon for so long, I find it difficult to conceive that he was little more than Cain's hand puppet."

His last words of advice to me were: "Believe it Son. I had hoped, as you grew older and more successful, that you would have developed a strong sense of self-preservation and intuitively understood these truths. If you have not, you should learn them quickly."

"At what point did your relationship as adviser to Rimush begin to erode?"

"Eventually the long-time King of Akkad, Sargon, had died and Rimush, his son, was appointed ruler over the whole of Babylonia. Because of my prior success in the court of Sargon, I was asked to step up and assume the same role of Chief Adviser to the court of Rimush. However, seven years had gone by and King Rimush had proven difficult to manage."

"In what way do you mean?"

"The most obvious problem was the man's inability to effectively use his advisers to help him make decisions in the kingdom. We were usually ignored, or worse, threatened if Rimush felt we had overstepped our position or attempted to contravene his decisions."

"Did this happen with some frequency?"

"It was ongoing, but especially of late. The less obvious problem, but equally dangerous, was that the Rimush was an utter fool. He took no thought of those who he insulted and disregarded those who had helped him maintain his kingdom. In short, he had made many enemies and his inner court of advisers was constantly trying to compensate or cover for his stupidity."

"Which event, in your opinion, pushed things over the edge such that the Clan became personally involved with the demise of King Rimush?"

"I realized this last battle with Rimush over the marriage of his daughter into the House of Mamagal would finally pit him against the one person in the realm who never lost a fight."

Jasher interjected, "So, at this point, you believe Cain became personally involved with the murder of King Rimush?"

"Cain must have been aware of this state of affairs as he had stepped in to ensure the success of Babylonia in spite of the fool who sat upon the throne. He seldom dismissed a ruler through incompetence as this ineptitude would likely be viewed as a reflection of his own lack of proper management for having made the appointment in the first place."

"Surely Cain does not simply remove a ruler on a whim. What is his usual method to prevent the incompetence and mismanagement of one king to spill over into other areas of the realm?"

"He usually attempted to borrow the strengths of one nation and tie them to a weaker one by means of politically arranged marriages as this would stabilize the weaker supreme ruler as well as the realm as a whole. But Cain was a micro-manager; he insisted on selecting the man and woman for the betrothal and he expected to be obeyed. If the ruler ignored him, he was removed, much as King Rimush had discovered too late."

"So, this disobedience to his instructions was the primary factor behind his removal."

Nadim leaned closer to Jasher as if to make a point, "Rimush refused to obey the arranged marriage between his daughter Antu and Prince Elam of Kish. His father, Mamagal, was incensed over the rebuff and reported this matter to Cain through his own advisers. I was unable to convince Rimush to reverse his decision even to the point of reminding him of his oath to the Brotherhood."

Though Jasher could guess, he asked, "How well did that fare for you?"

"That effort got me thrown into a hell hole for a week and I was lucky that the King of Gassur needed a Chief Adviser or I would still languish in that pit. When I was released from the king's dungeon, I was demoted then reassigned and tomorrow I leave for some back-water camel stop, but at least I leave with my head."

Jasher had listened patiently as the man had spent his energy with his tale of woe. It was hard for him to feel much sympathy for Nadim, but he managed to smile encouragingly or offer a word of understanding at all the appropriate moments in the story.

"Nadim, it would appear that you did all things according to your protocol and were simply the unfortunate adviser caught in the middle of two willful men."

The next question would have to be carefully crafted. "As you were imprisoned at the time, I understand that you could not have been directly responsible for the murder of King Rimush, but would you have any idea who might have been involved?"

Nadim seemed surprised at the question. "Well, obviously it was Cain. Oh, he may not have drawn the dagger, but I can assure you that it was on his orders that Rimush was killed. If I had to guess as to who actually performed the task, it was probably a servant. Cain's spies and operatives are everywhere; this is the power he holds over the kings and their courts. There are members of the Clan of who everyone in the Society is aware then there is the secret, Inner Clan of which only Cain is aware."

Nadim picked up his cup and brought it shakily to his lips then drained the draught in one gulp. A nervous tic appeared from one eye as he glanced toward the entrance to the tavern. His eyes fell upon a large man who had just entered who seemed to have taken especial interest in his direction.

Jasher was making mental notes, trying to comprehend the extensive power the Clan had over the region. When he was satisfied that Nadim had revealed as much as he intended, he commented, "Nadim, thank you for taking the time to explain this matter to me in detail. Is there anything more that you would like to share with me at this time?"

Nadim looked about furtively and hurriedly whispered, "I must go. I have already said too much." He abruptly arose and before his departure he pleaded, "You must not reveal a word of this to anyone, especially of my involvement. Most would disbelieve you anyway and those that would believe would take my life faster than a viper would a field mouse."

CHAPTER 8

SIDON, THE ASSET

The sons of Noah were Japheth, Ham and Shem. The continent, as it existed before the separation, consisted exclusively of the people of the lineage of Japheth located either in the lands of Javan, Magog and Madai on the west while those of the lineage of Ham and Cain, including some descendants of Ashkenaz, resided in the land of Babylonia, which Cain called Shinar. On the east, the descendants of Shem had mingled with those of Seth. Many of the latter had survived the Flood and had migrated westward from the area wherein was located the mountain vault. In no area of the realm was any one group primarily concentrated except that of the west in Javan.

Cain was seated at a darkened back table of a tavern on the edge of Nineveh. There in the waning afternoon of another day, he patiently awaited the arrival of his chief assassin, Sidon. So as to minimize any noticeable relationship between the two, as usual, Cain had left word with him at his nearby palace to meet at an out of the way location. Sidon walked in slowly and glanced casually around the room to ensure there was no one who appeared too interested. When he was satisfied, he walked to the rear and found Cain who had already ordered drinks. His benefactor nodded his head to indicate the chair opposite him and Sidon, once seated, slowly picked up the cup and took a sip of the local wine.

"Are you ready to serve the Clan once again, Sidon?"

As usual, Sidon's manner was respectful, yet relaxed. He slowly took the next sip and declared, "I am".

Cain leaned forward as if to talk confidentially, and in a low voice began briefing him on his new assignment. "Sidon, you are to journey to the far western area of the realm to Magog and use that land as a central location for future expansion of the Clan. I want you to dig deeply undercover. You will use your skills as a mason to establish an identity that will enable you to create a working relationship with all trades and governments within Magog then, under the guise of your trade skills, you will move about throughout all the nearby provinces."

"To whom will I direct my interests on behalf of the Clan?"

"Slowly introduce the workings of the Society to tradesmen, money lenders, advisers and finally rulers. You will put them under oath and covenant to the Clan of the Scar and when you feel that our influence in those societies has reached a certain level of acceptance, you will report back to me and I will send official advisers to their courts. Do you understand all this?"

"I see. As you are aware, my Lord, I am uninitiated at that level of our Society. Will I receive this indoctrination before my departure?"

"You will. Before leaving, you will be introduced into the inner workings of the Clan of the Scar, and as a result you will be fully vested to present others into our Society." Cain paused a moment as if to explain the essential scope of his Order and the rationale upon which Sidon's mission would rest.

"Our Brotherhood will always be welcomed openly in those lands where the masses have a tradition and a culture for limited civil representation. If they have only known the yoke of subjugation, they will have no understanding of what they would mistakenly call personal freedom of choice. Moreover, they would have no comprehension of how to use such freedoms to their advantage in any event. Therefore, any attempt to extend such ideals to them would be a waste of time and resources. I have provided a Brotherhood designed specifically to minimize life's confusions by ensuring limited choices. In the end, I will guide each person toward the better good of an enlightened society."

"I take it those in the Western Provinces might have a different notion as to their freedoms."

"Sidon, nowhere else in the realm do the citizenry cling so stubbornly to so-called God-given rights to exercise personal agency. They revel in that which they have hardly a whit of understanding; in consequence, they must be educated of the fallacy of that notion."

"Very well, but why me? This type of assignment is far removed from my usual roles of subterfuge."

"I have selected you for this mission because you get results. Moreover, you can pass for a common tradesman and mingle among the public at all levels." Remembering the debacle he had experienced with the city of Zion, he declared, "You will not be suspected, let alone accused of subversion, because you will blend in seamlessly into their society."

"I sense there is something different about this mission. This will be a long-term assignment, I presume?"

"It will. I do not expect to see you again for at least fifteen years. You will set up a courier pigeon system in the meantime and keep me posted periodically."

Sidon nodded then pointed out, "A deep, long-term assignment will require a special role to be convincing. Do you have any suggestions other than that of a simple tradesman which will afford me a better chance of success?"

Cain looked at him and smiled, "As a matter of fact, I do. You must get married and have children, settle in deeply and push the work along slowly, but surely."

"Me, married? Are you certain?" He smiled at the notion.

Cain did not return the smile, but intoned, "Deadly sure."

Sidon realized almost immediately upon his arrival to Magog that Cain's warnings were correct. His work there in the West was slow, and for the longest time beset with failures. The citizens were less tolerant of the workings of Cain's Society and seemed to carry an inherent distrust of the power of bureaucracy in government, but being a patient, meticulous man he slowly settled into a routine. He took Cain's advice and married a local woman and began a family which lent serious credibility to his undercover role. He was, after all, a mason by trade and this gave him a respectful, comfortable life for his family. As time went on, he developed business associations, which as everyone knows, invariably lead to political ones. He was careful to accept only contracts for government buildings or residents with political ties.

Though he had been posted in Magog, he felt no particular affinity for remaining there and often traveled with his family on business to the neighboring provinces in search of possible recruits for government change. His reputation for being an exceptional artisan had been spread abroad in the land so after over thirteen years he was beginning to be a highly sought after commodity when it came to building offices for magistrates, senators and advisers. He, of course, no longer performed the labor, but represented himself as the owner and chief operator of highly skilled stone and brick masons. This naturally provided a means for social interaction with the right persons and eventually placed him in a position to introduce the Society as a benign, non-intrusive alternative to the current representative governments now popular in the Western Provinces of Javan, Magog and Madai.

Having relocated from Magog, for the past few years he had taken residence with his family in Javan the Northern Province. That government, similar to all the Western Provinces, contained a limited supreme ruler with representatives in roles much like the British Parliament would embrace many centuries later. With the right contacts, his relocation inevitably led him into close interaction with King Riphath of Javan and his ambitious son, Tubal. Being a respected businessman, Sidon was invited to various social and political events and at one of these he was given audience with the king and was subsequently invited to dine at his table.

Sidon had been seated comfortably next to Riphath and was quite conscious of the ruler's interest in his travels. As per his role, he presented himself as a well-traveled tradesman with many business and political contacts throughout the Western kingdoms.

In order to engage the supreme ruler, he grew expansive on his opinions of the local governments he had experienced. He commented, "My King, as an artisan now living in your enlightened nation I have grown to love and respect your citizens. As you know, I am from Babylonia, and we are governed in a more tightly controlled environment. As a businessman, I have concluded this has been done to promote not only our welfare as citizens, but to ensure our social and economic progress."

King Riphath nodded his head in appreciation of Sidon's comments and was anxious to share a few of his own. "As you have undoubtedly noticed, our land has a representative style of government allowing the average citizen a great degree of personal control and representation. As a result, as I am sure you can imagine, the process of legislation for change is slow and necessarily time consuming. Being a man of action, I have often found myself constrained."

Sidon was delighted that he had finally gained the ear of the chief ruler of the land and had decided to carefully make a few pointed observations. He realized he was treading lightly when he pointed out, "It has been my experience that the average citizen lacks even the vaguest notion of government and remains unappreciative of the sacrifices involved with those who represent them." He sipped his wine and added with a touch of cynicism, "Furthermore, it has been my observation that the street rabble simply wants things to work and they are scarcely concerned as to how it happens."

Tubal, Riphath's son had grown bored with the table talk and quickly drained his cup distractedly then demanded more wine from a passing servant. As he turned back to the dialogue between his father and Sidon, he attempted to follow the conversation, but as usual the wine had blind-sided him. As far as he was concerned, the only point worth discussing was the acquisition of an army. On that topic he would have much to say and realized that, at least in this kingdom under the current government that it would be unlikely if not an impossibility to attain what he most wanted. He had many plans for the future and the sooner his father died and he inherited the throne the sooner he could control his destiny.

Riphath, however, was trying to impress Sidon as the well-intentioned, enlightened public servant. He also observed dryly, "I, too, Sidon have observed this tendency of the common folk. They are demanding and take little interest in my sacrifices on their behalf."

Sidon felt he had hit the mark and decided to press on to see just how deeply Riphath's objections ran. He decided it was time to insert the wedge of doubt into the discussion. "Your citizens are warm-hearted and intelligent, but in order to take them to the next level of an enlightened citizenry, they must be presented with a more deliberate manner of government." He paused to ensure he had the king's full attention. With feigned, yet obvious reluctance he added, "As a businessman, I have noticed your people are willful and distrustful of your leadership." He uttered an audible sigh as if reluctant to proceed.

"Please, go on," the king added with a nod of encouragement, but deep inside he felt a foreboding with this new revelation. He was deeply concerned that his rule had been found wanting among those who had recently relocated to his territory.

"Perhaps it is time to guide them wisely to a new era of government."

"I, too, have seen the need for change, but here in the far provinces we are behind the times and lack the understanding and sophistication of such matters that our more enlightened brothers in Babylonia have achieved."

Sidon shook his head in sympathy then added, "I have known many a fine leader who tried to hold on to dated notions of government at the expense of progress. A good leader knows when the time is ripe for positive change on behalf of his citizens."

"My people, as you have noted, are belligerent and would obstruct any such efforts on my part to change the government, even for their own good."

It was now time to drive home the wedge and create the separation. "My King, for someone clearly sincere for positive change, such as yourself, I have been provided with the authority to extend such an invitation to you and your son into a Babylonian-led Society that can guide you wisely and offer continuing support of a progressive government. Would that be something which would appeal to your obvious desire for service to your people?"

Riphath immediately saw the benefit of such support. Being a man that eschewed any ideal of a representative government, he had always admired the personal control that the Kingdoms of Babylonia, Nineveh and other similar domains enjoyed over their subjects. As a king, he had always felt ham-strung by the tedious efforts of listening to the voice of the citizenry. Moreover, he had grown weary of the public committees and endless debates that had side-lined him, more often than not, from making judicial decisions that had resulted in marginalizing his control.

After a moment, he quietly interjected, "I would welcome such support, and if you were in the position to reach out to your contacts in Babylonia, it would be greatly appreciated."

"It would be my honor and pleasure to extend to you the services of my Brotherhood, King Riphath."

Tubal made note of the last comments between his father and Sidon. Perhaps this man had the influence whereby they could eventually procure the support of a large standing army. If so, then maybe the social changes he had in mind for Javan could be realized much sooner than later.

Within a year, Sidon had inducted the king and his son into the Clan of the Scar and had sent for several of Cain's advisers to serve directly to the court of Riphath of Javan. This effort established a base of influence for future expansion of the Society into neighboring kingdoms. After reporting to Cain, he relocated to Magog with his family and continued his efforts there for similar successes. He had scarcely returned to Magog before he began to hear disquieting rumors of King Riphath's inept rule of Javan and lack of respect for the advisers Cain had sent to counsel and guide that region.

CHAPTER 9

SEEDS OF DISCONTENT

After Jasher had completed his latest recordings, which included the testimony of Nadim regarding the deposed King Rimush of Babylonia, he took all his accumulated records and made the long trek eastward to the mountain vault where he stored them for safe-keeping. His journeys back to the West took him through many of the newer civilizations still untouched by Cain's Society, primarily of the lineage of Shem mingled with that of Seth. After he had so-journed fifteen years, he eventually made his way back to the far western regions of his homeland where he entered the city of Javan, principal city in the land of his birth and it was in this kingdom that he met his future wife Miriam.

Miriam, the fourth daughter of Admah through the lineage of Javan, son of Japheth, was in deep conversation with her mother, Rachel. The courtyard under the maple trees was cool and it made their discussion of her upcoming betrothal bearable, if inconclusive. Miriam was pointing out, "Mother, we have gone over this before. My engagement to Tubal would be a mistake and I feel I must break it off. His father is a tyrant with our people and Tubal is no better."

"Of course his father, King Riphath, is a tyrant because his wives were either too lazy or too self-absorbed to be bothered to teach him proper manners. That is, after all, the duty of a wife," declared her mother. She added, "When you are married, and using proper charm, you, too, will be able to bend Tubal toward a more socially correct attitude toward others."

Miriam, knowing Tubal to be a brainless thug, was disinclined to believe he was capable of being reached by her female charms or any other charms for that matter. She was more concerned about his violent nature. "Mother, we are simply incompatible. The man I wish to marry should be kind and gentle, not an overbearing oaf a man."

"Miriam, you simply have to allow your parents to decide what is best for you in these matters. Tubal's father is our ruler and his son, his only heir, will one day inherit all and follow in his footsteps. This marriage makes it possible for our family to bask in the shadow of those who control our nation." As an added point she commented self-righteously, "You have no right to be so selfish."

"Mother, it is my life and I will decide what is best for me. I have seen and heard how miserable my older sisters are in their arranged marriages."

"They are miserable because they have chosen to be so, hardly because their husbands are incompetent. Each of them is an adviser in the courts throughout the land and is highly influential in guiding the course of our people."

"Yes, each marriage was a social arrangement to appease your untiring need to become a social figure in the kingdom. Even Father lacks the interest in such things."

Her mother huffed at that remark and replied, "You are quite correct about that! Your father has many fine qualities, but ambition has never been his strong suit. I have had to drag and push him every step of the way to reach the position of influence we now enjoy. Your marriage to Tubal represents the culmination of years of positioning our family into the light at just the right moment and you will not disappoint me in this matter."

"Mother, this discussion is pointless. I will inform Tubal tonight that the engagement announcement is off."

"Then you would insult the king's son by this decision? Do you have any idea what this refusal could imply? It could bring a harsh retribution down

BILL W. SANFORD

upon us all. Would you at least consider a postponement of the marriage to allow you time to think it over?"

Miriam was weary of the battle so reluctantly she considered her mother's request. Given the possible repercussions of her decision to break off the impending engagement, it did seem to be the best solution. She was reluctant to postpone the inevitable decision, but decided the best course of action was to placate her mother.

"I will speak with Tubal tonight and push back the date of the marriage announcement, but I don't see how this will change my mind."

"It will allow you more time to get to know the boy and mollify your perspective in the matter. Also, it is a reasonable request without giving offense." Additionally, she reflected, this would give her more time to wear down her daughter's hard-headed attitude.

Tubal was unhappy. Since he was used to getting his way he was unfamiliar with the concept of denial of anything he wanted. Nevertheless, tonight he was getting an education in rejection which had led to disappointment and hurt pride. Although his rage was mounting, he did strive to maintain a degree of calm as he commented, "Miriam, I refuse to believe that you would want to postpone the engagement."

Miriam was sick of listening to this overgrown, spoiled child. She was making every attempt to be patient and calm in her deliberation of her feelings. "Tubal, I think I have been quite clear on this matter. I need more time to evaluate our relationship and what it may bode for us in the future."

Tubal, now taking an argument from her mother's playbook, pointed out, "Why can't you just accept that, in these matters, our parents may know more about what we, ourselves, may need. It has always been our tradition and I see no reason why we should stop it now. Besides, how would the community react to this postponement? Not well, I assure you." He was seething and his tone of voice had gotten louder the more he thought about the delay and what it might signal socially.

"Tubal, I simply need more time. If that is beyond your comprehension, then perhaps we should end the idea of an engagement tonight."

4

At hearing this, his ire and hurt pride had burst forth and his hand reacted faster than his better judgment, though he immediately felt better for having done it. As he backhanded Miriam forcefully against the right side of her jaw, she reeled backwards, the blow having been administered hard enough to draw blood. She managed to catch her balance against a nearby wall, but as she slid away to avoid more blows, he grabbed her roughly on her upper arm then dug in his fingers dragging her closely to his glowering eyes.

"You will obey me woman! This is the first lesson you will learn and I can assure you there will be many more to come!" With a glee of victory now etched across his face, he clamped his fingers in more deeply into her upper arm; she was now openly cringing in fear. His smile was merciless as he implacably intoned between clenched teeth, "The engagement stays on schedule. I will make the announcement on the morrow."

With that, he pulled Miriam to the door way; then he threw her out of his room into the courtyard, the door slamming behind her. She looked down fearfully at the bruise already appearing on her arm, and as she wiped the blood from her now swelling lip, a feeling of hopeless terror flowed through her as she began to sob at all the hurt that was yet to come.

Jasher was happy to be home again. It had been well over one hundred years since he had left with Noah on the long trek eastward to the mountain vault wherein he had first viewed the records of his ancestors. Since then he had visited the Western region only once to see his parents and to conduct interviews. During that time much had changed. Thriving communities had sprung up throughout the land and the Kingdom of Javan was beginning to spread its tentacles of influence throughout the region. Nevertheless, he wasn't home long before rumors of the king's tyranny over the citizens began to reach his ears. After having seated himself in preparation for the evening meal, Jasher listened patiently while his father explained the political state of affairs in the country.

"My son, you must understand that King Riphath has grown drunk with power and no longer leads the citizenry peacefully as did his fathers before him."

"I have heard that he has raised taxes over the objections of many of the delegates to his court."

Nodding, Elisha pointed out, "He has taxed the citizens past reasonable endurance just to feed his lust for power and indulge his appetites for orgies of food, drink and women. Even more of a concern, he has also used these same taxes to double the size of his personal guard. His political advisers are frightened of his temper and just last month one of them was publicly whipped in the town square because he had displeased the king by counselling more temperance towards the public and a reduction of taxes."

"The man was publicly beaten? Did Riphath give the order for such actions? I thought only the elected magistrate was responsible for that."

"As his son, Tubal, was seen there to personally oversee the flogging, it was suspected that his son had instigated the punishment on his father's behalf."

Jasher reflected on all he had seen in the realm of Babylonia under the control of Cain and commented, "Father, you must realize that as bad as the affairs in our land may be, at least here, for now at least, we are beyond the reach of Cain and the influence of the Clan."

"As you know, Jasher, we have several contacts and kinsmen in Javan who serve on the inner courts of the government and there are rumors that his Order has already begun its work of subterfuge. Though thus far the effort has been met with limited acceptance, nonetheless, Riphath's newest advisers are foreign to our land and have come to us from the East. Those in the know have whispered they are of the Clan."

This was a new development. "Have you been unable to redress Riphath's excessive behavior?"

"Sadly, our elected representatives have been systematically ignored. It is now clear he no longer heeds the voice of the public nor is he any longer intimidated by our resistance to his reign."

"Can it be confirmed that Cain now controls the nation through Riphath?"

"The latest violence would suggest that Riphath has grown emboldened with his power, thus it would hardly surprise me if he has already been approached and admitted into the Clan of the Scar. I fear he is getting support from those outside of our region and eventually they will help him build up a large, private army to support his reign while he dismantles our government."

"The land of Babylonia is still far removed from this isolated sector of the realm. Perhaps this distance will be enough to give us time to prepare a sufficient defense."

Elisha shook his head sadly. "What we truly fear is that when Riphath passes the kingdom on to his son, Tubal, we will enter a period of pure terror."

"I have never met Tubal. What do you know of him?"

"If his father is a tyrant, then his son is that and much worse. His son enjoys inflicting pain and he openly flaunts this behavior in public and his father refuses, of course, to restrain him."

"Does Riphath have other sons who might be less inclined to support his father's excesses and proposed changes to the government?"

"He is the only son and he is accustomed to getting his way. Eventually, Tubal will inherit all, including his father's personal guard, which includes several of our kinsmen, and all have indicated that when he inherits, he will reign with blood and horror. Lately, they have overheard him boast that he will increase the size of the guard to a standing army and suspend all civic representation. I tell you that bad times may be on the horizon." Elisha rubbed his now wrinkled hands distractedly and reflected, "I am an old man and it troubles me that my land may yet fall under the yoke of despotism before I die."

Due to his mission which he had accepted many years earlier, Jasher had been absent from the social progress and political matters of his homeland, and consequently had no idea of the degree of fear which seemed to permeate Javan upon his return. Before talking with his father, the notion of a rebellion had never entered his mind, but having witnessed first-hand the results of the influence of the Clan in many other parts of the realm, he was determined that Javan would not fall under Cain's tyranny.

"Father, could a well-planned uprising topple Riphath's rule before he becomes too powerful?"

"I have considered that as a possibility, and such a suggestion has been whispered among our people. Some feel that, though there is danger, it could be done, but we must work quickly because Cain's influence is steadily making the inroads for a complete takeover. The question remains: could we make it work or is too late?"

Jasher pointed out, "In Shinar, as Cain has too many spies afoot, such a public uprising would be detected long before it gained acceptance; moreover, any organized resistance to topple a king's rule would be ruthlessly quelled and the leaders executed."

"Has he ever been opposed once he has taken control of a nation?"

"Cain's influence is so complete that whoever succeeds as the replacement ruler of any country under his control is immediately inducted into the Clan and if he refuses to obey or later is found non-compliant to Cain he then is murdered."

Both men grew pensive at this description of political and social conditions under Cain's Brotherhood. Finally, Jasher asked, "Can we count on the immediate support of the public if we begin this effort now rather than later? Otherwise, the success of our efforts diminishes if we wait."

"If the evidence of the influence of the Clan was sufficient, I know there would be public concern."

"How can we measure the resolve of the people?"

Elisha pondered the question then pointed out, "There is a large family reunion planned for next week and I suggest we talk with our kinsmen at the event and there decide upon the best course of action."

Rachel, Miriam's mother, despised family reunions and she was seldom quiet about her opinion of them. A reunion, in her estimation, must lead to a social or political advantage in some way and from what she had observed over the years, her husband's family was neither socially nor politically connected enough to be worth the attendance. Of course, on those occasions in which she reluctantly attended, this deficiency seldom prevented her from imbibing the wine to excess. Consequently, she was again on her way back from the wine table and was already well taken in drink.

Her vison, due to her inebriated state, was now myopic at best and was equal to her conversational skills. With an uncaring shrug, she had spied her husband deep in talk and had stumbled to his side. Now leaning on his shoulder for support, she made a poor attempt to whisper and instead slurred a little too loudly, "Admah, as usual, your relations have about as much notion of social finesse as a barnyard cow. This whole reunion has become tiresome."

Admah, seeing his wife indisposed, motioned for his daughter Miriam to collect her mother before she fell down and injured herself, which had on occasion occurred at previous reunions due to her aforementioned disposition. Miriam had been watching her mother and knew from experience that when she had reached a certain stage of inebriation she had to be carefully guided in the right direction with gentle reminders. When she noticed her father give the pre-arranged signal, Miriam began moving toward the men to remove her mother.

Jasher had been in quiet debate with the men in his group, attempting to solicit support and interest in his plan to remove King Riphath, when Rachel, wife of Admah, had drunkenly sidled up to her husband. It was clear she was near to collapse when Jasher became aware of a beautiful woman walking in their direction. After taking control of her mother, she smiled ruefully at the men then excused them both. When the two women were out of range, the conversation renewed.

For Jasher, the conversation was over. He had suspected that there might exist love at first sight and had even heard rumors of its existence, but until the moment he saw Miriam, he thought those notions were more a myth than reality. Elisha, noting the distraction of his son and inwardly smiling, suggested, "Jasher, there is another group of men on the far side of the courtyard. Would you circulate among them and assess their interests?"

"Of course Father, I will move around to get a better idea of the prevailing opinions." Actually, his only interest was wearing a loose-fitting, rose-colored robe and leading her mother to a chair under an arbor.

Miriam had her mother seated next to one of her older female cousins. The cousin commiserated with Rachel's condition and began a discussion relating to the illness of a distant relative. Due to her drunken state, Rachel was oblivious of the woman's chatter and would scarcely have cared to engage in it even if she had been coherent, but it did give Miriam an opportunity to observe a rather tall, attractive man approaching in her direction. His manner was courtly, and as though he had traveled and seen much, he carried a confidant grace and maturity about him.

Jasher nodded toward the chattering cousin, but gave her only brief attention as he had only eyes for Miriam. He bowed and his introduction was cultured, "I am Jasher and happened to notice your mother was feeling ill. Is there something I can do?"

Miriam felt something peculiar pass between them. With an open smile, she thanked him with for his concern and explained, "Mother becomes dizzy and light-headed when she has had too much to drink. Perhaps if she can sit in the shade for a few moments she may recover her wits."

Rachel began to snore lightly. Jasher and Miriam both smiled indulgently at the noise emanating from her mother's direction. She turned back in his direction and introduced herself. "I am Miriam, by the way. Thank you for your concern, Jasher."

His tone was courteous as he replied, "Of course. Please let me know if I can be of any help." He smiled then dismissed himself with a slight nod and walked over to some men in the far corner of the courtyard. In a few minutes it seemed to Miriam he was deep in conversation.

Jasher was explaining to his kinsmen the nature of his travels and began to relate to them all he had seen and heard regarding the Clan. The debate had become quite agitated. One commented, "Now see here, Jasher, the Clan, as it is called, seems benign to me. I lived in Nineveh for many years and was impressed by the level of government and its treatment of the citizenry in general."

Jasher patiently explained, "What you were unaware was the removal of governmental leaders if they dared to step out of line and extend better representation to the public or openly defy the Clan."

"How do you mean?"

"During my last visit to Babylonia, some fifteen years ago, in the city of Akkad, King Rimush was murdered on his own throne for refusing to accept the betrothal of his daughter to the son of King Mamagal of Kish. A source highly placed in that court assured me that an assassin, most likely a servant, was placed close to King Rimush and executed him for disobedience to Cain, the Master Mahan of the Clan." This last revelation created quite a stir among the assembled men.

Miriam had observed the discussion among Jasher and the other men, and being curious by nature, as well as out-spoken, decided to investigate. While making his last comment, he had overlooked the arrival of Miriam who had strolled over in their direction and began to listen to the end of his pointed commentary.

Jasher continued, "If we add this level of violent behavior to what you have already witnessed here in Javan from King Riphath and his son, Tubal, it becomes clearer to understand the degree of oppression which is to come."

Upon hearing Jasher's conclusion, Miriam could scarcely believe that someone besides herself had pieced together such a scenario of tyranny and fear. Knowing from first-hand experience the violent nature of Tubal, she decided to ask, "And what is it you suggest we do, Jasher?"

Jasher noticed the men turned to Miriam when the question was asked. It was a good question, one they all had, so none censured the woman for listening in on the conversation.

Jasher's eyes fell upon her and replied simply, "We remove our king and his son before they gain the full support of the Clan. Otherwise, if we wait, their power will have grown as well as their military strength and we will have no chance for success."

Miriam spoke for the assembled group of relatives. "I wish to hear your plans."

Jasher met her gaze then looked around the group. "We will meet tonight at the home of my father Elisha. As we can ill afford to be infiltrated by spies at this point, inform only those whom you trust outside of our family regarding this meeting. If this is to work, we must have the element of surprise and justice on our side."

CHAPTER 10

THE UPRISING

**You have enemies? Good. That means you've stood up
for something, sometime in your life.**

----- Winston Churchill

Shortly after the meeting had started, Jasher had made a convincing case against the methods of the Clan and gave his justifications for an insurrection. Given the likelihood that the influence of the Clan had already reached the king and his court advisers, it would only be a matter of time before the oppression of the population began in earnest. The only thing that remained to insure this came about would be the establishment of a large, standing army to enforce the tenets and policies of Cain's Society through Riphath. Jasher pointed out that if the king could provide a convincing reason to increase the size of the army, he could appeal to Cain and get his army then his power base would be complete. All knew that the uprising being proposed would, in all likelihood, result in that justification. Consequently, they had to succeed, regardless of the odds; it would be now or never.

Jasher explained, "Brothers, it has been my sad experience to watch the freedoms of other kingdoms crumble to dust under the mere threat of invading armies. Once the Clan gains a foothold, they will intimidate from without and Riphath will in all likelihood get his army to ostensibly be used as a defense for his territory, but in reality it will be used to defend his throne against his own citizenry."

Several plans had been proposed, but the only one that seemed workable and had the most potential for success involved a diversion using Tubal as the bait. Ironically enough, the plan had come from Miriam, the one person who stood to lose the most from Riphath and his son being removed from their rule. Jasher was reluctant to involve Miriam directly with the operation, but given her unique relationship to Tubal, she was the only one who could have pulled it off so easily. Besides, it was clear she would rather die trying to fight for their freedom than become a punching bag for Tubal's rages. As Jasher had inadvertently discovered at the meeting on the night following the reunion, her passion was evident and she was determined to see it through.

His concern was warranted, but fortunately, there were those on the inside, a few kinsmen on the staff of the palace guard and at least one adviser, who were eager to disengage from Riphath's ambitions and Cain's society. Each would provide needed information and support that made the success of the operation feasible. The plan was simple, but in Jasher's opinion, it contained too many unknown variables for an assured, quick victory.

Jasher listened in disbelief as Miriam enumerated the tactical points of the operation. His reservations during her briefing of the plan were more personal than operational and though most of the men agreed in principle to its feasibility, some, like Jasher, were concerned for her safety. His objections, however, were more vocal.

"I intend to request an audience to meet with my intended husband Tubal in the late evening hours to discuss a marriage date. Since this was what Tubal had wanted all along, the meeting will be easily granted. At some point, I will lure him outside where he can be easily abducted."

"How do you intend to lure him outside?"

"Once I am inside the palace and safely alone with Tubal, I will convince him to accompany me outside so that we may talk of our impending marriage announcement in private."

"How will you insure his compliance?"

"I will hint of an intimate encounter later. It is what he has always wanted, so why not provide the expectation as an incentive?"

"And after he is abducted, then what?"

"I will then inform the palace guard of the abduction then those guards, privy to our plot, will accompany me to the king. I will pretend desperate fear that Tubal will be harmed unless immediately recovered."

"How will you convince Riphath? Suppose he suspects you are in on the abduction?"

"I will have help. The guards, along with the adviser also in on the plot, will insist that King Riphath allow as many as possible of his personal palace guard to pursue the abductors until his son can be found. Immediately after the majority of the palace guard has departed in pursuit, the uprising can occur and the insurgents can take over the palace then lock up the king and his remaining advisers. Soon thereafter, they should proceed to raid the armory and arm themselves in the event the guards return later with the intent to give aid to Riphath."

"And when the main guard reappears from their fruitless search for Tubal? I doubt they will stand idly by as King Riphath is trussed up like a holiday chicken and tossed unceremoniously into his own dungeon."

"Any organized opposition should stand down an attack for fear of injuring the king and by then, in any event, he would be outnumbered by the now armed citizenry."

"Miriam, how do you know this plan will succeed? There are so many pieces that have to come together."

"As I see it," she pointed out, "the key to success is the removal of any potential resistance to our attack. This must be dealt with early in the engagement or we will lose the advantage of surprise and be slaughtered before we can get close to the king. So, we use a diversion or ruse to lure off the palace guard and then we capture him and arm our people."

Jasher, though clearly impressed with her assessment and tactical understanding, was nonetheless reluctant to allow her to place herself in harmsway. With deep concern, he ventured, "Might there be some other way to lure him outside without risking you any bodily harm in the assault?"

Miriam, being an astute, practical young woman, realized that Jasher was expressing his doubts of the plan based upon his feelings for her rather than because he thought the plan would fail. Inwardly she felt a tremor of affection for this kind man, but needed to convey outward strength to reassure him.

She met his eyes defiantly and declared, "Tubal must be unsuspecting of any treachery and it must be done the way I have described or the plan fails before we can even set it in motion."

Jasher realized by the set of her jaw and intensity of her eyes that she had made up her mind. There would be no way to talk her out of her part in the abduction. All the men in the room agreed that her plan of action was flawless and her conclusions sound. Each was openly confident of its success; all save one.

He looked around the room and met every eye then declared, "Every plan is flawed because we are flawed. We must prepare for the worst possible circumstances to arise," he added.

The remainder of the evening was dedicated to the discussion of contingencies in the event that the original plan failed or needed to be adjusted because of unforeseen occurrences. All throughout the remainder of the meeting Jasher's eyes never left Miriam and his foreboding grew deeper. At the close, it was decided that they begin the revolt the following night. To delay the uprising meant giving the opposition more time to prepare, especially should the Riphath be informed of their intentions, and they would need every advantage if they were to succeed.

Miriam was the last to leave. Jasher was standing next to the hearth, deep in thought as she approached him. Taking his hand, she quietly asked, "Jasher, we must talk. Will you walk me home?"

As they walked in silence, she reflected that all evening it had seemed he had wanted to reveal his true feelings and perhaps she had intimidated him with her pointed opinions. Nevertheless, if the rebellion was to succeed, there must be honesty between them.

"Jasher, as you have noticed, I am outspoken when I feel the cause is just. Please feel free to speak what is truly on your mind."

They walked on silently in the cool of the night. His eyes were on the stars but his mind was elsewhere. Finally, he asked, "How is it that you are so willing to be a part of this uprising? It would seem to me that your marriage to Tubal would be of great benefit to you and your family. Of us all involved, you would be least likely to benefit from its success."

"You do not know Tubal as I do. I am engaged to a man I despise and fear."

"Was your betrothal so set in stone? Surely, if he understood your true feelings for him he would not press you to move forward on this marriage."

"His feelings are too muddled by his pride. Before you arrived, there was no way out of the marriage that permitted my family a peaceful existence in the kingdom and I felt like I was caught in a trap with no way of escape. This plan gives me hope for my family as well as for our nation."

"It gives me physical pain to know you might be in danger while this plot unfolds."

Miriam stopped and turned to him, her eyes catching his own and seeing his face etched in worry, she said quietly, "When this is over and behind us, you and I will have a proper starting point for our feelings. Until then, we must be patient and put them aside. Can you understand?"

"I do understand but I don't like the risk."

"Then we must succeed."

The day of the revolt began overcast and rainy, but by noon day the dark clouds had given way to sunshine and Jasher then began last minute preparations by meeting with each group leader to ensure that each understood his specific tasks. Each leader, in turn, notified every member of his own group to ensure that the plan came together seamlessly. By mid-afternoon, Jasher had to admit that their chances looked good, assuming, of course, Miriam could lure Tubal to a concealed location on the terrace where the abduction could take place out of sight from the palace guards.

Jasher found a quiet corner behind his father's farm to contemplate the upcoming events and determine if there was anything left he needed to address. He could find no fault with the preparations and yet, he felt, that there was something missing of which he needed to be aware. He was thus in the act of self-examination when he noticed a man walking toward him along the pathway leading to the woods. As the man approached, with each step he became more familiar until he was standing before him as he had some years before.

"Joseph, or should I say Seth, I did not expect to see you again this soon!" Jasher smiled, genuinely happy to meet the messenger once again.

Joseph smiled in greeting. "It is never up to me to decide what the message will be or when the message is to be delivered. As I said last we met, I am only the messenger."

"I doubt you could ever be only a messenger," he countered. "I can only conclude by your timing that you have come as regards to our upcoming revolt. It is necessary, you understand."

Joseph's smile was quick, but he pointed out delicately, "I am not here about that matter, though I must mention that your involvement is outside the purview of your mission. Nevertheless, you will always have your freedom to make choices and if you must use your agency for these matters, ensure you do it for the right reasons."

"I feel that my reasons are just. These are my kinsmen and yours as well. I could hardly stand by idly and watch as Cain corrupted them in the same manner as he has done before. They have a right to experience freedom and if they choose to abandon those rights at least they will have had their chance."

"Well said, Jasher, and it is for that specific reason that I have arrived, to give them that chance, and by the way, your uprising will be successful if you stay the course on this plan."

"You know this for a certainty or do you mention it simply to assuage my anxieties?"

"There are things I know and you will better understand with time and acquired wisdom. But, my message does not concern your current plans. I have a special mission for you to complete; the first of many I can assure you."

"I can only assume this new task will deviate from my current role here in Javan."

"In a way, it will. Within a month, the appearance of a celestial object over the night time sky will signal your mission here in Javan will be complete. This object will be hurtling towards the earth and when it impacts our world, it will cause a cataclysmic event so tremendous that it will cause the earth to shake and our land mass to break up."

"I have travelled across our land mass, and though it is vast, if such a thing were to occur, would it not push our oceans over the land and cause another Flood as in the time of Noah?"

"The Creator has assured us there will never be another Great Flood. But, this event will cause our land to break apart into two major masses separated by a great ocean on both sides. In due time, the earth will continue to shift thereby producing other smaller masses that will subsequently create islands and other minor land forms."

"Where will the major break occur?"

"After the collision has taken place, this land upon which you now stand will shift and be divided from the land inhabited by Cain and his Society by a great ocean. This separated land here will be special and will always serve as a land of promise, choice above all others. You will, of course, record the incident."

A promised land? What a peculiar idea, he thought. "And what will make this land so unique above all others?"

"It will be a land of freedom for all men and women to exercise the right of choice and only here will exist a full opportunity for personal growth and social freedoms for several generations. They will have their chance; what they do with it is for them to decide, but regardless, this land will always be preserved for that special purpose alone. But, it will come with a price. Where much is given, much will always be expected."

Jasher was quite openly astonished at this news, but could only murmur, "If Cain learns of this, he will attempt to thwart the plan somehow."

"Yes, and no doubt he will hear of your insurrection by one means or another and will attempt to replace your new government with one of his own. Jasher, your mission is to warn him not to interfere; he must not be here when the land separations occur."

"Why should he listen to me? The last we met, I received nothing but a cursing and threats to stay out of his way."

"Coming from you, he will understand the message. You will have six months at most before the object hits the earth and precipitates the changes I have described. I would suggest you be long gone and much farther east by that time."

"So, I am not to remain here in the west with my people?"

Joseph looked at him compassionately and murmured, "I think you already know the answer to that question." He noted the concern on Jasher's face and with a knowing smile he declared, "But, you may take Miriam with you."

Jasher smiled, a little embarrassed by the messenger's astute observation. He said, "Joseph, you really don't miss much do you?"

"Why Jasher, whatever do you mean? I am only the messenger and I have delivered my message." Smiling, he bowed, turned and started up the road. Once he turned off the road to enter the woods a light could be seen in the distance. Without hesitation he entered the light and simply disappeared.

While Jasher was deep in discussion with Joseph, at the same time Tubal and his father had been in session with his advisers of the Society and by the end of the morning Tubal was in a dark mood. It seemed that for everything Riphath had wanted, the advisers had cautioned him to wait and have patience, so this debate was scarcely achieving Tubal's aims. Once again, he felt betrayed by an ongoing counsel for patience and forbearance, and if his father was not man enough to stand up to them, eventually he would have to take action and make the decision for him. With disgust, he concluded that the message that had been sent by way of the public flogging of the previous adviser had left hardly more than a token impression on the others.

Tubal need not have been too concerned. King Riphath seethed with anger over the latest counsel and protested their pointed advice. He cried, now outraged at the constant delays to his requests, "I must have a larger army to bolster my position. Cain wants me to increase the taxes and send him the proceeds, but the citizens grow restive and belligerent. In time they will overthrow my rule."

The Chief Adviser, Phut, was of Cain's Inner Clan and he was weary of listening to the tantrums of this cretin who would be king. "Sire," soothed the chief adviser, "If this is all done gradually, then you will have your army. Given time and with enough insistent pressure from within and from without, the citizens will insist that you have a larger army to protect them, but if you move too quickly, then they will resent your rule and will see your army for what it will truly be: a means to preserve your power over them."

"So, what am I supposed to do in the meantime, Phut? Hope that their love for me grows while I increase the taxes?"

"For the time being, we caution you to be patient and allow our counsel to guide you. For this reason, I and the other advisers have been sent from Cain to assist you in this process. I assure you, this has been done many times before with great success."

"Fools," cried Riphath. "Our people here are different and would accept Cain's dogma with difficulty. The only thing they will understand is the whip, so your counsel is useless. Moreover, if I had my way I would bury you all up to your heads and turn the sows loose upon you."

"Sire, you must be patient and understand that you will eventually have everything you want, but if it is done in haste, the result will be an uprising that will spiral out of your control."

"I swear that if I hear anymore inept counsel from you, all of you will share a similar fate as the last councilor who dared lecture me on how to run my nation. He still languishes in my dungeon and will stay there until I decide otherwise."

Phut looked coldly over at King Riphath and his son then intoned, "I am well aware of your action against our colleague, but I warn you to take care. If your conduct is repeated, then prepare to have your kingdom invaded. The two of you will pay dearly for any further outrages to Cain."

"Tubal, take this fool to the market square and make an example of him as you did with the previous adviser who was foolish enough to cry for patience when action was clearly indicated. This time, I suggest you send a harsher message."

"It would be a pleasure, Father. I have just the whip in mind."

Riphath added, "As to the rest of you, you are all under house arrest. I am weary of your incessant dithering thus you will taste my dungeon until I have received what I need. In the meantime, one of you must personally inform Cain to send me an army so that I can protect myself." With that, he stormed out of the chamber followed closely by Tubal now pushing the chief adviser out the door at the point of his sword.

The remaining advisers looked at one another and realized that they had a serious problem with Riphath. Mizraim, as now Senior Adviser, ventured an observation, "Cain will need to know, but which of us is foolish enough to take the message?"

The other advisers stared balefully in his direction and their look left no room for doubt as to who would be nominated.

Later that evening, as the revolt was unfolding, Miriam entered Tubal's bed chamber closely followed by her intended husband. She realized immediately that he was troubled and would have to be skillfully manipulated in the right direction if their plan was to succeed.

With false concern she asked, "Tubal, please tell me what is bothering you. Is it the execution in the market square today?"

"Well, of course it is you, silly twit! My addled-brained father ordered me to execute our chief adviser today, so now we will surely be invaded by Cain's army."

Naturally, Tubal neglected to point out that if his father had refused to take action, then he would have taken the initiative. Also, he had rather enjoyed the public display of his power. He thought, *It was a pity that the man had been too weak to endure the flogging; his death was unexpected, but well worth the spectacle.*

"Tubal, I understand you are upset, but surely Cain will understand the pressures you are all under." She sidled herself closely to him and kissed his neck. This seemed to mollify him and when she kissed him openly on the lips, his sexual interest seemed to heighten dramatically, driving away all other thoughts. He was about to push her to his bed when she took him by the hand and led him out to the open terrace.

"I will have you now!" His voice was demanding, insistent.

"There will be more time for that later," she promised. "Let us get some air and talk of our marriage. I think we should discuss our business before we indulge in our pleasure." Her voice was husky and insinuating, leaving no doubt what she had in mind.

"Very well, but I will hold you to that promise," he replied, revealing an oafish, leering smile of expectation. His face had a high sheen as he contemplated the consummation to come.

Now on the terrace, the two began to talk of their impending marriage. Tubal was in the midst of an explanation when he was suddenly accosted from behind. He thrashed around and tried to resist his attackers, but one cudgeled him squarely on the back of the head with a club and he crumpled to the ground. A few other men emerged from the darkness and began to tie him up while one thrust a burlap bag over his head. When Tubal was securely bound, his abductors threw him in the back of a cart and began hauling him away.

Before they departed, Miriam whispered to the abductors, "I will give you a few minutes to make good your escape with Tubal then I will raise the alarm. Good luck."

A few minutes went by then Miriam, according to plan, rushed from the chamber room to the main hall sounding the alarm to King Riphath and his guards that Tubal had been attacked and then abducted from the terrace.

With tearful eyes she beseeched Riphath to pursue them as soon as possible. "Please, my Lord, they have taken Tubal and I overheard them say they were taking him to the forest. I fear for his life," she wailed.

The king's greatest fear had come to pass. Some group had abducted his son as retribution for the increased taxes and public punishments. He cursed Cain and his advisers for not providing him a standing army for his protection. Miriam's performance and her pleas had hit the mark.

"Miriam, where have they taken him?"

"Sire, they rode off to the east of the city. Surely your soldiers will rescue him before they can reach the forest."

Abdon was one of the soldiers, the Senior Captain of the Guard and a kinsman of Miriam, and he knew his part would be critical to the success of the insurrection. With a firm voice he declared, "Lord, we must dispatch the entire palace guard in pursuit. If those cowards reach the forest, we may lose them."

"How many shall I send? I cannot send everyone and leave us defenseless here in the castle!"

"They may also have confederates who will lay in wait to ambush us, so the more of us that are sent, the greater the chance for our success."

"Who then?"

"Allow me to take your men in pursuit while, of course, your personal guard will stay behind to protect you with a small contingent." Abdon realized he could have volunteered to stay with the smaller detail, but either way he was ensuring that a small force was left to deal with a large group of insurrectionists.

Riphath could see no alternative on such short notice, so he quickly agreed, "Dispatch everyone, but Captain, you will bring them back to me alive. I want to deal with them personally. No one insults my rule and lives to boast about it later!" he shouted.

Miriam had decided, of course, to withhold the true direction they were actually taking Tubal. In reality, they were holding him a few streets away at a kinsman's home. Immediately after delivering Tubal to the home, they all vanished quietly into the night in separate directions where they would meet up later with the main body that would assault the palace. A few minutes passed and there was a flurry of activity as the palace guard raced through the streets on their way to give chase. Once the guards had cleared the gates of the city and were now riding towards the forest, the signal was raised for the assault to begin.

The attack on the palace went according to plan. Jasher led a large group of men armed with torches to guide their way and a battering ram that had been acquired to be used to force open the main gate. After applying the ram to the door, the men swarmed through and overpowered the few remaining guards who had been left to protect the king, and once inside, they confiscated the weapons and disarmed the remainder of the Palace Guard. Eventually, Elisha and the attackers burst into Riphath's chamber and found him cowering against the wall behind one of his wives.

"What is the meaning of this outrage?" demanded the king.

Elisha looked at him dispassionately and declared, "Your despotic rule is over Riphath. Until we have decided what to do with you, you and your son will languish in your own dungeon and join your advisers." He turned to Jasher and asked, "Where is Tubal?"

"As was planned, we have him tied up at your brother's home."

"Go and fetch Tubal. He will, of course, want to share the same fate as his father."

After the castle defenses had been successfully breached, several men had entered the armory and began the confiscation of the weapons. They quickly began to disperse them to as many citizens who had been alerted by the noise in the street and had come to investigate. When all were armed, Elisha had posted them in key locations around the palace.

Jasher re-entered the castle a few minutes later with Tubal in tow. While he was led bound and disheveled down to the dungeon, as was to be expected, he was breathing out all manner of threats and curses.

"I will have you skewered for your cowardly attack on me and my father. You are all dead men," he screamed.

The cell was open and he was roughly pushed into the corner on top of his cringing father, also bound. In frustration and anger, Riphath viciously kicked out at Tubal and snarled, "You useless oaf! You allowed that silly tart of a girl to get the better of you and now look at where we are!"

Tubal turned on his father and screamed, "What do you mean, you old goat?"

Miriam had just entered the dungeon, and needing no encouragement called out, "He means Tubal that the marriage is off. I would sooner mate with a jackass than you." This caused general laughter from the attackers now clearly in control of events.

Tubal, upon hearing this cutting remark, rushed up to the cell door and began kicking it with futile results. Ignoring his threats, the insurgents posted a few guards to the dungeon then Jasher led the remainder upstairs to prepare for the return of the larger contingent of the Palace Guard who had departed earlier in hot pursuit toward the forest.

The group, led by Abdon, returned later that night and as they passed through the palace gate, they discovered it had been battered into pieces and lay unhinged and on the ground. Once inside the enclosure, an armed body of citizens appeared from all directions and boldly stood facing the soldiers. Now knowing the insurrection had been successful, Abdon turned to his men and commanded, "Throw down your weapons. King Riphath has been taken captive and his rule is now over. If you resist, you will die."

The soldiers looked at each other and one by one they discarded their weapons. Apparently, they felt no obligation to support a despotic king either, especially when it was now obvious he no longer ruled.

When the insurrection was over, Jasher sent for the Chief Adviser, Mizraim. After being released from the cell he shared with the others in the dungeon, the adviser now stood before him, uncertain as to what this would all mean. One thing he was sure of was that this disaster would reflect badly upon his career.

Jasher declared, "Mizraim, I have a message for Cain, which I will want you to deliver personally. You will leave in the morning and will travel as quickly as your horse will take you. I stress *quickly* because time is short." He then related to Mizraim all he had been told by the messenger, Joseph.

At first Mizraim was skeptical and commented, "Jasher, how do you expect me to explain such a story to Cain. He will not believe it."

"Inform him he no longer has a place here and he has been warned to stay out of the West. Also, if he wants a visible portent, tell him to look upwards in the night sky."

Mizraim left the next day with a small entourage for protection. The message to his master may have been cryptic, but he feared unless it was delivered, Cain would hold him personally responsible for this failure in Javan.

CHAPTER 11

THE LAND DIVISION

*Charles Hapgood is perhaps best remembered as the earliest propo-
nent of a shifting earth theory. His book, <u>The Earth's Shifting Crust</u>
(1958), includes a foreword by Albert Einstein in which Einstein
partially supported the theory. Later, in a follow-up book, <u>The Path
of the Pole</u> (1970), Hapgood, building on a much earlier model,
speculated that the ice mass at one or both poles over-accumulates
and destabilizes the Earth's rotational balance, causing slippage of
all or much of Earth's outer crust around the Earth's core, which
retains its axial orientation. Based on his own research, Hapgood
argued that each shift took approximately 5,000 years, followed
by 20,000- to 30,000-year periods with no polar movements. Also,
in his calculations, the area of movement never covered more than
40 degrees. Hapgood's examples of recent locations for the North
Pole include Hudson Bay, Iceland, Norway and the Yukon. Later,
Hapgood conceded Einstein's point that the weight of the polar ice
would be insufficient to bring about a polar shift. Instead, Hapgood
held that the forces that caused the shifts in the crust must be located
below the surface.*

*In 1974 Flavio Barbiero, an engineer and explorer, theorized
that a shifting of the Earth's axis took place 11,000 years ago and*

caused what was subsequently recorded in myth as the destruction of Atlantis and Mu. He also suggested that this shifting of the earth's crust was probably caused by the impact of a comet on the Earth's surface and that the current position of Atlantis has to be sought under the Antarctic ice sheet.

In all natural disasters through time, man needs to attach meaning to tragedy, no matter how radical and inexplicable the event is.

— Nathaniel Philbrick

For over two months Mizraim had been on the road from Javan and had only to-day reached his destination. Though he would have preferred to have taken a more leisurely route back to Nineveh where Cain now kept a permanent home, the constant travel of his trip overland by horse had caused him to arrive weary and sore. Nevertheless, knowing Cain would need to hear this news with sufficient time to act upon it, he had ridden hard to arrive as soon as possible. Moreover, before departing Javan, he had sent a message by courier pigeon relating the desperate circumstances now existing there, but he doubted that the message would be understood unless he was present to explain it.

In consequence, before he delivered his official report, he knew he should have his story well-rehearsed before his arrival. With reluctance, Mizraim reviewed the events of the past year since his appointment to the Kingdom of Javan. The political conditions there had steadily deteriorated since King Riphath and Tubal, his son, had been admitted into the Clan. Neither had desired nor demonstrated self-restraint and moderation in their rule which was the hallmark of all provinces initially placed under control of Cain's Brotherhood. This was, of course, counter-productive to the manner of the Society which preferred to direct the populace to surrender their rights and freedoms of choice gradually, but willingly. Riphath's callous behavior and oppressive government had given way to dissention which had resulted in revolution within the boundaries of Javan. Unless stopped, this cry for more freedom would no doubt spread throughout all the western territories. After attempting so many times to carefully insinuate the influence of the Clan into the fabric of those provinces, Cain would be displeased to know that so much ground had been lost.

Upon arrival, Mizraim had been given immediate audience with Cain and he was apprehensive to be the bearer of such disturbing news. He was admitted to a large open room with high ceilings wherein Cain was bent over and facing an open hearth, busily stirring the coals.

"Report," he ordered.

"Sire, I have news from Javan and I fear that it is disquieting."

Cain still had not turned around to face him. Mizraim was afraid that either his master had misheard him or he was displeased at the interruption and was now gathering a rebuke.

Cain continued to stir the coals. "I am listening, report," he intoned as if indifferent.

Trying to keep the tremor from his voice, Mizraim took a deep breath and began to relate the story. "When I left Javan, King Riphath and his son Tubal, along with his court and his personal guards had been attacked by a street mob. The rabble had succeeded in storming his palace and they had, in fact, tied up him, his whole family and his entire court then placed them all in the king's own dungeon."

"And just who are the ringleaders of this unruly group of oppressed citizens?"

This was the part of the news that Mizraim had feared the most, but there was no way to soften the blow, so he bluntly declared, "It was Jasher." Mizraim braced himself for the outburst to come.

Cain immediately halted his stirring, and as if it had grown immensely hot, he dropped the poker he had been using to stir the coals. It clanged noisily to the floor and the echo resounded and reverberated throughout the open room. He slowly turned around to face the adviser.

"You tell me this now, after the fact? Why was I kept ignorant of the deteriorating circumstances until after that idiot king and his doltish son were overthrown?"

"Sire, the uprising occurred so swiftly and was so well organized that neither I nor any of the other advisers were aware of the planned takeover until it was too late."

"What did that fool Riphath tell them about my plans," he demanded? "Or did he spill his miserable guts without any coaxing?"

"I am afraid that he and his son were all too eager to blame you on the state of affairs in their kingdom. Also, King Riphath made it clear that you had definite plans for sending more spies and advisers into the neighboring regions to the south."

Cain was seething, now angrier than he had been in many years. His efforts in Babylonia, Nineveh and the surrounding territories had steadily over time yielded wonderful results. They were all highly organized and he had subjugated their people quietly, but surely. Standing armies had been formed to prevent any resistance from the citizens should they find fault or grew dissatisfied with the leadership or Cain's agenda. General peace in the area had proved a means to allow Cain an opportunity to experiment with many new social projects. Several plans were now in place which would further limit their personal freedoms and he was anxious to see just how far he could push his dominion. He fully expected his power would grow exponentially as the freedoms of the subjugated citizenry slowly diminished, but it had to be done gradually, not in an oafish, ham-fisted manner as Riphath and that idiot son of his had attempted.

"Where were you and the other advisers when that fool began to lose control?" he shouted. "I sent you there to teach and advise him, not let him bully you about like some cheap street thug."

"Sire, your chief adviser made a concerted attempt to warn Riphath to use caution and be more patient with his citizens while a suitable army could be formed and dispatched to his kingdom. He further admonished Riphath to restrain his son from openly flaunting his power until after a more favorable government could be established to permit his excesses. For his honesty, he and another adviser in separate incidents were publicly whipped and hung up in the town square. Tubal was responsible."

"And what excuse did he cook up to rationalize his behavior?"

"Tubal excused his excesses, of course, that it was done for their disrespect and impertinence to his father, the king. The first adviser was publicly flogged while the other, your chief adviser to his court, Phut, was also whipped and later hung in the market square after he had expired."

"And where was that witless ruler when all this was taking place?"

"It was he who had put Tubal up to the public hanging, Sire."

"And you all stood by as useless as jackasses in a horse race?"

Mizraim's mouth had gone dry with fear as he reported, "King Riphath grew embolden by the public hanging and had placed us all under house arrest since the incident. While in the dungeon, no one was able to escape and get the information back to you until after the insurrection."

"So, how did this revolt take place? Did not that incompetent king have any guards with any balls to stand up to the rabble?"

"Jasher and his men abducted Tubal and led off the King's Guard while another group stormed the palace gate. By the time the guard returned from a futile chase around the kingdom to locate Tubal, the insurrection was over and Riphath and his son were securely trussed up in his own dungeon.

"Again, why am I being informed of these matters after the fact? I do have a messenger system in place, do I not?" He realized that he now had to take matters in hand personally.

"Sire, once the takeover was complete, I was the only one allowed to leave. By this time, Jasher and his men had destroyed my pannier of carrier pigeons save one, and I was only allowed to send one message, which I did, but it was brief."

"Yes, I received that message, though I dismissed it as being incoherent. It simply stated that I should not leave Babylonia."

"That was all I was permitted to send. Thus, I was left with a desperate ride across the country to reach you with another message Jasher claimed was for your ears only."

"Why should Jasher and the rest of the rabble allow you to leave? They have to know that I will bring my armies to destroy them!"

Mizraim hesitated at this question. He knew that how Cain would react to his real message would determine his fate, but again it was necessary.

"Jasher directed me to inform you to remain outside of the Western territories. If you venture into the region, you will die. Those were his exact words of warning, Sire."

Cain was livid and unable to speak for some moments. Finally, he blurted, "The impertinence of that weasel is beyond belief! He dares to dictate to me what I will or will not do in my own realm? If I find him, I will have his whole family diced up on my cutting table and afterwards fed to the dogs."

The idea of revenge was so great, that it actually calmed him and made him pliable, even affable now that he knew what he would do. "So, do tell, why is it that I should fear for my life?"

"Jasher says that the earth will part and our land mass will be divided into two large land masses separated by a great ocean."

Cain's brow furrowed as if he had misunderstood, then as he began to piece together the meaning, he roared laughter. When he was finally able to contain his mirth, he asked, "And exactly what are we supposed to do to avoid this great catastrophe?"

"Jasher said you are to remain in your own land and avoid crossing over into the West."

Cain had heard enough. He would have to set matters straight and put paid to this business and soon. "Well, that advice does not suit me," he replied irritably. "He and his whole family of traitors and assassins will pay for toppling my government in Javan, and you, Mizraim will accompany me and my army back to Javan; there I will have my revenge on that self-proclaimed prophet turned renegade."

Mizraim, to say the least, was not overjoyed with the news.

Jasher and Miriam had been on the move eastward for nearly three weeks. They crested a mountain and noticed an army had encamped below them and had found rest for the upcoming night. Miriam shakily murmured, "I am frightened. Is it Cain?"

"It is and we must be careful. My instructions were to warn him away and that is all."

"If he is as dangerous as you say, will that be enough?"

"I honestly don't know. But, I do know we are to avoid engaging him in a prolonged conversation or bait him in any way. His anger is ever-present and if his pride is hurt he would simply ignore my warning and invade Javan before the object hits the earth. He must be elsewhere when the division occurs."

"Jasher, I am still trying to understand the *why* of it all." Why not just allow him to blunder into Javan and be destroyed once and for all?"

He was quiet for a moment then replied with a measure of disgust, "It has to do with who he is and who I am. Our missions are inextricably linked somehow in a way that I do not yet comprehend, but one day I intend to understand it. For now, all I know is that he must live and it brings me no joy to warn him."

It was an hour later when they entered the encampment and were stopped by a roving patrol. Jasher and Miriam announced who they were and requested an audience with Cain, the leader of their army. A few minutes later, the couple was escorted into the tent of Cain and Jasher was once again confronted with the full force of the man. Cain smiled beguilingly, hoping to extract information from Jasher willingly before he resorted to more physical persuasion, specifically to his woman since it was not permitted to persuade Jasher vigorously enough to extract all he needed to know. Either way, he intended to have the truth before he pushed his army farther west.

"Jasher, I see my last suggestion to you has gone unheeded. What have you been doing in Javan?"

Jasher, not desiring to goad the man, responded quietly with little emotion, "I have provided the people a chance at a real government which will allow them to make choices for themselves."

"Jasher, what a naïve notion! The people have no idea what they want and never have and never will. It has always been up to me to help them make the hard decisions, which they would in any event want to avoid."

"Nevertheless, I felt it my duty to ensure they were given the chance that you would surely have denied them."

"As you would undoubtedly lose, it would give me great pleasure to debate with you over the issue. But, I digress", he replied reasonably. "So again I ask; what have you been doing in Javan?"

"The rule of Riphath the King and his son, Tubal, has been abrogated by the citizens of Javan who now demand a better government."

"What have you done with them?"

"They have been banished to wander the backroads of the nation they once ruled. When I last saw them, they had been stripped of their royal colors and were no longer in a mood for discussion."

"Jasher, you cannot hope to thwart my influence by this witless campaign to topple the government in Javan. My army will pound the people into submission and they will beg me for a government of my choosing."

"You will not get the chance, Cain."

Cain stared stonily at Jasher then abruptly shifted his gaze to Miriam. He offered her a charming smile and she warily made eye contact. "So, this young woman is now your wife?" He leered at her openly. "Does she know about you, Jasher?"

"She knows enough!"

"Miriam, as long as you are with him, your life will be in danger." Cain looked her over and his eyes appraised her beauty. "Because of his misguided belief in his mission, you will perish or will eventually fall into my hands. It is inevitable."

Miriam flinched as if slapped.

"Your discussion is with me, Cain!"

"Yes, it is." With typical arrogance, he turned his attention back to Jasher. "My adviser has informed me of your warning. I gave it only brief consideration because of its absurdity. But, do explain it to me," he added as if interested. He was provided a field chair and sat down, now surrounded by his guards.

Jasher had been rehearsing how he would explain the message he had received from Joseph, but until now, he was unaware of just how dangerous Cain was and how he might react once he had received the warning. In spite of the warning, he was also aware that he was very close to losing his usual calm exterior. Cain had certainly hit a nerve when he noticed his eyes moving over Miriam.

"Cain, as you know we now live on one large land mass. More than enough explorers have ventured out and have mapped our earth to confirm it. A celestial object, a comet, will hit the earth in a matter of days and will cause our land mass to break into two large areas separated by large oceans on the east and on the west. If you continue to bring your armies any closer, you will be caught up in the destruction as the earth is ripped asunder."

Cain's face was covered in obvious doubt. "I remain skeptical. How do you know this?" he persisted.

"I have two witnesses. Look up into the night sky. Even now you can see it approaching."

Cain arose from his seat and pushed by Jasher and Miriam on his way through the tent flap, closely followed by the couple. Once outside the tent, he looked up and observed a bright object that was brighter in the front and seemed to taper off toward the back as though it had a tail.

"That is it? It looks too small to do any real damage," he scoffed.

"Nevertheless, when it strikes the earth, it will cause the damage I have described."

"Sorry, I remain unconvinced. And your second witness?"

Cain was becoming bored with this line of conversation and was weary of dealing with this man. He wondered how his beloved Miriam would look back in Nineveh servicing his advisers in his personal brothel. He smiled in anticipation.

"A heavenly messenger visited me and delivered a message of this event."

Cain's frown clearly indicated that he was both exasperated and incredulous with this line of talk. "I don't believe you. Who is this heavenly messenger and why would he visit you?"

"He is someone who you would know and recognize, Cain. In life he was known as Seth, your brother, and he proclaimed that he would deliver me messages from time to time."

Cain seethed. *Even in death my brother plagues me,* he silently cursed. "And Seth told you all of this just to save my life?"

"No, the warning was issued to keep you and your army out of the West."

"What nonsense are you babbling on about? I will take my army wherever I so desire and do not need your leave or that of my dead brother if I decide to take the field of battle."

"You are to avoid being in Javan when the division takes place and if you make any further attempt in that direction, you will be destroyed before you can arrive there. That is my message and it is for you choose what you will do with it. We will leave you now to decide."

Jasher and Miriam turned to go, but Cain indicated to the guards to restrain them both. While he decided what he was to do with the pair, Cain decided to toy with them a few more minutes.

"Why should I allow you to leave? I will only have to deal with you later so why not finish it here and now?"

"You already know why, Cain."

His frustration had finally burst forth. "Yes, of course, we must all follow those ridiculous rules of engagement. My soldiers have already gone through your belongings and I know you have no records, but take care to write only what you know and not what you may suspect. Now, get out and leave me to my thoughts." He had had the last word, but it felt like bitter lemons to his taste; the recollection was so reminiscent of his dealings with Seth.

After the two had left the tent, Cain dismissed the guards and informed them he wanted no further disturbances for the remainder of the night. He sat silently in the lotus position and closed his eyes. After a few minutes, his breathing became shallow and he began to meditate his options.

Presently a form coalesced; an old friend had emerged and said, "Cain, you have no other options. You must turn back and avoid the destruction before you are destroyed. It will do our work no good if you are killed in such a fashion."

"He has no right to deny us that territory," Cain opened his eyes and responded heatedly, "We were so close!"

"It makes no difference. We will still win their hearts, but it will just take a little longer."

"What are you talking about?"

"Do you not recollect sending a spy over to the West after taking care of that problem with Rimush?"

"You mean the assassin, Sidon?"

His mentor replied confidently, "Of course. Was he not fully indoctrinated in our ways and fully endowed to practice the rites of our Society and spread its message?"

"Yes, but it may take many years before we can determine the success of his mission. Too much time will be wasted in the process."

"We still have time," was the confident reply.

When the two were safely out of the encampment Miriam began to replay the events and comments that were made. She had felt Cain's malevolent force and feared it, yet there was a weakness to his character she would have been unaware if she had never met the man.

At length she turned to Jasher and asked, "Has he always been that way? I mean, he has an obvious outward strength and glamour, but he lacks something fundamental."

Jasher had had time over the past few years to draw certain conclusions regarding Cain, and his personal observation on the two occasions he had met him seemed to confirm his impressions. "So far as I know and have been told, there is something essentially lacking in him. He has strength of will, but no strength of character. He has knowledge, but lacks wisdom. He will never achieve his end goal, not for lack of trying, but for lack of vision."

Above, the evening stars were ever-present, the moon clear giving off its celestial light. Also present was an unusually bright object of unknown size with irresistible force. The couple, now rested, arose and holding hands continued their trek onward back towards the east and away from home.

The comet struck the earth near the southern section of the great land mass where the population was as yet non-existent. Subsequently, its impact was sufficient enough to send a strong tremor up and down the length of a great tectonic plate buried under the surface of the earth which twisted its way from the south to the north. Suddenly, the earth began to shift and move and then wrenched itself into two land masses with the one on the east significantly larger. Finally, a third mass, though smaller than the other two began to form and it drifted farther south until it rested as a southern sub-continent. There was incredible devastation along the fault lines and much flooding that followed the event, but fortunately there still existed scarcely any people along the lines of separation, thus the population as a whole was only marginally impacted. In spite of significant break-offs and drifting of land in all three directions for centuries after the cataclysm, in time, great societies sprung up on both the major continents as well as the innumerable islands that were formed due to the damage.

Before Sidon had arrived in the Western Provinces, no operative from the Clan had ever had any degree of success establishing relations in that region. With his connections to Riphath's government in Javan, Cain finally had the wedge he had always desired and he fully intended to exploit it. Following his report of success to Cain and before his return to the West, Sidon was rewarded for his devotion and loyalty by receiving a full induction into Cain's inner circle and received the personal mark of the scar along his left cheek as a sign of his devotion to the Clan of the Scar. In addition to the Kingdom of Javan, it was expected that Sidon would continue to have similar success in the other provinces as time when on, and that would have indeed been the result had not the insurrection in Javan resulted in such disarray for the Clan in that region. As his assignment was to avoid breaking his cover as a businessman, Sidon was directed to remain out of the affair in Javan by Cain's personal advisers to Riphath's court. Even when it was evident that a debacle of the Society-led government was imminent, his orders were still not to break cover but to await Cain's personal involvement for follow-up instructions. Unfortunately, Cain never arrived. The government of Javan fell and shortly thereafter a new representative government was established in its place.

While Sidon was supervising a construction site a few months later in Magog, suddenly the land seemed to sway to and fro. He was thrown to the ground, and like everyone else, he was in a state of bewildered anticipation hanging on to whatever could be grasped. The swaying motion continued for some time, then finally subsided. One by one, and then collectively in groups, the frightened citizens began to wobble slowly and shakily to their feet. Many were violently sick and if they were found near falling debris they suffered the range of slightly bruised to those seriously injured. Fortunately, there were only a few mortalities incurred by the event, but all were highly curious as to the cause.

A few weeks later, bewildering news from the east arrived at Magog and it was met at first with skepticism then after several had ventured eastward, their worst fears had been confirmed. They were now isolated from those in the East by a great ocean of water. Sidon was now alone and the sole agent of the Clan on the western side of the ocean. But he was, after all, a fully endowed member of Cain's Brotherhood and fully vested to introduce new members into the oath and covenant process.

After dinner that evening, he had walked out on the porch of his home and was looking up at the night sky when it occurred to him it would be many years before he was able to make changes along the guidelines of the Clan of the Scar. But, being a meticulously patient man, he saw no need to be overly concerned or have any second thoughts as to his mission. The fact was, he had remained unassigned and his mission had not changed.

Sidon's wife walked out on the porch to join him. The evening was mild and she enjoyed a few minutes alone with her husband away from the usual night time struggle getting the children down for the evening.

"Husband, you are certainly quiet tonight, even more than usual. Is it the news from the East that concerns you? I know your kinsmen were all from Shinar and it will be a hard thing to never see them again or know of their fate."

"It is a small thing. My life is here with you and the children now and that is all that matters, I suppose."

"You are much stronger than I would be. Sidon, you are a good man and a fine father." With reluctance, she added, "And, it is time I put your children to bed." She touched his shoulder with affection then turned to go inside.

Sidon had decided he would continue with the original plan for as long as it required; the mission would always come first. With a last glance at the stars, he walked back inside his home and began helping his wife with the evening routines.

PART 2

CONFUSION OF TONGUES

*5 And the Lord came down to see the city and the tower,
which the children of men builded.
6 And the Lord said, Behold, the people is one, and they
have all one language; and this they begin to do: and now
nothing will be restrained from them, which they have
imagined to do.
7 Go to, let us go down, and there confound their language,
that they may not understand one another's speech.
8 So the Lord scattered them abroad from thence upon the
face of all the earth: and they left off to build the city.
9 Therefore is the name of it called Babel; because the
Lord did there confound the language of all the earth: and
from thence did the Lord scatter them abroad upon the face
of all the earth.*

—— Genesis 11: 5 - 9

And from the beginning there was one language and one speech. And the people gloried in their own wisdom and felt no restraint to do whatever they so desired.
And from the land of Shinar the people found materials to burn brick and slime for mortar and they began to build a city which they called Babel. And from the city they built a tower from which they supposed they could reach heaven. And the Lord God was angered and therefore confounded their language that they knew not the speech of their brothers nor could they complete the tower. And the Lord scattered them abroad throughout the earth. And Cain was wroth and his brotherhood was also scattered and he swore vengeance upon all men for his oath's sake.

—— The Abridgement, Chapter 16

History and experience tell us that moral progress comes not in comfortable and complacent times, but out of trial and confusion.

—— Gerald R. Ford

THE TRANSLATION, CONTINUED

Usually, after a long day of translation, Jasher was weary from the effort and the stress, not to mention the worry of whether his revelation to the world would be accepted. This evening, however, he was in an affable frame of mind and intended to teach rather than merely listen and make occasional comments to the evening discussions. Thus, after the translation session for the day had concluded and security matters were addressed, he joined Professors Bedford and Levinson for the nightly routine. The topic turned to the most significant events in history and Jasher was quick to point out that, for him, it was the confusion of languages.

Isaac found this opinion remarkable given that so little was known of the origin of language. "Jasher, as a linguist, I would like to agree with you, though many would consider the invention of the movable printing press or the harnessing of electricity to be more significantly impactful to human progress."

"Here, here," added, Bedford. "As you are all aware, as far as most scientists and linguists are concerned, the study of the evolution of the different languages has become a point of only token interest. This stems from there being no consensus on the ultimate origin or age of human language."

Levinson added, "One problem makes the topic difficult to study: the lack of direct evidence. Still the question lingers: why change the language when everyone is comfortable with what they have?"

Bedford pointed out, "Darwinism speaks of the natural evolution of the species and most suppose that language was simply part of the process and seldom is the *why* of it all a topic of much interest."

Jasher, though nodding in agreement to their conclusions, offered a differing perspective. "In my opinion, to understand the *why* is the most compelling point of all. Humans need other humans to fulfill a basic sociological need and so the instinct to congregate is strong and what better reason to congregate when you have a common language? A change was needed to disrupt the flow of history to that point."

Bedford declared, "So your point is that human progress had grown too stagnant and needed a change?"

"Precisely. When you think about it, we are at our best and most creative when we remove ourselves from the daily routine and mundane everyday occurrences. Otherwise, a stagnation of thought occurs. That was the social state of existence just prior to the confusion of tongues."

Levinson commented, "Jasher, since hardly anything can be proved as to what the original language was, it is difficult to follow the reasoning of the development of so many languages. For lack of a better description or theory, they simply happened and most scientists are unconcerned as to the *how* or *why*."

"But, suppose this need to congregate around a common language eventually led to the stifling of progress? All the great population centers following the Great Flood were established around a central hub with Babylonia at the center, and unless the population was dispersed, there would have been no other unique civilizations, and history as we know it would have been denied a chance to begin. Furthermore, if there had been no cultural and language diversity, many of the stimulating advancements in our social evolution would have been absent."

Isaac considered what Jasher had just explained and added, "I would have to concede that your point is compelling and this would explain the *why*, but I am curious about a related cause of these phenomena that our translation has uncovered that might explain the *how*. Would you care to comment on that?"

Jasher paused a moment to collect his thoughts. Finally, he nodded as if he were recalling a key detail from some long ago event. "The other reason is less sociological in nature and more spiritual, though at times there is so much overlap between the two that I can scarcely remove the one from the other. It is ironic, in my opinion, that the *why* and the *how* are so inseparably connected."

Bedford, not being a man who depended upon metaphysics to answer complex scientific questions, was doubtful. "Spiritual? How would that fit into the reasons?"

Jasher continued. "According to our canon, The Old Testament speaks of the intent of the early Babylonians to build a tower to heaven. In spite of being taught the truth along the lines of Noah's teachings, the people of the time were worshipping a myth or totem which would physically lead them to Heaven rather than preparing themselves for a spiritual journey. This digression from the truth was so greatly disturbing to the Creator that he caused a confusion of tongues to spontaneously descend upon the people. The result was, as is recorded in our biblical text, that this event so confounded the population that there was no more desire to continue the construction of the offensive structure. If we can concede that our Old Testament relates an accurate historical event, then this *how* it happened is as germane as any other theory that has ever been proposed. Who is to say differently since there are no other historical records to dispute it? And now that you have *The Abridgement* translated to this point, there are now two such historical witnesses."

Levinson added, "I see. Since we lack any other differing historical evidence, the *how* can be traced back to the time of the Tower in ancient Babylon. The Lord God was so displeased at the arrogance of man, he confused their language."

Jasher continued his discourse, "Correct, but was there an additional *why* involved? Other than to remove the hideous offense of the Tower or promote cultural diversity, what other reason may have the Creator had in mind to confuse the language? The answer is Cain."

Both professors were shaken by Jasher's claim. "How do you figure?" asked Isaac. "Was he at that time so influential?"

"By this time, through trial and error, he had developed a systematic process that had proved extremely successful in subverting the agency of man. This early civilization centered in Babylonia between the Tigris and Euphrates Rivers was the pattern by which all other peoples would be subjugated. As far as Cain was concerned, and it was his plan, all subsequent territories would eventually be annexed and fall under his control from one centralized kingdom. In short, if left unchecked, he would control the social and spiritual development of mankind by ensuring that it was regionalized in that area and all other provinces would branch out as spokes on a wheel with Cain and his kingdom at the hub. Try to understand that, for the Creator, there is no difference between the social and the spiritual."

Bedford saw where Jasher was going with this logic. He interjected, "So, you are saying that other the Creator caused languages to spring up spontaneously to cause a social disruption significant enough to temporarily check Cain's progress and allow social and spiritual growth."

Levinson added his final comment, "Moreover, if we follow this line of logic, this may have also been the reason for the continental division that we have only recently translated."

Jasher nodded in agreement. "Of course. The Creator had in mind the establishment of other civilizations throughout the world that would be separate and unique in order to provide diversity of thought and cultural progress. Clearly, Cain's model would have denied this potential. Placing him on the side-line, for at least a few centuries, was the only way to ensure it could happen."

CHAPTER 1

THE GREAT TOWER

One who is too insistent on his own views, finds few who
agree with him.

— *Lao Tzu, philosopher and poet of Ancient China*

Jebus was a tall, middle-aged man with tremendous strength. It was due to this physical attribute alone that he had risen to the level of responsibility he was now forced to endure. He and his family hailed from Elam, a land to the east that would one day be known as Iran. A few years earlier, his nation had been overrun by the Babylonians with the result that he and his family had been taken captives back to Babylon and were now used as slaves for the building up of the cities between the two great rivers. As was his custom, he awoke early and slowly padded out to the eating area of the hovel which he and his family now called home. He watched his wife in the corner listlessly going through her morning ritual of preparing a meager breakfast of dried fruit, nuts and bread. He glanced in the opposite corner and observed his three children were beginning to stir from their sleep.

Shaking his head to clear the memories of his once humble, but proud home in Elam, he walked toward the doorway and gazed upon the early morning sky to the east. He paused there in the threshold and waited as the sun began to peek above the horizon and throw its dim light on the beginning of the new work day. After a few minutes, his eyes followed the morning rays out over the awakening city and beheld the project which had consumed his reason for living during the last three years.

Weary from a long day cleaning office buildings of court officials, his wife, Anshan, had slept little the night before. Even though exhausted, she had arisen early to prepare breakfast for the children also working as day laborers for the city. They would need something to eat, inadequate though it might be. The state provided for the basic care of the housing and food for the slave quarters, but the daily caloric and fat intake was usually inadequate to support the needs for those involved with hard labor. Owing to his position, Jebus alone received more food which he obtained at the construction site and when the opportunity permitted, he was able to extract additional food for his family. The foreman was a good man and so he often looked the other way when he observed Jebus gazing longingly at the food left-overs from the day. Jebus knew he should avoid complaining; there were those who had less.

"Husband come, your breakfast is ready,"

Jebus turned from the doorway and cast a loving glance toward his wife, now turning into a drab before his eyes. She had been the most beautiful woman in their village just outside the city of Susa, and though she was still a young woman, the hard daily toil she was forced to endure had taken its toll on her once soft, inviting body; worse, it was sucking the life from her. Moreover, she was ill-treated, but to her credit she refused to complain.

Trying to appear outwardly assuring, Jebus replied with a note of encouragement in his voice. "Feed it to the children. I will have sufficient at the work site for my needs."

Anshan made no effort to dissuade him. She was too weary to argue. "Very well, Jebus." After a moment of reflection, and knowing his love for the project he supervised, she ventured a question, "How goes the construction?"

"Excellent," he answered with passion. "The men are quite committed and work with enthusiasm, so I am confident that soon we will have achieved our goal."

"And what is that, husband?" She occasionally asked him this question, not out of any real interest; little existed of their current lives that was noteworthy. It was out of some vague sense of duty to what was left of their former selves before slavery had robbed them of the value for honesty.

Jebus was alert to her question, and at an earlier time, his smile may have been contagious and encouraging, but the lackluster look of her eyes and face now told a different story. Actually, there was seldom ever a note of optimism that reached her anymore.

Jebus pressed forward with his oft repeated mantra, "We have been assured that we will reach the abode of our supreme God." He had convinced himself that reaching this exalted location was the only way that he and his family could somehow extricate themselves from their current abased condition and the Tower was the earthly means to achieve that goal.

"Of course, Jebus."

His wife envied her husband's distorted sense of reality. Since being captured and pressed into slave labor, he had never really accepted the undeniable circumstance of the daily bleak condition of servitude and she had lacked the will to disabuse him of the delusion. His acceptance of the blatant lie of the final destination of the Tower was simply another facet of the same denial of the essential truth: they were slaves and would always remain so. She could see how he would need to accept the lie regardless of the absurdity of the dream; it took his mind off the desperation of their plight. It gave him something to hope for in the midst of the absolute finality of their existence. Unaccountably, there seemed to be many in the slave quarter and the city that shared this delusion, and some even rivaled her husband's enthusiasm and passion.

Jebus decided to get an early start at the work site that day. He gave his wife and children an embrace and was off before the sun had fully risen. He wasn't really blind to what his wife was experiencing, but he simply needed to hope for more and so he set off down the hill for another day at the site more buoyant than the effort should have demanded. The Tower was magnificent, he marveled with an optimism borne out of desperate hope.

The mid-morning air lay hot and still on the workers who labored near the Great Tower. Though the land between the two mighty rivers of the Tigris and Euphrates was fertile, in the distance, and especially at this height, one could envision a very different outcome should the desert ever reclaim its hold. Babylon was a paradise surrounded by a stark landscape that was blasted by incessant heat and blowing sand.

King Su-abu was irritated and the discomfort was etched upon his tanned face. Though early yet, the heat was already oppressive and he could feel a drip of sweat running down his back between his shoulder blades. Glancing to his right, he took note of his visitor who seemed unaware of any displeasure. His face, by contrast to the king's, was serene and reflective.

Now reporting before the supreme ruler, the construction foreman, Sabtah, furtively appraised the progress of the Tower out of the corner of his eye and found it acceptable, but in his heart he knew the project was utter foolishness. Nevertheless, his job was neither to judge nor criticize, but to ensure that the Tower was built. As was the daily custom, each morning Sabtah arrived with a written and oral report to the king which outlined the measure of their progress for his approval. If warranted, he also informed King Su-abu of any issues. "Sire, as you can see by my report, assuming our building materials hold out and our supply of slave labor remains inexhaustible, we will continue to make good progress, and consequently, we should attain our goal."

As he perused the written report, King Su-abu wiped his brow with a linen cloth, and without looking up at his chief foreman, asked without much interest, "And what is that goal, Sabtah?"

Sabtah's eyes gazed out over the terrace and rested reluctantly on the Tower. This was the part of his report he always dreaded because he was always asked the same question and his answer always seemed to lack passion. He pulled his gaze back to the king and with more optimism than he thought possible replied, "It is to reach Heaven, Sire." As much as he tried different word inflections or stresses of speech, his answer always seemed to fall flat in his mind.

Every day King Su-abu watched his construction foreman for a moment listening for a sign of truth to his response, but he never found any. He shrugged inwardly and reflected that it mattered little so long as the construction went on and on and on, but he supposed the daily routine had to be followed.

The king considered a more optimistic dismissal, but was unable to think of one. "I look forward to your daily report, Sabtah. It is a great comfort in knowing we agree so much on this vital work to our kingdom. You are excused." Even this routine response was part of the daily ritual.

It was just prior to the noon-day break when Sabtah raised his hand to block the glare of the ever-present sun and gazed below as Jebus, the chief slave, if such a thing could be imagined, slowly walked up the spiral stairway to where Sabtah stood. Now wiping the sweat from his brow, by way of greeting, Sabtah offered a word of observation.

"Jebus, I see the men are hard at work and need hardly any persuasion today. Is there sufficient water?"

"The water is sufficient, but the work is back breaking and dangerous. Three men have already died this morning. That makes thirty-seven this week."

Sabtah was hardly irritated by the response. It was, after all, the truth. He looked up into the hard, blistering blue sky and muttered, "I fear there will be many more before we have reached our goal." He attempted to change the subject. "How is your family, Jebus?"

He was unsure why he had developed a familiarity with this strong, silent man. Perhaps he had needed the companionship and could turn to no one else or he needed a way to pass the time with each mind-numbing day. Or perchance it was simply that of all the men around him, Jebus seemed to be one of the few who still believed in the work and Sabtah fervently hoped that one day he would discover how that was possible.

"They are all fine, My Lord. They, too, look forward to our completion as our tower takes us closer to the gates of Heaven. Perhaps we shall all see this glorious vision soon. After all, how much farther can it be?"

Sabtah listened closely to his comment, hoping to hear a facetious tone of implied disbelief that might rival his own. Disappointed, he realized that Jebus actually believed what he had just said, and after a moment, he discovered he envied the man his faith.

Su-abu had a marvelous view of the Tower as it slowly inched its way upwards. He sighed in boredom. The Tower was unlike any other structure having been built in the city since the days of King Shu-turul, some one hundred years earlier. King Su-abu usually took interest in these buildings and looked forward to the completion of each. A visionary man, he saw his city full of buildings of unique styles, colors and materials, but due to the incredible demand for manpower and materials, The Tower was preventing the other projects from starting. With disgust he thought, *and, as any intelligent man could see, it was never going to be completed. How could it? A stairway to Heaven, indeed!*

He turned to his companion seated next to him and dryly commented, "Good news, Cain. My foreman informs me we should reach Heaven by the end of the week."

"It was inevitable, wasn't it?"

It was too hot to laugh, so the two leaders settled for a cool drink that an awaiting servant brought and carefully lay on a nearby table between them. Wishing to avoid sounding too impertinent, Su-abu needed to be reassured of the logic behind the mind-numbing inanity of this project.

"Cain, my city architects grow restive for the need to build more housing, gardens and parks. This tower project has put them on the sideline wondering when they can get back to building with a purpose. Please re-explain the need for this hideous thing."

Cain sipped his cool wine and patiently explained, "Common people need a singular goal or purpose around which they can hang hopes and dreams for something more glorious than their daily, pointless lives. I have provided them with such an ambition. The whole of Babylonia awaits the completion of our glorious Tower. Of course, no intelligent man would embrace such nonsense."

The king nodded in agreement, but ventured a tentative question, "How much longer will we need to endure this project?"

Cain thought a moment and asked, "How long have we been working on the Tower?"

"Three years, five months and a few days", replied the king. And to think it had been grinding along that long! It was mind-numbing.

"That seems about right."

Cain was in an affable mood and so explained, "This falls under the category of urban pacification. Until I have a newer experiment in mind to pursue, we will proceed a few more months with this one."

"You feel the people need to be pacified?"

"The people need a distraction in the form of hope, even if that hope is groundless. As the means to attain a heavenly reward, The Tower serves that purpose."

"So, Babylon is to be the portal for their heavenly abode?"

"Don't be patronizing. The reality is that The Tower is a symbol, nothing more."

Cain slowly closed his eyes, trying to envision his realm in the centuries to come. A smile was etched across his face as he casually explained, "In time, I see my realm a series of numerous provinces and city/states branching outward and interconnected with Babylon as the hub. Each population center will be separated by farming communities which will support our city centers with the food we will need to support a huge population."

"There will be those in the region who may resist this expansion."

"Those who persist in their refusal to accept my model of planning and building our cities will regrettably end up as slaves to service the building projects for still more cities."

"Can your plan absorb so many more slaves? They still have to be fed and housed. Besides, after a point, I don't see where new slaves can be so easily acquired."

"You may have noticed that the recent slaves have been requisitioned from our eastern and northern provinces. Unfortunately, the rulers there were too slow to accept and support our grand scheme of growth and now they have paid for this stubborn behavior with the loss of all independent status. Their citizens now serve me and my agenda. Not to worry, there are always more slaves to be found."

Su-abu slowly nodded his acceptance, but was deep in thought. *What can I do, after all? Cain is the Master Mahan, and if he wanted, he could have me thrown from my terrace and have a new king installed before I hit the ground. He would scarcely break a sweat at the effort and would lose absolutely no sleep over my absence.*

As if to continue the conversation, the king ventured another inquiry. "Do you perhaps have a follow up project in mind?"

"Actually, it is curious you would ask that. As a matter of fact, I was thinking of a venture involving a large sporting arena. It would be built in the shape of an elliptical amphitheater, tall enough and large enough to hold fifty to sixty thousand spectators."

Su-abu was intrigued. "And what would be its purpose?"

"In addition to sporting events, it would serve to provide a wide variety of social spectacles. Try to imagine mock battles, animal hunts and eventually a public stage for executing political prisoners. The rabble enjoys spectacles and gambling and this project could provide it on a grand scale."

Su-abu, now wanting something, anything, that would serve to interest Cain long enough to move him on to the next project, was quick to encourage this discussion. "And this entertainment value, as you say, what social need do you envision that it would serve?"

"It would provide common citizens something on which each could hang their pitiful hopes and aspirations. Even heroes could be provided to act as surrogates for their own drab lives."

"And what short term benefits do you see from such spectacles?"

"Urban pacification will be the key to managing a large population, especially when many of the people will be of the working class and slave laborers. Again, when your life is a pointless parade of wretched, tragic events, it is imperative to have an actual distraction to dream about, even if it's just temporary."

"So, these construction projects when completed will be designed to give the common people something gratifying to experience rather than think about the desperate condition of their lives?"

"Yes, these projects will pacify the masses and take their minds off any loss of freedoms, that in any event, they would lack the wisdom to exercise properly anyway."

Su-abu had to admit it was a good idea. "I would be happy to assign my architects to that labor when it suits you."

"Thank you and please reassure them that the Tower project will be completed in a few months." With a smile he raised his wine cup and toasting the Tower added cynically, "Regrettably, the stairway to Heaven will go nowhere except up."

CHAPTER 2

ON THE ROAD TO OBAL

No man was ever wise by chance.

— Seneca

Mahonri was a Shemite from the land of Mesha and had been born the third son of Jobab, a kinsman of Peleg. If not for an encounter on the road that day to Obal, his life would have remained simple, worry free and considerably less interesting.

As he began his journey that morning, he noted the day had dawned clear and vibrant which showed Mount Sephar in its panoramic splendor; most concluded this was always a good portent for the day ahead. For much of the year, he reflected, the mountain was shrouded in fog this early in the morning and it was usually difficult to discern the pinnacle so distinctly.

He was late for a family reunion, thus as he slowly ascended the steep incline of a foothill, he tried to pick up his pace. He reflected that his step was somewhat slower than it once had been; old age, he had discovered, was the most unexpected thing to have happened to him. In spite of the distance, though, the yearly gathering of his family was now a priority and a personal presumption. As he was invariably celebrated as the family patriarch, the reunion for him and others was always an anticipated event and a reminder to him of the advantage of close family ties when one grew older. Though his wife had recently died and all of his children were now married and had children of their own, he was as content as could be expected.

At a bend in the road, he became aware of a man walking steadily towards him. He had seen many people on the road the past few days; indeed, he had even passed the time by walking with a few fellow travelers. It was, after all, a public road and heavily used, but for some unaccountable reason, a tremor of expectancy coursed through his body. As the man drew steadily closer, he was left unprepared for the singular scene and discussion that unfolded.

The first thing Mahonri noticed about the man was that he was exceptionally clean for someone who had been walking the foot paths of Mesha. Unsurprisingly, the road tends to be dusty in dry weather and when it rains, as it often did during this season of the year, the public ways can become choked with mud. Since it had showered the previous day, there was still water standing in places. No doubt the average traveler, if on the road for any length of time, would have swept up dust, attracted mud and animal droppings onto his robe or sandals. Yet, the travelling clothes of the approaching man were almost pristine in appearance. Then, it began to occur to him that the stranger intended to stop directly in front of him and so was unsurprised, though curious, when the man did just that.

Now offering a smile of greeting, the stranger said, "You would be Mahonri, I believe. I am Joseph and am happy to finally meet you." He made a quick bow from the waist to indicate a respectful greeting.

Mahonri was struck by the meticulous cut of the man's hair, which was beginning to silver along the sides. Most men simply allowed their hair to grow at will and cutting it only when necessary, but his seemed to be naturally short and well-trimmed. While his piercing blues eyes captivated your attention, he seemed to be examining you, as if the man was marveling at a new and undiscovered species of flower. Mahonri's overall evaluation was that the stranger was a handsome, affable man that exuded confidence as well as mystery. And puzzling still, the man had called him by name, though they had never met before that day.

"May I walk with you down the road, Mahonri?"

"Of course and please forgive me for staring, but you seem most unusual." He added hesitantly, "I feel I should know you, but your greeting seemed to imply otherwise. Have we met?"

The man only smiled, but made no comment then joined Mahonri on his trek and both resumed the walk towards Obal. The air was especially clean and crisp that morning. Birds could be seen and heard going about their natural and instinctive rounds. While the butterflies looped about complementing the color and glory of the honeysuckle and primroses on which they settled, a jay scolded and warned all other birds that he was master of his domain. Bees could be heard slightly humming as they darted here and there, selecting one flower then the next as they, too, completed the full measure of their existence.

Joseph did not speak for a few minutes. He seemed, instead, to be enjoying the beauty and solace of the day. Finally, he commented, "Morning was always my favorite time of the day and it appears that the Creator has favored us with another beautiful day of possibilities."

His smile was contagious and as he looked over to Mahonri, he, too, was unable to withhold his feelings of gratitude. He nodded his head and offered a smile to confirm his own recognition of the beauty of a new day. But, curiosity had gotten the better of him and so a moment later he asked again, "How is it you know me, though we have just now met?"

As the two men proceeded down the road, Joseph quietly explained, "In a manner of speaking, we have met, but not in this life. Mahonri, I am Joseph, an angelic messenger, and have been sent to deliver you a message and extend a calling." Joseph paused to insure Mahonri had clearly heard him.

To say that Mahonri was surprised would have been an understatement. He was so astonished he gazed over at his road companion and could only nod his head that he had heard, but making sense of it all was still beyond his current state of mind.

"You are to proceed to the home of your eldest daughter and her family. As you know, they are in the midst of a family reunion, and while at the affair, you will declare to them that they and all of your family and friends are to be led to a land of promise far from your home on the other side of a vast ocean."

Mahonri frowned slightly, as if trying to comprehend his part in all this. "As you have pointed out, I am attending the reunion, but I fail to understand my role in this declaration I am to make."

"You are to be their prophet and patriarch for as long as you shall live and if you are true and faithful to this calling, you will experience much joy and personal fulfillment during your life. All of you are to meet in Babylon in the land of Babylonia, or as is commonly known as Shinar at the home of your kinsman, Jared, who lives in that city. An event of especial significance is about to occur in that land, so your journey to Babylon must be accomplished within two months."

"I understand the meaning of patriarch as it relates to family matters, but the only prophets I have ever heard of lived before the Flood, well before my time, and as you have noticed, I am quite old."

"Nevertheless, you have been called to be one of the first since those days." He glanced over to Mahonri to ensure that his walking companion fully understood of what he had just been informed. When he was thus satisfied, he then began to explain that many of his kinsmen at the gathering would be prepared to receive his message. Each in his own way would either accept or reject his message, but their agency to choose would be inviolate; none must feel coerced. With a smile, Joseph politely asked, "Did you understand my last explanation?"

"Yes", he replied. Then, he attempted to expand his response into some type of understandable context, but his mind was busily leaping from one question to the next, so he only managed to stammer out a question, "But, why me?"

To his surprise, Joseph began to smile, the mirth evident around his eyes. "Do not take offense, my friend. Your response was the most unpretentious I have ever heard. I find your spirit to be calming and your touch with people to be guileless. These qualities will serve you well as you serve others."

After a moment, Mahonri, still in mild shock, could only utter, "What more do I need to understand about this calling, as you put it?"

Joseph paused for a moment then proceeded to repeat his message and added a few more details regarding their destinations, Mahonri's and that of his family and close friends. Then added, "You will declare unto your kinsmen all that you have seen and all I have told you. You will testify from whom you received this message and your special mission as their leader then you will instruct your family and those who wish to follow them to meet you in Babylon. You, however, will journey to Babylon alone by a different route."

Now curious, he asked, "But, why alone."

"Your journey to Babylon will differ from their route because you are to spend time in the desert to better acquaint yourself with the specifics of your mission."

"Why the desert?"

"There is a cleansing solitude there that can be experienced in no other way."

"I see, at least I think I understand. And you say I am to go alone?"

"As this singular experience will be meaningful for only you, no one else is to accompany you, but you will not be alone. There will be others like myself who will meet with you to discuss your role and answer any questions you may have. At length, you will meet up with your family at the home of your kinsman, Jared. Do you understand the message I have just delivered to you?"

"I have a thousand questions, but I have a feeling that I am about to learn more than I had ever dreamed possible, but again, why have *I* specifically been selected? Why am *I* so special?"

"I cannot reveal the answer to you because that answer is not for me to understand, but for you only."

"Joseph, this may be more than I am prepared to comprehend."

"Do not despair that this all may be too much for you. The ways of the Creator are neither mysterious nor curious. He is omniscient and if we are patient he will reveal the truth of all things to us when we are ready to accept them and are fully prepared to observe them. My message has been delivered and I must now leave you."

"Joseph, will I see you again?"

"Over that I have no control. I am merely the messenger." With that Joseph turned and walked toward the forest, but before entering he turned and gave Mahonri a slight, encouraging wave. As he passed into the forest, a light slowly opened up in front of him and he melted away out of sight.

By early afternoon Mahonri had arrived at the gate of his eldest daughter, Bathsheba, and her husband Timon. There he found the reunion was already underway, and as was the custom, he was welcomed as the honored guest and family patriarch. While he made the rounds to be welcomed by family members who had come from many parts of the land of Mesha, he was happy and content to bask in the attention of his dear ones.

As the light began to fade and twilight had begun at the end of another day, he felt the time was right to make the announcement to his sons and daughters. Actually, he was quite worried that they would think him a madman or, even worse, an old man on the verge of senility. It was, after all, an enormous thing he was about to ask of them whether they would heed his message and leave for Babylon or remain. Regardless of their choice, nevertheless, on the morrow he must leave and discover what awaited him in the desert.

As the festivities began to wind down, Bathsheba became acutely aware that her father had become more subdued, almost detached from the gathering. She slowly walked over to him as he stood next to the wall under the shadow of an ancient oak. She took him by the hand and asked with concern, "Father, you are saddened. What bothers you?"

Mahonri would never openly admit it, but of all his children, he found Bathsheba the most caring and observant; she was a woman so much like her mother. Reluctantly he confided, "It is not sadness that weighs me down, dearest, but what I must reveal that has disquieted me."

"What do you mean, Father? Are you feeling ill?" she asked, now truly concerned.

"No, but I have been asked to make an announcement and I fear that what I have to say will make me sound foolish and that all of you will think me mad."

She placed her hands firmly on her hips, arched her eyes slightly in an endearing way she had and chided, "You should give us more credit." Then she gently coaxed, "Please explain what has happened."

Mahonri sighed and shook his head with the enormity of the impact of his message, but it had to be delivered. "Bathsheba, I have been visited by a heavenly messenger who has informed me that I and my family must leave the land of Mesha and journey to a land far away across a vast ocean of water. The land was described to me as a land of promise, superior to all other lands upon the earth. We are to leave as soon as possible and all of you are to meet in my brother's home in Babylon within two months. I am to travel another way, but will arrive there soon after." He was ready to hear his daughter laugh derisively, shake her head in doubt or openly scoff, but instead a curious thing happened.

Bathsheba crossed her arms across her bosom and slightly lowered her head. She grew pensive as though considering his words, then after giving his message serious thought, she looked up and replied, "I believe you. Now you must make this announcement to the rest of the family." Smiling, she took him firmly by the arm and led him over to the assembled crowd. Turning to him, she commented with enthusiasm, "This will be an exciting journey! What a wonderful idea!"

She ushered him before his family and now smiling declared, "All of you, please listen! Father has exciting news that he wants to share with us!"

All began to congregate. Looking around, he found a wall to climb then sat down as his family and friends drew near. Within the congregated crowd of family were more than three hundred people, but his voice was strong and clear and carried his message to the awaiting throng. When completed, there were none who appeared skeptical or contentious. The visitor Joseph had counseled Mahonri to allow each to make his own decision to either heed his call for the journey or to remain in Obal. After some silence a discussion began as to the simple logistics of such a trek to Babylon, but in the end all agreed that, with careful preparation, it could be done.

Mahonri glanced over to his daughter and nodded his head that he was pleased at the response. Bathsheba nodded back and began to circulate and give counsel. She listened carefully to the concerns, but added her own observations to clarify what her father had said. In the end, all of the family and a few close friends were in general agreement that they could begin a journey within a few weeks. Mahonri was humbled at the manner in which his family had placed so much faith and trust in him and he was determined that he would never allow a situation in which their trust in him would falter.

At the end of a long evening, he and Bathsheba walked along the short pathway back to the home of her family. She was quiet for a few minutes then confided, "It will be hard to leave what we have, but if the Creator has decreed that we will have a special land for our inheritance then it will be well worth the sacrifice."

"I, too, agree Bathsheba, but there are other reasons for leaving also. We live in a bounteous land here in the Kingdom of Mesha, but our land is situated at a cross-road and as time goes on others will decide to take what we have worked so hard to preserve as our own and they will do it at the point of a sword."

"And this land to where we journey, you say it will be a land of promise?"

"I have been assured that where we journey, the land has been preserved for us as an inheritance and will always be ours for all future generations throughout time. This is our Creator's promise and so we will place our faith in Him and follow His will."

She nodded her head in agreement, but one other matter did bother her and she commented, "Father, you say you are to travel alone to Babylon. It would be safer to journey with us, so please reconsider your decision."

"I understand your concerns, but the Creator has determined that I must better prepare for my mission as your leader and patriarchal head and this must be done in the wilderness. There is no need to worry as I will be in His safekeeping."

After a moment Bathsheba responded, "Father, I will concede you will be in His care, but I will still continue to worry. Just make sure you return to us."

Jared was an astute businessman and over time had acquired the means for a comfortable living for himself and his family. He had left his home in Obal in Mesha many years earlier with a tapestry dealer who owned a magnificent warehouse of the finest rugs and tapestries in the land of Babylonia. He finally settled into the home of this fine man who had everything except the one thing he needed more than anything else, a son. He had assured Jared, and anyone else who would listen, that by far his daughters were the most exquisite of all his possessions.

He had been blessed with twelve beautiful daughters and his wife had been too old to bear him anymore children. So, he took Jared into his home and loved him like the son he never had. In time, he died and left Jared with his home, his business and all he possessed, including the youngest of his daughters, Martha. Jared always joked that Martha was his true compensation for all those years of hard work to keep up with the old man. She had provided him with a lifetime of companionship and fourteen children. Friends and associates always found him affable and quick with a smile or an amusing anecdote.

His life was blissful but relatively uneventful. Of late, however, he sensed something was amiss, a change was coming. He had few regrets save one: he missed his kinsmen who lived far away in his homeland of Mesha. Though he had made the occasional business trip that passed through his country and had become reacquainted with his family, it was still hardly the same thing. Being a wealthy man and knowing of the difficulties that farmers had to endure, he had wanted to assist them in financial and material matters. Moreover, he had wanted his own children to grow up knowing their cousins. He always left them with the promise of his return and extended them an open invitation to visit him whenever they could, but the distance was always so great, and being mostly farmers, they were unable to leave tended fields and livestock for any length of time. Of late he had pondered over this lack of casual interaction and had the strongest impression that it would soon be remedied.

A week later, Jared was in his warehouse taking inventory with his foreman when his youngest daughter, Esther, rushed in breathless as though she had been running. His first thought was that an emergency had occurred at home. After a moment, she caught her breath then exclaimed, "Father, you must return home immediately. Our kinsmen from Mesha have just arrived!"

Jared was overjoyed at the news. He reflected that he had just been think-ing of them the past few days and now it would appear that his premonition was justified. "That is wonderful news! Which ones have arrived, Esther?"

His daughter, in her haste to inform her father, did not expect his ques-tion. With eyes wide open in bewilderment she exclaimed, "All of them, I think!"

CHAPTER 3

IN THE DESERT

Solitude is the place of purification.

— *Martin Buber, Austrian-born Jewish philosopher*

In the desert, you can remember your name, 'cause there ain't no one for to give you no pain.

— *America, "Horse with No Name"*

In the Hebrew Bible, the Urim and Thummim are closely associated with the hoshen (High Priest's breastplate), divination in general, and cleromancy, in particular (Deuteronomy 33:8). Most scholars suspect that the phrase refers to specific objects involved in the divination process.

Thummim is widely considered to be derived from the consonantal root meaning innocent, while Urim has traditionally been taken to derive from a root meaning lights; in consequence, Urim and Thummim has traditionally been translated as lights and perfections or, by taking the phrase allegorically, as meaning revelation and truth, or doctrine and truth and it appears in this form in the Vulgate, in the writing of St. Jerome, and in the Hexapla.

Although at face value the words are plural, the context suggests they are singular words which are pluralized to enhance their apparent majesty. The singular forms, Ur and Tumm, have been connected by some early scholars with the Babylonian terms urtu and tamitu, meaning oracle and command respectively.

The description of the clothing of the Hebrew High Priest in the Book of Exodus portrays the Urim and Thummim as being placed into the sacred breastplate and worn by the high priest over the Ephod as a vest (Leviticus 8:8). Where the biblical text elsewhere describes an Ephod being used for divination, scholars presume that it is referring to the use of the Urim and the Thummim in conjunction with the Ephod, as this seems to be intimately connected with it. Similarly, where non-prophets are portrayed as asking for guidance, and the advice isn't described as given by visions, scholars think that the Urim and Thummim were the medium implied. In all but two cases (1 Samuel 28:6 and 2 Samuel 5:23), the question is one which is effectively answered by a simple yes or no.

The sun was setting on another blistering day in the wilderness east of the land of Ur. Knowing that the desert temperature would soon plummet by forty degrees after sunset, Mahonri was quick to find a suitable location to make his night as comfortable as possible. In the distance, perhaps only a mile, he could see the remains of an ancient village partly covered in sand, but close enough to a small oasis to make it worth the extra walk. A half hour later, he carefully stepped through the broken walls and made his way over to the overhanging shadows of several palms blowing listlessly in the desert winds that were now turning cooler with each passing minute. A small, underground water spring was still evident near the middle palm so he decided to make camp nearby. Still unable to see any sign of recent domestic animals, he wondered absently if this oasis was still used as a stopping point on some trade route. From his pack he pulled out a water skin, a type of *bota* bag, and began to replenish his water supply from the nearby spring. The water was sweet, and retrieving a few dried dates and flat bread, he began the evening meal.

The first visitor appeared as he was bedding down for the evening. At first Mahonri was unaware of anyone then a light caught his attention; this was followed closely by a slight disturbance a few paces behind the palm. A voice calmly announced, "I am Ethan; please do not be alarmed. As Joseph has alerted you to expect me, I have come to offer instruction in regards to your calling."

Though the sudden appearance of his visitor should have evoked some sense of dismay, nonetheless Mahonri remained calm, yet eager to hear his message. He decided that it must have been the serene tone of the voice that had quelled any feeling of foreboding.

"Thank you" was all he managed to say by way of greeting then added, "I am happy that you have been sent; it is obvious I am far from ready to perform this role into which I have been placed. Where should we begin?"

Ethan began by explaining the most eternal of all truths, that man's agency has always been inviolate and had always existed, even from the beginning. He sat down opposite Mahronri and asked, "Mahonri, how much do you know or even suspect of our pre-mortal existence with regard to what some refer to as The Great War in Heaven?"

"Ethan, I know pitifully little of our pre-mortal life, as you refer to it, other than to presume that since we are here, we were once somewhere else before here and when we die, we will undoubtedly be in a different existence, no longer here."

"Your answer is simple, yet correct," responded the messenger with nodding agreement. He continued to explain, "When the plan that would govern our agency was presented for discussion, all of us, then as spirts, were permitted to either accept it or reject it. Most of us accepted it because we understood its necessity for our intellectual and emotional growth once we were born into mortality. Nevertheless, one very powerful and persuasive spirit by the name of Lucifer concocted a counter-plan aimed at ensuring himself of all control, power and glory over the destiny of mankind. This he would do by demanding absolute obedience for each person in mortality to follow his will and his plan every step of the way. In essence, one had merely to attain a body without any real test of personal growth then would be elevated unconditionally to immortality at death. Once this process was complete and all of us were safely immortalized, then Lucifer intended that he be recognized and receive all the glory for his infallible plan."

Mahonri sat pensively trying to grasp the intent and scope of such a plan. "This war, as you put it, must have had a favorable outcome for us because, for the most part, it would seem that we have freedom of choice in spite of whatever forms of oppression exist. I take it that Lucifer's plan was rejected?"

Ethan nodded his agreement and continued, "Our immortality is not only qualified by our personal growth through our freedom of choice, but is the defining characteristic of its reality. Since Lucifer's plan would have denied us this growth, it was rejected as being unworkable given the Creator's objectives for our emotional and spiritual maturity."

"I have heard of Lucifer, of course, but he has always been depicted as a monster, someone used to frighten little children and the uninformed."

"Actually, his reality is much more subtle and therefore more dangerous. In his anger and frustration at not having his plan accepted Lucifer openly refused to support the plan of agency as presented by the Creator. Fully one-third of our spiritual brothers and sisters swore allegiance to him and refused to acknowledge the agency of Mankind. This alliance cost them dearly for they were all denied the privilege to obtain a mortal body, so in their anger they swore to take this battle to those who did receive a body."

"By those who received a body, you refer to everyone on earth?"

"Everyone who has ever lived or will live in mortality is their target. In consequence to his rebellion and of his denial to support the plan and his avowal to cause havoc and chaos, Lucifer and those who followed him were cast out of the presence of the Creator."

"And these other spirits who have followed Lucifer, as you have mentioned, where do they exist?"

"While the rest of us with mortal bodies follow the Creator's plan of agency and personal growth, these others now roam the earth as spirts of wrath determined to undermine our progress whenever they are permitted the opportunity."

And before leaving him that night, the messenger had taught Mahonri regarding the indispensable nature of agency as well as many other related matters which Mahonri would be instructed to teach his people.

The next night, just as he was finishing the evening meal, another messenger arrived. He announced he was Jacob, and his voice, also reassuring, provided Mahonri with much needed practical understanding of his mission. "Over the next few thousand years, your role will be the first of many such callings which will be extended to men through the lineage of Noah. Their roles will be identical as well as the preparation involved." He then went on to explain the sacred nature of one called as prophet, seer and revelator. Additionally, Mahonri was shown a breastplate wherein was fitted the *Urim and Thummim* and was then instructed in the use of those special devices which would be used to reveal the word of God to his people. The messenger finished up his instruction with a word of warning. "You must use your calling and acquired wisdom as a means to serve others and to carry out the Will of our Creator. There will be many who will scoff at the singular nature of your calling and role, but remember that it is not to men that you must answer for your actions, only to your God."

Mahonri had been in the desert for the metaphorical period of time of forty days and forty nights. The amount of time may have been figurative, but to Mahonri it seemed to be just long enough for him to make sense of the mission. Joseph had promised him that he would be visited by several messengers who would explain his calling and he was true to his word. After the first few visits, the knowledge he gained was cumulative in nature, though some instruction was repeated, but much he gained by simply listening and pondering, and of course, asking many questions. He was assured that this would be a similar pattern of preparation for holy men through the ages, and always it would be the desert to which they would turn for solace and wisdom.

The light was beginning to fade on another day when Mahonri crested a hill. In the distance he saw two things, an oasis and farther away a huge tower which was being built high above the other buildings of a city. Nodding his head, he realized he had finally arrived and being weary from his walk and nearly out of water, he decided to stay over at the nearby oasis for the night and press on to the city of Babylon in the morning. As he got closer to the oasis, the dimming of the light had already set in, and though it was now difficult to see, he was sure that he could just discern a man reclining comfortably under a nearby palm.

He reached the resting stop just as the last of the sun's rays had all but faded over the stark, bleached landscape. A desert wind, which would have been searing hours before, now blew cooler as the last of the heat of the day began to dissipate into the dry, evening air. A man was indeed resting under the nearby palm and appeared to have his eyes closed in silent meditation. When Mahonri drew closer, the man's eyes gradually opened and a smile appeared. His greeting was familiar as he announced, "Good evening, Mahonri. I was hoping we could meet again."

Mahonri was happy that it was Joseph. Of all the messengers who had come and gone, he alone had stood out as the most compelling and charismatic of the group. "Joseph, it is wonderful to see you as well. Can you stay through the night and keep me company?"

"It would give me great pleasure, Mahonri. By now you and I would have much in common, you see, but, alas, the time is still not appointed for an extended visit, even between friends."

"Then I can hope one day that will change."

"I, too, look forward to it."

Mahonri offered Joseph water and dates, but he declined to eat any. It occurred to Mahonri that none of the other messengers had eaten when they had visited either. So being curious, he felt inclined to ask.

"I have observed that you messengers neither eat nor drink. Is that not permitted?"

"It is simply unrequired. We are of a different order and in time we will be allowed to partake out of simple courtesy even as you are still required to partake out of necessity as a result of your mortal condition."

"I see." But, of course, he scarcely understood and so he sighed and with some resignation he admitted, "There is still much for me to learn."

"There is always more to learn; it never ends." Joseph's smile was enigmatic. "Now that you have spent time in the desert, would you have it any other way?"

Mahonri thought on that for a moment and replied, "I thought so once, but now I am changed, somehow different, more open to possibilities. If a man can be compared to a receptacle of water, I suppose there is now more room than I had before. I feel almost bottomless. Is that not peculiar?"

"It is strange, but true. That is why all prophets and seers will be tested in the desert. They enter full of impurities and self-doubts and exit considerably lighter and perceptive. It is time well spent."

The two were quiet for a few minutes, enjoying the still of the evening and the brightening of the night sky with it all its limitless glory. Mahonri waited for Joseph to break the silence, but he seemed content just to gaze up at the majesty of the heavenly display.

Eventually, Mahonri stirred then asked, "My mission really begins tomorrow, am I right?"

Joseph gazed out over the immense night, which was now alight with stars from distant galaxies. He reflected it would be easy to sit and contemplate their importance and expound upon all he had learned while in life and since then about stellar order and movements, but that would have to be for another time and place.

Reluctantly, he turned back to the here and now and declared, "In truth, our missions began before we were even born. It is only when we contemplate the infinite expanse of the universe that we can grasp the full significance of who we are and what we can become." He was about to rush into a more arresting discussion of such matters of time and space when he realized that the moment was still yet to arrive for a serious discussion of such lofty concepts.

He sighed as though loathe of the mention and substance of more mundane matters. He was now more serious, less introspective. "You will meet a man tomorrow on your way to Babylon. His name is Jasher and he is not a messenger, but a man with a special mission, though unlike yours."

"Has Jasher been prepared even as I here in the desert?"

"Your mission requires the solitude of the desert to give it proper perspective. Jasher has been prepared in other ways. Once you meet him, you are to declare to him your mission and he will accompany you to the home of your kinsman, Jared. There you will all wait until an extraordinary event has occurred. The event is personal and will affect every man, woman and child on this part of our world."

"An earthquake? Surely not another Flood."

"No, something quite different. While in the desert, you were taught of the man Cain who still walks the earth and about his abominable mission to destroy the agency of Man as an agent to Lucifer, our common enemy. Cain is on the verge of understanding a great truth which will greatly increase his influence and accelerate the fulfillment of his mission. This success must be checked until a time in the future when he can best be fought on more even ground."

"Checked? Sorry, I don't understand."

"The Creator has decreed that our language must be diffused into several different languages to create so much confusion and social havoc that people will flee from Babylonia in every direction to find those with whom they can communicate. Cain will have no choice but to restart his process of subjugation as he, too, will have to seek out only those with whom he can speak. It will take him many years to rebuild his empire."

"And this will only block his plan temporarily?"

Now, speaking as only one with personal knowledge of his subject, Joseph replied, "Cain is cunning beyond your understanding and he has had a long lifetime to perfect his plan. No, for now we can only slow him down and make him rethink his strategy. He will have to regroup and this will give us enough time to offer a stiffer resistance later."

"I take it then that Cain's work among us on the earth carries as much impact for those who have already died as well as those yet to be born?"

Joseph was impressed by the observation and answered straightway, "Of course. What is done here on the earth will always have repercussions on eternal matters which is why the Creator must keep a close eye on all events to ensure His desired outcome without a compromise to agency. Agency is inviolate for everyone, even for Cain." He added wryly, "I told you that your time in the desert would be well spent."

Mahonri was less certain and responded, "We shall see." It then occurred to him that he and his kinsmen might also be affected by the confusion and chaos.

Joseph seemed to read his mind. "You, Jasher and all your family and friends will be untouched by the confusion of our language. Jasher is well travelled and has been instructed to direct all of you to a special location where you will build vessels and embark on a voyage to a distant, but blessed land. There you will obtain an inheritance for your future generations and be free to live for many years without interference from Cain's Society. That is my message. Do you understand?"

"Yes, I fully understand." Though he should have guessed, he nonetheless asked, "When will we next meet?"

"Who can say? I am merely the messenger."

CHAPTER 4

BABYLON THE GREAT

Babylon was a significant city in ancient Mesopotamia located in the fertile plain between the Tigris and Euphrates Rivers. The city was actually built upon the Euphrates and divided in equal parts along its left and right banks, with steep embankments to contain the river's seasonal floods. Babylon was originally a small Semitic Akkadian city dating from the period of the Akkadian Empire circa 2300 BCE.

The town may have attained independence as part of a small city state with the rise of the First Amorite Babylonian Dynasty in 1894 BCE. Claiming to be the successor of the more ancient Sumero-Akkadian city of Eridu, Babylon eclipsed Nippur as the "holy city" of Mesopotamia around the time Amorite King Hammurabi created the first short lived Babylonian Empire in the 18th century BCE. From there, Babylon grew and South Mesopotamia came to be known as Babylonia.

It has been estimated that Babylon was the largest city in the world from 1770 to 1670 BCE, and again between 612 and 320 BCE. It was perhaps the first city to reach a population above 200,000. The estimates for the maximum extent of its area range from 890 to 900 hectares (2,200 acres or 3.5 square miles).

In the Bible, the name appears as interpreted in the Hebrew Scriptures' Book of Genesis to mean "confusion," from the verb bilbél, "to confuse." The modern English verb, to "babble," or to speak meaningless words, is popularly thought to derive from this name, but there is no direct connection.

The morning was already warm and by mid-afternoon the heat would be severe enough to bake bread on the pavements. Jasher abhorred the heat and especially the extreme temperatures of this climate. Over the past month, he had observed the land between and around the two rivers was fertile enough, but everything else in any direction was fit only for the scorpions. Sweat from the heat had begun to form on his upper lip so he took a moment to wipe it away with the sleeve of his robe. He had been waiting about an hour just outside the gates of the city when he spied a lone man apart from the moving throng of travelers and on foot approaching from the south.

As the man drew closer, Jasher reflected on the curious turn of events that had led him to the south gate of the city that morning. A vivid dream had come to him in the night which had left him puzzled, but because of its nature, he felt compelled to act on those impressions. In the dream, he was in front of one of the city gates to Babylon and he seemed to be waiting for someone then in the distance he could see a man on foot walking towards the city toward the southern entrance. Although he was certain that he had never met him, he nonetheless was left with the impression that he was someone who would need his help. Moreover, some important event was about to take place that would involve him, and the stranger, whose name was Mahonri, was the link.

In the dream a familiar, intimate voice whispered to Jasher: "Go out to the city gate to the south and accompany Mahonri to his kinsman, Jared, a dealer in rugs and tapestries." He was then provided with an impression of the kinsman's residence in Babylon. Additionally, the voice instructed, "You will listen to his story and accept all he informs you. When the appointed time is right, you will lead him and his kinsmen north and west to a port on the Western Sea where a boat can be built suitable for a long voyage. Once you have completed this assignment, you are to return and resume your primary mission." He then received a detailed view of the port, of which he was acquainted, then the dream had ended and he had awoken.

He lay there in his bed contemplating the singular nature of this deviation to his usual labors. He had never before received such a dream with such stunning clarity and the manner in which the message was delivered was as if someone had penetrated or slipped seamlessly into his consciousness and was in control of all he saw and heard; he had been merely a spectator.

Miriam had arisen earlier than usual that morning and had gone out to buy food for breakfast. Jasher appeared to be deep in sleep, which for him was unusual, so she had allowed him to sleep longer than was normal. She was now preparing the morning meal when she heard him stirring in the next room.

The message was still fresh on his mind so he hurriedly dressed and prepared himself for the task ahead. From the bedroom she heard him say, "Miriam, something urgent has come up and we must talk."

She was unable to recollect any such discussion of the night before, so she was momentarily perplexed when she heard his comment. She replied with curiosity, "Husband, what has changed since last night?"

"Judging from the dream I just had, it would seem our day has become more eventful." He entered the small living area where his wife had just placed the breakfast on a small table.

"Come again?" she replied with some disbelief. "Since when do you have dreams that tell you what you will do with your day?"

He sat down opposite her and began eating. "Since last night," he commented between bites. He changed the subject knowing it would irritate her. "Miriam, your cooking has improved considerably since first we met."

"Never mind that," she quipped. "What's all this about a dream?"

Jasher grinned at her response. Her cooking was always excellent and she knew it. "Apparently, I am to exit the city towards the south and meet a man by the name of Mahonri, who will have just crossed the desert. From there I am to accompany him to the home of his kinsman living here in Babylon."

"That seems like a simple task. Any guide in the city could provide that much information."

"Very true, but now this is where it really becomes curious: I am to escort him out of Babylon, along with a large group of people and guide them to a port along the western coast of the Great Sea. From there he and the whole group are to journey by boat across the Great Ocean."

"Am I going also?" she smiled mischievously.

"Of course, are we not a team?"

"Only always". It was a private joke of affection between them and they both enjoyed saying it. After a moment, she asked curiously, "Where is this port?"

"It is known as Tyre, a Phoenician port."

"And their destination?" she asked.

"I suppose it is to be the western land that was separated from our land mass over a hundred years ago."

She laid down her food and asked expectantly, "You mean our old homeland?"

"I do, but do not get too excited. We cannot take the voyage with them because my mission remains here until I hear otherwise." Jasher could tell she was disappointed, but as usual, she hid it well.

With a slight shrug she replied, "Then we must ensure that they deliver our love to them." She went back to her breakfast.

"Of course. Now, I must be off. Can you have everything packed and ready to go by the time I return?"

She rolled her eyes and replied, "That depends upon how much time you have given me for the task."

"I have the impression that our visitor from the desert has just ended his journey, so we shall be back here in a few hours. Does that sound soon enough?"

"It will do, I suppose," she responded with a pretended sigh of disapproval. They kissed and Jasher made his way to the door and waved as he departed.

Over one hundred years had passed since the parting of the earth's land mass, though there had been reports, more like rumors, that there had been several other divisions, thus creating new lands and islands now separated by water.

As Jasher was concerned that the mountain depository in the east would now be inaccessible, he had decided that, once his current mission here in Babylon was completed, he and Miriam must make the long journey eastward. This was not only to satisfy his curiosity as well as his own peace of mind, but moreover he needed to deposit his recent accounts and collect additional plates for future needs.

He had been in Babylon for over a month now making notes of all he had seen and heard. As he passed the Tower he wondered if this dream had something to do with this ugly, atrocious tribute to Cain's latest attempt to disrespect the Creator. He had interviewed several noteworthy citizens, including a few architects and a construction foreman, and they all unanimously agreed that its purpose was pure nonsense. What he was surprised to hear from the common people and slave laborers was their near universal acclaim that its completion would end their suffering and servitude. This news was disturbing because it meant that Cain's current experiment might be having the desired effect he had sought and he would no doubt consider it for future reference and use.

As the man walking from the desert drew up to face him, Jasher declared, "I am Jasher and you must be Mahonri. Welcome to Babylon. I have been instructed to escort you to the residence of your kinsman, Jared."

As Mahonri had been expecting him, he was hardly surprised and rather gratified that he was getting help with his mission from someone less angelic. His sojourn in the desert was over and it was now time to enter the next phase of his mission. The assistance had been priceless, of course, but his visitors were unable to remain with him for very long, and now that his education in the wilderness was completed, he could no longer expect their help, though he hoped that Joseph might return from time to time to help.

"Thank you, Jasher, and I appreciate the escort. I have never been outside my country of Mesha so the size and noise of Babylon would be overwhelming, particularly after spending so much time lately in the wilderness."

"That, too, was my first impression of Babylon since relocating back to the area. In just a short time it has grown from little more than a camel stop near an oasis to a bustling city of thousands."

While the two men had walked through the great, sprawling city of over two hundred thousand citizens, Jasher had pointed out several notable attractions of architectural beauty. As they drew closer to the Tower, however, Jasher halted his discourse and grew quiet, more introspective.

They had scarcely arrived near the construction site when Mahonri remarked, "Even in Mesha we have heard talk of the building of this great tower. From what I have been informed it is being built as a stairway to Heaven." Ruefully, he shook his head in disgust. "That must be a very sore affront to the Creator."

"It is typical of Cain's dark humor to have such a monstrosity built. Since he, above all others, realizes the absurdity of the project, I am sure he will break it off soon enough and move on to the next grand experiment that amuses him."

"So, it is Cain who is behind all this."

"It is. He has been responsible for every powerful kingdom of any size since the Flood and his hand is behind the blasphemy you see being built."

Jasher spied a small inn ahead and suggested they get a cool drink and discuss upcoming plans. After the two travelers had been served, Jasher looked at Mahonri, leaned forward discreetly then quietly declared, "I was told you had a message for me and that I should believe all you relate."

Mahonri was impressed by Jasher's careful, cautious manner. He concluded that in spite of his obvious youth he gave the impression of a man of maturity and highly intelligent in the ways of the world. Given the proper time and opportunity, he suspected they would become good friends. He began by telling his story, "A few months ago I was approached by a messenger who extended me a special mission to lead my kinsmen to a country far away from our homeland. He indicated the journey would be long and not without its dangers, but once we arrived we would be blessed to receive a land of promise for our inheritance. He further pointed out that we were to travel to a location along the seashore, and once there, build barges for a long voyage. After leaving Babylon, you were to lead us to the port from which we would depart."

"I sense there is something more afoot here than simple guidance to a distant port. What more did you learn from this visitor?"

Mahonri tried to formulate a comment which would describe the other, more compelling reason for their departure and Jasher's assistance. Unable to find one he simply declared, "Our language is about to be confounded by the Creator. Afterwards, there will be many new languages and the result will be temporary social havoc and chaos, enough such that the citizenry of Babylonia will disperse to all the corners of the world to discover those who have a similar language."

Jasher was stunned and yet highly impressed with the Creator's simple, but effective manner of dealing with Cain's success. "I must admit that I continue to be humbled by the wisdom and omniscience of our God. Cain's influence of deceit and subjugation would be quickly addressed with a simple act of language confusion. What a masterful stroke!" His enthusiasm subsided somewhat when he seemed to realize what this would also mean. "When this confounding occurs, how will you and I and your kinsmen communicate?"

"The visitor declared that we, that is, you, I, and my kinsmen are to be spared the confusion and that we will retain our understanding and be able to communicate with one another."

"There is sure to be absolute chaos in the streets when this confounding occurs."

"Agreed. As that event unfolds, we are to leave in the midst of the resulting social disorder and journey to the northwest." He added thoughtfully, "As this condition will occur soon, we should hurry and make preparations for our journey before the confounding begins."

Jasher immediately thought of his wife, Miriam, and suggested, "If it would not be too inconvenient, we will take a short detour and collect my wife and our belongings. In any event, she will need to be present with us before this confusion is unleashed."

The two men finished the drinks and set off quickly in the direction of Jasher's residence. When they arrived, they found Miriam waiting and ready with travel belongings and gear. A few minutes later, the three made their way through Babylon to the home of Jared, the tapestry dealer and brother to Mahonri.

Jared, being a prosperous and well-known tradesman, owned the largest estate that abutted the marketplace in that sector of the city and given he had nearly three hundred house guests; it was probably a good thing. Since many of the visitors could be reasonably well provisioned in his vast nearby warehouse, he was not bothered at the number. If this was a problem, then it was a happy one because he felt fulfilled that he could do so much for his family and friends. Nevertheless, he was puzzled by the unique circumstances of the visit, and in spite of the initial surprise, Jared and his wife had sat happily for two days listening to relatives discuss their journey from Mesha. Unfortunately, his guests were unable to provide much information other than they were to begin a journey to a choice land and that the stay in Babylon would be only temporary. Jared had an opportunity to speak with Bathsheba to get her personal impression of the whereabouts of her father, Mahonri. As his brother, he too, was concerned and noting her worry, he asked her to explain.

"He left a few days following our last reunion, and though he appeared anxious to get started, I could tell that he had reservations."

"If Mahonri felt strongly about his decision, then I am sure he had his reasons, but, like you, I wished he had accompanied the main body of the family during the journey."

"I know he has promised that the Creator would preserve him, but it is still an arduous trek for a man his age and so many things can go wrong." She rubbed her arms distractedly in anxious agitation and worry.

"My brother may be old but he has always been wise beyond his years. He will not take unnecessary chances with his life. We must trust the Creator in this matter. I am sure he will be with us soon."

Within the day, his brother, the patriarch Mahonri, arrived with a stranger and his wife. Soon, the full story would emerge and all questions would be answered, but Jared worried that the answers could bring more change to his world than he had ever imagined. His warehouse was the logical place to have a large group reunion and meal so he and the men rearranged the building to accommodate the event. The women had quite naturally gone out in search for food at the local markets that morning, and on their return, they and the servants had begun preparations for an early dinner. Mahonri had confided that he had wanted to wait until after the evening meal had concluded to disclose the full reasons for this unannounced visit. Now the attentive host, and no longer having to idly speculate the reason for his family's arrival and worry for his brother wandering in the wilderness, Jared was eager to please and be of service.

It was to be a festive occasion and Mahonri reflected it would probably be the last for many months to come. Even though his family from Mesha had been informed of their journey, he had yet to reveal the full story and was reluctant to do so because of the inherent dangers involved. They were to remain in Babylon until the confounding and that meant they would be faced with the pure chaos of a frightened citizenry.

The feast was served early as was customary for reunions and would continue well into the night. Every delicacy selected of vegetables, fruits and meats that could be prepared, was well represented at the table. Only the finest wines were brought forward to refresh and enhance the palate. Later in the evening, musicians entertained and made festive the gathering of Jared's family and all members cheerily danced and sang until exhaustion finally drove them to finish up the gladsome affair.

After the large dinner table was cleared by the servants and the musicians had been dismissed for the evening, Mahonri arose and thanked his brother Jared for his gracious hospitality. It was seldom that the two brothers had been together and it was a momentous and cheerful occasion for them both. After acknowledging his brother's kindness, Mahonri felt it was now time to reveal additional information regarding his mission. As all gathered together, there was a moment of hushed silence which lent solemnity to the occasion.

"My family and my new friends, Jasher and Miriam, my brother Jared has made it possible for us all to be together this evening. He has neither probed nor speculated aloud as to what to make of so many of us descending upon his home in such a fashion. It is time for him and all of you to know every-thing." Mahonri went on to narrate what most of them already knew regard-ing his mission. He then mentioned his sojourn in the desert and subsequent visits by several messengers who instructed him on the tasks and his respon-sibilities that lay ahead. In addition, he confessed, "What has impressed me the most is your resolve and disposition to follow an old man to a new land and a new inheritance for your children. Your faith and trust makes it pos-sible for me to lead you and now deliver to you a special message of an event that is imminent, and could descend upon us even as I speak."

Looking out over the somber, assembled group he declared boldly, "I have been informed that, within a day, a confounding of our language will descend upon the land of Babylonia and all neighboring kingdoms. Other languages are to appear spontaneously to confuse and confound the citizenry to incite them to disperse to all corners of the world in search of those who speak a similar tongue."

Immediately after hearing the announcement, the hush turned into sur-prised chatter and loud speculation. Knowing all too well how this revelation would upset and cause anxiety to the assembled group, Mahonri raised his hands to solicit quiet. Bathsheba noticed that few were watching her father and with a loud voice shouted, "Please, allow Father to finish. I am sure that all our concerns will be addressed." The gathered throng slowly began to quieten and finally all were once again looking toward Mahronri attentively.

"All of us within this room will be spared the effects of this singular event, which is to say we will retain our original language. Understandably, there will be social chaos in the street and we must depart on our journey through the midst of this confusion. Though we could depart sooner, a cara-van of our size will attract attention and we should avoid being followed and possibly detained. If we stay too long, we will be caught up in the subsequent social upheaval and eventually we will be sought after regarding the reasons why we were unaffected when so many were. It is hoped that anyone attempt-ing to pursue us or prevent us from leaving will be caught up in the same turmoil happening everywhere. Thus, our timing for our departure is critical. It is very likely that our gathering has already been observed and reported.

Thus, we must prepare to leave on the morrow and be ready at a moment's notice. Are there any questions?"

There were a few. Most wanted to know why this event was occurring and how they intended to slip out unnoticed by the populace. There was only one man within the group who had been informed sufficiently regarding the specifics of their departure that could be called upon to make relevant comments. In spite of the short time in which they had become acquainted, Mahonri and Jared had developed a close trust in Jasher and both loved Miriam as though she were a daughter.

Mahonri turned to Jasher and asked, "My friend, you are qualified to answer these questions far better than I. Please step forward and brief my family and friends on your impression of this whole affair."

Jasher began by telling them his history and his part in the journey onward. "By now, you are all aware of the great mission which your leader Mahonri has received. He is to be your patriarch and seer for the remainder of his life, moreover, he is to teach and guide you in the ways of the Creator. My role will be much simpler and considerably more temporary. Because I am familiar with the terrain and locations to which you will travel as far as the Great Sea, I have been asked to be a part of your journey and guide you to that point of departure from which you will sail to a land of promise."

"Equally important, I am to serve as a witness and record the consequences of unusual events which influence the course and progress of civilization and I can assure that this upcoming event more than qualifies for my close observations. Mahonri has declared that a great confounding of our language is imminent and I can assure you this action is neither a random occurrence nor a capricious decision on the part of our God."

A hand went up in the middle of the crowd. It was Bathsheba who asked, "I suppose what we all are wondering is *why*, rather than *how* this event is to occur. The Great Flood occurred, or so we have been taught, because our ancestors had grown wicked. God, in his anger, swore to cleanse the earth with water and destroy them. But, why is this confounding happening?"

Jasher replied, "The Creator has seen the debilitating influence of Lucifer upon the earth and his agent Cain who carries out his plan of corruption. You need only gaze westward from here and observe the latest tribute to Cain's handiwork, that disgraceful Tower he is building, but the Tower is only part of the abomination. There is much more Cain is planning once he tires of this experiment. The Creator intends to disperse the people of this land and all surrounding provinces of Babylonia to all corners of the earth in an attempt to slow down the effects of Cain's depraved influence."

This time it was Timon, Bathsheba's husband with a question. "Jasher, why are we not to be affected by the confusion?" Not that any of us would want to be part of that chaos, but why were we chosen for this journey?"

"Though clearly there may be more long-term reasons for the dispersion of languages, my experience with such matters tells me that this one point stands out as being the most immediate reason for your journey: you will be part of this universal dispersal to escape becoming caught up in Cain's next experiments. But, unlike all others, you will leave with your language intact, possibly to permit you to communicate with those who you will encounter once your journey is complete."

Jared remarked, "Jasher, I think I speak for all of us when I say that we truly appreciate your guidance in this matter. Since you and Miriam have arrived, we have all felt a calming affect which has softened much of our initial anxieties. What can you tell us about this land we are to inherit?"

Jasher now confided, "Most of you already know that I am of the lineage of Japheth, which makes us all distant cousins, as each of you is of the lineage of Shem. I and my wife Miriam were born in the land of Javan, part of the territory affected by the Great Division which took place several years ago and our homeland no longer exists on this land mass in which we now stand. That is the land to which you are going. For obvious reasons, we have had no word of our family since that event occurred and for reasons known only to the Creator, Mahonri and all of you have been called to settle that land on the other side of the Great Ocean that now separates the two land masses. In time you will meet those of my lineage who survived the Great Division and will all share a common inheritance."

Mahonri commented, "While in the desert, I was instructed to keep a detailed record of our travels, but unfortunately, aside from parchment which

I might be able to acquire along our journey, I have none. I was told, Jasher, that you would make such recording material available."

Jasher smiled and slowly nodded his head as if remembering a detail almost overlooked. "Mahonri will carry several records with him of our journey as well as those which I have held back for a special purpose. Before now I was unsure why I was guarding them nearby, but it appears that they were meant to join you on your sojourn to this new land. I will be making my notes of our progress westward up to your point of departure and record any events that occur along the way."

Mahonri stepped forward and thanked Jasher for his perceptive views of events to come. "My family, we must prepare, for on the morrow the confusion of our language will occur."

During the entire discussion, no one had been aware of a lone man by the name of Calah standing in the shadows making a mental note of all that was said. After the reunion was ended, he slipped quietly back into the shadows of the night.

CHAPTER 5

THE CONFOUNDING

The origin of language in the human species has been the topic of scholarly discussions for several centuries. In spite of this, there is no consensus on the ultimate origin or age of human language. One problem makes the topic difficult to study: the lack of direct evidence. Consequently, scholars wishing to study the origins of language must draw inferences from other types of evidence such as the fossil record, archaeological evidence, contemporary language diversity, studies of language acquisition, and comparisons between human language and systems of communication existing among other animals particularly other primates. Many argue that the origins of language probably relate closely to the origins of modern human behavior, but there is little agreement about the implications and directionality of this connection.

This shortage of empirical evidence has led many scholars to regard the entire topic as unsuitable for serious study. In 1866, the Linguistic Society of Paris banned any existing or future debates on the subject, a prohibition which remained influential across much of the western world until late in the twentieth century. Today, there are numerous hypotheses about how, why, when, and where language might have emerged. Despite this, there is scarcely more agreement today than almost two hundred years ago, when Charles Darwin's theory of evolution by natural selection provoked a rash of armchair speculations on the topic. Since the early 1990s, however, a growing number of professional linguists, archaeologists, psychologists, anthropologists and others have attempted to address with new methods what some consider "the hardest problem in science."

Over the past few months, as the building of the Tower began to wind down along with his interest of the structure, Cain knew sooner or later Jasher would make an uninvited appearance and begin to make notes of the progress or lack thereof. So, he decided it was time to monitor the flow in and out of his city in the hopes of intercepting his intrusive nephew and confiscate any recordings he attempted to make.

A month earlier, Calah had been at his usual post overlooking the northern entrance to the city of Babylon. He had gazed out over the entering and exiting flow of humanity and the arrival of a certain man had been detected accompanied by his beautiful, young wife. Of all the spies in Cain's stable of informers, he alone had been selected for this duty because only he had ever seen Jasher and could identify him on sight. It was especially hot that day on the entrance tower, and while Calah was wiping the sweat out of his eyes, he nearly missed seeing him, but it was Jasher. Even from the wall high above the gate he could detect the handsome profile and aristocratic bearing, but as his wife removed her headscarf, a type of *hijab*, what surely caught his eye was Miriam's reddish-blond hair. Their appearance immediately set them apart from the usual throng of travelers that permeated those hurrying into and away from the city.

Calah descended the steps and began following them at a discreet distance. His job was to follow and observe their living quarters, frequented destinations and make note of any habitual routines. Since he had been led to believe that Jasher would eventually begin to record, Calah had noticed for almost a month that he had done scarcely more than wander about the city with his wife, occasionally discussing the Tower with one person after the next as though making mental notes. He was never observed writing as that would have alerted others to his activity, but being a careful man, while both Jasher and Miriam were attending to other matters, Calah had entered their residence and made note of all possessions. As Jasher would not have been in Babylon unless he had a good reason, he suspected that his target was waiting for something or someone. Nevertheless, Calah had not noticed much of importance, so he had reported back to Cain who told him to continue his surveillance.

Calah reflected that the daily routine had become predictable, even repetitious, and hardly worth the effort, but he reasoned that since he had yet to be dismissed from the detail, he should continue the usual rounds of watching Jasher and his wife shop and busy themselves with trivial pursuits of personal interest. However, a few days ago just after sunrise, Jasher abruptly changed his routine and his new movements confirmed to Calah what he had begun to suspect, that he was waiting for someone. When he became aware that Jasher was exiting the city through the southern gate, he immediately climbed the wall stairs to get a better view of his destination. In the distance, a lone man could be seen walking towards the city isolated from the other groups on the common highway. After a few minutes, Jasher and the man seemed to come together on the road and greet the other. A short conversation occurred and the traveler followed Jasher back into the city. Calah surveilled them as they sat down at a local inn and had drinks then seemed to discuss matters of mutual interest. Later, and now in more of a hurry, they passed by the residence where Jasher and Miriam were staying, whereupon the three emerged and walked to the home of a successful tradesman, Jared, a rug and tapestry dealer. He observed also that a large number of relatives were staying at the businessman's home.

Yesterday, Calah made an additional discovery by following the women into the market center for food. Though he overheard a few women discussing a journey they were to make soon, none of the information alone had much meaning, but putting Jasher with Jared and his family made his movements more significant. Still, he felt there was more to this arrangement than he was actually seeing, accordingly he waited until later in the evening and overheard the strange declarations made by Mahonri and Jasher, as well as their plans for an early departure on the morrow. Calah had finally made the connection, but the facts made no sense, at least not in a way that he could interpret. Clearly, though, it seemed that they would all be leaving the next day so he decided to report to Cain that night.

It was late, but Cain would hold him accountable if he allowed Jasher to slip away without knowing where he had gone. Besides, Jasher had publicly announced he was in possession of records and that was more than enough reason to involve Cain at this point. He was aware of the lateness of the hour, but he had noted that regardless of the time of day, Cain always seemed to be alert and ever attentive to detail, and knowing Cain's predilection toward being informed of any new developments, he intended to withhold nothing of Jasher's whereabouts and activities.

Many years ago, Cain had discovered that he had required little sleep each night, consequently, as the years went by, he actually grew to resent the intrusion to his plans that sleep demanded. It was late night, and as he sat pondering his most recent social experiment, the Tower, and its subsequent effect on the masses, he was on the verge of deciding the details of his next project, the coliseum, when his reverie was broken by a discreet tap at his door. Glancing out to his terrace he became aware that it was well into the night, but as usual, he was wide awake and so he responded to the knock.

His servant was outside waiting deferentially. "My Lord, your observer, Calah, has returned and wishes to make his report."

Cain, though unperturbed, realized the hour was late and so thought about postponing the meeting until the next morning and so announced, "It is late and I wish to be alone."

"I am sorry, Sire, but Calah insists on seeing you tonight. It is urgent: those were his exact words. Shall I send him away?"

Cain knew that Calah was the only trained observer he had who knew Jasher on sight and if he said it was urgent, perhaps now would be a good time to see him. "Very well, send him in."

Now seated behind a large desk, Cain awaited Calah while the servant presented him before his master. Cain's only comment was: "Report"

Omitting nothing, Calah presented all details of his observations regarding Jasher's latest movements in and around the city then he began to report what was declared by Jasher and Mahonri during their discussion at the reunion. As he began to relate Jasher's mention and use of the records, he could see that Cain appeared to have reacted visibly by Jasher's criticism to his activities regarding the building of the Tower.

Finally, his anger erupted. "More lies! The man has no shame to speculate on my activities in my own realm!" He fumed. "I will not be second-guessed by that meddling, self-righteous fool! What else was said?"

Calah was momentarily thrown off balance by the sudden outburst of anger, but, knowing Cain's reputation, it was hardly unexpected. In spite of the momentary distraction of his tirade, he pushed on with the briefing. He continued, "My Lord, Jasher publicly declared that the records he had been guarding nearby here in Babylon would be accompanying the group on the journey westward."

"Well, now we are getting somewhere. The man thought he could parade about openly in my kingdom collecting ridiculous lies for some future journal that would implicate me of wrong-doing." With mounting rage, he shouted, "The wretch is no better than my spineless brother!"

"Sire, where would they be going with those records?"

Cain thought for a moment. Then it occurred to him there was a connection between Jasher, the records and that particular group of pilgrims. He concluded, "Jasher is not only acting as guide for these people to the other continent separated by the Great Ocean, but he intends to send them on their way with his own treacherous version of events as he has interpreted them here." He nodded with grim satisfaction and declared, "Well, if that is his intention, then he is sadly mistaken. No one of his group is leaving Babylon before I have taken possession of those lying records he has been hoarding." Cain then began pacing about the room as if contemplating how to proceed without alerting Jasher and losing the records.

Cain was about to dismiss Calah when his spy added, "Sire, I am unsure how to interpret the remainder of the declarations of Mahonri and Jasher. There was talk of a most unusual event that is to occur tomorrow. It was announced that a confusion of our language will descend upon us all, confounding our understanding of the language. Furthermore, after tomorrow there will be not just one language, but many languages. What did they mean, Lord?"

Cain halted his pacing as though considering this latest matter. He was silent for nearly a full minute then his eyes narrowed and he went absolutely ridged with anger. He had heard enough, now he needed consultation with an old associate. "You may leave. Continue your surveillance and let me know the moment the group actually leaves and the direction they intend to go."

Cain was furiously pacing the floor, muttering under his breath. Finally, he could endure it no more and he picked up a nearby urn. With a ferocity born of frustration at having his efforts again come to naught, he angrily heaved the object against a nearby wall fetching a satisfying noise of breakage. The act brought only scant pleasure, however, and he returned to his pacing.

"How could this happen, yet, again?" He screamed, causing the echo to reverberate mockingly back to his own ears. For years he had worked patiently to rebuild all that of which he had been unfairly robbed prior to the Flood. All the painstaking hours of planning and strategy would again be frustrated. "It's not fair!" he screamed.

In his reverie of anger and self-pity he had paid no attention as the room had become increasingly cooler. "Cain, you must calm your anxiety and anger," soothed a voice from behind him. His only friend and mentor had finally arrived.

"Well, I must say you took your sweet time and pleasure letting me in on this little debacle," Cain replied sarcastically. "These people may exaggerate on occasion, but they never lie so there must be some truth to it. Why was I not informed sooner?"

"I have only just recently been informed myself," was the reply in a placating tone.

"I seriously doubt that! I don't know why I bother listening to your counsel if it is always too late to act upon!"

"I have been busy attempting to eke out a compromise, but the best I could do was allow you to retain your original language."

"Your attempt is witless. A fat lot of good that compromise is going to do me while everyone else around me is running amok in the streets!"

"Granted, this setback is a clear violation of the spirit of our arrangement, but it is hardly unexpected. I warned you to cease building that tiresome tower and you continued pushing it forward long after good taste and common sense had departed by the boards."

Cain tore at his hair and began rubbing his scar. "How else was I to test my social experiments?" he replied heatedly.

"The Creator was unamused and he blames me for that monstrosity!"

"He has no sense of humor!" he answered petulantly.

"No, he hasn't. So, we will muddle through this the best we can as we always have. We will regroup and take with us all that we have learned and reapply it at a later date."

Cain sulked, but understood the finality of this reversal of fortunes. "How bad is this confounding to be? Will I be left with anyone who can understand me?"

"The focal point will be here in Babylon. I was able to negotiate better concessions for the city of Nineveh, your capitol and primary place of residence, but elsewhere in Babylonia, including the nearby provinces, the confounding will be near total. I suggest you depart the city tonight to avoid the understandable chaos in the streets tomorrow."

"Before I slink out of here like some whipped dog, I intend to exact revenge upon Jasher and that gang of rabble he purports to lead out of the city. His group should not be left untouched by this madness."

"You are wasting valuable time and risk being caught up in the bedlam and confusion which will reign on the morrow. I counsel you to simply leave and be grateful for the warning you have received."

"No, not enough" he angrily replied. "You are dismissed and I will call you again when I need you, which I sincerely hope will not be for a long time to come."

With that, he turned and walked swiftly across the hallway to his personal guard. "Assemble my men. We are going on a hunt."

His guard visibly blanched as he saw the slow smile of a feral beast appear on the face of his master. He was very quick to gather the armed guard.

While Cain was anxiously pacing around his study awaiting the appearance of his mentor, Mahonri abruptly awoke up from a dream-filled sleep. In his dream he had seen an army of men approaching the home of his brother, Jared, led by a demented, demon of a man. He quickly arose and ran to Jared's bed chamber and quickly roused his brother from a deep sleep. After explaining his dream, they conversed and it was decided that the group would need to depart that night ahead of schedule. They both rushed to the sleeping area in the warehouse where Jasher and Miriam had been billeted and whereupon finding him, Mahonri related to him the dream. Jasher immediately concurred with the two men that they all should depart as quickly as possible.

The entire group had been briefed beforehand to be ready to leave at a moment's notice, so they were assembled, along with all bed gear, tents and food, then made ready for a swift departure. Jasher was grateful for their foresight in this matter so that they only had to arise and leave a few hours earlier than planned. This had ensured minimal disturbance to the neighborhood while they passed along the early morning streets of Babylon.

Mahonri gazed around the warehouse full of his family and friends and announced, "We will now begin the hazardous trek through Babylon." He turned to Jasher and asked, "Jasher, will you share any thoughts you may have at this time."

Before retiring for the evening the night before, and trying to anticipate what Mahonri's family would need to hear on the eve of the departure, Jasher had spent a few hours contemplating the upcoming journey. This new complication, however, had thrown him temporarily off-balance and more concerned for their welfare.

"My original intent had been to carefully guide you through the streets of Babylon in the midst of social chaos, but it appears that we have been allowed to leave just before the confounding descends upon the city. However, this new development will be beset with danger because Cain has been made aware of our plans and will be on his way shortly to prevent us from our goal."

Bathsheba was concerned for her family and so asked, "Jasher, I agree we should depart now, but are we in any immediate danger?"

Jared, too, was concerned. "She is right. Do we need to prepare ourselves for an armed conflict?"

Jasher glanced over toward Miriam who shook her head encouraging him to deliver an honest assessment. She was well aware of what Cain was capable of doing; she had met the man and understood his resolve.

Jasher replied, "Knowing his disposition for violence, some or most of us may be harmed in the process, but if we conduct ourselves quietly, I feel we can avoid any armed engagement. At this hour of the morning, few persons will be wandering the streets, nonetheless Cain will have sent out spies to detect our passing. If you should take note of anyone that makes even a casual observation of our movements during our escape through the city, inform me immediately. Again, let me remind you, if we proceed quietly and confidently, we will illicit less attention than an unruly mob of desperate citizens." Jasher then led his group of nearly three hundred people through a still-darkened city.

The passing of the cautious crowd of pilgrims from the building left scarcely a sound, even from the children. As they cleared the building, Calah was on his way back to the warehouse and thus was unaware of their early exit. A half hour after they had proceeded unnoticed from the business district, he arrived now winded from his early morning run through the city. After catching his breath and trying to clear his mind, he reminded himself that he really had little to worry about; the group would remain inside until later that morning in any event. He did feel it was prudent, however, to make an occasional round of the warehouse to ensure they were securely tucked away for the night.

He walked carefully around the premises and expected minimal, if any, security patrols on the part of this amateur collection of farmers and business people. It was nothing he could not handle, anyway. If he met up with someone he would simply bluff his way out declaring he had mistakenly taken a wrong turn in the street, or if things got really nasty, he could always break a neck or two. He had done it before.

His movements were cautious as he walked through the entrance of the storehouse and peered inside. He expected the usual nighttime noise of sleeping people: a crying baby, a snoring old man or the inevitable insomniac stumbling about in the dark. He was surprised, however, at hearing the echo of an empty room. Trying to discern any movements, his eyes darted to all areas of the darkened room and once his eyes had adjusted to the dimness of the light, he realized with rising alarm that it was now empty. *How had they slipped by me so easily?* He berated himself.

Without further remonstrations, he ran out the building then began to sift about the detritus along the street for clues of the unexpected departure. After a few minutes of panicky searching, at the end of the street he observed a child's toy which had been dropped, but never retrieved. He ran along the expected departure path they may have travelled and looked for more discarded evidence of the early morning flight through Babylon.

Once Calah had deduced Jasher's proposed northerly route outside of the city, he turned around and dashed back to Cain's residence on the far side of the sprawling metropolis. Day had begun to dawn when he became aware of a cloud forming low upon the area, but in view of his current task, he had paid it only token attention, however, while nearing Cain's residence, he noticed that the cloud he had observed earlier had become a fine, grayish mist. With mounting concern, the cloud had descended upon the area and it began to envelope him. He felt a slight queasy feeling of nausea, but there was no pain then a noticeable tingling sensation coursed up the length of his body. As he drew closer to the residence of his master, he felt a small headache that he attempted to ignore.

From within the palace gate could be heard the canting and shuffling of horses being prepared to leave in haste. Suddenly, the gate flew open, exposing armed men now ready for battle, but unaware which direction to proceed. Cain recognized his spy, Calah, in the early dawn light and demanded, "Calah, to which direction have they fled?"

Calah could hear that Cain had spoken to him, but his words were incomprehensible. Now baffled, Calah began to speak, but before he had completed a sentence it was obvious that even though he could understand what he was saying, no one else could. He continued to speak and the soldiers all looked bewildered at him as though he was raving. Behind Calah came rolling toward them the mist, while Cain upon realizing what was happening, spurred his horse and directed his soldiers in the opposite direction.

The Captain of the Guard shouted to Cain over the noise of the horses, "Sire, what strange nonsense was Calah babbling? I was able to understand scarcely a word of what he said."

"That makes two of us."

Cain was desperate to put as much distance between them and the fog as was possible. He directed his soldiers to a nearby street corner and up ahead they saw the mist roiling in the morning air and it blocked their path in all directions.

The city was beginning to awake for another blisteringly hot day, but an unusually large, dark cloud hovered above, partly dampening the effects of the early morning light. As was normal, however, shopkeepers began setting up wares in various markets about the large urban centers of business. One by one, each shop was opened and the owners prepared for the usual morning rush to purchase food, clothing and household goods. As the early morning sun could now be detected peeking over the eastern horizon, above them could be seen a light vapor which descended from a cloud that eventually covered the full area of the city. The storeowners and early shoppers remained calm at the unusual sight, but curiosity of the event caused many of them to look at one another as if for an explanation. Meanwhile, the mist circulated among the shops and was inevitably breathed in by the shoppers and storeowners alike; all seemed to pause at the same moment. Then each began to experience the same symptoms as Calah, a slight tingling followed closely by a small headache. After a moment and trying to comprehend what was happening around them, the people as one began asking questions to those around them, but as each began to reply, they all looked at their neighbor quizzically and with suspicion.

When it was obvious that no longer could anyone communicate verbally, panic set in causing each to bolt away in search of someone who could explain to them what was happening. This reaction spread like a wildfire throughout the market centers and eventually spilled over into all residences of the city where the citizenry, now curious at the noise, flung open doors to investigate the commotion. This, of course, allowed the mist to stream insidiously and unabated into each household and immediately was breathed in by all of the family. Before long the residents added their screams of confusion to the vendors which added to the general chaos of the already substantial disorder insinuating its effects throughout Babylon.

Jasher had led the group through the final gate of the city and proceeded in a northwesterly direction. From the outset, it had been slow going, due inevitably from small children and the aged, but there had been minimal disturbances so the morning trek had gone unnoticed. Now the feeble early morning light of another day began to push gently away the long darkness of the night. They had walked almost a mile outside the city when a disturbance occurred that was so loud they were unable to refrain from stopping and looking back. Mahonri called a stop for rest and after a few minutes, there was enough light for them to notice toward the south a large cloud that had formed over the city and from within the cloud emanated a gray mist which was slowly wafting down onto the urban district below then spreading outward like tentacles of an octopus in all directions.

As they watched the darkened fog approach, Mahonri called out, "Do not fear the mist. We are protected from its affects, but as you can hear, the citizens of Babylon are not immune and they are experiencing the confusion which has been foretold."

And just as was predicted, an incredible howling could be heard as people ran wildly through the streets accosting anyone that impeded a headlong exit from the city to the countryside. Jasher turned around and bid his fellow travelers to follow him, but before too long, now bent on escaping the mist, a mass of citizens had quickly overtaken them on the road. They were all trying to escape the results of the cloud, of course, but the exodus was in vain as the damage had been done. Once the old language had been confounded and a new one acquired, the change was permanent. Ignoring the chaos around them, the caravan led by Jasher resumed their trek toward the northwestern horizon; the journey had now begun.

Unfortunately for Cain and his men, they were unable to escape ahead of the encroaching mist. They had bolted headlong into the fog and all, save Cain and a few guards, received the full measure of the affects. People milled around them in a crazed demented manner. They pulled the soldiers off their horses in an effort to expedite a swifter escape from the surrounding chaos. Now reacting in typical military fashion, the soldiers struck back as any armed men would do: swords were unsheathed and the men on horseback began hacking a way through the thronging crowd which produced even more pandemonium to the already frenzied citizens.

The terror had reached such deranged proportions that the mob was no longer concerned with self-preservation and now, with utter disdain for their lives, they threw themselves head-long upon the hapless soldiers, bringing them all to the ground and tearing them to pieces. The soldiers, now equally affected by the mist were alone and unable to communicate a tactical retreat so, out of fear for their lives, they swung swords out at random, slicing through one man and cutting asunder another. Nonetheless, the guards were now on foot and heavily outnumbered, their horses stolen or chopped up by the frenzied crowd. With fear etched on their contorted faces, they stood isolated and the rabble descended upon them with cudgels and axes.

After nearly all the guards were cut down by the frenzied mob, a woman, now traumatized from the violence, jumped maniacally upon the back of the remaining soldier. While hysterically shouting in an unknown language, she pulled a dagger and sliced it into his throat. Meanwhile, an approaching woman, screeching hag-like, descended upon him from the front with a hatchet, burying it deeply within his shoulder bone. His reflex pushed his sword upwards into the neck of the oncoming woman and all three tumbled to the ground, the blood now spilling out all around them. And the insanity rolled over them and continued throughout the city.

Once he realized the converging mob was bent on murder, Cain had called a command and a few soldiers recognized what he was saying. After the order, those few who understood and were left alive gamely followed him to relative safety away from the mob in a nearby alley way. He then commanded, "Dismount. Discard all weapons except your daggers." Looking out into the seething mob and seeing that the killing spree had actually escalated, he screamed over the din to be heard, "From here we walk."

A soldier shouted back, "Lord, why dismount and discard our swords and take only the knives?"

"The horses they see as a means to escape the madness around them and the daggers are viewed less of a threat. I just want to get out of here with as little confrontation as possible."

Bewildered and frightened, the remaining soldiers followed Cain through absolute chaos. If there had ever been any civilized order to Babylon, it was now in the past. The citizenry could be seen shouting and raving above the frenzy trying desperately to communicate with anyone and once they had found someone with a language in common, they gathered in groups. Finally, in spite of the bedlam of confusion all around them, each group fought their way slowly out of the beleaguered city and began the remainder of their now shattered lives. Husbands, wives, sons and daughters, whole families, regardless of their station in life, were divided because of the language differences and all sought only those with whom they could communicate.

Construction on The Great Tower to Heaven was abruptly terminated and permanently forgotten. The gray mist could be seen reaching out in every direction now, diffusing its tentacles of havoc throughout the land under Cain's control. There were few to escape its debilitating effects.

Cain and what was left of his retinue hobbled steadily northward back to Nineveh along a road now choked with refugees. As a result of the confrontation in the street in which he had been pulled roughly from his horse, he was limping and holding his right arm. He hadn't commented much since the retreat, but as he looked back over his shoulder he saw the mist slowly wafting in their direction towards the north and the land of Nineveh. He shook his head miserably then turning around angrily muttered a curse.

It had been two days short of five weeks when the caravan led by Jasher finally arrived at the small port of Tyre on the Eastern Coast of the Great Sea. Two weeks later, as another day came to an end with the sun setting gloriously in the west, Jasher, Miriam and the brother of Jared, Mahonri, had climbed a tall hill overlooking the port, admiring the sunset.

Miriam was the first to break the silence. "I will miss this sight more than I would have imagined." With a note of wistful finality, she asked, "So, Husband, I suppose we are to return to the desert tomorrow morning?"

Jasher knew what Miriam was thinking. The building of the barges down below had begun, but they were a long way from completion. "Yes, Miriam, I am afraid we must depart soon or we shall never do so." He looked over at Mahonri now silently commiserating with Miriam. Jasher commented, "I, too, feel a kinship with Mahonri and his people. They have become our family and it will be harder to leave them next month and the month after even harder."

Mahonri nodded in agreement. "Miriam your destiny is with Jasher and his mission will be on this side. The sooner you accept it as your mission, the easier it will be to follow him in spite of his hard-headed ways," he commented light-heartedly.

The three grew silent again as they watched the sun slowly extinguish into the twilight of the early evening. It was Mahonri who began a final commentary, "Jasher, I am in the way of knowing that one day you will reach out to us over there in the West. And when that day arrives, you will come in pursuit of our historical records. I will insure that those who follow me clearly understand that and realize the importance of making a record worthy of your journey."

"I thank you and appreciate your assurances. I hope that you will all enjoy many years of happiness and peace."

Mahonri was thoughtful for a moment then replied, "It will not last forever. Men will eventually begin to seek after power and attempt to deny us our freedoms contrary to the plan of agency that our Creator has provided us. And when those sad days once again descend upon us there will be those among our people who will record it. Never doubt, the records will be there awaiting you."

The sun dropped below the far western horizon leaving the twilight of the first stars of the evening. All three sat and admired the mystery of creation and pondered over their own pre-ordained place in the flow of history.

After leaving Mahonri and his followers, Jasher and Miriam started a long journey eastward. During this sojourn, they made note of many geological changes that had occurred because of the impact of the comet years earlier. Along the way, they met a number of people who spoke the old language who were of the opinion that the land changes and separations were still on-going. Many were also heading eastward with the intent to find new lands to settle. Jasher reflected that it was exactly what the Creator had intended.

Nearly six months later, Jasher and Miriam, now carrying their belongings packed on donkeys, walked into a valley on the eastern side of the continent. They were met by a now elderly woman, a matriarch by the name of Sariah who had seen much change in her long life. Though elderly, she still had much spring left in her step and felt unrestrained happiness at greeting the two young people who would in time bring so much joy and pleasure to her remaining years on earth. Incredibly, her language had remained unchanged, along with those few who still remained in her valley. She nodded her head at the sight of them and with hands on her hips, her first words to Jasher were, "How long can you stay with us this time?"

Jasher looked around, now holding the hand of Miriam, and for the first time in many years, he felt that he had finally arrived home. After a smile of welcome and a fond embrace, he answered with a joy he could scarcely contain. "For as long as my wife and children live." He paused and whispered, "And I hope that is a very long time."

As it turned out it was.

The Translation, Continued

Having received a note from Dov Hacohen that another attack on the compound might be imminent, Jasher had just left the translation room on his way to check with his contact in Nicosia. Before leaving, however, he had provided the professors with his take on the necessity of the division of the land masses, as well as an explanation of the confusion of tongues. Levinson and Bedford settled back into a quiet meditation. Levinson was the first to break the silence.

"What did you make of Jasher's explanation for those two events?"

Bedford considered the question at length and replied, "According to Jasher, he was a contemporary of Peleg and was a first-hand witness of those occurrences. He said they both coincided closely with his first encounters with Cain."

Levinson commented, "Yes, the division of the land and confusion of the language, so he reports, was necessary to separate Cain and his influence from those who would inhabit a land choice above all others and he termed it "a land of promise".

"It is a curious use of words, wouldn't you agree, that Jasher referred to the New World, specifically North America, as this land of promise."

Bedford expected Levinson to smile indulgently and express his own doubts over the description. It was, after all, a highly jingoistic comment and beyond the decorum of modern day expectations of thought.

Instead, Levinson remained somber and pensive. At length, he replied, "William, you and your forebears are fortunate to have lived in America for centuries and have grown understandably complacent with your concept of freedom and liberty, but there is a significant portion of former immigrant American citizens who remember the oppression of their former nations of origin. Those fears were real and the experiences traumatizing. They would have no trouble accepting the term, *land of promise*. My parents and grandfather were immigrants, refugees really, and in spite of all its imperfections, they never ceased their praises of America. There is a near palpable spirit there which embodies freedom. Yes, I think they would see it as a land choice above all others." With a slight pause, he added, "I would also have to add my belief as well."

Now missing their home, both men settled into their private reveries and pondered that ephemeral and yet necessary concept of freedom.

PART 3

INTO THE TWILIGHT

War does not determine who is right – only who is left.

— Bertrand Russell

The Olmec were the first major civilization in Mexico following a progressive development from those in the southwest area of Chiapas who had been in that area since 5000 BCE. Their eventual migration led them to the tropical lowlands of south-central Mexico, now the present-day states of Veracruz and Tabasco.

The Olmec flourished during Mesoamerica's formative period, dating roughly as early as 1500 BCE to about 400 BCE. Pre-Olmec cultures had flourished in the area since about 2500 BCE, but by 1600–1500 BCE, early Olmec culture had emerged, centered on sites near the coast in southeast Veracruz, Mexico. They were the first of the Mesoamerican civilizations and laid many of the foundations for the civilizations that followed, such as the Maya, Aztec and Toltec. Among other "firsts," the Olmec appeared to practice ritual bloodletting and introduced the Mesoamerican ballgame whose players all played to the death, both hallmarks of nearly all subsequent Mesoamerican societies.

CHAPTER 1

THE RESCUE

General Manasseh and his Chief Captain, Jacob, had known each other since childhood and had developed a mutual respect and love for their country, Nahor. It was not surprising then that both men had become warriors and had served with distinction. Both had sons who had served and died in defense of his country, and as a result, the two men had reached personal, though opposing conclusions regarding war. Having decided that war was a necessity to ensure national freedoms Manasseh was more sanguine about embracing his natural aggression and had become a career soldier. He understood that without the sacrifice of their sons to carry on this service, there would be no lasting peace for any of them to inherit one day. Jacob, on the other hand, was a reserve officer and preferred a quieter life, considering the act of war personally repugnant if not demeaning.

Jacob's youngest son, Aaron, was still a young man when Manasseh had chosen a time of relative peace in the land to come to enlist him as well as all the other youths of the surrounding settlements. An argument between the two old comrades had become bitter as Jacob, now weary of war, was intent on sheltering Aaron from discovering his darker side as only war could bring out in a man.

"Jacob, what of your son, Aaron? I know you have trained him well in the art of combat. He must fight for his country and people!"

Aaron was quick to interject his own opinion. "Father, allow me to fight to save our nation. The enemy is even now preparing another invasion!"

"And have you become traumatized by the murder of innocent women and children? Never!" he shouted and the argument and denials persisted. An angry exchange between father and son then ensued and before long both were shouting.

The women of the house, Jacob's wife and four daughters, heard the shouting and came running and realized that the men must have been talking war to incite Jacob to such an agitated state. Abish, his wife, took his hand and murmured, "Husband, do not excite yourself further." Turning to her youngest daughter she directed, "Beulah, fetch your father some herbal tea to calm him." She then gazed pleadingly at the General and said, "Manasseh, try not to upset him. He has been feeling ill of late and this discussion is not helping his state of mind."

The General grew quiet then nodded his agreement. Turning to Jacob, he stated reasonably, "I know Aaron is young, but you have prepared him to defend his people and I have in mind to use him for special tactical missions."

Jacob, now exasperated with this talk, at length agreed. "I know he must fight. All his elder brothers fervently believed in our cause and their bodies are now moldering in some distant jungle somewhere. He is of age and I have done the best I could to prepare him, but Manasseh, I hold you responsible for what he will become."

Afterwards, what followed for Aaron were months of intense training in various techniques of tracking, stealth insertion and assassination. He learned to use all weapons of war, especially the dagger for close encounters into enemy strongholds and encampments. This latter skill was his primary role and his skills were utilized to infiltrate camps and remove the enemy commanders on the eve of battle. By thus throwing the chain of command in sufficient disarray, he provided a slight field advantage to General Manasseh on the battlefield the next day.

Under the General's management, each settlement in the land of Nahor became a fortress of prepared bastions of defense. Moats were built and each city had dug bulwarks of dirt which encircled each settlement to provide a rampart between them and an invading army. Nevertheless, despite all creative defenses and attempts to secure a lasting peace, the land of Nahor was continually under siege from the southern armies. Their enemies of the South were persistent and thus began a series of relentless incursions into the northern territory of Nahor which removed any chances for a prolonged season of peace. This aggression would occupy the services of Aaron for many years to come.

Though all kingdoms of the realm, save one, were controlled by the Clan of the Scar, the northernmost kingdom, Nahor, located I the present-day state of Hidalgo, had managed to avoid any such political entanglements. To their south was Chalco, located in the present-day state of Oaxaca, and though both kingdoms shared a common ancestry, language and many customs, a civil war had broken out centuries before causing a rift that had never healed. This divisiveness had been exploited by the Clan decades earlier, and since that time Chalco and Nahor had been involved in an ongoing civil war with few years of peace.

Of the more dubious, but time-honored traditions of the Kingdom of Chalco, the abduction of members of the royal family of Nahor stood out as the most distinctive. Aside from its obvious signal of temporary predominance of the realm by one nation over the other, it had the more significant by-product of throwing the latter into a state of confusion as to royal succession. The captive was never held for ransom; he simply languished in a dungeon until he died or could be liberated. As can be imagined, in times of war, this had significant consequences. The question of royal succession was a constant worry for the ruler, and without a clear successor to the throne, the kingdom was vulnerable to enemies both from within and without.

The guard on duty, Dibri, scratched his beard from the lice that infested the dungeon, but hardly gave such matters any real room for serious thought. He knew what he wanted that night; he had been thinking about it all day and decided not to delay his needs any longer. He sauntered casually over to the cell containing Libnah, son of King Gilead of Nahor. During his captivity, Libnah had proved to be pliant and easily controlled and therefore a prime target for abuse should the guards find themselves bored in the early hours of the morning. Dibri had been assured he could amuse himself with the captive so long as another guard was present, but at this hour of the night he reasoned that he would need little, if any back-up. Taking out a whip from within his sleeve, he pulled back the lock from the cell door and with a leer of amusement he confidently entered the cell, all the while slapping the whip against his leg. He was hoping the diminutive, subdued young man would offer up some resistance to his advances that night. *It was always more satisfying if they put up a little fight,* he reflected.

Libnah was a quiet, unassuming man who had been avoiding confrontations his whole life. He also happened to be born at the wrong time and had been the first casualty of the latest civil war between his nation of Nahor and the southern land of Chalco that had erupted following his abduction. Being reserved and retiring by nature, he normally stayed close to home, but on this one occasion he had been out hunting and had strayed too far south when his hunting party was suddenly surrounded by a team of trackers who had been waiting for just such a moment to present itself. His hunting party, consisting of himself and half a dozen guards were set upon with the result that his security detail was cut down and he was wrestled to the ground, trussed up and returned south to Chalco for imprisonment.

He had no idea how long he had been left to rot in the dungeon, and knowing the usual predicament of those abducted during a war, he had long given up any hope of a rescue. He slept on damp, rotten straw and had been bitten by every crawling, filthy animal and insect that lived in this dank and dark hell-hole which he now called home. His food was hardly fit for swine and tonight, for amusement, he was sure the guards had fed him rotted, maggoty meat. In his hunger he had eaten it anyway and when most of it had come up later, he had heard the drunken roar of laughter outside his cell door.

Knowing his reserved disposition, the guards, especially Dibri, had often used a whip to terrorize and humiliate him. On occasion, this behavior had excited the jailor and unsurprisingly had led to sexual abuse of his captive, and tonight it appeared there would be a repeat performance. Though the room was dark, Libnah had long grown accustomed to the dim light and easily spotted the guard as he made his way slowly across the damp stone floor. The guard halted then stood over him, slightly swaying from his recent inebriated condition. Eventually his breathing had become accelerated by his lust; Libnah knew what awaited him that early morning.

He whispered, "Please, Dibri, not tonight, I beg of you."

The guard continued to slap his leg and while doing so seemed to consider the man's plea for mercy. Of course, he was merely toying with him and with a regretful tone answered, "Can't do it, Libnah. You were a bad boy tonight and did not finish up your meal. One should not waste food in times of a war, especially with so many people going without and having to sacrifice. It tends to set a bad example."

"Please, don't. The meat was rotten and I could not finish it." In a pleading tone, he pointed out, "Later, you heard me vomit it up."

The guard chided him as he would a child. "Libnah, the meat may have been a trifle undercooked, but we all ate of it. Times are hard and so you must be taught a lesson. After all, we cannot all live as a prince and eat on a whim as you have your entire life. You must show the proper gratitude for all we have given you."

With a casual flick of his wrist, the turnkey struck out at the small man, catching him across the face with the tips of the whip. The sound had a satisfying slap to it the guard appreciated, especially once Libnah cried out in obvious pain. To avoid being struck again, he rolled over to a corner into a ball. Ignoring his captor's desperate attempt to protect himself, Dibri's obvious lust washed over him and he again advanced upon the defenseless prisoner, all the while flicking his whip menacingly. While his captor cowered helplessly in the corner with his hand up to protect his face, the jailer was about to strike out again.

A leering smile of satisfaction had just crossed his face when he suddenly felt a pain in the small of his back followed closely by a searing burn to the neck. Dibri dropped his whip and his now free hand flew upward as he tumbled to his knees clutching his throat. It was no use, the blood was spurting through his fingers and his last conscious thought was that he would be denied his pleasure with Libnah that night.

The guard was roughly shoved to one side and a strong hand went out to the cringing prisoner, catching him below the arm and pulling him upwards. A voice quietly, but urgently whispered, "Libnah, remain calm and follow me out of the dungeon. If all goes well, I will have you safely home within the week."

In his weakened condition, Libnah stumbled, but caught the man's arm and allowed his savior to carefully guide him through the cell door and down the hallway. The cool wind of the courtyard was the first breath of fresh air he had experienced in many months and as he breathed in the gentle breeze, he noticed bodies lying about every twenty paces, now bleeding out, the men silent as the tomb. He followed the man slowly and wherever they encountered someone, each was eliminated in the same manner as Dibri, a knife to the back and a thrust to the neck. In time, they reached relative safety and knowing that Libnah had been severely weakened during his incarceration, his liberator provided food and drink he had stashed a few miles from the jail.

It was a beautiful evening, and Libnah, who had been denied the reassuring sounds of nocturnal birds for so long, now reveled in their night song. After he had wolfed down the food and had savored every drop of the wine, he managed to ask, "I wish to know the name of the man who has saved me."

"Aaron." The man explained, "I was sent by your father Gilead to free you. I regret it has taken so long, but your exact location was difficult to discover."

"I suspect the war has made everyone suspicious of strangers."

"Yes, I had to pose as a citizen for nearly six months before I could get close enough to get answers. I admire your ability to survive under such circumstances."

"Another day and I am sure they would have broken me."

"Many would not have lasted as long."

Libnah remarked gratefully, "Thank you for trying. I will never forget it."

"Thank me when I have you safely back home."

Libnah remarked between bites, "You must understand that King Shiz of Chalco will be angry he has lost a key means to extort his will over my father. He will take this rescue as a personal affront."

"I know. He will undoubtedly send man hunters to find us and unless we are quick and cunning, they will have you back in that dungeon in a few days. Can you walk?"

"I will bloody well fly if I have to. I am not going back to that hell-hole."

Aaron smiled, admiring his determination. "Very well. Please rest, but we must leave within the hour."

King Shiz of the Southern Kingdom of Chalco, never a bibber of wine to excess, seemed to be in the attitude of making an exception on this occasion. His anger had got the better of him and he now paced the floor in front of his advisers, one hand firmly around his goblet, occasionally taking a bout then asking for more wine.

Finally, out of frustration, he threw the chalice of wine against a nearby wall and shouted, "Bring all the guards who were responsible for this mess last night. I will punish them myself; I am considering a public castration!"

With as much decorum as he could manage his chief adviser and representative of the Clan, Eber, cleared his throat and quietly informed him, "Sire, I do apologize but I must inform you that none of the guards who were on duty last night survived the attack."

The king was in mid-stride, still trying to fathom how he could have lost his best bargaining chip in this civil war. "What? You are telling me no one survived the assault? So, we have no way of knowing who or how many were responsible?"

"That is correct, Excellency. Nevertheless, I dispatched our best team of trackers to investigate the massacre inside and in front of the dungeon. I was on hand when he completed his preliminary investigation. Apparently, this is the work of just one man. The lead tracker, Cush, has identified him by his killing methods and stealth. We are dealing with a man well-versed in the art of infiltration and extraction, killing or whatever it takes to get the job done. He is the best."

"Can your team capture them before they cross the northern border into Nahor?"

"I have complete confidence in Cush. If anyone can overtake them, he and his team can get the job done."

"As soon as they have completed their review of the attack at the dungeon, dispatch them immediately in pursuit. King Gilead will be less inclined to press for a conditional surrender to save his throne if his son escapes. We will no longer have any means to extort the man."

"I agree, Sire. Libnah was our best chance to avoid an all-out war. You realize we were on the eve of negotiating the surrender of Nahor when this escape took place. Our whole strategy for this current conflict was based upon that eventuality."

"Eber, I still fail to understand why we have sought a conditional surrender. Why not just enlist the Army of Sidon and overrun Nahor with the combined armies and raze everything in their path?"

"It was Sidon's wish that we insist that King Gilead surrender their records to avoid an all-out war. His son was merely a means to bring them to the negotiating table. He will be displeased at our failure to ensure their cooperation in this matter."

King Shiz shook his head in frustration. The last thing he needed now was to have Sidon breathing down his neck. "You need not remind me. We must avoid incurring the wrath of the Master Mahan at all costs. When Cush has recovered Libnah, have him report to me at once."

Libnah was somewhat familiar with the southern province of his father's kingdom, but never before had he ventured this far into the interior. The jungle noises were deafening at night and threatening during the day; moreover, he had never known such dense undergrowth and canopy from above blocking out the noon-day rays of the sun. The heat and the pace were taking a toll on his stamina. As they took a quick turn in the underbrush, he glanced over toward his travelling companion and noted his lack of concern and confidence in such an alien and forbidding landscape.

Libnah remarked between intakes of air, "I never expected the route to be this circuitous back to our nation. It feels like we are moving in circles."

"We are."

Libnah was surprised and more than just a little exasperated. His idea of a straight line was the shortest distance between two points. He grabbed Aaron by the arm and halted their jog through the near impenetrable jungle. They had been running for two days and should have been at the most a few days short of crossing into their homeland by now and would have achieved that goal if not for this detour. Catching his breath he managed to say, "Explain."

"We are being tracked and if we had stayed on our original course, we would have been overtaken already."

"That seems hard to believe given our pace."

"Believe it." Aaron refrained from telling him that this slow progress was due to Libnah's weakened condition from his long incarceration.

Libnah thought of the dank dungeon from which he had escaped and said, "What is our plan? At this rate we will never get home."

"We will never get home unless we do the unexpected. By now those who pursue us know I am with you and you are slowing me down, so it was necessary to throw them off by creating this unanticipated charge through the jungle. Up until now, our route and their pursuit had been going according to their plans and they had confidently expected to overtake us, but I have now given them something more to think about and to consider another strategy. While they are pondering our next move we are going to use both this confusion and the jungle to our advantage."

"How so?"

"I intend to reduce their numerical edge by leading them into a few well-set traps I created a few months ago."

Libnah shook his head as though he had misunderstood. "I don't understand. You have set them already?"

"I anticipated this pursuit in our headlong flight and mapped out an escape route ahead of time. It pays to plan in advance, especially when you know you will have murderous trackers hot on your heels every step of the way."

Yesterday Cush and his trackers were confidently certain they would quickly overtake their prey by nightfall. An unexpected change of route by his quarry had left him momentarily confused. He called his men together to discuss the possible implications. "Our prey has changed direction and is now headed through the jungle. This can only mean that they are aware of our pursuit. I need to know what they are planning and why."

"They are frightened and hope to lose us in the dense forest?" commented one.

Another interjected, "They have changed their minds; they no longer consider Nahor attainable so intend to hole up somewhere in the jungle."

Still another declared, "We should assume this flight through the jungle was a feint in a desperate hope to lose us; then they will cut back toward the original direction. We should wait for them along the original path farther north and grab them as they emerge from the jungle."

Cush considered all these possibilities and more. Finally, he decided. "We will test the will and cunning of the leader. He is leading a small, weakened man and I intend to run them into the ground and leave them no room or time to formulate a workable evasive strategy. I agree this feint into the jungle was simply a means to not only confuse us, but also make us second-guess our resolve. Libnah is slowing them down and if they have deviated from their original course, it is out of desperation. Brothers, by nightfall the leader will be dead and Libnah will be in our net."

Aaron and Libnah had spent most of the afternoon completing a dead-fall which consisted of a small pit, about four feet deep and six by six feet on each side. The pit, Aaron explained, had been dug weeks beforehand, and all that needed to be added were the sharpened staves which would lay point-up and coated with a local poison, curare. After carefully completing the task inside the pit, they placed covering fronds from nearby ferns and laid them over the trap. Aaron examined the completed trap and nodded his head in satisfaction. It was at the foot of a small hill and the trackers, with the proper motivation, would rush head-long into it and the forward momentum would pull them directly into the pit, impaling them. The poison tipped stakes would ultimately kill them if the fall didn't. He turned to Libnah and said, "All we need now is the bait."

"The bait, what do you mean?"

"You."

Five minutes later the two were jogging back along the original path through the jungle. As they slowed, in the distance, Aaron sensed rather than heard the approach of armed men bent on the hunt. A movement within the lush underbrush convinced him they had been heard and the hunters had then made a slight route correction along their path. Aaron turned to Libnah and whispered urgently, "Stay on my back and do not drift away for any reason. This has to look like two men desperately trying to stay one step ahead of their pursuers."

"That should not be too difficult for me. I have been feeling desperate since you liberated me, but I would rather die than go back."

"If you do as I say, it will not come to that. Let's go. I can hear them approaching."

As both men set off at a steady pace, a light mist began to fall, and this, along with the diminishing light of the day buoyed Aaron's confidence for the success of his traps. They slowed their pace, allowing the trackers to gradually gain on them. It was nearing the end of the day and between the dimness of the sunlight and the dense jungle canopy, the pathways had darkened considerably. Aaron and Libnah took a sharp turn down the hill which left the trackers temporarily uncertain at what they were running into as they hurtled head-long toward the bottom. At the foot of the hill, of course, lay the dead-fall and this next maneuver had to be convincing. Aaron, and Libnah close behind, carefully skirted the pit by inches yet not appearing as though they were trying to avoid it. The trackers had to be convinced there was nothing amiss until it was too late.

Cush and his men had been pushing hard throughout the day and they all had one goal in mind: to reach their quarry before they lost the daylight completely. Suddenly, up ahead in a slight clearing, Cush noticed two men had emerged from the jungle and knew immediately they would catch them soon. In their excitement, his men let out whoops of victory and increased their speed past Cush, each trying to be the man to draw first blood. Initially, Cush too had felt a rush of excitement, but as they turned a hard corner and began to plunge down a hill he sensed something was wrong. Cush and the other trackers all noticed the smaller man to the rear was Libnah who instinctively glanced back over his shoulder as he and Aaron shot through the underbrush. His men seemed to ignore the peculiar, slight deviation of their prey then slowing down, almost as if they wanted to be followed.

Four of the trackers hit the bottom of the hill at roughly the same time. The front two fell immediately into the pit, closely followed by two others who attempted to brake once they became aware of the fate of their brothers who had hit the trap, but they slipped on the now greasy, wet undergrowth. Their own inertia carried them forward inexorably and they tumbled into the trap on top of their screaming brothers already impaled on the curare tipped stakes. It took all of his efforts for Cush to avoid slamming into them himself but he managed to halt his progress and pull the other two behind him to relative safety to the left side of the pit, avoiding the pit by inches. Four of his men were either dead or dying as Cush and the other two trackers looked on helplessly.

Inside the pit, one tracker lay face down and dead, his neck and upper body impaled. Of the four only he had died cleanly without the assistance of the poison; meanwhile the others were writhing in pain from the wounds as the poison worked its way throughout their bodies, slowly choking them. The poison is alkaloid and functions by causing a weakness of the skeletal muscles, and when administered in a sufficient dose, eventually causes death by asphyxiation resulting in paralysis of the diaphragm.

Recognizing the effects of the poison, Cush knew nothing could be done for them. He glanced at the others and angrily ordered, "Finish them off and let's keep moving."

One of the trackers commented, "Cush, surely there must be something to be done for them."

"No, they are done for; if you want to help them, give them a clean death. Meanwhile our quarry is getting farther away and the daylight diminishes by the minute."

His remaining two trackers from the team withdrew obsidian-tipped arrows from slung quivers and fired them from their bows at the remaining brothers who were still gasping for air inside the pit.

When the deed was done, the other hunter asked, "Cush, who is he, the one who liberated Libnah?"

"Never mind who he is. There is still time to catch him before we completely lose the light." But, Cush knew who they were up against and he longed for the sweet, cold revenge against an old enemy. Now trying desperately to beat the oncoming dimness of the daylight, the three men set off at a frantic pace to end the hunt.

A half-mile later they ran into the second trap. Cush may have been angry but he had decided he would not die stupid. He sent the other two men on ahead, and as he was behind them only a few paces, that more than anything else had saved him for another day. By now the sunlight had been gone from the day, thus they did not notice that the clearing ahead had a strange viscosity to it until they were right on top of it. It was not unusual in a jungle to encounter a shallow, stagnant pool of still water; however what they did not notice was that this was no pond, but quicksand. In their haste, the two point men had simply plunged in up to their waists without thinking and immediately encountered stiff resistance from the viscous goo. Somewhat quicker to assess the situation than his brothers, Cush managed to halt his progress and avoided the trap that the others had blundered into; he too, had entered into the pool, but only up to his thighs.

From the bush on the opposite side of the pond, two men had emerged and watched as Cush and his two remaining trackers struggled with the mud. Aaron withdrew an arrow from his quiver and set it in the bow to await the outcome. They made no effort to provide assistance, but waited as the jungle grew gradually dimmer and the sounds of the night creatures began to announce the end of another day.

Cush, having had some experience with quicksand, looked frantically at the other trackers and shouted, "Stop fighting it and slowly move your legs back my direction."

But the other two had panicked, and with agitated movements had only made the viscous sand more dangerous and soon it began to creep up to their chests then to the chins. Then, in desperation to avoid their helpless plight, with mouths open they screamed only to have the wet sand pour into their mouths and down their throats. In the end, they both sank as they desperately pulled on one another for a last frantic hold on life.

As Cush gradually worked his way through the quicksand he thought of the past few days tracking at a desperate pace and his frustration at being bested angered him. When he had obtained relative safety back on the original path, he noticed that all his weaponry had been lost in the sand and, of course, the weapons on the other two trackers had followed them down to the bottom of the pool. Now disgusted over his failure, he sat down to catch his breath and quell his temporary panic and anger. Then, looking up, he took note of the men quietly watching him from the opposite side.

Aaron commented, "Cush, you should have brought more men."

Cush did not bother getting up; he glared at the men on the opposite side and exclaimed, "Well, what are you waiting for? Finish it!"

Aaron lowered his bow. "Not today, Cush. No sport in it."

There was murder in his eyes as he announced, "Aaron, you may have won this round, but our paths will cross again one day and next time you will not be as lucky."

"Cush, when next we meet, luck will have little to do with the outcome."

"I pray to my gods that it may be soon."

"As they are false, it would do you little good."

With that said, the two men turned and jogged back into the jungle towards the north, leaving Cush to seethe at his missed opportunity.

CHAPTER 2

THE SIEGE

It was now six months later and Gilead, the King of the North, paced nervously in his audience room listening to the report of his chief adviser, Dekar. There was much for which he should worry; his government was disintegrating and fracturing from within and his enemies from Chalco to the South were nearly at the gates.

Before the adviser could complete the report, the king angrily interrupted him, "Dekar, your report is useless and your advice is witless. If I am to commit what is left of my Army and throw it at the invading horde from the south, I need the counsel of my General Manasseh."

"But, Sire, as you know, the main body of the army under Manasseh is in the field and is even now engaged in a battle to the west. I doubt seriously he is even aware that the fight he is now prosecuting was little more than a ruse to draw him away from our chief population centers. He would have no idea that a smaller army attacks from the south."

"Dekar, only he would have some idea of what we are now up against and what awaits us if we continue to dither and postpone what should now be obvious. Unless we act, we will be overrun in a matter of days."

"Perhaps we could mount a defense. The General left a garrison to guard the city."

"How many men do we have to defend us?"

Dekar was reluctant to say, but quietly declared, "Less than five hundred."

"Who is here to defend us? Surely Manasseh has left someone with experience in nominal command?"

"Yes, Sire, he did and the man Jacob and his son both wait in your outer chamber and wish to enter to discuss our options."

"Well, why haven't you said so? Send them in!"

Aaron's father, Jacob, normally a reserve officer, had reluctantly born the armor of a military man for many years, and though he loathed the idea of taking a human life, he performed his duty well. So well, in fact, that he had been quickly promoted over others to assume a large command against the army of their enemies to the South. His force was always the best trained and the most motivated because he was beloved by his men for his integrity and pureness of heart. These were exceptional and unusual characteristics for a man that had been repeatedly called upon to spill the blood of other men, but, as the wars in which he fought steadily took on the hue and stench of genocide, these morals were the only thing which maintained his sanity and separated him from the sociopaths which were even then rife in the Armies of the North and the South.

In the event of an unexpected incursion from the south, Manasseh had left Jacob in command of the garrison which protected the city of Nahor. Of all the captains under the General, Jacob was the only commander capable of repulsing an assault of this size and providing Manasseh enough time to return to save the city of Nahor if it became necessary. His son, Aaron, accompanied him and both would provide the ruler and his city the best tactical advantage to prevent the kingdom from being overrun. Both walked in and presented themselves before King Gilead.

The king knew Jacob by reputation and, of course, knew Aaron personally as he had been directly involved in the successful rescue of his eldest son a few months earlier and had masterminded their escape.

"Captain Jacob, please report your assessment of our chances to successfully repulse the invaders from Chalco."

"Sire, since receiving word of their intentions, I have been mustering my men in an effort to offer a defense. Our enemies are formidable and would have a clear cut advantage in the field of ten to one."

"My God, we are doomed."

"I suggest we buy as much time as possible by preparing for a siege. All persons living in the immediate area should retreat to within the walls of the city and will assist us in the defense. They should bring with them as much food and water as possible. The bulwarks of dirt and the moats we have built around the city should slow them down."

"What are our chances for survival?"

"Slim, but fortunately, due to our previous experience during the last siege of the city, we have since dug wells throughout Nahor. Moreover, the walls of the city have been built up to withstand a frontal assault and can defend us in any prolonged engagement with the enemy. Undoubtedly, they will be aware of this and thus they have probably altered their strategy since our last meeting. Whatever they have planned, it will probably involve something quick and decisive; they will not want to wait around for General Manasseh to return with the bulk of our Army."

The king thought a moment and asked, "How many soldiers do you have to offer in our defense?"

"Four hundred."

King Gilead was stunned; it was less than he had been led to believe. Only four hundred men stood between them and a massacre. There was no point in bemoaning the fact, it would have to do until the main army could return and intervene. "Aside from preparing a defense for a siege, what other strategies have you devised, Captain?"

Jacob glanced toward his son and informed the ruler, "King Shiz, in my opinion, has committed a grave error in strategy by dividing up his army. The army to the west is much larger than the one which even now is near our gates here in Nahor. But, if we can hold off his smaller army to our south and can reach General Manasseh in the west and turn our army back in our direction, we may have a chance; so, time is critical. My son, Aaron has devised a plan, and though it is somewhat unconventional, he says it has a chance to work and buy us more time."

Aaron had rehearsed his plan with his father and neither could find fault, though as his father had stated, it was unorthodox. Nevertheless, since the defense of the city rested on that success, it was imperative that he pull it off.

"Excellency, sometimes small efforts can yield large results. Since time is what we need the most, I propose throwing enough confusion among the advancing army to our south to temporarily disrupt their plans."

"How do you intend to do that?"

"I will enter the tent of the army commander and jab a knife in his neck."

The king thought he had misunderstood him; the scowl on his face indicated his doubt. His son, Libnah, sitting next to him in the audience room, on the other hand, smiled and merely said, "Bravo."

Gilead looked over toward his son to confirm Aaron's bold assertion, but saw no doubt, only honest admiration. The ruler turned back to Aaron and asked, "Then what?"

"Once I have dispatched the Commander, I will proceed westward to locate our General and inform him of your situation here in Nahor. With their commander gone and the line of command in question, there may be enough confusion in the ranks to delay an armed attack. If my father can hold off the approaching army for two weeks, I think it will be enough time for our forces to return and to turn the men of the Southern Army back to Chalco, their homeland."

Libnah asked, "Aaron, how soon can you set this plan in motion?"

"I leave as soon as we have concluded our report and have received your permission to carry it out."

The king shook his head in disbelief, but smiled and looking at Jacob said, "You were right; he does have an unusually bold plan. I take it this has been done before in the field?"

Jacob, knowing that in the field anything could happen and usually does, was reluctant to be overly optimistic, but replied, "Nothing on this level and with so much riding on its success has ever been attempted, but yes, it could work. At this point, we have few alternatives. If Aaron can buy us even a few extra days, it might make the difference between life and death for the city."

"Then you have our leave to try whatever is necessary."

Before the two men departed the castle, Libnah cornered Aaron in the hallway and embraced him as a brother. Their banter was light-hearted in spite of the seriousness of the occasion.

"Aaron, it is good to see you once again and I see you have not changed much nor your tactics have faltered any."

"Excellency, it gives my heart great pleasure to greet you again and to know that you will not be accompanying me on my latest adventure."

"What? Are you suggesting I would slow you down?"

"No, merely pointing out that by the time you had arrived to the tent of General Manasseh, I and the army would be halfway back to Nahor."

"Oh, ho! He boasts."

"Let us just say that I will be travelling fast and I will not have time to count the bodies or look over my shoulder for any stragglers."

Libnah was serious again. "My Friend, I have not forgotten all you have done for me and our nation. May the Creator of us all bring you back to us unharmed and quickly." He would be sorry to see Aaron leave, but if anyone could pull off this miracle, it would be him. In a way, he almost felt sympathy for those who would get between his friend and the camp of Manasseh. Then he remembered the conditions of his captivity and their erstwhile hospitality and his sympathy for them vanished like smoke.

It was two evenings later and Aaron sat on a hill overlooking the tents below of the smaller of the two Southern Armies from the land of Chalco. Behind him lay the two bodies of a scouting party he had ambushed nearly an hour earlier. The officer of the party was securely tied up and gagged, seated against a nearby tree.

Aaron turned around and said, "Well, Lieutenant, it is time we became better acquainted. I assure you, there is only one reason why you are still alive while your comrades lay dead at your feet. You have information I need and once I have it, I will leave you alive to die for your country another day. If I don't get it, I will continue asking, quite persuasively I assure you, until I am satisfied you have given me all I need. When I direct a question to you, your gag will be removed and you will whisper your answer. Any attempt to shout and give away our position will result in a loss of your tongue then you would be free to gesture with your hands the rest of your life. Also, do not attempt to deceive me with false information. I already know much about your invasion into our kingdom, so I will know when you are lying and any attempt to deceive me will result in a loss of something vital to your body." Aaron pulled out his knife and slowly pulled the blade across the man's stomach leaving a small sliver of blood to trickle down to his navel. "Do you understand?"

The officer nodded in the affirmative.

"Excellent. First question: When do you intend to attack?"

The gag was removed and though there was defiance in his eyes, the prisoner knew he was on a short leash and his answers, while imperfect and lacking absolute truth, nonetheless had to be genuine.

"We attack in two days" he whispered.

And the questions continued until Aaron was satisfied that what the officer had to reveal was mostly truth, at least according to his limited knowledge of the overall invasion plan. He pulled the man up to his feet. One last question remained, however, with his personal immediate plans.

"Take a look down below. Where is the tent of your field commander?"

The prisoner hesitated. Aaron had expected as much, in fact, he would have been surprised had he been immediately forthcoming. No doubt he was wondering what could be done with the information, given the tent would be so heavily guarded.

"I know what you are thinking; I would not have a chance to reach the tent. Well, if you believe that then there is no reason not to give me the information I need, is there?"

Aaron moved up directly in front of him. The knife he had been holding now moved quickly with the point just under the man's jaw; in fact, Aaron was sure he could feel the blade, given he had just broken the skin and blood began to dribble down the officer's neck.

"In the middle, the one with red and black standards."

The knife went into the throat just a tad deeper, drawing fresh blood. "There are many down below carrying those colors."

For the first time since the interrogation began, fear was clearly etched across the officer's face. "All right. You are a dead man anyway, so I will be happy to send you on your way. It's the largest of the group and the tent is blue."

"I believe you."

He sheathed the knife and began to remove methodically the man's breastplate and armor as well as any identifying markings or insignia which would indicate his rank and station. He then pushed the man heavily back to the ground.

The push angered the officer and convinced him that Aaron had no intention of keeping his word to spare his life. Thinking he was to die anyway, he spat in Aaron's direction and said, "Now that you have left me half-naked, I suppose you will kill me now in spite of your earlier promise to spare me?"

"No, but you may have much time to wish I had."

He replaced the gag back in the man's mouth and turned him over on his stomach. With a quick, practiced movement of the knife, he sliced the blade deeply into the area of the Achilles heel, severing his feet along with the tendons of each. If he ever walked again it would be with a distinct limp; his days being a soldier were definitely over.

All the while the man thrashed and cursed on the ground, Aaron slowly dressed in the man's clothing and armor trying to resemble the man as closely as possible. When he was clothed and satisfied of his appearance, he placed upon his head the officer's battle helmet. He looked down on the ground at the now helpless man, pulled out the gag and since he would not be running anywhere soon, he cut his restraining cords then asked, "Well, how do I look?"

"Like a dead man," the officer whispered between gritted teeth.

"We shall see."

As the night began to converge upon the jungle, nocturnal creatures crawled and flew about; their night sounds alerted Aaron of the close of another day. He waited around until full dark had covered the land then mounted the Lieutenant's horse and carefully made his way down the side of the mountain towards the camp fires below.

The art of stealth, as Aaron had learned over time, was about becoming whatever he needed to be. The more he got into the role, the more convincing the guise and the easier the engagement became. He had often wondered how it was that he had become so successful at this art. It had finally occurred to him that it was because he enjoyed it so much; no one said a dirty job had to be despised.

His current role required that he be a scout returning from his patrol and reporting to his commander. He reminded himself he had a reason to be there so he could act with confidence and appear bold as he stated his objectives should he be detained or questioned. Thus he rode with purpose through the encampment directly to the tent of the enemy Field General and, of course, there were two armed guards posted in front of the entrance and several more surrounding it. After dismounting his horse, he walked with deliberate strides up to the tent and held out a parchment so that both men could clearly see he held something of importance, though, in reality it was hardly more than a prop being used for the role he was playing.

"I have an important dispatch for the commander's eyes only. Please let me pass."

At this point the plan required that he adapt very quickly to the fluid situation. If the guards demanded to see what he had then he would react one way; if they appeared to let him pass, then another, but regardless, one way or another he was getting into the tent. The guards took notice of what appeared to be a dispatch and also made note of the insignia of an officer. They glanced at one another and the larger of the two parted the flap and allowed Aaron entrance.

Once inside, he saw that two men were standing over a table examining what appeared to be a field map. This was even better than he would have imagined; instead of dispatching just the General, he would also have a sub commander under his knife. The General had been expecting an intelligence report from the front lines, and seeing Aaron enter the tent then noting the parchment in hand, concluded that he had brought the latest assessment of the enemy's strength.

"Lieutenant, I hope you have brought us news of the military capabilities of the city of Nahor and its possible disposition in the field."

The sub-commander joked, "We would not want to wake up some morning next week and discover General Manasseh had crept up on us in the night and had decided to join us for breakfast."

Both men laughed at his wit. Aaron, now wholly into the role, decided to return the moment of levity with an indulgent smile and comment.

"Of course, Sir, I would rather it be us outside of his tent one morning."

By now he had positioned himself in front of the two smiling men, and after handing the general the parchment, the officer turned to his second-in-command and they both began to peruse the dispatch. While they were both occupied, Aaron pulled two daggers from his belt and thrust each upwards into the jaws of the two officers where they stood and he buried both blades up to the hilts. To reduce the noise, Aaron caught them both slightly as they toppled forward, but they were dead by the time they hit the ground, their life's blood spilling out across their now useless breast plates. He removed the daggers, and looking around the room, he discovered a wash towel and cleaned the blood off his hands and arms, as well as any which had spattered over his armor.

A few minutes later, he quickly exited the tent, and once outside, turned to the two guards and announced, "The General wishes to be alone with his sub-commander for the rest of the evening. He has left strict orders that they are not to be disturbed by anyone until he says otherwise."

As the General had been expecting news of the upcoming engagement, neither of them was surprised at the orders. "Of course, Sir," they both replied.

Without rushing his movements, Aaron mounted his horse and with a practiced calm asked the men, "I have not eaten all day; where is the officer's mess tent located?"

The men both smiled and directed him to a location on the other side of the encampment. He smiled and saluted them and they, in turn, returned his salute. He rode slowly in the direction they had indicated and once outside the camp, he turned to the west and began a head-long dash towards the camp of General Manasseh.

It was three long days of hard riding, but he finally entered the tent of the General, and now hungry and desperate to return back to Nahor, he made his report. Within the day, the General had disengaged his attack on the larger army of Chalco and pulled his army back toward the east. He left a rear-guard contingent to slow down the other army in case they decided to give chase.

If it had not been so tragic, if would have been laughable. By the time Aaron had reached the army of Manasseh, the great siege from the Army of the Kingdom of Chalco had died still-born. The morning after Aaron had made good his escape, the bodies of the Field General and his sub-commander were both found lounging in field chairs in a corner of the tent where he had left them, mostly bled out and quite dead. Before the day was out a half dozen field captains were all vainly attempting to wrest control over the Southern Army from Chalco and all the commanders refused to recognize the authority of the other. After a few hours of harangues and threats, the situation finally escalated to open combat in the encampment when one battalion commander and his men attacked the others and then the whole camp was engulfed in its own private civil war.

Before it was over, Jacob in the city of Nahor had received word of enemy insurrections and his four hundred men left Nahor and attacked what remained of the Southern Army still encamped nearby. In the ensuing confusion, he sent the remnants scurrying back to the south into the land of Chalco. There they met up eventually with the now depleted army which had engaged Manasseh in the west. A week later, General Manasseh and the Northern Army re-entered the Kingdom of Nahor and relieved Jacob and his company, allowing them a well-deserved rest.

King Shiz of the Southern Kingdom of Chalco was so angry he was shaking as though with palsy. Before him stood two of his surviving field captains, all that was left of any authority which existed of his once proud Army of the South.

"Fools! I should have you both put to death, but then I would have no one left with any command experience in the field. Please explain how this debacle could have happened."

Before either of them could interject a word in their defense, the king's chief adviser, Eber, hurried into the room. "Sire, the Master Mahan is here and demands an immediate audience. What should I tell him?"

"Can he be stalled for time while I interrogate these idiots?"

"Sire, he insists on seeing you immediately. I already tried a delay, but he knows of the defeat at Nahor already and he is quite put out as you can imagine."

Shiz put a hand over his eyes and shook his head in quiet desperation. With eyes still closed in misery, he muttered, "Well, send him in. Don't keep him waiting."

The Master Mahan, a direct descendant of Sidon who called himself Sidon as were all his predecessors before him, was angry and his deliberate stride into the audience room reflected his current state of mind. With mounting fury over this lost opportunity to bring down the government of Nahor, he was in no mood to brook any feeble defense or excuses for failure. He began a harangue of King Shiz and his advisers which would last the better part of the next half hour.

He shouted, "For your incompetence, I should have everyone one of you beheaded."

"Sidon, I am just as appalled as you over this setback, though I assure you it is only temporary." The ruler was trying frantically to buy some time and convince the man that taking his head would only make matters worse, though he wondered privately just how much worse it could be.

"Shiz, do not try my patience by trying to weasel out of this failure. I told you why I needed that territory under my control and you assured me you were the one to deliver it to me. And now it looks like I am going to have to go farther afield and bring my own Army into play." Save for Nahor, the small enclave to the northeast, Sidon was the undisputed lord of the realm which encompassed all lands to the north up to the Great River and South to the narrow neck of land which separated his territory from the great un-known land southward.

"Sidon, I regret that my field captains had a falling out and these two standing before us are all that remain of those who commanded my once great army."

Sidon turned his attention to the two men, now quaking before the man who could give life or take it on a whim. Tartan was no fool and he and the other captain, Paphos, had worked out an explanation beforehand, which though not completely the truth, was nonetheless possible. At least, there were very few still alive who were willing to come forth and contest it.

"Captains Tartan and Paphos, we are all waiting on some explanation for what happened at Nahor."

Tartan explained, "It all started when we discovered General Nabal and Sub-Commander Janeel dead in the General's tent. They had both been stabbed in the throat by an unknown assailant during the night."

At this point, Tartan had been interrupted by Sidon. "Were there no guards to prevent this assault from happening? Surely they performed some function."

Paphos spoke up and said, "Sire, they were part of my company and from what I was able to ascertain the next morning they reported allowing access to a messenger the previous evening who claimed he had an important dis-patch for the two officers. He was also an officer so the guards allowed him entrance."

Sidon's interrogation was rapid. If he could, he intended to catch them in a lie then pressure them into revealing the whole truth.

"You lie! They never would have allowed access to the tent without veri-fying the man's story or notifying the General first."

Tartan answered, "Excellency, the General was expecting a dispatch from the field and he had what appeared to be a parchment communiqué. Knowing the general would not want to be delayed getting this needed infor-mation, they allowed him immediate entrance."

"What were the guards doing while their commanders were being butch-ered in their tent? Buggering one another in the bushes?"

"Sire, they overheard the General inside talking with the messenger then a few minutes later he exited the tent then gave the guards instructions that the General did not want to be disturbed for the remainder of the night. The next morning, after discovering the two men dead, we came to the conclusion that the unknown officer had to have been the murderer as he was the only visitor that night."

"I should very much like to question these guards myself."

Paphos glanced over to Tartan and said, "Regrettably, Excellency, those two guards are dead; they were killed while helping us put down the insurrection later that day."

"How convenient."

It was obvious the details of this assassination, and possibly the truth, were going to be absent from the day's discussion. He looked sternly back to Tartan and said, "Explain what happened in the camp later that day."

Tartan knew he would have to be careful not to implicate himself and Paphos, so taking a deep breath began his explanation. "The next morning all the company captains reported to the General's tent for the morning briefing, and not getting any responses from our entreaties outside the tent, we began to be concerned. We entered uninvited and therein we discovered the bodies of both men. The guards were questioned, of course, but we learned no more than what I have already reported."

"Yes, yes. Go on. I am most anxious to hear how this discussion among professional soldiers ended up in such a colossal failure to communicate!"

Tartan, though frightened by Sidon's anger, continued his report. "A discussion as to who would lead the Army and the attack on the city of Nahor then proceeded to occupy our time the rest of the morning. Finally, after a heated debate it was clear that only two of us, myself and Captain Paphos, would support a temporary field commander of the Army, but there was no agreement on who that would be or how that would be determined. When it became obvious that the other four captains would not even be willing to cast lots for the temporary command, Captain Paphos and I withdrew from the tent while the others continued the argument."

"Why did you two not stay and attempt to regain some semblance of control back to the command structure?"

"The meeting had erupted into such a state of disorder that we left to work out some form of workable strategy between us on our own. We were in the process of deciding upon a compromise when the arguments within the tent spilled out onto the rest of camp. After that, chaos and pandemonium ran amok within the army."

Sidon interrupted, "So, of the six company commanders, only you and Paphos were in favor of some form of temporary command?"

"Yes, Sire, those were the conditions. As the altercation spilled out into the rest of the camp, the results were that each captain took his company and attempted to enlist the support of the lieutenants from the other groups."

"What? You are telling me that not one professional soldier in the army was capable of wresting temporary command without bloodshed?"

Paphos interjected, "Sire, the rivalries among the commanders ran deeply. It was clear that any professional decorum had turned to dust once old animosities and accusations came to the forefront."

"Old animosities? Explain yourself, Paphos!"

"Sire, you have to understand that these hard feelings go back years. One commander had even had trifling affairs with the wives of two other commanders. It was not surprising that the conflict was inevitable."

Sidon was appalled. He looked angrily back over to King Shiz who was quaking at this new revelation. "Shiz, I suppose you knew nothing about these sordid details before these men received field commissions?"

"Of course not, Lord."

Sidon's disbelief turned quickly to disgust. He turned his attention back to Tartan and said, "Well, go on!"

"Sire, these defections among the men had disastrous results which caused the camp to break up into different loyalties and allegiances. One group accused the others of treason and fomenting an insurrection. By the end of the day, there was open warfare and many lay dead, the rest having fled the scene."

"How did the garrison commander at Nahor get wind of all this?"

"I suspect they had sent spies among us. Somehow this insurrection must have come to the attention of the small contingent defending the city of Nahor and while we were fighting among ourselves, they fell upon us and finished the slaughter. Captain Paphos and I assembled what was left of our men and retreated south. Eventually, we met up with what was left of our army that had been engaged with General Manasseh, but they were in no condition to give a serious fight to Nahor once Manasseh had returned home. Moreover, their own general had been killed and his sub-commander severely wounded during the engagement with Manasseh and only a company commander was in nominal control."

Sidon shook his head in disgust and looked balefully over at the other Captain. "Is that your story, too?"

"Yes, Sire, and that is the truth."

"I seriously doubt that, but it appears that we will have to accept that for now, but I will be interrogating your lieutenants and if I feel that their stories are seriously out of line with yours, I can assure you both there will be executions. For now, you two are reduced in rank and you and your companies will be folded into my own Army. The next attack on Nahor will have you and your soldiers in the front lines taking the worst of the fight. You are both dismissed. Now get out of my sight before I change my mind."

"Yes, Sire!" came the response. On the way out of the audience room, they glanced at one another, relieved they were leaving with their heads intact.

Sidon now turned his attention back to his quaking advisers and the king. "You blithering fools! I told you why you were to take that city and kingdom and bring them all under the control of the Clan peacefully. You were there to intimidate them and force them into a conditional surrender. We missed our chance six months earlier when they recovered Libnah and now it appears that you have failed me yet again."

Shiz replied, "Excellency, the Army of Nahor proved to be more formidable that we had expected. Those cowardly assassination tactics could not have been anticipated."

"Do you think I fear one whit about that little piss-ant country? My army could have taken it any time, but I did not want that crazy prophet Manti to panic and realize I was behind the invasion. Those incursions into that region had to appear as though it was a civil war between rival kingdoms, yours and theirs, not an invasion by the Clan. My instructions were for you to attack the nation, sue for at least a conditional surrender and confiscate the records, then bring Manti to me for further questioning."

Shiz ventured a question, but was afraid he may have overstepped his position. "Sire, what does he have that would cause the Clan to fear? Surely we are more powerful that some raving old man."

"Fear is not the issue! Your job is to do what I tell you to do! I have to know where he has stashed all the remaining records of our people and have them destroyed. Those records and that man stand between me and complete control over the realm. Now it appears I will have to initiate the next invasion myself as it is evident you are incapable of doing it on my behalf."

"Sire, is there anything I can do to restore your faith in me?"

"There is only one thing left to do. I will use your kingdom as a staging ground for the next invasion which my own army will prosecute. I will fold what is left of your pathetic military forces into my own and, hopefully, I will not be blamed for this debacle and our future invasion in that old man's records."

Shiz was desperately playing for time in the hope Sidon would spare him his control over Chalco. He had a bad feeling that very little would be left of his kingdom if Sidon his way. "Sidon, when can we expect the next invasion?"

"It will take time to plan the next one, but I assure you that if I am the one to prosecute it, there will be no follow-up invasion. It will be the last one. In the meantime, Eber, you will come with me and between us we will attempt to get the records without destroying everything in Chalco and Nahor in the bargain. There is a plan I have been working on that may yield us what we want with minimal effort."

Eber had been an adviser to the court of King Shiz for many years now and realized that if Sidon was openly taking control of military matters then Sidon's strategy for Nahor had taken on a different direction. "Very well, Sire. As always I value your counsel." He straight way departed out of the room with the Master Mahan of the Clan.

King Shiz turned to his own advisers and took his fear and anger out on them. "We were all lucky this time, but Sidon will accept no further failures. Whatever happens to me, the same will befall you. I suggest you all think about that before you attempt to give me any more witless, pathetic counsel."

CHAPTER 3

NEGOTIATIONS

Eber sat uncomfortably before King Gilead, his son Libnah and their court advisers, along with Manti the Prophet. Aside from King Shiz of Chalco, his court and Sidon, and of course the Inner Clan of Advisers, no one else in the realm was supposed to be aware that he represented the Clan of the Scar. Yet, he had the impression that their holy man, Manti, was aware of whom he truly represented and it was not Chalco. Sidon had made it very clear that he was to broker a peaceful negotiation which included access to the records of Manti. In return, Chalco would cease the military hostilities and incursions and abide with a treaty of peace. It all sounded simple, but Eber sensed that the rulers and people of Nahor might be unwilling to give up the records without a fight.

The discussions had proceeded well enough; both sides seemed amenable for a lasting peace and the talks had progressed to the point of addressing the specifics. King Gilead pointed out, "Eber, our two nations can live in peace despite our social and religious differences. So long as we both can agree to stay within our borders, there should be no reason why we cannot coexist."

"King Gilead, of course you are quite right, but to ensure that hostilities remain a thing of the past, we should give consideration to redrawing our borders to minimize contact until we have given this peace an opportunity to become part of our cultures."

"Please explain what you have in mind, Eber," replied Libnah.

"To minimize future misunderstandings, we propose to establish a buffer or free zone between our two territories along your western and southern borders."

King Gilead was concerned over what he was now hearing. "Why would such a zone be necessary?"

"There are several ancient sites which we both claim as holy, two in particular which we consider sacred above all others, El Opeño to your west and Tula to your south. Both are located within this proposed zone and we would request access to both as our religious customs dictate periodic pilgrimages are made to those locations in honor of our gods."

"We, too, have similar religious and social needs, thus we would have to share the sites, particularly the El Opeño site. Tula, however, though now deserted was more of an economic center so I do not see how that could possibly interest your people for a religious pilgrimage."

The negotiation at this point was critical. Sidon had informed Eber that the records were likely at either El Opeño or Tula, thus both had to be secured for the Clan. How he had acquired this information, Eber was unaware, but knowing the Clan, it had entailed either extortion or murder, possibly both.

"I do not pretend to understand the depth of religious fervor, but I have been assured that both sites represent religious significance for my people. As you know, this disputed land has been a source of our unrest for many years now."

"Eber, the only thing I know," countered Gilead, "is that our territory has been repeatedly under attack for many years and if you say that it has been over religious differences, then it is news to me. What I do know is that your king wants something, but I do not think it is religious in nature."

"Our two peoples have a long history of differences and our religion should be the first issue to be addressed. Our gods are not yours and yours are not ours, and my proposal makes it possible for us to share both sites and any others within this zone and still maintain the peace."

"As simple as all that?" Libnah scoffed.

"What is the alternative: more fighting and more dying?"

"You have a point," Libnah replied reluctantly.

"Of course. It is after all the only logical solution to our problem. We, too, are weary of war and death and it is time we all got back to living."

Eber could tell both King Gilead and Libnah were in favor of a lasting peace at any cost, even if it meant surrendering dominion over those two sites, including all the disputed land encompassing those areas. Only one last bit of negotiation remained and now that the bait was set, he hoped these fish would bite.

Gilead was reflective for a moment, but concluded, "Your proposal has merit, but what else did you have in mind?"

"Really a trifling thing and when you consider that lasting peace hangs in the balance, it should be a relatively small matter to concede."

"Go on," replied the king.

"We know you are a record-keeping people and we, too, are also interested in our past. Since we share a common language and history, would you be willing to share these records with us that we might review them for our personal edification and education?"

"No." It came from a voice at the other end of the negotiation table.

Gilead turned reluctantly toward the sound and knew, of course, to whom the voice belonged. It was the Prophet. "Manti, please explain. Their offer appears genuine and their interest seems benign. We are all weary of war so why not share the records we have?"

"They have no more intention of honoring a peace treaty than they do in reviewing our records for their education." Manti turned his attention back to the adviser and asked, "Eber, who are you truly representing here today, King Shiz of Chalco or Sidon, the Master Mahan of the Clan?"

Eber was appalled that Manti had seen so clearly through his deception, but Sidon had made it clear that he wanted those concessions from Gilead. With an effort, he attempted to appear confused at the question. "Sorry, come again? Who?"

Gilead and Libnah were equally perplexed over Manti's assertions. "Manti, we have never provoked Sidon or his society. Why should they be involved in all this?" asked Gilead.

Manti turned back to the king and replied, "Is it not obvious? They not only want access to the records which I have kept but also those that have been maintained for centuries in our sanctuaries and temples."

"And what is so wrong with that, Holy Man?" demanded Eber.

"Their intent is not to be edified by the contents of our history and records but to destroy them and all mention of the activities of the Clan of the Scar."

Libnah had never heard of this matter before. He looked quickly to his father but Gilead was busily averting his eyes. "The Clan of the Scar? Sidon? Who are these people? Father, what is all this affair?"

Manti gazed over to Gilead and intoned, "Either you tell him or I will. One day he will be king and he is going to know sooner or later in any event."

Gilead shook his head miserably and replied, "My Son, the Clan of the Scar is the real power behind the realm; nothing happens of any consequence without their approval. The kings, including Shiz, are little more than marionettes dangling upon strings. Sooner or later it was inevitable that our kingdom would come under attack. If Manti is correct then they want our records because of the damning comments regarding their nefarious society."

Manti further pointed out, "I would not be at all surprised if this continuous civil war in which we have been engaged for decades with Chalco is not connected to their efforts to obtain the records. This negotiation is little more than a smokescreen for the real reasons. Up until now, I still had held out hope that this war was just between Chalco and Nahor squabbling over disputed territory; now I know differently." Manti turned his gaze back to Eber and declared, "Eber, your work here is finished."

Eber had listened to the dialogue with mounting concern and when it finally became obvious that Manti had subverted the peace process, he glowered at the men seated before him and demanded, "You will turn over the records and you will tell me where the rest have been hidden. Moreover, you will surrender Manti to our interrogators or Sidon will destroy your entire kingdom. Those are his exact words and I have been authorized to declare them."

Gilead was inclined to sue for a peace at any price, but it was obvious that Manti would not accommodate their terms willingly. To save his nation, he must give them Manti and the records; there was no alternative. He turned to his son, Libnah, and murmured, "We are trapped and I see no other way out of this dilemma. If Sidon is behind this, he will eventually take whatever he wants and the destruction and death he will cause will hardly matter a whit to him."

"Father, what are you suggesting?"

Gilead looked over to his advisers and each nodded their heads in agreement. They, too, had all come to the same conclusion. "We must surrender Manti and the records."

Libnah sat stunned by this father's words. "Can we not continue the fight? Surely they will tire of this madness eventually." Libnah glared at Eber, angrier than he had ever been. He had not forgotten his imprisonment at the hands of King Shiz of Chalco.

Eber pointed out, "Once Sidon has decided, he will not retract his words or his resolve. As your father has so astutely pointed out, King Shiz and the other kings are his hand puppets. They will do his will and unleash their armies upon you."

Libnah turned to Manti and asked, "What is the significance of these records to Sidon and The Clan?"

"The records stand as an earthly testimony against Sidon and his murderous society. Sidon believes, even as do I that without the damning witness of our writings, the full weight of justice will pass him by. I assure you, he is highly motivated to destroy them and anything that gets in his way of attaining that goal."

Eber declared, now growing impatient, "Sidon has shown as much restraint as he has been willing to extend you. Until now, these incursions into your lands have been half-measures designed to pressure you into surrendering your records. Since you have continued to resist, he has been left with this ultimatum: you will agree to his demands or your nation will be annihilated."

Gilead turned his attention back to the prophet and said, "Manti, what is your response to this?" Of course, the king knew what his answer would be, but he had to allow the man a chance to surrender the records before he was forced to make the hardest decision he would ever make.

Manti was quiet for a moment, but it was not fear etched upon his face, but anger. "Eber my answer is: Sidon will never have the records while I draw breath. I will not divulge their whereabouts."

The king was also angry, but weary from so many sleepless nights and he knew there were many more yet to come. He glanced behind him and shouted, "Guards, remove Manti and place him in the dungeon until I can decide how best to deal with him."

Libnah began to protest, but King Gilead held up a hand and shook his head to indicate no further talk in the presence of Eber. Apparently, he wanted to continue the discussion in private.

While the guards were escorting Manti out of the chamber room, Eber nodded his head in agreement, but commented, "Gilead, you will have Manti placed in my custody and ready to be transported back to Chalco as soon as possible. My master, Sidon, will brook no further delays in this matter. I will be leaving tomorrow morning with him in chains." Eber arose and walked toward the door, all the while a look of triumph on his face. Before exiting the room, he turned and intoned, "Do not disappoint me."

That night, Manti was brought again before the king, but this time it would be a closed session. Neither Libnah nor the advisers were present, only Manti, he and Eber. The final decision had been made. King Gilead was weary of the incessant attacks upon his kingdom and had decided that the lives of his people were more important than the recordings and ravings of an old man. He had asked Eber to be present so that regardless of how things turned out, Sidon would know of his sincerity.

"Manti, will you reconsider your position in this matter and turn over the records?"

"I have already given you my answer and it has not changed."

"Then you force me to choose between the life of one man and the lives of many."

"It is not that simple."

"What do you mean?"

"Has it ever occurred to you that the only reason our country has never been overrun is because we have valued our freedoms and have protected the records?"

This is getting us nowhere, thought the king impatiently. "We have never been overrun because of our army and our superior field commanders."

"Wrong. I am surprised that you have never made the connection. The Creator preserves us to fulfill a purpose. When you have removed that purpose then we have become no better than our enemies."

"So, if I give you up to Sidon, we lose the protection of the Creator? You think you are that important?"

"I will not divulge the whereabouts of the records, no matter what Sidon does to me. Then he will come for you again and the next time you will be on your own."

Gilead looked over to Eber who appeared both impatient and bored. "Manti, this discussion is pointless. You are not making any sense and we have no idea what you are talking about. My son and I, along with my advisers, have come to the conclusion that you are an expendable liability to our kingdom. You will accompany Eber and his retinue in the morning back to Chalco. From this moment forward, you are hereby banished from our land and if you are seen again, you will be put to death."

Manti reluctantly declared, "King Gilead, from this point forward, you will taste of nothing else except defeat."

King Gilead, now impatient with the line of talk, shouted, "Guards, take this man back to the dungeon."

The next morning when the guards went in to collect Manti for travel, his cell was empty and no trace could be found of him anywhere. Eber's final words were a threat: "Either find him and turn him over to Sidon or face an all-out invasion."

CHAPTER 4

THE FINAL BATTLE

The following year, General Manasseh, now desperate for every experienced man in the kingdom to serve his country, had enlisted the help of Aaron to help him convince his father to return to the war.

"Jacob," began the General, "the war is going badly for us and we need every capable man in the field."

"Manasseh, as you know, neither side is negotiating nor taking hostages. Our freedoms have been suspended and our own citizens are being forcefully conscripted into this conflict. Those who have refused to serve have either fled to the north or have been executed."

"Jacob, if we don't destroy them, they will exterminate us to the last man, woman and child."

Jacob had reached the point in which persuasion had ceased to reach him. With disgust he replied, "Manasseh, this conflict is pointless. Can you even remember why this bloody war began?"

"No, Jacob, I can't and as God is my witness, it no longer matters. The reasons are immaterial and no one is either talking about surrender or a cease fire. This is a war to end all wars. It is either them or us and I would prefer that it be us. Do I have your support?"

"General, look at my leg! The last campaign robbed me of my freedom to move about and now you would have me take a crutch into battle? No, you ask far too much!" Jacob was remembering that campaign and the unbidden details came rushing back to haunt him now even as they did much of his sleep:

The forced march westward had taken Jacob and his men steadily into a different climate zone: the jungle canopy was dense with a myriad of flora and the tropical breeze off the western ocean was muggy, gravid with moisture. Its proximity, however, alerted them that they were nearing the enemy strongholds. The closer Jacob and his men moved toward the attack zone the more signs of combat and its horrific aftermath appeared. As the great jungle had spread out before them, bodies were strewn about where the men had been ambushed from above and below. Clouds of flies hovered over bloated corpses of those who had been killed or wounded then stripped of their combat body armor and left to die slowly of thirst and exposure.

None of this was a new sight for the men under Jacob's command for they had seen much of it before on many fields of battle. What they viewed next was something far different and unexpected, however, and once they experienced it they would remain forever traumatized. Along the western edge of their territory, the jungle eventually gave way to a large clearing where a small city had been built long ago at the foot of verdant surrounding mountains. A large enemy recon and scouting party had passed through the area a few days earlier and had left scarcely anything alive, including the animals. As they approached the altars of the city temple, the decapitated bodies of women and children could be seen lying below and it was clear that, one by one, they had been taken to the altar and beheaded, their bodies then tossed irreverently below to become entangled with those already on the ground. For the enemy, this was an offering to their gods in propitiation for their lost loved ones and as a token of their bravery in battle. For Jacob and his men, it was blasphemous, a scene hideously beyond imagination and an affront to the true God of their Fathers, the Creator. Realizing their loved ones left behind in Nahor could meet a similar fate, the men reacted with wild cries of anger and a call for vengeance.

Jacob, a seasoned veteran, knew that this scene of carnage signaled a change in field strategy. The enemy had escalated the level of its ferocity and now it would be nearly impossible to restrain his own men from resorting to the same level of bestiality. He quickly called his lieutenants together and commanded them to sort out the men and move them farther west skirting away from the city, and though many of the men wanted to remain and bury the bodies, there was insufficient time if they wanted to get ahead of the quickly approaching army.

Jacob's battalion had reached the area a day before the oncoming army from the south and this had allowed them the much needed time for rest and preparation. The plan succeeded, perhaps too well; Jacob's men fought as though possessed. The enemy was caught unawares by Jacob's flanking maneuver and as the battle proceeded, the southern army was driven steadily eastward under an onslaught of obsidian tipped spears and arrows. As the dead piled up, Jacob's men insisted on collecting trophies of their kill and he was unable to dissuade them otherwise. His men left a bloody path of ear-less and nose-less faces as they pushed the enemy army inexorably eastward until they met the main army under General Manasseh.

Jacob was sickened by the carnage that followed. The enemy army was caught in a pincer between two determined forces. Now surrounded and outflanked, Sidon's army desperately turned on their pursuers, but were hacked to pieces by the main army. The enemy, realizing they were outmaneuvered and now outnumbered, threw down their weapons in surrender, and knowing of his men's thirst for vengeance, Jacob made every effort to dissuade them from continuing the fight, but was unable to restrain them while his men continued the slaughter. General Manasseh's main army, also weary of the enemy's constant incursions and refusal to abide a total cease fire, turned on them as well. The General had decided to end this latest incursion without captives; every man was hewn down and mutilated then tossed into a nearby lake.

After the massacre, Jacob resigned his commission. Notwithstanding General Manasseh's pleas for his support, he rejected all his requests to return. During the last battle he had been wounded in the leg which rendered him incapable of any further field campaigns, though in reality, the aggression had turned into a war of genocide and he wanted no part of it. He had refused any further service and the General was unable to convince him to serve even on his staff.

The General looked over to Aaron for support, but knew that father and son had grown distant the past year, their conversations strained. Jacob would not talk about the incident, but Aaron knew it had something to do with the last campaign that had taken him westward with his men. The bitterness ran very deeply and each effort Aaron attempted to discuss the matter evoked an argument. During the last meeting, Jacob had asked him to desert from the army altogether before he lost his soul to the corrupting influence of war.

"Father, with you in the field, at least on staff, we have a greater chance of victory. The men will follow your example and will take heed of your counsel."

"Aaron, will you renounce this war and turn your back on it before it is too late?"

"No, father, I cannot. You have raised me too well to reject my country in its time of need. The enemy is relentless and will never stop until we have rejected our freedoms and beliefs."

With resignation Jacob quietly submitted, "Do with me as you will. It is all over for us, anyway. To save our nation, we must be reduced to the same level of our enemies. What kind of victory would it be if this is to be the cost?"

Manasseh rubbed a tired hand across his face and shook his head to clear his mind. He was also tired of the constant stress and conflict of open combat. His reply reflected his own lack of optimism.

"Any victory is better than none at all; from this point forward, our defeat will signal our death. We are nearly out of time and options."

In retrospect, Aaron reflected, his father had been right. This was a war of continual attrition and no one was spared on either side. Invariably, when one army was victorious, they sought out the civilian populations and began a slaughter until they were driven away by the opposing army. At the time, being in the midst of genocide, he never wondered at the reasons why the war was being waged in that fashion. It had become the only type of war he would ever remember and he simply had no frame of reference to compare it with the way wars should be prosecuted. He had been told that there was no longer any alternative: it was either them or us. When it came to a mission, the General simply pointed him in the enemy's direction and Aaron performed flawlessly.

Moreover, reports were coming back that the enemy, when a city was taken, would raid the learning centers and destroy every record that could be found. To Aaron, it was hard to understand the sense of it all. It was almost as if the records were the justification for the attacks.

After so many years of the bloodletting, since Sidon had taken over the reins of absolute command of all armies of the South, that which occurred that last year would never be known to the world at large. Sidon had decided that since there was no negotiated way to subjugate the people of Nahor and obtain the records of Manti, only complete annihilation of the enemy, their learning centers and temples would bring him what he wanted. Finally, there were very few population centers remaining; the populace had either been murdered to the last person either because they had been too slow to flee or they had managed to escape to the far north or slipped through the lines south past the narrow neck of land. What remained on both sides, including men, women and children had formed two great armies, Nahor in the north and Chalco of the south, which had been augmented by Sidon's personal army.

Both armies squared off in a large open valley a few days travel east of what is now Tula in Central Mexico. Both sides had access to the nearby obsidian mines to replace damaged daggers, clubs, arrows, and spear points. The rules of engagement were simple: there would be no peace treaty, no negotiated truce nor even a temporary cease-fire. Battle would be waged until the one side was completely vanquished to the last man, woman and child. No army would leave the valley unless victorious.

The first day of battle continued from daybreak until dusk. Then, each side rested with weapons ready for the following day then the battle continued until dusk the next day. Thus it went daily until only a few remained. Aaron met with the General in his tent on the eve before the last day of battle.

"General, only a few of our forces remain. What is your order?"

As Aaron awaited the General's reply, he became aware of several bodies lying about the tent. An elderly man was the only non-military man inside and his presence in the corner of the tent on the ground caught Aaron's eye.

He also appeared to be dead, but stirred slightly when he heard the discussion between the two men.

"General, is this the man?" the old man inquired tiredly.

Manasseh was weary from lack of sleep and his voice lacked hope. He glanced in the old man's direction and replied, "It is, Manti. Now would be a good time to deliver your message. After tomorrow morning, nothing and no one will remain." He motioned for Aaron to step over to the elderly man prone on the ground.

Aaron slowly made his way across the tent filled with the wounded and soon to be dead officers of what was left of Manasseh's personal guard. He knelt down to get a better look and to better hear the man in the tattered, blood-spattered robe.

"I am Aaron. Do I know you?"

Manti's reply was faint, but understandable. He had received a wound a few days earlier that had festered. Now a raging fever could be detected on his brow and neck while agony was etched across his exhausted face.

"I have little time left so I will make this brief. I am in the way of knowing that you will survive our final stand but you must leave soon to avoid the conflict."

"Leave? I cannot desert my post, old man."

"Aaron, listen to the man," ordered the General.

Manti continued, "Once you escape, on the road, a messenger will visit you with a mission to finish an important work for our people. The world must know what has happened to us and only you can insure that will occur."

"And who is the messenger I am supposed to meet?"

The old man, with his last breath, whispered, "Go to Tula and protect the records." Manti blinked twice then the light began to fade from his eyes, and before closing they seemed to stare off to a distant point in space.

Aaron slowly stood and walked back over to the General. He didn't know what to make of the old man's final message or how it could possibly apply to him. "General, who was that man? His ravings made no sense."

"He was a holy man with a message and he insisted that you would arrive and that you were to leave as soon as his message was delivered. That is as much as I know." He shook his head dejectedly and seemed to dismiss any further conversation of Manti.

"General, what are your orders? Shall I lead the last attack?"

"My last order is for you to flee this valley of death and report to your father at his home. I dismissed him before this last campaign began and ordered him to protect your mother and sisters."

"But General, what of the battle on the morrow?"

"It is lost. There will be no victory for either side. Our nation, our citizens, our great cities are gone. No one can claim victory and only the carrion eaters will benefit."

"Captured officers of the Army of Chalco have rumored that Chalco only wants our records. Surely our leaders can negotiate a truce or even a surrender. Can't they simply give our enemies what they want?"

"King Gilead is dead along with his son, Libnah. There is no one in control still alive to negotiate anything. No one can turn off the murder. Whatever it is that King Shiz has wanted, there will be very little left for him to inherit."

"Is there nothing more to be done?"

The General's last words were desperately final. "No, nothing. There is only death here." The General gathered the last of his strength and said, "Tell your father I am sorry, he was right about this war; there was no point to any of it. I hope he is still alive to receive my message and the return of his son."

Aaron quietly slipped away early the next morning. As he had been taught, he moved with stealth and evasion down the mountain plateau towards the northwest and his father's home. Having evaded any enemy contact, and while dawn was beginning to break, he reached the last pass through the mountains. He looked back at the carnage spread out below and realized the General had been correct. Only a few would meet in battle that morning and there would be no victors. In retrospect, those who did walk out of the valley that day had only one mission left in mind: the complete annihilation of Aaron's people and the destruction of the records that they had so carefully maintained for over fifteen centuries.

CHAPTER 5

THE VISIT

Since leaving the valley of death behind him, Aaron had kept a difficult pace trying to put as much distance between him and any trackers or hunting parties in the area. Eventually, however, his retreat had taken him back into the northern regions of his homeland. On the third day of his travel, he had reached the farm of his parents, and the homestead, like most others he had observed during this journey, had looked as if a battalion of soldiers had marched through it, and in fact, they had.

His enemies, what remained of them, were swarming about the countryside of his nation in search of any traces of his people, and after putting them to the sword, they burned all possessions to the ground. After a careful inspection of the nearby area, he came upon his parent's decapitated bodies outside their home. Each of his sisters had been violated then mutilated nearly beyond recognition. The sight should have made him angry, even nauseated, but he was weary of battle and the trauma was nearly complete. It was, after all, more of the same that he had already witnessed. As he walked dispiritedly around his home, he realized that he was now one of the few surviving members of his people, but having seen how they had laid ruin to a once proud civilization, he felt no obligation to carry on any of the traditions, save one. After burying his family, he sat under a tree and contemplated what he was to do with the rest of his life.

He had been trained to live off the land, kill or be killed, to win by attrition, but no one had taught him how to be a survivor when there was nothing left to live for. So, he sat and rested and at the end of the day he could scarcely think of one reason why he deserved to live when so many had perished. Though his inner turmoil interfered from any serious thought, he nonetheless began to ponder whether to allow his enemies to capture and torture him to death or simply end it all by throwing himself upon his own sword.

He was thus considering his demise when he saw a man walking up the path to his home from the south. Even at a distance, it was obvious the man was cleanly attired and not some bedraggled, half-starved refugee. Unlike so many others he had seen on the roads the past few days, he seemed to stride with a purpose and a confidence that so many of the glassy-eyed survivors seemed to lack. On closer inspection, as the man approached the tree under which he rested, Aaron's curiosity changed abruptly to wonder. Everyone else was battle weary or traumatized beyond repair. Why was he so different?

The man stopped in front of Aaron and sat down opposite him under the tree. He openly gazed at the war-torn, weary face of abject misery; his smile was compassionate and gently declared, "I am Joseph and you are Aaron. I have been asked to visit you and extend to you a special mission. By now, you must have asked yourself whether there is any further purpose to your life. I can assure you there is. Would you be willing to perform one more service for your people?"

"What people? There is scarcely anyone left of my people either in Nahor or in Chalco."

Joseph, undeterred by the reply, and given the circumstances was hardly surprised by his response. In an attempt to persuade through reason, he continued, "You may find it hard to believe, but even though your people are all but extinct, a small number of survivors are scattered here and there. They will ultimately mingle with other groups of this blessed land and will yet again be a mighty force."

"To what purpose? So they can start the killing up all over again?"

Unperturbed by the reply, Joseph continued, "I have come to offer you a way to find meaning for your loss. The day will arrive when your descendants will need a written record of your long history and civilization to remind them of how to avoid the same pitfalls which led to the downfall of your people. Would you be willing to accept the challenge to abridge a history of your nation for future generations?"

"You would want me? Why?"

"Who better to account the struggles and ultimate act of self-destruction? Moreover, there are those who are responsible for this ruin who will evade accountability unless you record what you have seen and heard."

At the mention of indicting those accountable for this destruction, a spark of interest flitted quickly across his mind. "That might be well worth the effort. But, what makes me so qualified to perform this work?"

"Remember, you have been taught in all the ways of your people, including a written knowledge of the language and you have a cunning and singular skill for survival, and more importantly, you understand commitment. These are all highly admirable qualities for the task I have in mind for you."

"I am exhausted in body and mind and have seen and done things for which I am not proud. I just don't know if I am equal to your high expectations. You should look elsewhere for someone to perform this work."

Joseph attempted one last effort to reach him. "You have been contemplating suicide and I am giving you a reason to live. This work is essential and no one else is more qualified than you to perform it."

Aaron jerked at the mention of taking his own life, and now realizing that this man was in possession of his deepest thoughts, he managed to stammer, "If you know so much about me then how is it you have sought me out when I have no training in this art? How am I to learn, as there are no more teachers left alive to teach me?"

Joseph seemed to recognize that what he had answered was not a dismissal of the responsibility, but more of a plea to understand. He was aware of the look of reluctant acceptance on Aaron's face so he continued, "Are you familiar with Tula? It was, before abandoned, a learning center and it is to there we will walk. Along the way, I will teach and you will listen and ask questions. Would you be willing to accept this task on behalf of your people?"

A glimmer of interest, even curiosity, began to take hold of Aaron as he contemplated these new possibilities. But, he had seen and experienced too much brutality to be convinced anything he could do at this point would make a difference. His reply to Joseph's request was slow, but when his response came it was more oblique than direct. "Just who are you?"

"I am a messenger from our Creator," he declared with a smile.

With a cynical shrug, Aaron replied, "Then I suppose I am the man you have been looking for." Thus, a partnership had been established in which the battle-hardened and weary warrior would be instructed, as had others before him, by the messenger Joseph, in life known as Seth.

CHAPTER 6

AARON, THE RECORDER

That which remains of the ancient city of Tula is located in the southwest of the modern day state of Hidalgo, 75 km north of the current location of Mexico City. Geographically, it is in the Tula River Valley, at the south end of Mesquite Valley in a region that indigenous records called Teotlapan (land of the gods) by the Toltec. This area has an elevation of between 2000 and 2200 meters above sea level (elevation approximately 7,000 ft.), with a semi-arid climate known as the altiplano, or high plains. It has only three continuously flowing rivers and streams, the largest of which is the Tula River; there are also a number of arroyos that flow during the rainy season. The earliest well-defined settlements in the Tula area appear around 400 BCE and Tula was probably settled originally by people of various ethnic backgrounds which may have included the Nonoalcas and the Chichimecas from the south and north respectively. The area probably was under the political control of Teotihuacan in the Epi-classic period (200 BCE – 100CE) according to Teotihuacan designs found on Tula pottery. The area's lime deposits were probably an important source for the plaster used in its construction of that great city to the south.

At that time, Tula was a fertile region near obsidian mines and situated on an important trade route. Its economic base was agriculture and the mining and crafting of obsidian. It appears the craft was practiced by about half of the occupants, along with the working of travertine and ceramics, taking over this function from Teotihuacan. Tula probably did not rule the Toltec empire, but may have ruled a regional state.

Joseph and Aaron had been on the road for almost three days. The climate of the *altiplano*, though semi-arid, did provide occasional rain evidenced by the run-off of the arroyos into the Tula River. It was this vital resource which had made it possible to support the water needs of the weary traveler as well as a small urban population center.

Tula was now an abandoned city which Aaron's people had built centuries earlier. Because of its strategic location and proximity to obsidian mines the city had suffered the aggressions of war, and as a result, in the last few decades of warfare, the inhabitants had fled north to escape the incessant civil turmoil. Moreover, the recent conflicts had left much of the homes burned and the buildings of learning and worship destroyed. Aaron had visited Tula on a number of occasions earlier in his youth, but never since the civil wars had resulted in its abandonment and destruction. It was a little eerie walking through an empty city where once commerce had flourished and its citizens had lived out a social purpose.

As the two approached the central plaza, ahead Aaron observed several architectural designs chiseled in bas relief on the major temple of the city that indicated its dedication to the Creator. Once the two had neared the remains of the temple of worship, they slowed their pace, and though Aaron was unfamiliar with the layout, Joseph seemed to be quite acquainted with it. Once they entered the structure, he moved through the empty rooms without difficulty, scarcely throwing a small echo to indicate a passing. A small library had been constructed inside the synagogue and Joseph went directly to a corner wall and pulled a small switch tucked under an ornately chiseled symbol of the sun.

There was a slight tick signaling the location of a concealed panel and then a hidden door opened slightly, revealing a stairway to the basement. Joseph found a lamp at the door opening, and after locating a small vial of oil that had been placed nearby, he had carefully lit the lamp throwing light before their descent. So as to avoid a fall or any noise that would arouse unwanted attention in the event someone was listening, the two descended quietly down the basement steps. At the base of the stairwell the two entered a spacious room which had been used as a record depository for many generations and in it was stored all the ancient historical records of his people as well as several curious artifacts, including a leather breastplate wherein was placed stones of a unique color and shape.

Once inside, Joseph signaled to a wall stacked high in every direction with records which had been preserved on bronze plates. A table and chair had been placed conveniently in the middle of the room as a work area for recording; writing tools had also been provided nearby to facilitate this process. The records from which the abridgment would be made lay stacked near the recording table and on the table itself laid a stack of unused plates. Upon these the redaction would be written and to bind them all together in a readable fashion, each plate had been laid and fastened together with a metallic binder.

Immediately, Joseph began the process of instructing Aaron regarding all the details of abridging the records before him, including the writing of a preface on a blank plate by way of introduction to the writings to follow. His would be the task of sifting through the stacked plates nearby, reading and studying each for details of the history of the long and bitter struggle of the civilization of his people and recording the relevant information pertaining to its rise and fall.

Aaron looked on with open amazement at the repository. In spite of Joseph's careful and perceptive teachings along the trek to Tula, the true nature and scope of his task never really penetrated his understanding until he stood in the midst of so much history. "How far back into our past do the records extend?"

Joseph gazed over the formidable number of records before them and replied, "From the time that Noah's descendants were commanded to write a history." He also added, "You will discover many compelling points of history of which you neither had knowledge nor access until now."

"How will I know which type of information I am to abridge?"

"You will confine yourself to the historical facts and leave the recording of religious teachings to others; those records before you are of historical value. You are to write exclusively regarding any mention of the Society of Cain, known also as the Brotherhood as well as the Clan of the Scar, its origins, methods and influence upon the civilization of your people."

"I have never heard of such a Society. Who are they?"

"Very few of your people have ever been aware of their existence. They represent a Brotherhood of men committed to the subversion and overthrow of governments and societies which uphold and support the freedoms of Mankind. The founder and father of this society is Cain of ancient days."

Aaron nodded his head in acceptance, though he was still unsure how the Clan fit into the destruction of his people. "Which specific information regarding this society am I to record? There are numerous plates nearby and yet you want all the relevant material to be recorded on just one set of plates, am I correct?"

"That is correct. Where there has been a direct cause of any civic upheaval as a result of this Society, you will note and record it."

"Was this group responsible for the civil war which destroyed nearly all of the people of my land, both in Nahor as well as Chalco?"

"It was. And you must record how this occurred. There are sufficient records in this vault that I have collected for you which relate directly to that civil war instigated by the Clan."

"How does Manti fit into all this? It was he who instructed me to seek you out."

"The most recent and most important of these recordings regarding the Clan were written by Manti before he died and they are located nearby. These must be an integral part of your abridgement."

Aaron scanned the room and noticed a separate stack of records next to the writing table. He walked over to where they were located and asked, "Who wrote these records?"

Joseph responded, "Men with similar missions as you were asked to make recordings during their lifetime. In time, this repository was built as a place to store the records and, as I have mentioned, it is from that group of records that you must write the abridgement."

"Once the abridgement has been completed, then what? Keeping it here would defeat the purpose of exposing the Clan."

"Once your task is finished, you will wrap up the plates you have abridged and place them in a pack." He indicated to a leather satchel in the corner into which the redaction would be placed. "You will then proceed as quickly as possible to a location near the Eastern Ocean to a place of many rivers and streams known as Lamanai."

"Lamanai? I have heard rumors of it, but the area is very remote and it is said the city is difficult to locate. Is there a specific person I should contact to deliver the plates or did you have a hiding place in mind?"

"You will find a remnant of your people living within the settlement and you will be directed to a temple site which has been consecrated for the purpose of burying the records; within that ancient temple you will bury your abridgement." Joseph paused to allow Aaron to grasp this point. When he was satisfied, he continued, "In spite of all your best efforts, there will be those committed to prevent you from reaching your goal. You will be tracked, hunted and harried every step of the way, but it is essential that you deliver the plates and place them within the temple building; only then will they be safe."

Up until now, Aaron had expected that the mission would be without danger. He was unprepared for the warning he had just been given, but he understood now why he had been chosen. "Who will be tracking me and why?"

"You must come to realize the importance of this mission. Your enemies who instigated this civil war, which resulted in so much destruction and bloodshed, will be bent on not only learning the location of this repository in Tula, but to prevent you from delivering the abridged plates to a safe location. It will be in their best interest to prevent you from making a record of those dealings and influence which contributed directly to the downfall of your civilization."

Nodding his understanding he commented, "Then I am to expect seasoned trackers to be on my trail once I leave Tula."

"The Clan has dispatched a group of well-trained hunters and assassins to prevent you from completing your mission and the moment you complete the abridgement and have begun your journey eastward, the records will be in the open and you will be in constant danger. Moreover, you will have to make use of your considerable survival skills to elude capture."

"I should not be surprised then that they have orders to kill me. After the final battle of our people, no one was left alive and anyone who was had been tracked down and murdered."

"Regrettably, you will probably have to kill them for they have been instructed to continue with the hunt until they have brought your head and the records back to the leader of the Clan, a man by the name of Sidon."

A look of disappointment could be read upon Aaron's face. "I had hoped that part of my life was over. Now it appears that it will continue after all."

"No matter how many times you are forced to do it, the taking of a man's life is no easy thing to do, but the mission at hand rescinds any such considerations. It is far better for a few men to die than to allow the records to fall into the wrong hands and be absent as a witness of the atrocities caused by Cain's Society. I regret that I must put it in those terms, but the Creator has so decreed it, so it must be done."

Then Joseph spent the better part of the remainder of the day demonstrating the use of the abridgement tools and acquainting Aaron with the records to be abridged. Near the end of the day, the messenger asked him to accompany him to the exit. Joseph then took him down a long winding underground path that egressed on the other side of the abandoned city then turning toward Aaron, he counseled, "Aaron, you must take care to avoid staying here any longer than three days. The hunters will be on your trail soon so you must be gone and on your way before they arrive. Make your abridgement thorough and I promise that you will make your selections correctly."

"And when my mission is completed, then what?" He had been wondering about this for a few days now and felt the time had come for an answer.

"Our life experiences always lead to that question, but the answer is different for each of us and I cannot pretend to know what will be best for you when that day arrives. But, I will promise you this, that when you complete the mission, you will know what it will be. At the present moment, you are unable to see it, though it has always been there before you."

Aaron was left wondering what the messenger meant by his last comment and the cryptic smile on Joseph's face indicated that he was aware of the confusion. He inwardly shrugged and concluded, for now at least, it was beyond him to understand it.

Aaron decided to ask one more question before the messenger departed. Up until now, he had not considered asking the reason for the destination of Lamanai other than as a place to deposit the abridged records. He concluded that there must be some significance to this far-flung part of the country. He asked, "Joseph, for who are the records intended?"

As he considered an answer, Joseph's eyes sparkled with an inward reflection then confided, "A man, much like you, will retrieve it one day. His name is Jasher. He was promised that such a record would be available to him when the time and opportunity presented itself, so we should not disappoint him, should we?"

The two parted at the exit of the shaft, and before Aaron closed the access door, to his surprise he saw Joseph step into a light and a moment later was gone. His mind played over that singular event, and for the remainder of his life, he would be unable to forget and fully explain it. For now, though, the abridgement of the records would be the first priority, but later the hunt would begin, and as on many previous occasions, he would be the hunted.

CHAPTER 7

THE TRACKERS

After receiving word of his ultimate victory, King Shiz of Chalco had been in a pleasant mood and both his advisers had been quick to congratulate him on a job well done for his part in the final victory over the land of Nahor. What was left of his and Sidon's victorious armies was now mopping up the countryside and dispatching all remaining enemy survivors.

His advisers had been toasting their fortunes when the king's servant entered the audience hall. "Sire, Sidon has arrived with Eber and wishes to enter your presence."

"Excellent. May I know of Sidon's disposition?"

"Sire?"

"We expect him to be in a festive frame of mind. After all, we have just prosecuted a great victory on his behalf. So, how does he appear?"

The servant was reluctant to say, but clearing his throat he formally announced, "Sidon, the Master Mahan has demanded to see you forthwith. His adviser to your court, Eber, accompanies him. If I were to gauge their disposition, I would describe it as being highly agitated."

Shiz had been assured by his own advisers that this scheduled visit would be congratulatory. The news that Sidon's mood might be just the opposite was unexpected. After all, the results on the battlefield had been gratifying, yet something was amiss.

"Send him in and leave word that we are not to be disturbed under any circumstances."

After giving leave to allow audience to the High Priest of the Clan, the king and his two advisers were now guarded and awaited the true meaning of this visit. At the end of the hallway, as the Master Mahan strode into view, he could be heard hurling threats and insults at any and all in his path, his adviser trailing behind and having difficulty keeping the pace. The scar on Sidon's left cheek was livid with the hue of anger and expressed his displeasure at the missed opportunity of the conflict that had taken over a year to plan and execute.

He lost no time getting down to the business at hand. Pointing at Shiz and his advisers, he bellowed, "You blithering fools, you may have won the battle, but you have very likely cost me the war!"

Shiz sputtered an apology but was unsure why he needed one. "Excellency, please explain your displeasure and I will make it right."

"As it is probably too late, I seriously doubt there is anything that can be salvaged! You were told to bring back alive that senile old prophet Manti for questioning. Instead, he was chopped up along with the rest of that stubborn bunch of misguided followers of his." Sidon began pacing and gesticulating his anger.

"Manti, the prophet and recorder?"

"No, Manti the Great God of the Underworld!" he replied with sarcasm. "Of course, Manti the prophet. Who else have I been searching for the past twenty years?"

The king and his advisers had never seen the Master Mahan in such a state of mind. He was usually calm and deliberate, but his anger had created someone far more dangerous than any of them had ever witnessed. They were all in trouble and they knew it to be a fact.

"Now I must assume some other recorder has been recruited to replace him and I have no idea who he is or where he is going. I only know that Manti was seen talking to someone before he expired and that person is the only man who walked upright away from that massacre north of here near Tula. My operatives, once they had entered General Manasseh's tent, had found the old man dead and the survivors too weak to talk."

"But Sire, per your instructions, our men had questioned all of Manasseh's staff officers quite vigorously, but very little information could be gleaned. Most were dead, including Manti, when our men arrived and the rest were severely wounded."

"I told you to have your men secure the tent and wait until my men had arrived so that they could interrogate the prisoners properly. Vigorous torture was not part of your instructions. Instead, your men had beaten out whatever confessions that could be extracted, but hardly anything was learned except that the man I now seek was seen slipping away in the early morning hours on the final day of battle. He may have walked towards the northwest, but your incompetent head-breakers didn't bother to pursue him and now I am in the position of losing the advantage forever."

"But, Sire, how were my men to recognize Manti in the field when so many were fighting?"

"Are you joking? He could barely get around without a cane, much less heft a sword and swing it with any strength. He was an old man with a beard down to his navel! You witless fool. I told you that I needed Manti alive! He was to be captured on sight if engaged on the battlefield; instead he was cut down like everyone else."

Even after Sidon had briefed them on several occasions, King Shiz still had not comprehended the relevance of the records. "Sidon, I am still at a loss for your anger at the death of the old prophet and the need to find the location of his hidden records. If he is dead as well as his followers, then his writings and his memories die with him. No one who discovers them, assuming they do, will have any idea what they meant nor even care."

Sidon had lost his patience. "Are you completely dead from the neck up?" he screamed. He turned to Eber, who was standing nearby, and shouted, "Tell him!"

Eber, shaking his head in exasperation, pointed out, "Those records contain the details of our plot to overthrow the government along with the specifics as to the workings of the Society. Moreover, in spite of all efforts to shield Sidon from direct involvement, they will undoubtedly contain mention of his influence in this genocidal war that we planned and masterminded. This is precisely the information that needs to be concealed from future generations. No record of our dealings in this matter must survive."

"But, why?" ventured the king.

Sidon replied, "I have explained these matters before, but it is clear that my explanations have fallen on the ears of the perpetually slow-witted!" With more patience than he thought possible, he calmly reiterated with rising anger, "Try to imagine a scenario where each of you, me included, is one day made to stand before a tribunal and explain how this civil war started and how it ended with the near complete genocide of this civilization. We can all claim ignorance and be acquitted if there is no written evidence to convict us, but if someone comes forward with the complete account of our dealings, each of us will face an everlasting condemnation. I, for one, have no intention to be found on the side where the maximum penalties are handed out. I have had a glimpse of that hell that awaits those that are found in that position and I assure you that you will want to avoid being part of that damned group."

The king was stunned with fear. He had to assume, of course, Sidon spoke the truth. "What can be done at this point?" he asked.

Sidon responded as though talking with a child. "I will send a team to track him down," replied Sidon. "If he leads them to the records, they will destroy him and whatever else he is working on. I had hoped that I would have Manti to provide hard details of that man's intentions as well as his identity, but it appears your failure to produce the old man will mean that I must depend wholly on second hand information before I send out my trackers."

"And suppose these trackers can't find him?"

"They will find him because they are the best, but I must have some idea where to start looking or they will lose valuable time trying to pick up his trail."

"Can you speculate on a destination at this point? Surely, you must have some idea where the prophet might have kept his records."

"It is highly likely that Manti, before he was killed, passed on to this man the final task of chronicling the events leading up to our final victory, so he will probably be on route to a depository where Manti maintained the records. Unfortunately, information as to the depository died with Manti, but I know that it must be somewhere in Nahor's territory and it is likely a learning center."

"Excellency, because of the war and your orders to burn all learning centers of Nahor, there can be only a few such places left intact."

"Correct, but the question remains which one; time is of the essence. We can ill afford to allow this new chronicler to finish his work and walk away. Bring me any remaining survivors from the tent of General Manasseh and I will personally question them myself. Following that, when I have as many details as I can gather, I will summon the trackers and have them begin the hunt. As you have pointed out, there are only so many of these learning centers which remain."

Three days later a team of determined and well-armed men arrived at the final battlefield. This was where the Southern Army of Chalco, supported by the army of Sidon, had slaughtered thousands, even whole families, and where their own people had been severely decimated. They had been victorious, not by any superior strategy, but only because there had been more of them to throw into the final assault. Even from a distance, the killing field was simple to find; the presence of carrion eaters could be seen endlessly circling the bloated dead and rotting bodies. On closer inspection, the packs of desert predators had found the bodies of the near dead who were too weak to defend themselves any longer, and the beasts had torn them apart. The trackers scrupulously avoided this area because of the overwhelming stench and the confusion of the numerous trails left by the few survivors who had succeeded in shambling or crawling away from the field of death below. They were looking for a man walking uprightly and left a definite path towards the north or west. In time and with patience they found what they were looking for. They sped up the pace and began to jog, all the while scanning for signs along the trail.

A few mornings later, with minimal stops for rest, and after eating a meager meal of dry meat and fruit, they resumed the hunt. Their patience had paid off and eventually they arrived at what was left of a homestead, still smoldering from a recent firing. Freshly dug graves indicated that the man had stopped there long enough to perform the ritual burying. The man they were tracking came in from the southeast, and later it appeared he had walked back towards the south. They quickly discovered a few miles later that he had then turned off in a south-easterly direction towards Tula, one of the anticipated learning centers of Nahor. As they had been informed, the man they were tracking was a recorder, accordingly the lead tracker, Cush, concluded the man was heading for the hidden records they had been tasked to recover and return to Sidon. The trackers quickly set off at a steady pace in anticipation of an early kill and Tula appeared to be the destination.

For the past few days, Aaron's focus on the records before him had been meticulous. He had combed through the plates that Joseph had stacked nearby for any mention of the Clan of the Scar and had recorded any ill effects of its influence over the history of his people. Of especial interest was the latest record left by Manti and this he had recorded in its entirety with little redaction.

Now that the abridgement was completed, Aaron carefully began to plan his escape. He intended to use the underground passageway Joseph had showed him which had been built as a secret exit years before. It had been well excavated; moreover, the builders had placed lamps with oil containers along the way to diminish the effects of the darkness. With grim determination he packed the records in the satchel, along with a small container of oil to light his way through the passage. As an afterthought, and knowing he might be on the road several days without a chance to hunt, he also packed a few meager provisions which would sustain him until he could acquire more. Carrying a torch light, he then set off down the dark entryway, and after he had walked several minutes, he reached the end of the tunnel then extinguished the flame.

His movements now had to be deliberate as well as quiet. If his pursuers were nearby, he intended to give as little notice as possible. He opened the exit door slightly then peered in all directions hoping to catch a quick glimpse of anyone who might be lying in wait. His eyes now had grown accustomed to the darkness, and once he was assured he was alone, he exited the building, shutting the door quietly behind him.

The night was clear and star-lit, and though this would work to the benefit of the trackers, he would also enjoy the same advantage. Relying on his considerable training, he had to accept the probability they were out there somewhere, undoubtedly spread out around the perimeter of the deserted city. For now, the element of surprise would be his as he was sure that they were unaware of his knowledge of their location and his considerable training. For now, he must dispatch at least two of them to give him some numerical advantage, even if only temporarily. Later, the sheer numbers would begin to work in their favor as they began to adapt to his level of expertise. With a stealth born of intense training and experience, Aaron kept low to the ground and stayed in the shadows, gradually working himself around to the eastern edge of the deserted city.

As anticipated, there was a man waiting near an outcropping of a low wall that had fallen into disrepair. Although the man was alone, someone else would be posted farther east to intercept him if he could get beyond the man at the wall. It was this multiple layered surveillance he had expected. If he could get through the two of them, however, he would be well on his way before dawn, giving him a slight, but necessary lead. Eventually, though, his tactics and his ease at removing their brothers would signal to the other hunters they were dealing with a professional assassin and not the amateur that they were expecting.

Aaron, positioning himself in the shadow of an adjacent building, tossed a rock into a nearby doorway. The sound echoed noticeably, and as planned, attracted the attention of the nearby tracker. The man hooted once, like a night owl; this was obviously a signal to his brother perched and watching somewhere nearby. Having been trained in man hunting techniques, Aaron concluded they were using the standard method for night communication: one hoot, a signal for alert, two hoots, a signal for danger and three hoots, an all-clear signal. His brother would be waiting for a double hoot if there was trouble.

Now with stealth, Aaron moved closer to the man's position then crept inside a nearby doorway, awaiting the hunter to cross his path. As the man walked through the entrance, he made a slight movement and blundered across Aaron's position. Once he was inside, Aaron allowed the hunter to pass him then he quickly sidled up to his inside, cupped the man's mouth and drove his dagger up into his back, pulled it out and delivered a second plunge up and into his neck, severing his carotid artery. His neck now severed and bleeding, he was unable to cry out and as the man slumped forward, Aaron caught him as he fell. He carefully lowered him to the floor of the abandoned house then went through the man's weapon arsenal. After a brief inventory of the hunter's belongings, he discovered a long, machete-like knife, and more significant, a blowgun with a quiver full of darts. From the scent, he concluded they were coated with the venom of a poison-dart frog.

Aaron quickly left the derelict house and moved up the trail. He hooted three times, sending the all-clear signal to the tracker's companion. He was hoping the other tracker would stand down the alert and resume his normal surveillance, but he was careful to check the path up ahead. Waiting a few moments, he then walked up the short hill, and as he looked to his right, he saw a figure that had blended into the shadows of a large rock. He was in luck; the man appeared to be asleep, but appearances could be deceiving and so he moved up closer to get a better look. He measured the distance between the two of them and made a decision to rush him. As he slammed into the hunter, he turned him over on his stomach then pushed his face into the hard ground silencing any cries for help. With unerring skill, he drove his knife down into the sweet spot of the man's back between the fourth and fifth ribs. He followed up with the blade to his neck; the man briefly struggled then lay still.

Aaron quickly pondered the events and his options. The tracker had been carelessly napping, so he had been taken by surprise. In the morning, when the others find the two he had dispatched, however, they will know who he was and take precautions. Mistakes would not be repeated.

While Aaron busied himself securing the weapons, he scanned the pathway for an escape route to the southeast, and once satisfied that the path was clear, he quietly clambered over the hill then made off into the brush of the *altiplano*. Though out of immediate danger, he knew as long as he was in the high plains area he would be an easy target to detect in the open. He stepped up his pace and ran through the night, his satchel with the plates tied securely to his back.

At daybreak the chief tracker, Cush, gathered his men and went looking for their missing brothers. It was hardly difficult to find them. After viewing the death kills, each concluded reluctantly they could no longer assume they were chasing an amateur as they had hoped, but, in fact, a professional with considerable skill and Cush knew who it was. He announced, "My Brothers, we are tracking the best. His name is Aaron and I have seen his work before, and if we are to succeed, we will need to adjust our attitudes and our strategy considerably. We will continue our pursuit to run him into the ground, but we must be cautious as he is clever and will make very few mistakes and will no doubt leave traps along the way to slow our pursuit. But, if we can tire him out and leave him no time to neither maneuver nor stop for food and drink, he might make just enough errors to give us a slight advantage."

CHAPTER 8

PURSUED

There is no hunting like the hunting of man, and those
who have hunted armed men long enough and liked it,
never care for anything else thereafter.

—— Ernest Hemingway

As the old female eagle surveyed her domain for any signs of prey to feed her young, she flew high over the central highlands area. Her visual acuity was almost four times that of men, so she easily spotted the lone man running at a brisk pace across the dry valley below. Since her eyrie was located in a niche of a nearby cliff, she kept a close eye on his progress across her territory. She did not fear him, indeed she feared no man, but her young were her first priority so she was naturally over-protective. In the gloaming at the end of another day, she caught a warm thermal air current and ascended an additional five hundred feet for a better view of the terrain. In the far distance she could see more men approaching, also running at the same pace as the front man. In her primitive, simple mind she made a note to watch them all until they had cleared her ancient territorial homeland. Generations of her species had dwelt here in peace without any encroachment or endangerment from the follies of men.

Aaron knew he was being pursued and the records he carried were now in the open. His trackers had nearly caught up with him on a few occasions, but, when many others of his people would have long perished, his training had kept him alive. To his knowledge he was one of the last, though he suspected that there were a few smaller enclaves of countrymen who had slipped away unnoticed across the narrow neck of land that had long existed on the other side of their enemies to the south. A few of his kinsmen had believed that, with careful planning, if a person or small group could journey far enough south and could manage to avoid the enemy, they could enter a vast land nearly uninhabited. He sadly concluded that even if they made it that far, there was scarcely anything to guide or remind them of who they were and instruct them in the language of their fathers. Since so few of them were around any longer, he surmised many must have attempted that journey or had died trying to avoid their enemies.

His father had taught him that nearly a hundred years earlier their enemies were even then so vast they easily crossed into the lands of his people, took what they wanted and killed when it pleased them to do so. *They are a mindless swarm of pure hatred bent on destruction and now that they have nearly destroyed us, would they then turn on one other?*

Darkness was quickly approaching so perhaps their chief tracker would overlook the cutoff point he made as he turned towards the southeast. Before Aaron made the directional turn he looked skyward and saw an eagle slowly turning in the air then she let out a shrill *skree* either in surprise or warning then was gone. Aaron was long accustomed to listening for portents, so he concluded that it was a warning sign. Realizing his pursuers would attempt to overtake him before nightfall, he quickened his pace to put as much distance between him and the trackers as was possible.

Taking a short rest at a ridge overlooking the valley below, in the distance, Aaron spotted the approaching men and by their pace it was obvious they meant to exhaust him. It would indicate they intended to make this a test of endurance. Reluctantly, he arose from concealment and continued his southeasterly run, occasionally chewing on cocoa nuts to maintain his stamina. He was making good time, stopping only when necessary, and in spite of being nearly overtaken a few times by his hunters, by the evening of the fourth day, he had cleared the high plains area and had entered a cooler, somewhat wetter climate zone. This had allowed him a respite from the arid desert-like climate he had been crossing since the hunt had begun. Also, and more important, he felt much safer since he could now avoid being constantly in the open. He was nearly exhausted, but pushed on until he could see the familiar twin volcanoes looming ahead and rested nearby for the night. This long run had pushed him to the edge of his stamina and wondered if his hunters were keeping pace. Regardless, he needed water and rest or they would eventually run him to ground then their hunt would be over.

For many years his ability to remain alert even when resting had saved his life on more than one occasion. Consequently, after only a few hours of rest, he sensed rather than heard the running footsteps of his pursuers. He climbed up out of a deep slumber and instantly became vigilant. It was the end of a clear, moon-lit night and from his vantage point about half way up the side of the larger of the volcanoes, there was just beginning to be enough light to throw the shadows of his trackers in definite relief against the surrounding countryside. He deduced his pursuers had declined to rest the previous evening and had decided to push ahead to make up time, but realizing the futility of stalking their prey with so little light, they, too had stopped for the night. Doubtless they would resume the hunt before first light to gain a slight advantage. He decided they might be too weary from the pursuit to take notice if he doubled back on them and eliminated a straggler. The altitude of the volcanic mountain had created a tree line, so he decided to climb a ficus near the logical approach path and wait there until morning light had fully broken.

When the hunters entered the tree line, he was waiting for them about twelve feet off the ground. They were jogging single file through the denser foliage and trees and from his vantage point he could see that one of the trackers was indeed farther back from the rest. After a quick and silent movement to the small quiver, he had retrieved a poison dart and readied the dart to his blowgun. He would be ready and in position when the straggler passed by.

The front group cleared his perch and Aaron recognized the lead track- er. *So*, he thought, *Cush had decided to make good his threat he had uttered years before*. Then, from below the straggler had entered his target zone. A mo- ment later, Aaron expertly blew the dart into the neck of the weary man and the poison hit the fatigued tracker as though he had been cudgeled. In spite of his short rest, the man was already exhausted, and once the substance entered his bloodstream, it had the effect of hitting him like a stone wall. Consequently, he immediately dropped to the ground, lying inert and his brothers up ahead neither heard him fall nor paid heed to his feeble calls for help. Aaron dropped from the tree limb, quietly removing any weapons the tracker had, then stowed away any item that appeared useful; everything else he tossed into the bush. He strained to hear if the men were returning, and satisfied they weren't, he darted quickly through the forest in a different di- rection, now towards the south. Since Aaron knew the lead hunter, the chase had now taken on a different dimension of interest.

Cush called for a short rest and realized they were now one man short which could only mean that Aaron had doubled back on them and picked off the first straggler he saw. Through his exhaustion, anger began to crease his forehead.

Though he already suspected, he still asked, "Where is our brother, Omer?"

Opher, the youngest of the trackers spoke up. "He was running behind me through the forest and when we pulled up for our rest, he was no longer there. We should go back and collect him. He can't be far behind us."

"Opher, what would be the point? He is dead, just like we are all going to be unless we keep our wits about us." He thought desperately for a few minutes then decided. "We have to avoid losing sight of each other; otherwise our quarry will become the hunter and pick us off one by one."

Cush tried to imagine Aaron's strategy then he slowly smiled and con- cluded, "Up until he turned up through this mountain forest he had been travelling southeast. Then, to confuse us, he turns north to set this ambush. I suspect that if we move back to the southeast we will once again cut his trail. If so, then he has signaled us his true intention. If we can move around and get ahead of him, we may be able to lay in wait for him to fall into our trap for a change."

"And if he has not turned southeast?" asked the next tracker.

"Then we may lose him altogether," replied Cush. "At this point I don't care. We cannot afford to play this game according to his rules. We must regain the advantage."

The hunters were all silent. One of his team, Gershon observed, "Sidon will not be pleased at our failure."

"My Brothers" declared Cush, "we will not fail. This strategy will work."

Then next day, Aaron rested at the crest of a hill and gazed back at the direction from whence he had come. The late morning sky was clear, the air dry so he had little trouble seeing in the distance. No one was in sight and that meant either two things: he had lost them in the forest or they had abandoned the trail he was leaving and had circled around and were trying to get ahead of him to lay a trap. He had to assume the latter was correct.

An hour later, he looked out over the terrain of tall dry grass waving listlessly in the warm breeze in front of him. An idea occurred to him and he decided on a rather drastic course of action. He left off his southerly course and set out due northeast. With patience he cut the trail a few miles later after he had satisfied himself of the truth of their signs. He began to work his way around them until he felt confident they would have their backs to him awaiting him along his expected southeasterly path. He found a ceiba tree and ascended up as far as he could climb. Reaching a high branch, he crawled carefully out far enough to observe the surrounding countryside.

In the distance Aaron observed a few trees surrounded by a sea of grass. As visibility was good from any direction and would serve as a natural resting stop, this would be a likely place for them to set a trap. He watched for some minutes for any overt movement from that direction and finally his patience was rewarded. A tracker stood up and bent over to urinate against one of the trees then quickly lay back down. Aaron climbed down the tree and looked around for a suitable location where he could start a small fire without giving notice. He found a small rise of the land where he could be concealed below it and could complete his task without giving up his location. He found rocks and made a clearing, then using his flint tool, he sparked some dried grass and branches to life, creating a tiny, but effective fire. He removed the arrows from his quiver, along with the vial of oil he had packed before leaving Tula then coated each arrow tip with the oil.

He had to move quickly; the smoke from the fire might begin to draw unwanted attention from the trackers below him still waiting in concealment. It was apparent that they were still expecting him to arrive in the opposite direction from the west, so that would be where their focus would be, not suspecting that danger would come from their backs from the east. With practiced speed and accuracy, he lit each arrow and let loose one after the other so that they fell in a semi-circle around the position of his pursuers who were oblivious of his position behind them. The high, dry grass began to burn immediately, and then spurred on by a sudden brisk, dry breeze, the fire was quick to spread out and everything in its path began to blaze. Once the fire was well fed, Aaron shot off a few more arrows which landed in front of his pursuers.

The trackers were slow to react and were caught in the converging fire-storm. In confusion and fear they began to run about directionless, urgently looking for an escape gap between the flames. In desperation, a few tried to run through the blaze in Aaron's direction. Aaron positioned himself about thirty yards from a location where he expected the desperate men to emerge the flames then readied his arrows awaiting their appearance. When two trackers emerged smoldering and coughing, Aaron took aim at the first and brought him down with an arrow tip lodged firmly into his neck. He fell roughly to the ground and as he kicked and yanked to remove it, the fire over-took him and he became a dying, burning thing. The other hunter, Opher, was pierced in the chest, and while trying to remove the arrow shaft, he tripped over his hapless brother and the two hunters ended up in a rolling pyre of arms and legs.

Meanwhile, Cush attempted to regain some semblance of control of the situation. He grabbed whoever he could and pushed them through a slight opening in the furious rage. Each staggered beyond the consuming fire, coughing and gagging, and once they had cleared the blaze, they began running back to the west to escape the quickly spreading fire. Cush looked around, now blinking hard to remove the sting of smoke from his eyes and discovered there were only he and four others who had survived the attack. One of the trackers, Omer, now coughing unabatedly and unable to speak, gazed at their leader with questioning eyes. Frustration now consumed Cush's face; his eyes told the story. Somehow Aaron had anticipated their move and had positioned himself ahead of them.

Having extinguished the campfire to prevent his pursuers from detecting his presence, Aaron now gathered all his equipment and weaponry then picked up his pack and raced back towards the southeast. Though his latest attack had dealt them a severe blow to any numerical advantage, he was curious to know if they would follow. But doubtless, if they stayed on task with their mission, they would be furious at this latest set-back. Before departing, however, he began to plan his next move and wondered if he could goad them into making a few more mistakes.

Cush was more stunned than angry. His previous experience tracking Aaron had also ended in defeat, yet this current team he led was the best with whom he had ever worked and his confidence had been high that he could expect a much different outcome. Not only did he have to retreat and find some way around the fire to continue the hunt, assuming they could reacquire the trail, but he would have fewer trackers to pursue this man. Running him to the ground was no longer an option; that had not worked and it was clear they would have to adjust their strategy.

Retreating up-wind from the fire zone, Cush and his trackers found a quiet, safe location and he contemplated this new dilemma. After nearly an hour, he regrouped with what was left of his team and laid out a new plan of attack: "We know he is going southeast. We will no longer run, but simply follow his tracks then when we arrive at his destination, we will give him no path of retreat. He will come to us and we will persuade him most vigorously to tell us where he has hidden the records. Either way he is a dead man and we will have our revenge; I swear it on my oath to the Brotherhood."

Each member of the team agreed and smiled with confidence at this new stratagem, especially since it permitted them a semblance of safety from future ambushes. A day later they had again found his trail and just as Cush had suspected, it pointed southeasterly.

CHAPTER 9

LAMANAI

Lamanai was occupied as early as the 16th century BCE and the site subsequently became a prominent center in the Pre-Classic Period from the 4th century BCE through the 1st century CE. The name "Lamanai" comes from the Mayan term for "submerged crocodile", attributed to the local reptiles that live along the banks of the New River, now located in the country of Belize. Moreover, the nearby dense jungle brims with exotic birds and hydrophilic iguanas. There is further evidence in the area of Maya life that dates through Post-Classic (CE 950-1544) and Spanish colonial times (CE 1544-1700).

Among the many important aspects of Post-Classic and early Spanish colonial period, Maya life at Lamanai is shown by the presence of significant numbers of copper artifacts. Copper indicates broader trade relations in the southern Maya lowlands, and as a reflection of technological change, the history of metal artifacts used at Lamanai is an invaluable element in the reconstruction of Post-Classic and early historical group dynamics.

These archaeological contexts in which copper objects have been recovered at the ancient Maya site of Lamanai in northern Belize indicate that these objects served a great purpose for the residents of the community during Post-classic time. Nearly all of the copper objects found at the site are distinctly Mesoamerican in form and design, and based on metallurgical analyses, it appears that manufacturing technologies were distinctly Mesoamerican as well. The presence of production materials and miscast pieces along with the results of chemical compositional and micro structural analysis support the idea that the Maya at Lamanai were engaged in the on-site production of copper objects by late pre-Columbian times (CE 1150). The term "copper" is used to describe the metal found at the site, but all of the copper artifacts found at Lamanai were alloyed with other metals such as tin or arsenic and could technically be considered bronze.

It was now a week later, and it was apparent that the trackers had called off the vigorous nature of the hunt. This had then made it possible to make excellent time arriving at his assigned location without the worry of attack along the way. His destination, as he had been informed by Joseph, was Lamanai.

As he entered a zone of dense jungle and low rolling hills, in contrast to the *altiplano* and later the high altitude volcanic zone, he had arrived at a land teeming with wildlife and fresh water. Rivers wider and longer than he had ever imagined were seen and had to be forded, but fortunately, there were villages along the rivers, and though the dialects of the villagers were different than his own, there was enough similarity to his language to reach some understanding.

Those that Aaron met who were native to the area were affable companions and all were eager to assist him on his mission. When he came to a river too wide to cross on foot, he simply followed the human signs until he found a village and there he found those who would ferry him across and inform him of other villages ahead. For the past few days now he had been making discreet inquiries in the settlements along the way whether he was taking the path that would lead him to his destination. According to villagers, the settlement he sought was along a great river that flowed out to the sea.

He had turned due east and was speedily approaching a village in which he could find someone who might ferry him upriver to his destination. By that afternoon, with the help of a local fisherman who knew the settlement quite well, he was at present able to set foot in the city known of Lamanai. Owing to its central location along the river and its ease of access of many trade routes, the settlement attracted a homogeneous mixture of various different tribes and dialects that were ruled by a king of a larger empire from the far south. After making a few enquiries, Aaron was able to locate a small enclave of his people who had migrated to this land several decades earlier. As he would finally be able to communicate his purpose and mission clearly, he sought out the elder from among that group.

A family welcomed Aaron then presented him to their sage, a man by the name of Shule. Until his home kingdom of Chalco had become infested with the influence of the Clan of the Scar, Shule had been a court adviser who had served with distinction for nearly forty years to King Shiz in a land located in the present day state of Oaxaca in southern Mexico. He was outspoken in his warnings of the Clan's impact on the government, but over time his warnings had fallen on deaf ears. Being an influential man, he had been approached on several occasions to join the Brotherhood, but had been successful at rejecting the usual offers of entrance without being overly offensive. In time, however, the Society had grown suspicious of his influence and had been successful in forcing him out of his position, but he never refrained from raising his objections to its effect on his nation.

Once Shiz, the ruler of the land, had gained the solid support and backing of the Clan, an era of unrestrained repression had set in. This influence was methodical such that over time, slavery, pagan idolatry and blood sacrifice had been inserted into the social fabric of the culture. Then began a long, protracted conflict with other territories of the realm and civil unrest became the norm. In an effort to check the growth of the Clan, the opposition leadership had coalesced around Shule, but over time, the resistance movement he had supported no longer acted on behalf of the citizenry. They cared now only for their own agenda and had adopted a creed and methods similar to that of the society they had once despised and opposed. Eventually, even they grew weary of Shule's concerns for the rights of the public, so in the end he concluded he would have been a party to replacing one oppressive government for another. He left with his family and friends and fled eastward before the civil uprising could consume them all. Eventually, he and his followers had found a home in a remote area of the land along a wide river in the Eastern Yucatán Peninsula. He often wondered whether events would have taken on a different hue and spirit had he decided to remain and fight for change.

After introductions were exchanged, Aaron began to relate his remarkable, albeit dangerous journey across the landscape to Lamanai. As he began to conclude his story, he added, "It has been nearly two months since I have last spoken my native language. I have had to get by with the varying dialects of the people I have met along the way, and though they were friendly, it was difficult to make my mission clear enough for them to understand."

As Shule listened to Aaron, he was curious as to the disquieting rumors he had heard regarding his old homeland of Chalco. After hearing Aaron's account of his harrowing journey, he readily extended their hospitality with an encouraging smile.

He declared, "It is our pleasure to see a fellow countryman after so many years in this isolated section of the land. Our city attracts many strangers, but none from such a distance as yours." Shule peered closely at Aaron, noting his strength and stature, as well as his weapons of war he carried confidently about him. He astutely concluded that he must be a soldier, and if such, he would know of the rumors of civil war and unrest of his native kingdom. "You are a warrior, I think, and therefore you must have some idea of the turmoil of our home and, of course being a soldier, it occurs to me that you are far afield from the battleground."

"I was a soldier for nearly fifteen years, though to be honest I saw few battles in the traditional sense of fighting. My skills were more specialized and specific to my mission. With time and training, I learned many arts of killing, but in the end, my specialty came down to survival tactics."

"So, you are a survivor. Did the civil war end badly for our people in your land?"

"In truth, there were scarcely enough survivors on either side to claim any real victory; we fell upon one another and took no prisoners. Thus, few survived and little now exists for any side to inherit, and my homeland, as I once knew it, is gone. Your homeland to the south fared much better in our civil war, but those numbers have been severely decimated. I suspect that in time, other countries will arise to fill the void caused by so much death and destruction, but for now very little remains."

Shule sadly nodded his head as if expecting to hear this news. "It has been almost forty years since I said farewell to my home. When I left, there were those who opposed the current regime which had been completely corrupted and taken over by a secret society led by a man by the name of Sidon. Have you heard of him?"

As Aaron had first-hand knowledge of the workings of the Clan and the disastrous end of his own people, he was unsurprised that he and Shule might share similar information regarding this man. Aaron nodded his head and added, "It is curious you should mention his name. I have had access to several records which corroborate your story. From all accounts, he and his society were the masterminds behind the last civil war which claimed so many lives."

"He was probably the same man, though it could have been the son who initiated the final battles. In any event, it is immaterial since they are all of the same blood line and all carry the same name and embrace the same dogma."

"That would support what I have discovered also. How were you able to escape the turmoil fomenting in your own land?"

"We left secretly by night and were not pursued; the king I suppose had other matters more pressing than to prevent a handful of disgruntled citizens from leaving. As neither side was willing to yield power to the other and neither had any interest to support freedoms for the public good, we departed after it was apparent that the opposition, too, had been infiltrated by the same forces."

"Yes, my study seems to indicate it was Sidon's way to insure that, regardless of the loser in a civil conflict, he and the Clan would always be the victor."

Shule concluded, "So, it took slightly longer, but the end result was the same. I suspect that the members of the Society didn't expect that their efforts would yield them so little. The evil of it is that they will simply move on until they infect other realms, eventually this one, and the process will unfortunately repeat itself." Shule paused to reflect a moment of personal discouragement then carefully commented, "If only there was a way to educate future generations of this disease."

Aaron became subdued as if weighing what he was disposed to reveal. "There may be a way, but it would require discretion and patience before their works could be revealed and it would also mean that we would have to leave a record for future generations. In our lifetime, we could only educate from our own knowledge and first-hand experience. Our progress would be slow and in all likelihood be ineffective in the short run."

Shule glanced at the satchel that Aaron carried protectively at his side. "And this record, I suppose you carry it with you?"

"As you might have guessed, I am not here by accident. I was asked to perform an abridgment of the records of my people on bronze plates then instructed to take my record to the city of Lamanai at the farthest reaches of the realm. Upon arrival I was to deposit it in a temple to remain until some appointed future date and time, where it would await the coming of one of our people, a man by the name of Jasher, a distant relative. Unfortunately, though I have arrived at your city, I am unaware of the specific location of the temple wherein it should be buried."

Shule appeared to consider then said, "Such a record could not be carried about, but would, as you say, need a resting place until it could be discovered and read by a people more advanced and enlightened than our own."

"Who would you suggest that might be most qualified to read and judge its contents?" asked Aaron.

"Once in the open, it would require the protection of a king or governor who would understand its worth and take the measures necessary to ensure its truth was properly disseminated among the people."

"Perhaps this Jasher, who is to reclaim the records, is such a person."

As if coming to a decision, Shule declared, "I know just the place you seek. There is a legend that one of our temples was built on hallowed ground, so it would seem an appropriate resting place for your records."

Relief was evident on Aaron's face. "Thank you. I will breathe much easier once this record is well hidden. I should warn you, however, that a group of dangerous men, hunters really, has been on my trail for nearly two months now."

"What possible reason could they have for hunting you down?"

"Their mission is to destroy my abridgement and kill me or anyone who knows the whereabouts of the records. They intend to leave no witnesses and nothing which would incriminate their masters of the Clan in any way regarding the last civil war. So, it would be best that the fewer that are aware of the hiding place, the better it will be for all."

Shule listened soberly to Aaron's warning. After thinking it over for a few moments, he concluded, "Very well, it will be our secret, but we must be cunning to avoid the scrutiny of curious eyes. Tonight I will take you to the temple I have in mind."

There were a number of greater and lesser temples in Lamanai dedicated to various gods, including the one great Creator of all, and it was to this site that Shule had in mind for the resting place of the bronze records. As was the custom of nearly all the citizens in this territory of the land, as one city was abandoned because of wars or famine, it was later re-inhabited by others who brought with them their own gods. Instead of destroying the older places of worship, the new inhabitants simply built over the existing structures, thereby adding their own uniqueness to the original sites. One such building known to Shule was in the process of being built over and the construction was near completion. It was here that Shule had discovered, quite by accident, a small entrance to the older temple beneath, and once he became aware of Aaron's mission, concluded it would be a suitable hiding place.

Darkness had fallen over the land, and as they moved about through the lush canopy of ficus trees, the spider monkeys and other beasts of the jungle could be heard moving about and signaling their nocturnal passing. Now carrying a small torch to light the way, Shule led Aaron unerringly through the darkened pathways which meandered circuitously along the principle hill of the area. Arriving at the temple site, Shule counselled quietly, "Keep the record inside your satchel as a covering. You will notice the opening to the entrance is just large enough now for its safekeeping, so push the satchel down and as far back as you can reach. Stone bricks are lying about and we will cover up the opening. By tomorrow, the construction crew will have completed this portion of the temple and by the end of the day a new staircase will have been built over the top of the old entrance. To ensure that the opening remains accessible, I will speak to one of the crewmembers tomorrow. He is a kinsman and can be trusted; he will make certain that the stone over the opening is not properly bedded."

For the next few minutes, both men busily uncovered the stones then finally slipped the satchel containing the plates inside the opening. After completing the task, Aaron stood back and examined their work and could find neither fault with it nor the selection of the site. It felt right. Within a half-hour, the two had returned to the hut in which Shule lived and each prepared for the evening meal and rest.

Aaron, now having this weight lifted off his back, had time to ponder over the deeper meanings of his mission. He looked over to where Shule was seated and deferring to his age and wisdom asked, "What makes men distort the truth so badly that they forget its original intent, so instead of trying to correct their failure, they simply try to cover it up and pretend they were never aware of it?"

Shule thought for a few moments and responded tiredly, "I find my mind wanders to such things more and more the older I become. Regretfully, we discover that life's greatest tragedy may be that we become old too soon and wise too late, so for what it is worth I will try to explain what I have learned."

He paused as if to collect his thoughts then proceeded, "When given the opportunity for power, many men will compromise integrity, and the truth is the first casualty. Eventually, they delude themselves into thinking that if no one is aware of their secrets then they cannot be harmed. Over a lifetime, they build a wall so wide and so tall with this repeated act of compromise that they finally reach a point in which they are unable to cross it and have instead built themselves a prison for their own delusions. This prison contains all their lies and empty promises and they guard it with all the dedication of any mother with her newborn child. It's not that they are inherently evil men. Eventually, they just can't see beyond the prison walls that they have so carefully built for themselves. The light of truth simply cannot penetrate the hidden refuge they have created and covering up the lies has become their only reality."

Aaron did not break the silence for some time. He pondered Shule's words at length and turned them over then examined them in light of his own experiences. As if coming to a similar conclusion of his own, he nodded his agreement.

A moment later, as they were turning in for the night, Aaron said, "I must leave soon. There are still those tracking me and I must draw them away from Lamanai. When they arrive, they will seek you out, so you must convince them that I still have the records and you last saw me leaving for the south."

Shule wore a look of doubt as he asked, "How do you know they will approach me and my people?"

"Because they are an elite group of hunters and if I could find you, they will also. Moreover, I know the man leading the group and he will not stop until he finds the records and kills me or I stop him."

"What would be the point of such a mission? If what you say is true, his home kingdom has been nearly destroyed and there will be hardly anything to which he can return."

"It would make no difference. He has been given an assignment and he will either fulfill it or die trying. It is a matter of personal honor."

Shule thought this over and said, "I am concerned for the safety of my followers, therefore we must make your departure a public spectacle. In the morning, I will announce to the neighborhood that we are withdrawing our hospitality and driving you out forcefully."

"It might just work, but it must be loud and public and very convincing for all to hear so that when your neighbors are questioned, they will corroborate your story. All must see my departure towards the south and that I am carrying a travel satchel."

It was early morning and the day had dawned cool and overcast. Shule's hut was only a few pathways from the common market and many had started the usual daily routines. Hoping he would convince all that Aaron had worn out his welcome among his people, he had orchestrated a departure scene. Thus, on his signal, a crowd gathered in front of his home and began shouting and screaming epithets at Aaron, which had the expected effect of attracting curious neighbors. His kinsmen had been convinced that Aaron's exile was in the best interest of all, so the show was even a better performance than either had hoped for.

"Be gone, you are a public nuisance and trouble-maker. We don't want to hear any more of your mission or your miserable records!" A loud brawl could be heard throughout the neighborhood.

Then a man was thrust unceremoniously from within Shule's home along with a travel satchel tossed uncaringly at his feet. Dejection was etched upon his face as he collected his weapons and travel gear then he walked off towards the south.

As Shule watched Aaron leave dispiritedly down the road, he reflected on the irony of which he was now a part. This man, who had risked so much, even his own life to reveal the truth to a future civilization was himself being treated no better than a pariah dog. He wished he could be sending him off with a blessing instead of this public denouncement and cursing. The angry crowd picked up stones and began flinging them at the direction of Aaron who was now walking miserably down the street and out of the city. Shule watched the scene with disgust then turned around and went back inside his hut to wait.

CHAPTER 10

LAST MAN STANDING

Cush angrily smashed his fist into the face of the old man. Once down, his men began kicking out at Shule and screaming for him to reveal the whereabouts of the records. In reality, this was only for show. Cush had questioned several neighbors, including Shule's followers, and he was satisfied that Aaron was only a day ahead of them at the most. Once he had extracted all the information he needed from the villagers, he intended to catch up to him before the day was out. The reports also indicated that he had been seen carrying a satchel, presumably carrying the records, so the beating that Cush was now administering was for his personal amusement and to relieve the pent-up frustration of being denied his prey. He was now confident that he would soon have Aaron trussed up and swinging from the limb of a nearby tree. The torture to follow would serve, in part, to make up for his loss of men and honor at having been outmaneuvered so thoroughly.

Cush was up in the face of Shule and screamed, "Speak, old man, or I will have my men cut you open and fed to the dogs who wander the streets of this miserable, pox-riddled pig-sty you call a town."

Aaron's warning of what was to come when Cush learned of Shule's involvement was truer than either had imagined. No longer dissembling, Shule pleaded, "You know I speak the truth!" Ask anyone in the neighborhood.

This fellow came into my home, demanding my hospitality and then began blathering on about records and a sacred mission."

"And you gave him sanctuary, I suppose?"

"As a fellow countryman, I felt obliged to provide him food and shelter, but when it was obvious he was attempting to enlist me and my followers into his own private delusion, we all quite rightly threw him out!"

Just to cross-check his story with what the neighbors had reported, Cush shouted, "And where did he go from here?!"

Shule did not have to pretend at being injured; he was holding his bleeding head in one hand while his other arm dangled uselessly at his side. "The last we saw of him, he was heading out of the village towards the south. That may or may not have been his final destination, but good riddance I say."

Cush nodded to his men to withhold any further persuasion of the old man. "All right, Shule, but when we find him, we also had better find the records he was carrying. If not, when we have finished our business with Aaron, we will be back for you."

He gave Shule a parting kick in the ribs which would leave him bruised and sore for a week. After Cush and his men had departed, Shule crawled over to the corner of his hut and muttered under his breath, "I hope he kills you all."

As long as he was in possession of the records, Aaron had placed his priority on ensuring their safety. With the records now hidden safely in the temple, his distractions were now minimal and he could focus on the immediate problem at hand, his personal survival. He knew that Cush was left with no more than four men in his team, and though the numbers were scarcely improved in his favor, he had faced worse odds before. The only question was how to use the jungle to his advantage and pick them off one at a time at his leisure.

As Aaron entered a small village, while he was walking up to the first hut, from inside appeared a friendly villager who stepped out on his porch. Pretending to be interested in a settlement farther down the road, he and the man talked at length. Aaron made several inquiries and the villager gave him information about a short cut through the jungle. Later, as Aaron departed, he made it obvious he was taking a path off the main road then disappeared into the jungle behind the hut.

It was the tropical wet season, and as the day had grown progressively more humid, his movements through the jungle was somewhat slowed. Nevertheless, as Aaron walked a mile into the dense growth of ferns and forest canopy, he discovered that in places the path was overgrown and in others it was visible. He knew that however the path appeared any change or disturbance to the foliage would be immediately obvious to experienced trackers. A fern slightly twisted or mud appearing on a root would indicate a deviation and that was what Aaron wanted Cush to see, therefore, he set out to leave just enough of a trail without being too obvious.

Five minutes later Aaron located the spot for his first ambush. The canopy of the jungle draped low over the ground, permitting very little light, but at the foot of a mahogany tree was a slight clearing; he had found his killing zone. Dead moss and ferns were lain about so the trap would blend seamlessly into the verdant background without appearing to disturb the surrounding foliage. He walked forward several feet and found another similar tree then began cutting several large planks from the bark of the tree with his machete-like blade he had taken off one of the hunters he had killed.

He retraced his steps back to the trap area and pulled out the poison-tipped darts from the small quiver and buried several of them tips-up and embedded into a few planks of wood then buried them randomly about the clearing. Finishing that task, he carefully covered the tips with the dead underbrush. Once he looked it over and could find no issue with the trap, he then crossed back onto the main path. He looked up through the canopy of green and became aware that a light mist had begun to fall then drip to the jungle floor below. As his intention was to complete the next trap before the rain descended in earnest, he knew he would have to hurry if he wanted to avoid making his task more difficult than he had wanted.

A few minutes later, he found a second small path that led off into the jungle. He looked around and noticed liana-like vines climbing throughout the area and decided the next ambush would require slightly more time to set up, but would be equally effective in reducing the number of trackers. Using the resilient, woody vines he began constructing a spring trap from wood of a nearby ceiba tree. Using the machete blade once again, he stripped and carved the wood into a paddle and embedded the remainder of the curare-tipped darts into the wood. When the trackers tripped the rope-like liana, the snare would spring outward from the same tree and impale anyone in its path with the paddle. In his experience, this type of trap on a larger scale had been effective in bringing down large game, so he reasoned a man should be no problem.

Once the two traps were set, he doubled back to the village to await the trackers. His patience paid off, when finally on the late afternoon of the same day, he sighted Cush and four men jogging quickly down the road from Lamanai. Because the light mist was still falling, he felt the men would be more concerned with the rain and footing than worrying about a trap. He observed them as they stopped at the edge of the village and talk to the villager he had met that morning. The man pointed in the direction of the short-cut path, which led into the jungle, and Aaron overheard part of their conversation. The villager mentioned that the man they sought was traveling light, without any travel bag, only weapons of war.

At hearing this news, relief was visible on the face of Asher who pointed out, "If Aaron no longer has the records then let us return to Lamanai and beat the confession out of the old man. I am certain he knows something more than he is telling us."

Cush's patience snapped and his anger spilled out and washed over the other frightened men. He grabbed Asher by the chin and shouted into his face, "There will be time to return to Lamanai when we have completed our business with Aaron!"

He pushed the frightened man back and he slipped to the ground. All could see contempt etched upon the face of Cush. He sternly reminded them, "Aaron must be interrogated thoroughly for the location of the remainder of the records. That parcel he has been carrying about for the last two months is but a smattering of the total cache that has been hidden in Tula. It must all be destroyed and only he knows its whereabouts. Besides, I refuse to allow him to escape our grasp now that we are so close. He probably thinks we have given up and gone back to our land, so if we speed up our chase we will overtake him before nightfall. We will deal with the old man once we have Aaron's head in our net."

Having made his point, Cush sped off into the bush with his tracking team following reluctantly behind. A few minutes later and they had found the path they were seeking. After they had passed, Aaron waited a few minutes then slowly followed them through the dense, wet undergrowth of the jungle. He had left his stalkers a trail of someone no longer worried about being followed, which is to say, that the tracks were carefully laid down to give that impression. Moreover, he also had left the impression with the villager that he was in no particular hurry.

All this signaled to Cush that Aaron had probably completed his mission and no longer carried the records. He had probably found a place to stash them and had assumed Cush and his team had given up the chase and no longer posed a threat. He reasoned that since Aaron had been seen just that morning, he would no doubt be a few hours away at most, also he would be more relaxed and unsuspecting that the hunt was very much still in play. An all-out run through the jungle would surely overtake him quickly then they could extract the whereabouts of the records and those in Tula and torture him at their leisure.

The more Cush thought it over, the more he began to be convinced that the records he had been carrying were back in Lamanai and if that proved to be the case, then he intended to return to the village and have a follow-up conversation with Shule. No doubt the records had either been left in his care or were hidden somewhere nearby just outside the village. Cush swore, if necessary, he would burn the whole village down unless he was given the location of the hidden records.

So, on they ran single-file through the narrow pathway. They rounded a slight hill with a small clearing at the bottom, and owing to the rain-slippery undergrowth, the front two trackers slipped and plunged head-long into the first trap. Their forward momentum caused the two men to step forcefully on the buried curare-tipped darts. When Cush saw his two point men go down and began screaming, he pulled up quickly and prevented the two following him to fall forward into the same trap. He cursed, knowing what was sure to follow. He had seen it before.

Before leaving Lamanai, Aaron had found an apothecary and had purchased curare in a very lethal form. Cush and the remaining two men watched helplessly as their brothers lay writhing upon the ground. Finally, the two began twisting, their eyes wide open in distress in a desperate attempt to find breath. Knowing nothing more could be done for them, the other hunters watched over the death throes, and within a few minutes, their brothers were both dead of asphyxiation. Cush was livid with anger over the loss of his two men, one of which was his biological younger brother, Lemuel. He looked at the other two who were clearly frightened and now no longer confident of the mission.

Gershon flatly declared, "We should leave and return home, Cush. We are beaten."

"You cowards can return home if you like, but may I remind you? There is scarcely anything of our home left for you to return and Sidon will find you and make you both account for your spineless retreat. You have only two choices: stay and fight or spend the rest of your lives looking over your shoulders."

Nabal, one of his two remaining trackers nodded his understanding of the current dilemma then suggested, "Aaron is sure to have more traps laid along this pathway. We should return to the original turn off and try to pick up his trail along the primary path. If he has wandered back, then we will cut his trail at that point."

Cush quickly agreed and he and the remaining two men ran back the way they had come.

When Aaron heard the bellowing cries from the jungle, he knew his first trap had been sprung. He was perched high up in a nearby mahogany tree when the two men went down. He watched while Cush and the remaining men hovered over their dying comrades and discussed what they must do next. Within a few minutes, they jogged by directly under him on the way back to the main pathway. Soon thereafter, he descended from the tree and carefully made his way to the next choke point where he had concealed the last trap. He would make his stand there and whoever was left would walk away the victor.

Now irate over the loss of his brother and with a determination he had never before known, Cush set out to end this chase once and for all. Cush reversed his route and easily found the main path. They continued along until they noticed where someone had come out of the jungle, crossed the path and had headed off to the other side. After examining the tracks that indicated Aaron had recently crossed over, Cush pushed the other men hard in that direction with himself in the rear. He knew with a certainty that Aaron had planted another trap along the way and he intended to be the one standing after it was sprung. Moreover, he knew that once his two men went down, it would flush Aaron out into the open. It was only fitting that the final confrontation should come down to just the two of them.

A few minutes later, all were breathing heavily and in single-file, Cush in the rear. The first man, Gershon, tripped over the liana vine used as a trigger that had been staked to the ground. The trap swung out from concealment and impaled the hapless stalker in the chest killing him as the poisoned tip entered his right lung.

Cush, though anticipating the ambush, was still astonished at the suddenness of the attack while Nabal pulled up in surprised wonder. Then Aaron, now in close range, used their surprise to launch an arrow into the neck of Nabal, who had been standing only a few paces away. The force of the arrow passed through his neck and pushed him back and into an allspice tree where the tip was driven firmly into the bark. His hands, now frantically pulled on the shaft to remove the arrow, but it was no use. Near the end, his hands dropped to his side and he slipped forward, now dead. The weight of his body pulled the shaft downward and broke it off from the tree, the arrow still firmly lodged into his neck. As he tumbled lifelessly to the ground, his blood mixed with the falling rain as it coursed from his neck wound across his body.

After allowing the remainder of his men to take the brunt of the final attack, Cush had hoped to draw Aaron out into the open. While Gershon went down in the trap and after Aaron had dispatched Nabal with an arrow, Cush dove for cover into the nearby dense bush then crawled away. He intended to circle Aaron and wait for a clear shot with his own bow. Cush had not forgotten the shame of being bested by this man during their last encounter a few years before during the hunt for Libnah, son of King Gilead.

From within the jungle came a goading voice, "Cush, it is now just the two of us. Since I know you will not withdraw, let us settle this as men on the battlefield, hand-to-hand."

"And what would you know about the battlefield, Aaron? Your art has always been about slithering around tents like a snake then using a dagger on helpless men in their sleep."

Aaron replied reasonably, "My art has been no less honorable than your own, Cush. You who would hunt men down in cowardly groups then torture them to death for sport."

"Well said, my Brother. Suppose I simply withdraw and we part company?"

"I will not be looking over my shoulder the rest of my life, Cush," He added thoughtfully. "We finish this now or I will become the hunter and you the hunted."

Cush refused to accept that end. "Throw out all your weapons save a dagger and I will do the same."

When this was done the two stepped out of the lush jungle and faced the other some ten few yards apart. The two enemies glanced up as the rain began to fall harder.

"At least you will die wet and clean, Aaron".

"That could well be said of you, also, Cush."

Cush intended to get in the first blow so he tried a distraction. "Aaron, I am truly sorry that it has come to this. There are so few of us alive, we should be embracing as brothers, hardly as sworn enemies."

Before the last word had left his mouth, he rushed head-long toward Aaron, intending to gut him with a surprise attack, but Aaron was too well trained and easily parried the jab, twisted around and drove the obsidian blade of his own knife deeply into Cush's lower back. Immediately, Cush went face down into the muddy ground then Aaron straddled his back and leaned on the protruding knife handle, breaking off the obsidian blade inside his back. Cush, now unable to move his lower body, began to thrash his head about, but Aaron had pinned him down. Pushing his face roughly into the mud and blood of the killing zone, Aaron leaned close to his ear and whispered gently, "You should have stayed home, Cush."

Cush blinked his eyes from the falling rain and mud then replied weakly, "What home?" He lay there silently until he had breathed his last.

The rain began pouring now in earnest. Aaron stood over the dead man and looked up into the dense canopy of the jungle, feeling the water stream down his face, and as he pondered his options, he allowed the feel of the rain to cleanse his mind.

He had been on the run for so long that he had given very little thought as to what he would do once he completed his mission and eliminated his trackers. He lay back under a nearby ficus tree and considered how he would begin the remainder of his life. Cush was right; everything that he had known in his home, including his family, was gone or in ruins. Sidon and his Society would surely be waiting and they would have a long memory, moreover, he concluded reluctantly that eventually he would be tracked again for the whereabouts of the records in Tula. As long as he was alive, the records would always be at risk for exposure.

After a few moments of contemplation, he arose and found the path back to the village. Once he had located the cross roads, he looked both ways then a thought occurred to him and he decided to return north back to Lamanai.

EPILOGUE

THE TRANSLATION

While Professors Bedford and Levinson continued a minute review of the day's efforts, Jasher had excused himself a half hour earlier to perform a security check. Both were satisfied that the translation that day had been an accurate rendering of *The Abridgement*. From the standpoint of the historian, it was an incredible chronicle of man's most powerful and influential civilizations for which there was already corroborating historical evidence from other outside sources.

Bedford shook his head and marveled at the manuscript notes. He commented, "What is unique is the detailed observation and insights of one man over time as he records these pivotal moments in history."

Isaac smiled and added, "Yes, our Mr. Jasher seems to have captured the historical spirit of each civilization, whether it was Phoenician, Greek, Roman or later the Muslim Empire of the Ottomans and concurrently the Holy Roman Empire.

They were deep in discussion over these matters when Jasher re-entered the room, and overhearing their comments, he quietly sat down.

Bedford asked, "Jasher, in addition to the more renowned civilizations of human history, you have also recorded details of a number of civilizations which have been heretofore unknown to the world. What is truly notable and consistent about your observations is that each civilization became more powerful and prolific than the last, almost as if men were learning the best manner of conquest and then, more significantly, how to consolidate and maintain their power over time."

Levinson asked, "To what do you attribute this success at empire-building, for lack of a better phrase?"

Jasher leaned forward to express his view. "I assure you that given the different languages and cultures involved since the confounding of the original language centuries before, that this success was no mere accident and definitely no simple feat to accomplish. It required men dedicated to the rise and development of empires with the intent to eventually form one whose influence would reach world-wide proportions."

Bedford could see where Jasher's point was going. "Are you suggesting that Cain's society was experimenting to find the ultimate system of subjugation?"

"Professor, Cain is no different from the rest of us in the sense that we do not accumulate all the answers to our questions at once. He had to adapt with the times and circumstances then apply certain principles to test his theories. Some of these civilizations grew and became highly influential upon our history, languages and cultures, but as they all failed to provide for personal growth through freedom of choice, they all fell short of his expected outcome, though not for lack of trying, but because the principles upon which they were founded were inherently flawed to our human nature."

Levinson interjected, "Additionally, they were all subject to corruption from within and attack from the outside."

"Precisely. Remember, the ultimate goal of his Clan was to attain world-wide dominance and until a few centuries ago, that goal was simply unattainable, not for lack of interest or effort, but because no delivery system existed powerful enough to ensure they could get there."

Bedford slowly shook his head in understanding and commented, "I take it then that he has reached that point and the system is now in place. Will it work?"

Jasher slowly leaned back in his chair and commented, "Modern technology, joined with his exceptional planning skills developed over a lifetime of trial and error, has now made it possible for Cain to consolidate his efforts. He has a powerful system in place and intends to implement it at the highest levels." He considered William's last question. "Yes, his system has the potential to work, but only if we fail to reveal the truth."

THE END

PREVIEW TO PART 3, THE BOOK OF JASHER

While William Bedford, Professor of Paleology and Professor Isaac Levinson, Professor of Ancient Languages filed quietly into the room, Benjamin Jasher sat dejectedly in the master living area. The professors had just completed the final editing of *The Abridgement*, an ancient bronze relic containing a record of mankind's greatest civilizations. What they had both discovered over the past month was that the translation had modern-day implications over international geopolitical affairs. Their lives had been in danger during the majority of their association with Jasher, but it was evident that the ominous message revealed by the translated records represented a greater danger. A heightened air of suspense had settled heavily upon the two men as they awaited the new developments which Jasher had decided to share.

"Gentlemen, it has come to my attention that we must move forward as quickly as possible with our announcement to the press. Walker Cain is gathering his considerable power and influence to destroy our work, consequently, in a few moments I will phone my media sources and announce our next attempt at a press conference. For security reasons, we will attempt to have the conference here on my estate in Cyprus, but barring that, we may need to reconvene back in Jerusalem. These are the only two venues that would afford us a degree of security and friendly support. I would prefer to remain here, but if we are expelled from Cyprus, it is quite likely we may have to flee to Israel for sanctuary."

"Why is that?" asked Levinson, now concerned.

"Cain's influence may be able to reach out as far as Cyprus and have us expelled. If so, we will need to prepare an emergency exit plan from my estate."

A few minutes later Jasher was on the phone with his media source, Franklin Pierce, at *Thomson-Reuters News Agency*. After placing the call on speaker phone to ensure the professors could hear the conversation first hand, he began by speaking directly with his contact.

His voice was tense with anxiety as he announced, "Franklin, the time has come to put into motion our plan to reveal the discovery and translation of my records."

"I see." replied Pierce. "So that business a few weeks earlier in Austin was intended to accomplish what purpose?"

"Franklin, the impromptu press release I had planned in Austin would have worked except that our opposition in high places had acquired more information over the contents than I had expected, thus they attempted to stop the release. The result was the destruction that followed."

"And the translation you have mentioned, where were you in that process when you had to flee the United States?"

"There were still a few matters left to complete on the first half of the manuscript, but essentially it was far enough along to reveal our message. I used the proposed announcement as a gambit to see if anyone was listening and to what extent they suspected about our project."

The newsman was surprised to hear the previously planned press conference was little more than a ruse to measure the resolve of the opposition. Jasher was playing a dangerous game.

"And now, how far along are you in the translation?"

"We have a full manuscript of the entire abridgment and we are now essentially ready for publication."

A pause was evident at the other end of the phone. "And now, you are prepared to move forward regardless of the danger?"

"Franklin, I have every reason to believe that it is now or never."

"Can you be more specific?"

"The forces that Walker Cain represents are formidable and he is dangerously near to setting events in motion that will change the history of our planet forever. If the future is any reflection of the past, and I think it could be, there is likely to be devastation and death the likes of which our world has not known for millennia."

"Jasher, I am going out on a limb for you on this because, frankly since I have known you, you have never been wrong before, but I assure you that if you are wrong on this one, the press will crucify you and there will be no way that I can protect your reputation nor that of Professors Bedford and Levinson."

"Franklin, the only serious regret at this point is if I am blocked from revealing what has been translated."

"Your records will have to indict Walker Cain conclusively for masterminding a world movement to take complete control."

"They will do that and much more, and for that reason I know he will make another attempt to move on us as he did in Austin."

"What do you mean?"

"He will be desperate to stop the announcement and publication of the records because he is fearful that the truth will expose him for what he is and cause him to lose the credibility he has worked so hard to establish."

"Surely, he has people who could spin this press release in his favor. Violence to you and your cohorts would seem an unnecessary risk."

"What we have to reveal is so damning he will consider the consequences unacceptable and he will not permit any more delays to his timetable. This justification will embolden him to take desperate steps to prevent us from uncovering his true identity."

"Just who is he, anyway?"

"I prefer to announce that at the press conference here on Cyprus." Jasher hoped that what he had already said was enough to solicit the support and interest of the press, but these matters had to be settled in their proper order.

There was a pause as the newsman thought it over. "All right, fair enough," replied Franklin, though it was obvious he was disappointed and concerned that he was putting his own reputation on the line. He did venture a follow up-question.

"What desperate steps is he likely to take?"

"He intends to prevent the press release from happening. If he can't do that, he will destroy us and anyone remotely connected with our efforts to go public with our discoveries."

"Not being too melodramatic are you, Jasher?" he replied reproachfully with a light banter to his voice.

"Just keep your eyes open, Franklin. We need to have this press conference much sooner than later, possibly tomorrow afternoon?"

"Give me until the following day. Otherwise, I can't guarantee the full coverage you will want."

Jasher was disappointed, but replied, "Agreed. Get back to me when you have it set up. I owe you a big one for this, Franklin."

"Just make sure you have all your facts together, old boy." He then rang off.

Jasher turned back to the professors and said, "We must prepare our statements and get all things in order. We are going to get only one chance at this and we must do it right."

Author Biography

Bill W. Sanford completed his first book, *The Clan*, in 2016. He recently finished the second book in the Book of Jasher series, *Shadow of the Clan*, and is hard at work on the third.

Sanford was born in Orange, Texas, and received his bachelor's degree from the University of Texas at Austin. He spent fourteen years teaching Spanish, and he very much enjoyed the twenty-one months he spent in Mexico as a teaching missionary. Sanford lives with his wife, Debra in Grand Prairie, Texas.

10953465R10166

Made in the USA
Lexington, KY
03 October 2018